THE
FINAL
NAIL

By Stefan Ahnhem

THE FABIAN RISK THRILLERS

The Ninth Grave (Prequel)

Victim Without a Face

Eighteen Below

Motive X

X Ways to Die

The Final Nail

THE FINAL NAIL

STEFAN AHNHEM

TRANSLATED FROM THE SWEDISH
BY AGNES BROOMÉ

An Aries Book

Originally published in Swedish as *Den Sista Spiken* in 2021 by Forum

First published in the UK in 2022 by Head of Zeus Ltd,
part of Bloomsbury Publishing Plc

9 7 5 3 2 4 6 8

A catalogue record for this book is available from the British Library.

ISBN (HB): 9781801109949
ISBN (XTPB): 9781801109956
ISBN (E): 9781801109925

Typeset by Divaddict Publishing Solutions Ltd
Cover design by Matt Bray

Printed and bound in Great Britain by
CPI Group (UK) Ltd, Croydon CR0 4YY

Head of Zeus Ltd
5–8 Hardwick Street
London EC1R 4RG

WWW.HEADOFZEUS.COM

In memory of Theodor Risk
* 25 March 1996

† 31 July 2012

PROLOGUE

3 August 2012

ERICA ANDERSSON HAD never been particularly fond of water. She didn't mind showering. Or spending an hour or two in the bath with a good book. Quite the opposite. What she didn't enjoy, and had never enjoyed, were lakes and the ocean. Splashing about, swimming, diving, or whatever it was people insisted on getting up to in the water when they were neither hot nor dirty.

She knew how to swim, more or less, though she was certainly in no position to brag about her prowess. In all honesty, four laps in a pool without swallowing a lot of water would be beyond her ability. Not to mention in open, frigid water full of waves, jellyfish, and disgusting seaweed.

And yet she had somehow been talked into squeezing her ample bulk into a tiny kayak that was so narrow and unstable it was nothing short of a miracle she hadn't tipped over. She was quite literally sitting in the water. The cold, dark water, whose unruly waves seemed to be buffeting her from every direction.

If Mikkel were to be believed, kayaking was a dry endeavour. He had looked her straight in the eye and told her that, at most, her forearms might get splashed from time to time.

His earnest assertions had turned out to be bald-faced lies, however, which was just like Mikkel, especially when he'd struck upon an idea he thought was brilliant. For a month, he'd gone on and on about how amazing it was to greet the sunrise from Copenhagen's canals, to become one with the water.

One with the water. Jesus...

The things we do for love. Well, she wasn't exactly beating eligible suitors off with a stick, and Mikkel was decidedly out of her league. He wasn't just good-looking; he had a real career as a programmer, too, with a salary most people could only dream of.

The only problem was that he was Danish, which meant she'd had to leave Helsingborg. Though in the grand scheme of things, that wasn't much of a problem. At least, not compared to her struggle to keep the kayak from capsizing.

It seemed like the tiniest ripple might tip it over; her stomach and back muscles were already aching from the effort of keeping it steady. And they were doing far better than her shoulders and arms. The real question was if they would fall off before they reached the end of Mikkel's overly ambitious route.

'Look around, take in the beauty of it all!' he called back over his shoulder.

She nodded. It really was beautiful. Kayaking genuinely did let you see Copenhagen from a different angle. But she was having a hard time enjoying it. Especially since leaving the calm, idyllic Wilders Kanal for the harbour, where there was a lot more traffic and consequently much larger waves.

She couldn't understand why he'd forced her out onto the open water. She supposed he wanted to show her everything, now that he'd finally managed to coax her into coming out with him. Or did he have some kind of ulterior motive?

That was a line of thought she would have preferred to ignore, but apparently it wasn't up to her. The idea had already taken on a life of its own and was rapidly unfolding.

Mikkel had been unusually on edge recently, and it had been almost a month since they'd last made love. At first, she'd figured it was a rough patch that would blow over. But things had continued to deteriorate. They were in the middle of their summer holiday now, and things had honestly never been worse between them.

Was he sick of her? Was that what this was about? Was that why he had forced her to come on this kayak trip from hell? To make her so unhappy she'd break up with him, saving him the trouble? Because he was too chicken? God, what a coward.

But then, he'd always been too good to be true. She'd known that from the start. What possible reason could he have had to choose her, of all people?

She could be hard work. She was very well aware of that. Especially when she got hung up on something. She was routinely unable to let whatever it might be go before it was too late. Like the time she'd been convinced Mikkel had been seeing someone else and hadn't hesitated for a second before going through both his computer and his phone.

If she'd just dropped it when she didn't find anything, everything would have been fine. But no, she'd obviously thought it was a great idea to follow him two nights later, like in a grainy old spy film, to make sure he really was just out with a friend. And then he'd spotted her, of course, and been really angry. No, he'd been furious. Just like that time when she asked one too many questions about his ex-girlfriend, who had apparently died in a car crash.

'And that's the new opera house!' He pointed with his paddle towards the magnificent building.

'Lovely,' she called back. 'But hey, would you mind if we turned back now?'

'No, come on! Look, the water is so calm and still this morning.'

'I guess, but maybe we could call it a day anyway? My arms are getting tired.'

'Well, just think of it as a good workout.'

'But Mikkel, I don't feel safe. Can you understand that? I'm scared and I've had enough. All I want now is to get back to dry land.'

'Erica, I promise. There's nothing to be scared of.'

And then that smile that invariably made her melt and say yes to anything. It was like kryptonite to her, and she had no choice but to heave a sigh and keep going, past the opera house and further out into the harbour.

He'd worn that exact same smile that night when he'd come over and asked if he could buy her a drink. She'd been in Copenhagen for a night out with some friends and had instantly fallen so head over heels that two weeks later she'd quit her job and moved to the Danish capital.

She'd ignored her mother's worrying about how things were moving too fast and how she barely knew the man in question. Maybe she should have listened.

'When we reach Reffen, we can turn back,' Mikkel called out after a few minutes. 'Okay?'

'I just don't know if I want to keep going,' she called back. 'Seriously, Mikkel. This thing is going to tip over any second, and...'

'No, it's not. Just relax and keep paddling, nice and calm.'

Why couldn't he just break up with her and tell her to move out, if that's what he wanted? Sure, she'd be sad and almost certainly angry. She would yell and accuse him of all kinds of things. She might even throw things.

But in the end, she would accept the inevitable and move back to Helsingborg, though she'd contact him a few more times before completely giving up. That was all he'd have to endure, if getting rid of her was what he wanted.

He just didn't have the guts. That was the only explanation. And granted, she did have a temper, there was no denying it. But it was really nothing compared to his.

Once or twice, he'd frightened her. Especially that time when she'd threatened to file a rape claim unless he let her sleep. He'd punched the wall just inches from her head, so hard his hand had gone through it.

But that was then. Now, he never wanted to have sex any more.

Just minutes later, when she spotted a cruise ship pulling into port less than a mile ahead, she suddenly realized what this kayak trip was really about. It dawned on her that Mikkel had a plan.

And with that realization came panic.

'Look!' he called back as she cast about for some way out, away from this nightmare. Away from him and back to Sweden. 'Those white sculptures!' He pointed towards a number of snow-white sculptures standing in a line at the end of a pier.

He must have sensed that she'd seen through his ruse and decided to try to distract her. The sculptures were probably lovely, gazing out across the sea in all their splendour, defying wind and weather. But a quick glance was all she could spare them. Her attention was firmly on the cruise ship.

It was probably docking at Langelinie, rather than going all the way into the inner harbour. But the waves it made would spread inward, and even though she couldn't see them right now, she just knew they were coming closer by the second.

She would capsize, she knew it, every part of her body knew it, and once she tipped over, she'd be doomed. And he knew it, too. What kind of psychopath was she living with? Was this what he did when he got tired of a woman? Just arranged a bizarre accident to get rid of them?

It was the only possible explanation for why he'd pushed for them to head out on virtually open water where there would be no witnesses. It would look like an accidental drowning. Just another reckless idiot who couldn't swim well enough to save herself, another datapoint added to the statistics.

'Help!' she screamed, and she started paddling frantically towards land. 'Help!'

'Erica, what are you doing?'

Still paddling, she looked over her shoulder and now she could see the wave. Or waves, actually. There were three of them, spaced about thirty feet apart. From a distance, they didn't look too alarming, but they were approaching fast, at a speed that was terrifying in its own right.

'Erica!'

She put her back into the paddling, but the kayak refused to obey. Instead of gliding forward, it insisted on veering left or right. Fuck, fuck, fuck! Why hadn't she just listened to her mother? How had she missed all the red flags? How could she have been so naive?

And there it was.

Just like she had known it would be.

She could feel it now, how big it really was, as she and the back half of the kayak sank diagonally down, only to be heaved upwards a second later. *Holy fuck* was her last thought before everything began to spin.

She closed her eyes. As though she were safe so long as she couldn't see what was happening. But no matter how hard she squeezed her eyes shut, she was now in the water, the cold, dark water, upside down, hanging from the kayak. She'd heard you could get back up by doing an Eskimo roll, but she didn't have to even try to know that was impossible. And her knees were stuck.

So this was how it was going to end. Hanging upside down under water. Strangely, she felt pretty calm. It was as though the panic that had gripped her just moments before had suddenly subsided. Maybe because she'd given up all hope and somehow accepted her fate.

She didn't know how long she'd been under water, but it couldn't have been more than seconds because she wasn't struggling to breathe yet. Maybe that's what it was like just before it was all over. That the seconds slowed down as time stretched out.

And for the first time in her life, she opened her eyes under water. She had always been too scared to do it before, but now she had nothing to lose. She was going to be dead in a minute, and she might as well face death with her eyes open.

It didn't hurt nearly as much as she had thought it would. It barely hurt at all. And it wasn't particularly dark, either. If anything, it was fairly bright. Light green. And blurry.

Then she ran out of oxygen. And as she did, she tilted her head to look down and spotted a car a few feet below her, and just like that, the panic returned.

The back part of the car rested against a large lump of concrete while the front hung suspended a foot above the sea floor. The windows were down, and a naked woman with long dark hair floated in the back seat. It might have looked like an advertisement, if it hadn't been for her open mouth and staring eyes.

Just then, the sun peeked out from behind a cloud far above her, improving visibility, and she realized there was a man in the driver's seat, dressed in a tuxedo, his head against the steering wheel.

She didn't have time to see much else before she was yanked up towards the surface. Only that the back of the man's head was one big, bloody crater.

PART I

A lot of us hope good will vanquish evil in the end. A lot of us wish humanity will eventually understand that we are stronger together. That despite our different skin tones, cultures and religions, we are one, and that with joint effort we can fight the big injustices, save the planet, and eventually even achieve peace on Earth.

Sadly, that's a utopian notion. The world, as we know it, wasn't built on the dream of a happy ending. Reaching out to help the weak is a beautiful concept. In theory.

In reality, other forces inevitably come into play. As soon as we gain something of value, someone tries to take it from us. Whenever anything is healthy, something else seeks to make it sick. This is true of everything, from the cells in your body to stars that collapse and turn into black holes.

According to a team of Chinese researchers, the explanation behind humanity's destructive behaviour can be found in the size of our brains. Simply put, the human brain is large enough to invent the atomic bomb. But it is not large enough to comprehend the consequences of that invention.

Another theory holds that goodness is by no means the guarantor of existence and survival. It is not what drives natural selection, constant evolution, the refining process that helps a lion survive on the savanna and spurs a tree to reach just a little bit further towards the light.

In other words, goodness is not to thank for us evolving from plankton to fish and from there all the way to our current form.

Evil is.

We have evil to thank for everything.

Evil in its purest form.

1

THE RAMSHACKLE OLD brick building on the western edge of Sankt Jørgen's Lake in central Copenhagen was full of contradictions. On the one hand, it was so unassuming that only a handful of the countless locals who had ever strolled around the lake had noticed it. On the other hand, it was, despite its modest size, grand in its own way, screaming out for attention.

Not least with its southern wall, which was painted black and adorned with a large relief in the shape of a chess pawn. Or with its tin roof, which had also been embellished with a black pawn in each corner. Exactly why and what they signified was unknown. The building had never housed a chess club. Nor had it been owned by a chess enthusiast. Perhaps the pawns symbolized that even the lowliest could, against all odds, grow strong enough to turn into a queen one day.

The interior was equally contradictory. Apart from a few nooks and crannies, a bathroom and a tiny kitchen, it consisted of a single room. A room that, with its white wooden floors, bright open floor plan, ample ceiling height and large atelier windows, seemed considerably larger than the building itself.

That said, for the past month the feeling had tended towards the claustrophobic because the room was filled with so much technical equipment it was more reminiscent of a recording studio crammed into a cockpit than an airy artist's studio.

Side-by-side worktables lined the street-side wall beneath a mullioned skylight, each laden with computers, screens, countless rack mounts full of flashing diodes and exposed circuit boards, connected to other devices by thin wires of every conceivable colour.

Whiteboards covered the walls on either side of the workstations. Someone had written Kim Sleizner in big letters on one of them. Underneath was a collection of photographs, all taken from afar, all zoomed in on the same man, on his way to and from the Copenhagen Police HQ, or talking on the phone, or sitting in his car, waiting for a light to turn green.

On another whiteboard was a jumble of diagrams, bars and curves, and a long list of phone numbers, each marked with a letter and various timestamps. Next to a large map of Copenhagen was a bunch of tiny flags, also labelled with letters.

To the uninitiated, it probably looked like chaos. But there was a system, a strategy dictating how all the notes, with their arrows, abbreviations and symbols, were meant to be used, or exactly where all the different electronic gadgets were to be placed and how to link them together to achieve optimum oversight and control.

As usual, this early in the morning, a kind of controlled calm reigned. As though all the equipment in the room constituted one giant, sleeping body with a resting pulse so slow it was barely measurable. Granted, several of the hundreds of diodes were flashing, but not with any real urgency. On the contrary, they took their time, slowly lighting up and fading, as though they were in a state of electronic meditation, in which they, together with the screensavers, could live out their dreams, each more inventive than the last.

Everything was idle but poised, ready for anything.

Anything at all, at any time.

In the same room, a few feet above a pile of toppled wooden chairs, hanging from a steel pipe that rested on several of the ceiling beams, Dunja Hougaard was inching her way into a one-armed pull-up. Hurrying just to get it over with was pointless. Endurance was the name of the game. Without it, she would have been lost, would have given up on this project months ago. She would have convinced herself there was nothing to find that would see Kim Sleizner, the Head of the Copenhagen Police, convicted.

But she was never going to give up. Not only because he was the exact opposite of what a senior police officer ought to be. Nor because he had relentlessly undermined her every attempt to do her job as a detective in the homicide unit, regardless of how many innocent people had had to pay for it with their lives. Nor because he had pushed his grimy fingers into her, tried to rape her, and then had forced her out into this cold that kept her fire burning. It was because of all the things they hadn't uncovered yet. All the things she was certain were there, just waiting to be discovered and dragged into the light.

Once her chin was above the steel pipe, she lowered herself as slowly as the lactic acid pumping through her muscles would allow. It hurt, but that was where she was going. All the way in, to the point where ninety-eight per cent of her wanted to let go, and the other two per cent clung to the certain knowledge that the ten-foot drop onto the upside-down chairs would hurt a lot more.

She grabbed the pipe with her other hand and once again began pulling herself up as slowly as she was able. She had four more slow pull-ups to get through, then her two-hour workout was over.

She had never been stronger. But then, she had been doing two long strength-training sessions and an hour of yoga every day since last spring. In just a few months, her body had undergone a transformation she wouldn't have thought possible. She had put on several pounds but was noticeably slimmer. She knew exactly where her body's limits were, and every day she pushed them a little bit further.

It had started as a necessary evil. If she wanted to stand a chance against Sleizner, she had to be both stronger and faster than him. A point she had likely already reached and passed, if the pictures of him were any guide. They clearly showed that he had neglected his own health to hunt her.

He had recently resumed his morning yoga, but even without it, Sleizner was not a man to be underestimated. For that reason, she didn't mind that working out had become something she had to do in order to keep from bouncing off the walls.

The surveillance was a different story. That had been futile so far. They hadn't found a single thing of interest. Nothing concrete enough to take him down.

And yet they had kept him under more or less constant surveillance for the past few weeks. They had listened in on every phone conversation he'd had. They had read and analysed every text and email he had sent or received. They had scrutinized his financial activities, and with the help of the GPS transmitter in his phone, they had logged his movements so they could, with very few exceptions, home in on the smallest detail and see what he was doing, where he was doing it, and, above all, when he was doing it. Often, they could predict with a large degree of precision all three factors in advance of them taking place.

In other words, the prick was completely mapped out, and

she had been surprised by how regimented and unexciting his life seemed. The most titillating part was that he regularly visited Jenny Nielsen, or Jenny Wet-Pussy Nielsen as she called herself, on Nøjsomhedsvej 4.

It was the same prostitute he'd met up with in the back seat of his car on Lille Istedgade almost three years earlier. The meeting had caused a minor scandal when it was leaked to the media. Especially since it turned out he had been on the clock at the time and had, as a direct consequence, missed an important call from the Swedish police in Helsingborg.

Fareed Cherukuri had, on his own initiative and without consulting Dunja, leaked the information to the tabloid *Ekstra Bladet*, which had in turn drummed up a media storm that led to Sleizner being humiliated on primetime TV and on the front covers of virtually every newspaper for weeks. Which had in turn led to, among other things, his wife leaving him and the National Police Commissioner himself, Henrik Hammersten, ordering him to take a leave of absence.

It didn't take a genius to figure out the whole thing must have been a devastating blow to a media whore like Sleizner, and for some reason he'd decided to blame her and her alone for it, which was why he had subsequently done everything in his considerable power to destroy her.

And that power had only grown after he somehow worked his way back in from the cold; now he seemed to have loyal friends in practically every part of the Danish elite. Bouncing back the way he had was implausible in the extreme, and how he had pulled it off was a mystery to her.

That he spent his free time frequenting a prostitute long past her prime was, unfortunately, neither scandalous nor remarkable, and not even illegal any more in Denmark. It may be sad and pathetic, but far from enough to bring him down. If anything, it would probably humanize him in the eyes of a lot of people.

In all honesty, she had expected to find something far more egregious, extravagant and decadent. A kind of double life with one foot in the police and the other in... And that was exactly where the big problem lay. She had no idea. The only thing she had was a distinct feeling that something was off. That despite all the time and energy they'd expended on this, despite all the equipment they'd purchased and put to use, they had barely scratched the surface.

That Kim Sleizner was the embodiment of pure dyed-in-the-wool evil was beyond doubt as far as she was concerned. Let him walk around, playing at being an upstanding copper. She could see right through the polished façade and was fully aware it was just a performance.

Which was why they simply had to keep looking until they found something. Keep listening, tracking and analysing his every move. Because somewhere, there was an entire cupboard full of skeletons that wouldn't survive a second in the light of day.

But time was growing short. Sleizner wasn't the type to rest on his laurels. He spent every waking minute shoring up his defences, pushing to grow powerful enough that no scandal in the world could bring him down, and from what she could tell, he was close to succeeding.

She pulled herself up again, defying the pain ripping through her muscles, oblivious to what was happening below.

It had started a few minutes earlier, with a diode on one of the many patch modules. Its flashing had suddenly changed. Not a lot, but enough to set it apart from the rest. Insistent and irregular. As though it had been roused from a peaceful slumber and realized it had overslept.

And like some highly contagious virus, the anxious flashing had quickly spread to fifty more diodes, and then several of the computer screens woke up from screensaver mode, displaying programs full of audiographics, controls and timelines that started up and began to record.

One of the many screens showed an opulent crystal chandelier above an unmade double bed. A naked, balding Kim Sleizner was sitting on the edge of the bed, stretching.

From a speaker next to the screen came the sound of him groaning and cracking his neck and vertebrae into place, then he stood up and walked out of the frame.

The sound made Dunja prick up her ears and drop down to land on all fours next to the pile of chairs. On her way to the screens, she glanced at her watch and noted that it was ten past five in the morning.

Sleizner hadn't come close to waking up this early at any point during their surveillance, which suggested something out of the ordinary was finally happening.

2

FROM A DISTANCE, the white Mercedes looked almost new, dangling in the air, about to be lowered onto the concrete pier. Fresh from the factory, ready to roll out onto the road. But the water leaking out of the open windows and the seaweed clinging to the bonnet, coupled with the outlines of the two bodies inside, gave the lie to that impression.

Jan Hesk was cheered up by the sight as he drove down the gravel road to the pier on the Refs Peninsula and parked at a safe distance from the mobile crane.

Granted, it was an ungodly hour, and he'd been forced to cancel a family trip just as they were about to pack themselves into the car and set off towards Jutland and, to the children's untold delight, Legoland. They had waited their whole lives to go, so he had no problem understanding their disappointment. What had surprised him was that Lone had flown off the handle and started a loud row right there in the driveway.

He, for his part, had managed to stay relatively calm, playing along with the others' dismay, blaming the circumstances, never for a second letting on that in his heart of hearts, he'd been counting the days until he could go back to work.

Ever since the first week of his leave, during which he'd held the fort at home while Lone did inventory in her shop, where she sold plastic-free baby things, he'd itched to get back to the station and get to work. But he had kept that to himself, set his jaw and built a treehouse, made pancakes, and cycled to Amager Beach Park whenever Benjamin grew sick of being in the house.

Now, he was finally back, and he had a brand-new title, too. A title he'd coveted since his first days on the homicide unit. The reason behind his elevation was the terrorist attack at Tivoli a month earlier. It had changed everything. For the world at large, it had been a terrible tragedy, and the victims' loved ones were, understandably, in a place so dark he couldn't even imagine it.

But for him, the event had proved a turning point. Never had he experienced a clearer before and after. Before, he'd been something akin to a loyal pooch for his boss, Kim Sleizner, to kick around, but now, he suddenly had his respect.

Sleizner had been so impressed by the way he'd acted and handled himself during the crisis that he had given him not only a raise and his own office, but, more importantly, increased responsibility as well. He was finally going to assemble and lead his own team.

Crime scene technician Torben Hemmer was already on the scene, busy unloading his equipment from the van, even though the crane operator hadn't even had time to undo the straps around the dripping car.

So far, he and Hemmer had only spoken on the phone, but he was already convinced the new guy was an asset. The focused energy he radiated as he organized and prepared his equipment for the impending investigation was exactly what they needed. A man who was here to work. Not drink coffee and shoot the breeze.

He was not, on the other hand, all that sure about Julie Bernstorff, who was walking towards him. He couldn't put his finger on why. Maybe she was simply too good-looking, with those almost unnaturally clean features, that dark, advertisement-curly hair, and those long legs.

She looked as though she worked in fashion or some other trendy industry, not here, where the slightest wobble in those high heels entailed a considerable risk of falling and getting hurt. The fact that it was Sleizner who had hired her and suggested she join his team did nothing to recommend her to him either.

'Hi, Julie Bernstorff,' she said, pushing her hair behind her ear with one hand as she extended the other. 'I'm the one who—'

'I know.' He cut her off and nodded. 'We've met.'

'Oh, that's right, I remember now,' she said with darting eyes that belied her statement.

'Last spring, before your interview with Kim Sleizner,' he said, to help jog her memory. 'We met in the hallway, but I'm sure your mind was on other things.' He was at least going to give her an honest chance before he put his foot down and had her transferred.

'Oh yes, that's right.' A smile brightened her face.

'Anyway, welcome to the team.' He took her hand, shook it curtly, and continued towards the Mercedes. He didn't care how attractive she was; on his team, looks would get her nowhere.

'I'm sorry, but there was something I wanted to—'

'Maybe it could wait until after we've dealt with the most urgent things,' he cut in without stopping.

'I don't know, you see, the thing is that...'

He stopped and turned to her. 'Listen, Julie. I'm not a complicated person. All I ask is that everyone do what they're supposed to, and when it comes to you, who, I'm given to understand, have no experience, the first order of business is to keep a low profile. Listen and take everything in without taking up space.' He gave her a tight-lipped smile and resumed walking.

The last thing he wanted was to become like Sleizner, the boss from hell, whom everyone smiled at and sucked up to but in secret hated more than anything else. But this wasn't the time for mentoring, discussing leave, or any of the other things that were part of his job description. Right now, a case involving two bodies fished out of the harbour was waiting for them.

Granted, it seemed pretty much like an open-and-shut case, from what little he'd been told. He considered this a great advantage. They had everything to gain from solving this quickly and efficiently, thereby proving to themselves, and even more importantly to Sleizner, that they were up to the challenge. Which was a prerequisite for being assigned more complex cases in the future.

'Hi, Torben.' He held out his hand to Hemmer, who was just about to zip up his protective overalls. 'I can see you've hit the ground running and just wanted to say hi and welcome to the team.'

'Thanks, but no thanks.' Hemmer nodded towards his outstretched hand. 'I don't know where that thing has been, and the last thing I want is to be contaminated in the middle of a crime scene investigation.'

'Of course.' Hesk nodded and held both hands up in the air. 'Though there's no need to fret. These fellows have been sanitized enough to get me nicked at a traffic stop.' He chuckled. 'Because they'd set off the breathalyser, you know.'

'Sure, but maybe we can talk more later, when we don't have two decomposing bodies to deal with, bodies that those people over there will want access to as quickly as possible.' Hemmer nodded towards an approaching ambulance.

'Of course, of course.' Hesk backed up a step and felt a wave of self-loathing crash over him. 'You get to it. I'm going to talk to the witnesses.' He looked around. 'But where are they?' He turned to Bernstorff. 'I thought there were two of them? A man and a woman.'

'Yes, that's correct.' Bernstorff nodded. 'That's what I was trying to tell you before. I already spoke to them.'

'Right, so you're saying you've conducted an interview on your own initiative, without consulting or even informing me?'

Bernstorff nodded. 'I was first on the scene, and they were hypothermic and in shock. Especially the woman, who was on the verge of a nervous breakdown, so I judged that she needed medical attention and sedatives as soon as possible.'

'Okay.' He nodded and finally felt firm ground beneath his feet, now that the focus had moved off his embarrassing interaction with Hemmer. 'But next time, I'd like you to contact me first.'

'I did. I tried to call.'

'Oh yes?'

'Yes, but you didn't pick up.'

It must have been during his fight with Lone in the driveway. Damn it. 'Fine, let's not get hung up on details. Did they say anything of interest?'

'Not much, other than that the man had taken his girlfriend out for some early-morning kayaking, and then the waves from one of the cruise ships overturned her right out there.'

Hesk nodded. She was probably right. It probably was exactly that mundane. 'You're right, that's not much. I hope you remembered to take down their contact information.'

'Of course. I emailed it to you, along with the interview report.'

So she'd already had time to do that. That was impressive.

'Great,' he said, in an attempt to start over, and as he did, a car door closed behind them. He turned around and saw Morten Heinesen walking towards them with that distinctive, slightly anxious gait.

Heinesen was without a doubt the colleague he'd worked the most with during his years as a detective. And he was one of the few of his co-workers he felt he could trust implicitly. Heinesen didn't gossip or have a hidden agenda, wasn't trying to climb the ladder. All he wanted was to follow the rules and regulations to the letter and do a good job.

And yet he always had a nervous air about him. As though he'd been bullied all his life and had to be prepared for the next blow at all times. It had given him an undeserved reputation as one of the dullest knives in the drawer, when in reality he just shied away from conflict and preferred to keep his opinions to himself rather than risk locking horns with anyone.

'Good morning, Morten,' he said, perking up, relieved to see someone arrive even later than he himself. 'Here comes someone who apparently needed his beauty sleep.'

'He actually got here right after me,' Bernstorff put in.

'Is that right? But then why...'

'I dropped the witnesses off at the hospital,' Heinesen said.

'I see.' Hesk wanted to sink through the floor. This morning couldn't possibly have got off to a worse start. He, who knew he couldn't pull off telling jokes, had so far tried to make clever quips twice, both times with disastrous results. What was he playing at? 'I'm sorry, I was just hoping you were as tardy as me.'

'Don't worry about it,' Heinesen replied with a smile. 'So, how are things going here? Find anything interesting?'

'I don't know,' he said, pulling on a pair of gloves. 'I wanted to give Torben a chance to start by himself. But let's head over there and have a look.'

Heinesen nodded and the three of them walked over to the car, where they found Hemmer leaning into the boot, taking pictures.

Hesk went around to the right side of the car, opened the door to the back seat and studied the naked woman lying supine across it. He was finally finding his footing. This was what he was supposed to be doing. Focusing on the investigation. That was what he was good at, that was what made him feel safe. His leadership skills would have to develop over time.

The woman was younger than he'd first thought. How young was hard to say. She was not ethnically Danish and her smooth, golden skin could as easily be fifteen as twenty-five. Maybe even past thirty. What was immediately clear was that she had been strangled. The dark-blue marks around her neck revealed as much.

He had been around the block enough times to know that in any investigation, you started with the low-hanging fruit. In nine cases out of ten, there was no reason to make things complicated. Because reality bore little resemblance to a film where a scriptwriter had tied themselves in knots to create one amazing plot twist after another, simply to keep the viewer entertained.

Granted, there were exceptions to that rule. Such as the cases that Fabian Risk and his colleagues on the Swedish side of the sound had had to deal with in recent years. But in the grand scheme of things, those were anomalies.

In reality, crime scenes usually looked like what they were. For a murder to have been executed according to a well-thought-out plan, or any plan for that matter, was rare, and once the deed was done, perpetrators almost never took the time to cover their tracks. In the rare cases where they did, they usually only succeeded in making new ones that were even more incriminating.

He turned to Hemmer, who parted the woman's legs with one hand and snapped a series of pictures. Hesk always felt a bit dirty when he saw a dead woman with exposed privates. Hemmer, on the other hand, seemed to harbour no such qualms; on the contrary, he leaned in closer and continued to fill up the camera's memory card.

'Good morning, everyone, how's it going?'

Hesk looked up across the roof of the car and saw a woman with short red hair and a lab coat walking towards them, trailed by two paramedics.

'I'm Trin Bladh and I'm from forensics,' she continued, raising her hand to greet them all collectively.

'So you're filling in for Oscar Pedersen?' Heinesen asked.

'More like I'm his new colleague. I'm sure he would have told me to send his love, if he'd known we were here. But how about it? Do you mind if we take charge of the bodies?'

'Not quite yet,' Hesk said. 'Give us a few more minutes.'

'All right. I can do a few more minutes. But no more than that, please. Once people have been in the water, things happen fast, you know.'

He could have hit her with a barrage of arch comments about who was in charge of this investigation. But he wasn't going to stoop that low. He was better than that, so he let her little lecture dissolve on the morning breeze while he opened the front passenger door and bent down to study the man dressed in a tuxedo, a white dress shirt and a bow tie, his head resting against the steering wheel, from which the airbag hung like a sagging balloon.

The bloody crater in the back of the man's head was so large he almost forgot that what he was looking at was a human being. But it was, and it didn't take a crime-fighting genius to conclude that the dark marks around the woman's neck had likely been made by this man's hands. In fact, Hesk had already seen enough to picture the entire scenario.

'Well, this doesn't look too complicated, or what do you reckon?' He turned to Heinesen, who nodded and shrugged at the same time.

'Sure, I suppose most signs point to him taking things too far, accidentally strangling her, and then killing himself.'

'Exactly what I was thinking.'

'The question is if they had sex in the car.'

Hesk shrugged. 'Her clothes are, from what I can see, not here, so I'd guess they were either in his or her home or in some unstaffed hotel.'

'So, in other words, just about anywhere,' Bernstorff put in.

Hesk turned to her, about to remind her to keep her thoughts to herself until she was spoken to. But he managed to stop himself and instead flashed her a smile. 'Well, not quite. My point is that he must have had the ability to bring her out and put her in the car without being seen. Since she's not in a bin bag or rolled into a rug. Have we found the weapon, by the way?' He turned to Hemmer, who had moved on to collecting samples of hair, blood and brain matter from the walls of the car.

'It was on the floor by the pedals.'

'And where is it now?'

'On the table behind you.'

Hesk turned towards a foldable table, on which lay a number of evidence bags, one of which contained a gun. He picked it up and noted that it was a semi-automatic, model number CZ75. A common model, made in the Czech Republic and readily available anywhere in the world. 'Julie, look up DK556919B.'

Bernstorff nodded and stepped aside with her phone.

Apart from his initial mishaps, this was actually going as smoothly as he had hoped. If it carried on like this, they might even be able to wrap this up in just a few days, and Legoland could be a wonderful surprise for the family.

The only thing that bothered him was the fisherman standing about a hundred feet away, outside the police cordon, swinging his casting rod from time to time. He couldn't say exactly what it was, but something made him borrow Hemmer's camera, zoom in, and snap ten or so pictures of the muscular man dressed in a fishing vest with several pockets and a hat with sewn-on lures.

'Torben,' Heinesen said behind him. 'Do you have any idea of how long the car might have been down there?'

'No more than a few days,' Hemmer said. 'If you want a more precise answer you'll have to wait until I'm done examining the car's electronics.'

A fisherman on the pier was hardly unusual. Especially early in the morning. But through the telephoto lens, he could clearly see that this man didn't even seem to know how to hold a casting rod, let alone how to cast. Not that that was necessarily significant. Everyone was a beginner at first.

He handed the camera back to Hemmer and turned to Trin Bladh. 'All right, the bodies are yours. Do what you need to do.' Best-case scenario, she found evidence for what they already knew. That would leave just the identification, which shouldn't be too difficult.

'Sorry, but I actually had something,' Heinesen said, with his usual index finger in the air. 'I'm sure it's not important, but just to be on the safe—'

'It's okay,' Hesk said. 'Just say it, so forensics can do their thing.'

'Like I said, I'm sure it's nothing. But I was thinking about the scenario we were talking about.'

'Yes, what about it?'

Heinesen swallowed. 'I'm not so sure it adds up. Especially the thing about him killing himself. Or I should say, the way he killed himself.'

'He put the barrel in his mouth and pulled the trigger.' Hesk shrugged. 'What's odd about that?'

'Nothing. What's odd is that he must have done it while driving off the pier, which I'm thinking isn't the easiest stunt to pull off. And besides, it feels, how to put it, a bit over the top.'

Hesk was about to say something dismissive, mostly so they could move on. But there was actually something to what Heinesen was saying. It was, in fact, a little odd. 'Can't it be a combination of two things?' he suggested at length. 'One, that he wanted to die as quickly and painlessly as possible, two, that he simply wanted to disappear and potentially never be found.'

'Yes.' Heinesen nodded. 'I'm sure you're right. I'm sure that's how it was.'

It was just a theory he had pulled out of thin air. That didn't automatically mean it was bad or incorrect. But now Heinesen was standing there, bobbing his head, even though it was obvious he didn't agree. The way everyone always did when Sleizner was in charge of a case.

'But you don't think so, do you?' he said.

'No, look, I'm sure you're right. Absolutely.'

'Morten.' Hesk walked around the car and went over to him. 'The only thing I'm interested in right now is to know what you're thinking. Never mind what you think I want to hear.'

'Something's not right here.'

That was, in fact, the last thing he wanted to hear.

This wasn't what he'd pictured. An investigation that had barely got out the gate before coming to a screeching halt and skidding, of course. He'd wanted to nail this thing faster than Sleizner had expected. Show everyone that the only thing wrong about his promotion was that it had been too long in coming.

But Heinesen was right. Something about the scenario was off. And the last thing he wanted to do was mess up. Overlook that one little detail that would later turn out to be the key to the entire case.

He turned to Hemmer. 'What do you think, Torben? On a scale. How odd is it for him to have shot himself and driven off the pier at the same time?'

'I'd say it's perfectly possible. He might, for example, have started by driving into the harbour and then shot himself. It does take a while for a car to fill with water and sink, after all.'

'But all the windows were rolled down,' Heinesen said.

'Sure, but I would still say at least twenty seconds, and he only needed one.'

'But?' Hesk said, and waited.

Hemmer met his gaze. 'Perfectly possible isn't the same as probable.'

'So you don't think that's how it happened?'

'What I think isn't what matters here. The only thing that matters is what I see, and not much points to him having shot himself in this car.'

'And how many things point to him not having done that?'

'Quite a few. The most obvious of which is that there's no bullet or bullet hole.'

'Right, but again, the windows were rolled down. Couldn't it have gone out of one of them and ended up at the bottom of the harbour?'

'Doubtful. Possibly one of the back-seat windows. But if

that were the case, it should have gone through the headrest, which is intact.'

'And why not through one of the front-seat windows?'

'The angle would be too extreme and uncomfortable. I mean, why turn ninety degrees the second before pulling the trigger?'

'Not that I don't think you're right,' Heinesen said, 'but the car was likely moving about quite a bit while it filled with water.'

'That's true.' Hemmer nodded and squeezed his earlobe. 'That's a good point.'

'Regardless, we should probably call in the divers and search the sea floor,' Hesk said.

'But there's the blood spatter, too. Apart from a few clusters around the inside walls, there's hardly any. Not even on the ceiling, and there definitely should be, unless he was lying on his back when he shot himself.' Hemmer leaned forward and pointed up at the ceiling. 'See? Spotless.'

'Okay, but hold on.' Hesk could feel the headache that had subsided since his row with Lone returning. 'The car was full of water. Is it any wonder if the brain matter, or whatever, was sloshed around quite a bit and in some places was washed off completely?'

'I can go along with that to a certain point. But not on the ceiling. Because there was a big air bubble there that kept the water out. See for yourselves.' Hemmer pointed to the uneven moisture line that encircled the padded ceiling.

Hesk nodded and failed to contain a heavy sigh. 'All right, but no matter how you look at it, there's clearly blood in here, which to my mind is strong evidence that this was where he shot himself. The alternative would be that he died somewhere else entirely, which means a third person must have placed him behind the wheel. And this person must also have collected the blood and brains from the original crime scene, don't ask me how, and then spread it out inside the car as best he could. Then he somehow made the car drive off the pier without being in it himself.' He spread his hands. 'I mean, you can hear what that sounds like.'

'That last thing about the car is actually not that complicated,' Heinesen said, his finger in the air again. 'You just have to stand right next to the driver's door, insert a stick or an umbrella through the rolled-down window and push the accelerator.'

'Perhaps. But if you ask me, that wouldn't even hold up in a bad episode of *Midsomer Murders*.'

'Well, I'm not about to argue that point,' Hemmer said with a chuckle. 'And I'm far from done here. Who knows? Maybe I'll find something to point us in a completely different direction.'

Idle assumptions and questions without answers. Clues and leads that contradicted each other instead of pointing in the same direction. If this kept up, he was sure to have a full-blown migraine before long.

'Yes, I'm still here,' Bernstorff said into her phone on her way back towards them.

Hesk turned around and realized he'd completely forgotten that she was there.

'That's right. DK556919B,' she went on. 'Okay, thank you.' She ended the call and turned to them. 'We have the name the gun was registered under.'

'Great, at least one thing we can check off. Let's have it.' Even before she replied, he could tell it was more than just a name, and when he heard the words 'Mogens Klinge', what little confidence he still clung to evaporated. 'Not *the* Mogens

Klinge?' he said, even though both he and his migraine knew it was.

'I don't know. How many are there?'

'Hold on here.' Heinesen pointed to the dead man behind the wheel. 'Is that the Head of Operations at DSIS?'

Bernstorff nodded. 'He's licensed to own multiple firearms.'

'Well, just because it's his gun doesn't mean this is him.'

'No, but I looked up the car as well, and that's registered to him too.'

'Okay,' Hesk said, nodding to buy some time. 'That certainly puts things in a different light. Morten, would you mind making sure we expand the cordon significantly before the media catch wind of this?' He went over to the driver's door. 'The longer we can keep this under wraps, the better.'

As Heinesen rushed off, Hesk opened the driver's door and studied the body slumped against the steering wheel. In order to be sure, forensics would obviously have to formally identify it. And that would take time, so for now, he would have to make do with pushing the body back against the seat.

The man's face was virtually unharmed. The only thing that revealed that something was amiss was the open mouth and the surprised look. As though he'd had no idea what the bullet was going to do to the back of his head. But yes, this was one of the most senior officers of the Danish Security and Intelligence Service, there could be no doubt about it.

Hesk straightened back up and turned away from the car, away from the others. Then he started to walk, past the cordon and all the way to the edge of the pier, where he gazed out across the sparkling water, over to the other side, where the first and most enthusiastic tourists of the day had arrived to gawk at The Little Mermaid.

He suddenly remembered the first time he'd seen it himself.

How disappointed he'd been when it turned out to be much smaller than he had expected. It was the same thing now. None of his expectations of this morning had been met, none of them, and no matter how tightly they tried to control the flow of information, the news about Mogens Klinge would soon leak and all hell would break loose.

3

Fareed Cherukuri was typing in commands, seated in one of the three chairs facing the wall of screens. Back when he'd been working for mobile network provider TDC, he'd spent every minute of his free time trying to hack through firewalls and listen in on various celebrities' phone conversations to keep himself from dying of boredom.

Next to him, his friend Qiang Who – another previously underutilized programming whizz employed by TDC's customer support – was monitoring the screen that showed the crystal chandelier in Sleizner's bedroom.

They had both been hired by Dunja, who in addition to modest salaries had given them an opportunity to do something other than defend why it was so expensive to let the kids spend all day on their phones while on holiday abroad.

'I don't get it,' Qiang said, without taking his eyes off the screen. 'When did he wake up?'

'At 5.08 a.m., if the sleep app on his phone is to be believed. Which is to say, seventeen minutes ago.'

The sound of a toilet flushing in the distance came from one of the speakers.

'And he's not just catching some kind of crack-of-dawn flight or whatever?' Dunja said behind them while Qiang pulled back the time marker to replay the video.

'Not according to his calendar.' Fareed clicked through the

menus on his screen, which looked like the desktop of a mobile phone, until he reached a long stack of alarms set for different times. 'And I don't think any of the alarms were set either, apart from his regular 6.30 one.'

'And no texts?' Qiang yawned and stretched. 'And no one called?'

'Well, it's on silent and he was in the middle of deep sleep. But hang on, let's see.' Fareed opened the texting app. 'No. Nothing there either.'

Now Qiang's screen showed Kim Sleizner sleeping on his back, eyes closed and mouth open, wrapped in his sheets.

'Looks like he's been sleeping badly.' Qiang pointed to the tangled sheets.

'For the past few nights,' Dunja said as Sleizner woke with a start and looked around as though he wasn't sure where he was.

'But maybe it was worse this time. Maybe all the anxiety finally caught up with him?'

'Are you seriously suggesting his conscience is bothering him?'

'Why not?' Qiang shrugged. 'Even an evil elephant can—'

'Please...' Fareed cut in. 'It's far too early for your elephant similes.'

'It's always too early,' Dunja added.

'Want me to tell you what it's too early for?' Qiang retorted. 'Huh, do you?'

'No, please spare us,' Fareed replied.

'Find out what happened instead.' Dunja nodded towards the screen, on which they could see Sleizner roll on to his side and out of the frame.

Qiang shook his head. 'It's almost enough to make me think he knows we've hacked his phone and is just toying with us.'

35

Dunja put a finger to her lips and turned up one of the speakers, and after a brief silence they heard Sleizner heave a long sigh. '*Fuck, fuck, fuck…*'

'That's not the sound of a man playing games,' she said, turning to Fareed. 'Wouldn't you agree?'

'I would. None of it's normal behaviour for this guy.'

The screen showed Sleizner roll back into the frame, sit up and swing his legs over the edge of the bed, and finally crack his neck loudly before standing up and disappearing from view once more.

'Try going back to real time,' Dunja said and Qiang clicked on a scroll-down menu.

The view of the crystal chandelier in the ceiling mirror remained unchanged, but from the speaker came the sounds of Sleizner coming back to the bedroom.

'Now be a good boy and bring your phone with you,' Qiang said.

But all they saw was a shadow passing by the edge of the bed, only to exit the frame as quickly as it had come.

'That's what I'm talking about. The bastard's toying with us.'

'I'll send him a text from TDC to inform him of new network settings,' Fareed said, getting to work.

'Didn't you say it was on silent?' Dunja asked.

'Not any more.' Fareed turned the volume all the way up on Sleizner's phone and fired off a service message, making the phone emit a series of loud beeps that sounded like a fire alarm.

Sleizner was back in the shot in seconds, picking up his phone, and then the screen filled with a close-up of his drowsy face as he read the message. When he was done, he put the phone back on the nightstand and disappeared from view.

Fareed sighed and turned to Qiang. 'How would you feel

about testing the TC 5, just to make sure he's not just doing his regular morning yoga?'

'Why not?' Qiang shrugged. 'It can't possibly make things worse, said the elephant, and stuck its trunk into—'

'Qiang...' Dunja cut in and shot him an insistent smile, which made him sigh and boot up yet another computer, to which he connected a controller with two joysticks.

An image slowly appeared on the screen. But the only thing they could see was something undefinable and grey that turned a slightly lighter shade at the top of the frame. Only when the whole image began to move upwards and the camera focused did it become clear that it was grey roofing felt on the roof of a building shaped like an infinity symbol encircling two large glass domes.

In front of the building, they could see blueish-green water, and on the other side a number of office buildings with steel and glass façades. Behind them, by the horizon, they could make out the silhouette of Vesterbro, and to the right of it, Tivoli with its gilded tower.

Using the joystick, Qiang turned the camera back and down towards the curved façade and the top floor, which consisted of one big balcony with floor-to-ceiling panoramic windows.

At first, all they could see was the drone reflected in the windows, but as soon as Qiang had adjusted its position and focus, they had a clear shot straight into Sleizner's living room, which was relatively spartan, with a large, inviting sofa and armchairs in the middle, a dining table, and an enormous flat-screen TV next to a painting that looked like it had been made by a gaggle of toddlers. But there was no sign of Sleizner.

'Looks like we're right,' Fareed said as Qiang steered the drone along the façade. 'No naked salutations or nudist yoga as far as the eye can see. Something's definitely up.'

'Looks that way,' Qiang agreed. 'And here he is.'

Thin curtains had been drawn in the adjacent study, partly obscuring the view. But there could be no doubt that it was Sleizner in there, leaning in close to his computer.

'And from what I can see,' Qiang said, zooming in on Sleizner's arms, which were both motionless, 'he's not just surfing around while he wakes up properly.'

'Could it be something on the news?' Dunja sat down in front of one of the computers. 'Something that...'

'*Fuck*,' they suddenly heard Sleizner exclaim. '*God damn fucking shit!*' And the screen showed him putting his face in his hands and shaking his head. '*I don't believe it. I don't fucking believe it.*'

4

Jan Hesk hadn't noticed it when the woman was in the back seat of the car. But when he stepped into the autopsy room at Forensics and saw her again under the powerful overhead lights, he was struck by how beautiful she was. Her big curly hair, her clean yet soft features, and her golden, almost shimmering skin.

And yet it was the body on the table next to her that drew his eyes. A body that was anything but beautiful and viscerally painful to look at, even though the blown-out skull was hidden under a green cloth.

Mogens Klinge was his age. The few times he'd seen him in interviews on TV, he'd come across as energetic and fit, with a casual sartorial style that consisted of jeans and sweaters. Now he lay there naked, no jeans, sweater, or the tuxedo he'd been found in, and the decline couldn't have been any more glaring.

The body wasn't just pale, it was pink, like a pig, and even though Klinge had most likely made sure his BMI fell within the normal range, the flab around his waistline swelled like newly risen dough. His body hair looked oddly patchy, but that was probably just because he'd been less than meticulous with his trimmer. And as if that wasn't enough, his penis had shrunk to nothing under his bushy pubic hair.

Would he look as revolting? He, who had never been fat,

but who in recent years had developed a gut even though he jogged twice a week. He, who had bought dumbbells, a balance board and an exercise mat. Was he going to lie there like that, when his time came, and make whoever was looking at him feel faintly nauseated?

He turned to the coroner, Trin Bladh, who was bent over the woman's parted legs, studying something on the inside of her thigh through a magnifying glass. She was so focused she hadn't noticed that he'd been in the room for almost two minutes, so eventually he covered his mouth with his hand and cleared his throat.

'Well, aren't you an impatient one,' she said, making no sign of interrupting her examination.

'I'm sorry, I realize you're just getting going. But I wanted to check...'

'Don't worry about it.' She turned to him. 'Impatience is a word invented by all the people who never get anything done.'

He nodded. 'The thing is, this is my first time leading an investigation.'

'I know.'

'You do? Did I tell you that, or did someone else...?'

'The only tattletales around here are the beads of sweat on your forehead and your stiff, slightly nervous air.'

'I'm not nervous. I just want to do a good job.'

She had seen right through him. 'Are you as good at analysing the dead as you are the living?'

'That remains to be seen.' She turned back to the dead woman. 'Hopefully that scar will speed the identification process along.'

Hesk took a step forward, leaned down closer to the woman's parted legs, and studied the scar on the inside of her right thigh. It was several inches long and shaped like a cross, and he realized it must have been what Torben Hemmer had been photographing so intently that morning.

'At first, I assumed it was simply an injury that had just happened to leave a cross-shaped scar,' the coroner went on.

'But?'

'Well, firstly, it's a very unusual location for an injury. Secondly, I don't see any sign of there having been stitches, which would suggest this was done on purpose.'

'You mean like some kind of torture?'

'Could be, but if pain was the goal, there are much simpler and more effective things you can do. Besides, if we assume she's a prostitute, it's a bit like marring the goods you're trying to sell.'

Hesk nodded. From this angle, the scar was certainly hard to ignore.

'If you ask me, I think she did it to herself. Like a tattoo. But like I said, I'm guessing.'

'A tattoo.' Hesk turned to the coroner. 'So, you're saying it had a specific significance to her?'

'No, I'm not saying anything. I'm just guessing.'

'But a cross, that's a symbol of death.'

'Sure, but also of a bunch of other things, and first and foremost it is, together with a skull, one of the most common symbols people ask to have tattooed on them. Don't ask me why. It's as incomprehensible to me as choosing to get a tattoo in the first place. But that's just me.' She shrugged. 'Now I'd like to carry on with my examination, if you don't mind.'

'Just one more thing, then I promise I'll leave you alone. What do you think about the scenario we brainstormed this morning? Have you found anything to support it, or do we need to start over?'

'And the scenario you're referring to is that Klinge

accidentally asphyxiated this woman during a sexual act and then shot himself as he drove off the pier?'

'Something along those lines, yes.'

'I've only just started, but so far, I haven't found anything that would rule it out.'

Hesk instantly felt a weight fall from his shoulders. Maybe this case would be solved smoothly after all. 'So you've been able to establish that they had sex?'

The coroner nodded. 'They did. But only vaginally, and it doesn't seem to have been rough. I could only see scar tissue from older injuries.'

'And what about the strangle marks? Will it be possible to establish that they were made by him?'

'I think that'll be a challenge.' She walked over to the other end of the table and studied the marks on the woman's neck. 'If he'd had a turned-in pinkie ring or something like that, it would have been a different story altogether. These marks could have been made by almost any...' She trailed off and started squeezing harder. 'Odd,' she said to herself after a moment, then she opened the woman's mouth and shone a small torch down her throat.

'Have you found something?' he said, stopping himself from moving in too close. The last thing he wanted to do was disturb her.

There was no answer. She continued her examination as though she hadn't heard him by pushing her fore- and middle fingers so far into the woman's mouth his own gag reflex was triggered.

Just then, the door was opened by a broad-shouldered janitor in blue overalls, who entered with a cart full of fluorescent lights and bulbs in various sizes and styles. 'Hello,' he said with an Eastern European accent. 'Just change bulbs.'

'Go ahead.' The coroner pulled her fingers out of the woman's mouth and turned towards a table full of equipment, from which she selected a pair of tweezers almost a foot long.

Even though Hesk was interested in what the coroner was doing, something made him keep his eyes on the janitor, who unfolded his ladder, climbed up to one of the light fixtures and began to take off the cover. He couldn't explain why. The only noteworthy thing about the man was that the ring finger on his right hand was missing.

Eventually, he turned back to the coroner, who was pushing the long tweezers deeper and deeper down the woman's throat, and when she finally began to retract them, slowly pulling something out, he went over for a closer look.

He didn't understand what he was looking at. Other than that it was a colourful piece of cloth, covered in glistening phlegm and saliva. Yellow, orange, pink, gold and green. Thin stripes in every colour under the sun, which kept coming out of the woman's mouth as though there was no end to them.

'Doesn't it look like a handkerchief?' he said after the coroner had unfolded the square of cloth on one of the side tables.

'It does.' The coroner nodded. 'Which suggests at least half of your scenario is out the window.'

'What do you mean?'

'This has nothing to do with breath play gone awry. This is about one thing and one thing only. Murder.'

Hesk nodded and was trying to fit this newest puzzle piece in with all the others when he realized the janitor was standing at the top of the ladder with a fluorescent light in his hand, staring down at them and their find.

'Excuse me, but weren't you just here to change the bulbs?' Hesk said, walking over to him.

'Right, bulbs and tubes.' The janitor gave a start and twisted one of the fluorescent tubes free.

'This might be a stupid question, but what's the point of changing them? I mean, they work.'

'Point?' The janitor shrugged.

'Yes, why are they being changed when they're still working?'

'I don't know. You want to talk to my boss? It's better. I can call him.'

'No, that won't be necessary. But I'd like to see some ID.'

'Some what?'

'Your ID. May I see it?' he said again. Just like with that fisherman, there was something not right about this.

'Why? I don't understand.' The janitor stepped off his ladder. 'I did nothing.'

'I never said you did. But we're in the middle of an investigation here and I want to make sure everything is as it should be.'

'But I don't have it here.'

'Okay, where do you keep it, then?'

'In our office.'

The door opened and another man popped his head in.

'Wratlov, what are you doing? We don't have all day.'

'It's him. He wants to see my ID, and I don't have it with me.'

'We're just changing some bulbs.' The man entered and walked up to Hesk. 'What's the problem here?'

'I just find it strange that you have to change these bulbs, which are clearly working, when the room is occupied.'

'We're changing all the bulbs to more energy-efficient ones. It's policy.'

'And my policy is that I want to know who's in the room with me during an active investigation. So either you show us some ID, or you get out.'

'Okay.' The man nodded. 'We'll come back to this room. When will you be done?'

'Don't ask me, ask her.' He nodded towards the coroner, who was now examining the woman's red nails through her magnifying glass. 'Though right now, I think she's too busy to answer.'

The man nodded to his colleague, who put the cover back on, climbed down, and folded up his ladder.

'And what is your name?' said the man while he helped his colleague with his equipment.

'Hesk. Jan Hesk.'

'Nice,' the coroner said once the two men had left the room and the door had closed behind them. 'You're hitting your stride.'

'I won't comment on that,' he said, even though that was in fact exactly how he felt. 'I just don't want any unauthorized—'

'Hopefully you're not striding too fast to have a look at this,' she cut in, pinching the nail of the middle finger on the woman's right hand with pliers and bending it back until it stood straight out at a ninety-degree angle.

'What have you found?' he said, walking over to her.

'This.' She scraped the underside of the nail with a long, narrow tool and showed him the blood-red residue. 'This is not hers.'

'Sure, I suppose she must have scratched him.'

'That would be a reasonable assumption.' She scraped the skin and blood remnants onto a microscope slide and held it up to the light. 'The problem is that there isn't so much as a single scratch on Mogens Klinge.'

5

IT WAS ALREADY after nine o'clock, just over four hours since Kim Sleizner had woken up and got out of bed considerably earlier than usual. After a trip to the bathroom, he'd spent half an hour in front of the computer in his study.

Unfortunately, they'd been unable to see exactly what he was doing in there. To fix that, they'd have to break into the flat and install key logger software on the computer, and so far they had deemed that too high-risk.

Then Sleizner had taken a quick shower and got dressed, arriving at the Police HQ about an hour and fifteen minutes earlier than usual, carrying his regular Friday smoothie with spirulina, seaweed and spinach, but, more importantly, having skipped his normally mandatory morning yoga session accompanied by chill-out music that was in equal parts spiritual and contrived.

In other words, Sleizner's morning had been anything but normal.

He hadn't begun to communicate via text and email until he reached his office. And then, nothing of what they'd read had revealed any clues as to what had made him get up so early.

It had just been the usual administrative trivialities that took up the greater part of his working hours. More specifically, budget discussions, hiring schedules, and a number of conversations about when they should make the new clearance rate public.

It had all been so dry, Qiang had begun to quip that it would be more entertaining to watch a tree grow. But they had still felt energized, and over the past few hours they'd worked more intensely than ever.

As had Sleizner, who had been unusually efficient behind his desk that morning.

Many of the emails he had replied to were several days old, some closer to two weeks. He had also cancelled his participation in all meetings for the rest of the day and was in the middle of doing the same for the rest of the week.

The only explanation they'd been able to agree on was that he was cleaning house. Which in turn indicated that he was preparing some kind of exit, or that whatever had happened was serious enough that he needed to put everything else aside. Either way, it meant he was under significant pressure.

Dunja went over to Fareed, who was looking back and forth between two screens, a steaming cup of tea in his hand. 'Found anything?'

'I'm not sure. Maybe. What do you think about this?' He pointed to one of the screens, which showed Sleizner's email correspondence. 'It was delivered to one of his private addresses three minutes ago.'

From: tablereservations@restaurantzeleste.dk
To: kim.sleizner001@gmail.com
Subject: Table Reservation

Hi Kim,

Thank you for reserving a table for three at Restaurant Zeleste.

You are hereby warmly invited on Friday 3 August 2012, 2.30–5.00 p.m.
Booking reference: 15962897
To cancel, click here.

Regards,
Restaurant Zeleste

'That's this afternoon,' Dunja said. 'Is there anything about it in his calendar?'

'Not yet. Right now, the whole afternoon is wide open, since he cancelled both the budget meeting between 12.30 and 2, and that blue-sky meeting with HR that was going to eat up the rest of the day. You know, where they were going to discuss the Police Authority's new core value words for a better work environment.'

Dunja nodded. They'd had a good laugh about that particular meeting. Sleizner had been the one to initiate it a few weeks ago, almost certainly to burnish his own halo and show everyone what a decent and empathetic boss he was. But apparently something had come up that was more important than *respect, empathy, equality* and *diversity*.

'Do we have any idea who he's having lunch with?'

Fareed shook his head. 'Qiang's on it. But judging by his terrible posture, he's not having much luck.'

'I'm not the one who's constantly complaining about back pain,' retorted Qiang, who looked like he was about to slide off his chair as he clicked around one of the screens.

'Have you checked Facebook?' Dunja asked.

'Yes. And Twitter. And Wordfeud.'

'Wordfeud?' Fareed said.

'Yep, he downloaded it about a week ago, and there's a chat

function in the game. But apart from the emails you've read, it doesn't look like he's been in touch with anyone. He hasn't even left the office to get his morning coffee and chat with his colleagues.' There was a ding and Qiang straightened up in his chair. 'Hold on, something's happening.'

'What?' Dunja walked over to where he was sitting.

'He just sent a text from his phone.'

'To whom?'

'Jan Hesk.'

'Hesk?' Dunja turned to Fareed. 'Isn't he on holiday?'

Fareed nodded. 'Yes, and not scheduled to be back until Monday the thirteenth.'

'Read it.'

'*Hi Jan, just wanted you to know you have my full confidence,*' Qiang read. '*Can't imagine anyone better suited to lead this case.* And he ended with a smiley face.'

'Case? What case? I'm completely lost. Was there a reply?'

'Yes, a thank you.'

'And then what? Is that it?'

'So far. Though I think Sleizner's typing something right now. But you know how slow his chubby fingers are.' Qiang seized the opportunity to walk over to the coffee machine and top up his mug. As he sat down, there was another ding. 'He's asking how the investigation is going and when the team is meeting.'

Dunja walked over to one of the free computers, opened the *Ekstra Bladet* website and searched for anything big enough to launch a full-on police investigation. But she found nothing but celebrity gossip and diet and holiday tips. The broadsheet *Politiken* wasn't much better, though they'd taken the time to test and review the season's new kettle grills.

'And here's the reply from Hesk,' Qiang said. '*Smooth*

49

sailing so far. I'm meeting with the others at 12.15. I've ordered lunch for everybody.' Qiang shook his head. 'Working lunch. Nothing worse.'

'Speaking of which, Sleizner just added his late lunch meeting to his calendar,' Fareed said, turning to the others. 'Apparently, he has a "dentist appointment" between 2.30 and 5 p.m.'

Dunja felt lost. What had they missed? What was so important that Hesk had been forced to postpone his leave and Sleizner had cancelled all his meetings to go to a ritzy restaurant for lunch instead, under the guise of a dentist visit? The only thing she knew for sure was that the day she'd been waiting for had finally come.

6

THE DARKNESS WAS like a large, deep hole that appeared out of nowhere. It was the same every time. Like a fuse that suddenly blew and made every light around him go out, made everything stop.

Go silent.

And with it came the cold. A cold that spread from his chest to the rest of his body, which began to shake. And yet he sweated. So heavily, beads turned into runnels that made the sheet underneath him cling to his back.

The first time Fabian experienced it, he assumed it was simply a bad dream. Now, he knew better. There were no twisted images from his subconscious here. No miniature peacock wandering along his arm like an indecipherable symbol.

He was awake, wide awake, but the only thing he could feel was a darkness so heavy the weight of it on his chest made it hard to breathe.

It had been like that every morning since Tuesday, when he'd woken up, clammy and panting as though he'd just run several miles. Now it was Friday, and he continued to fall helplessly deeper into the bottomless pit that enveloped him with anxiety as cold as it was corrosive.

Three days and nights that had already morphed into an eternity.

Back then, on Tuesday, at half past five in the morning,

when he'd been in the middle of that other life that was lost to him now, he'd had no idea what it was about. Where the black hole, the breathing difficulties and the anxiety had come from.

Quite the opposite: most aspects of his life had finally seemed back on track after years of struggling, suggesting a brighter future lay ahead, for him and his family.

A month had passed since he'd arrested his colleague, crime scene technician Ingvar Molander, for no fewer than five murders and two attempted murders. On the same day, just a few hours later, he'd also managed to arrest Hao Wikholm, or the Dice Killer, as the public had taken to calling him, with the help of a dice. Both perpetrators were now behind bars, awaiting their life sentences.

For the first time since last spring, things had been quiet at work, and he'd finally been able to take some leave without feeling guilty. And things had been better between him and Sonja than in a long time. True, there had still been a distance between them, but it had shrunk with every day they'd spent together. With every night they'd lain in bed, holding each other.

Matilda had improved too, slowly returning to her old self and calling him *Dad* again, instead of *Fabian*. Even Theodor's situation in Danish detention had looked like it was going to be resolved.

After being postponed repeatedly for inexplicable reasons, the trial of the alleged murderers of the homeless woman was finally going to resume next week. The outcome had, according to Theodor's lawyer, Jadwiga Komorovski, been impossible to predict. It had, on the other hand, been clear that the court was going to consider his son's involvement marginal compared to that of the other perpetrators and, if convicted, his sentence would be unlikely to exceed a year or two.

Granted, that had been a huge setback, but they'd got through it. After all, Theodor had only acted as the lookout, and he had been forced to do even that much by the others. In other words, things had turned out as well as could be hoped, given the circumstances. And yet there had been a pain in his chest, as though the oxygen in the room were running out. Just like every morning since.

He turned to face Sonja, who had kicked off the duvet and lay on her back, breathing so slowly he had to lean in very close to feel her warm, damp exhalation. He gently kissed her cheek. But as though she wanted to avoid being pulled into his darkness at any cost, she averted her face and pushed him away.

Three days and nights and they had never been further apart.

It was already quarter to ten. If they kept going like this, they would soon have completely reversed their circadian rhythms. Just like the previous three days, he let her sleep, tiptoeing out of the bedroom.

The adrenaline rush had him wide awake, and it was as good a time as any to do the exercises his physiotherapist had given him. It took no more than thirty minutes and consisted of equal parts stretching, strength and balance. Working out indoors had never been his favourite thing to do, but he'd doggedly performed every last exercise every day for a month, and it had speeded up the healing of his hip considerably.

True, he still had a limp, and walking for too long made the pain return, radiating down into his leg. But he was no longer in a wheelchair, and he'd put the crutches aside two weeks earlier. Which had to be considered significant progress, considering it had only been a month since Kim Sleizner shot him in the leg.

An act that had been in every way uncalled for, since he

himself had been unarmed and had only moments earlier apprehended one of the most prolific serial killers in Scandinavian history. The affair had prompted his boss, Astrid Tuvesson, to contact Sweden's National Police Commissioner to request that he make an official complaint against Sleizner and the Danish Police Authority. But the commissioner had declined, arguing that their relationship with the Danes was strained enough already. Besides, the best possible outcome was simply an official apology.

In truth, the bullet in his leg was payback for not helping Sleizner locate Dunja Hougaard. That he had no idea where she was only served to make the whole thing even more absurd. Nevertheless, he'd decided to let it go and have as little as possible to do with the head of the Copenhagen Police in the future.

After a minute or two in front of his record collection, he decided on *Ancient Future* by Christopher Willits and Ryuichi Sakamoto. An album he'd ordered the other week because the algorithms were convinced he'd enjoy it.

He'd never heard of Willits, but he'd been a fan of Sakamoto since the early 1980s, and had elevated him to the realm of the greats in his collection when he co-wrote 'Forbidden Colours' with David Sylvian.

It started out just as sweeping and atmospheric as he'd hoped. He turned the volume up slightly, rolled out his yoga mat on the living-room floor and started to warm up. But he couldn't find his centre. Despite the meditative music, the relaxing exercises, and the fact that his only focus was on not thinking, the adrenaline rush refused to subside.

It was probably because today was the day. The day he, Sonja and Matilda had been waiting for since that fateful phone call: it was finally happening. Hopefully, it would put an end to the limbo they were living in and maybe even mark the start of something new. Something that could bring them closer together again. Closer in their grief, which so far had only served to push them apart.

In the end, he gave up on his exercises and walked over to the kitchen island where his phone was charging. Exactly like he'd done on Tuesday. This time, there was nothing. No texts or missed calls. On Tuesday, there had been a voicemail from Komorovski. She had tried to call him at 5.32 a.m., which he realized later was exactly when he'd tumbled into the black abyss for the first time.

Hi Fabian, this is Jadwiga Komorovski, she'd said in a tone that was so neutral it bordered on unnatural. *I'm sorry to call so early, but I would like you to call me back as soon as possible.* As though it wasn't really her, but rather a voice synthesizer programmed to mimic her.

With his heart pounding in his ears, he'd found her number and called, and as though it were too early in the morning for phone calls too, his phone had taken several seconds to make contact with the nearest mast and connect.

Hi Fabian, she'd said. This time in a tone that had dropped any attempt at neutrality. *I think you should sit down before we...*

Somewhere around that point, the phone had slipped out of his hand, as though it were suddenly too heavy, and skidded several feet across the floor. But he hadn't needed to hear another syllable. He'd already understood everything he would ever need to. More than anyone should ever have to.

The realization had made his knees buckle, and he'd collapsed on the floor next to his phone.

Fabian? What's going on? a voice had called to him. But it hadn't come from the phone, it had come from the stairs, and when he looked up, he'd seen Sonja standing there wrapped in a robe, Matilda next to her. *What are you doing? It's not even six.*

Don't you get it, Mum? Matilda had interjected. *It's Theodor. Isn't it, Dad, it's about Theodor, isn't it?*

He'd tried to respond, but the pressure on his chest had rendered him unable to speak.

Fabian, is that true? Sonja had demanded as tears began to stream down her face. *Is Matilda right? Is she? Fabian, answer me? Has Theo...*

He had looked from Sonja to Matilda and back again, unable to squeeze out so much as a word.

I knew it! Matilda had screamed as she burst into tears. *I told you! It's what I've been telling you all along!*

Fabian had found himself unable to cry or scream. He'd tried but hadn't been able to summon the required strength. He hadn't shed so much as a tear. As though he were unable to comprehend that Theodor no longer existed. That his own son had killed himself.

And yet part of him had been scared he might. Just a faint whisper. A subconscious premonition that this was the only way it could end. That no matter how hard he fought to steer events in a different direction, all roads led to this. Like a black hole whose gravity was impossible to escape.

But maybe it would all change today, in a few hours, when they would finally be able to go over and see him.

Look at him with their own eyes.

Behold the unfathomable.

7

THIS PARTICULAR HALLWAY was one of the most nondescript in the triangular building that housed the Copenhagen Police HQ. It was long and had neither doors nor windows. Nothing adorned the walls other than an uninspired shade of beige just slightly lighter than the brown linoleum floor.

But it was without doubt the hallway Jan Hesk had walked down more than any other. Not just during his years as a police officer, but likely in his entire life, including everything from school hallways to the front hallway of his own home. The diarrhoea hallway, as it had become known on account of its colour palette, connected the office section of the building with the meeting room section, and it wasn't unusual for him to hurry back and forth at least twenty times a day.

But he had never done it to get to a team meeting he was in charge of, and never before had he looked over his shoulder so many times.

He couldn't help it. He felt like everyone was watching him, judging his every move. Trin Bladh was probably right that he was just nervous about messing up. About being exposed as a charlatan who had got by on pure luck until now.

Doubt made him torn between hurrying so as not to waste precious minutes and turning around and running away.

In a way, the ambivalence came as a surprise. This was what

he'd been looking forward to for so many years. A murder investigation that might lead anywhere and make his life anything but dreary.

True, he would have felt more comfortable with a simple case while he got his bearings, and sure, there was something disturbing about this particular investigation. Something that made him wary.

But those were feelings and confused thoughts, and he had no time for either right now. If he was going to solve this case, he had to keep his wits about him and make sure to focus on the right thing, and not go off on irrelevant tangents.

He rounded a corner, entered the newly refurbished meeting room section and discovered that the rest of his team were already seated around a table behind one of the many gleaming glass walls. They didn't seem to be chatting idly either, which meant they'd started without him.

Fine, so he was late, he was. Almost fifteen minutes. But still. This was his investigation. He was supposed to lead the discussion and chart their course. A little bit of respect, was that too much to ask? Apparently, it was. Fifteen minutes was enough to make the mice play.

He'd been in the bathroom. He'd needed to sit down and collect his thoughts, away from all the eyes. All the judgement. It had been his first break since the early morning.

Normally, fifteen minutes alone behind a locked bathroom door was something he enjoyed. But this time, his body had seized up and insisted on clinging desperately to something it really ought to have let go of. And instead of preserving his strength for what lay ahead, he'd strained until sweat beaded his forehead, cursing his inability to complete even the most basic of tasks.

In the end, he'd been forced to admit defeat, wash his hands, and splash the sweat off his face before rushing to the meeting room. What the water hadn't rinsed off was his self-doubt, and the moment he put his hand on the handle of the glass door, it became obvious the rest of his team felt the same way. No one had any faith in him.

'With some luck, I might be able to get the GPS working,' Torben Hemmer was saying to Julie Bernstorff and Morten Heinesen. 'That would allow us to map the car's movements over the past few days.'

'Hi, Jan,' Heinesen said with a smile.

'Hi,' he replied, closing the door behind him. 'I'm sorry I'm a bit late.'

'No worries,' Hemmer replied without turning around. 'So I would suggest we wait and see if the dry-rice method does the trick.'

'It worked when I dropped my phone in the bath,' Bernstorff put in.

'Sure, but it's going to depend on the model and his settings.'

'Okay then, good. So, in other words, we'll see,' Hesk said in an attempt to seize the initiative. 'That's that, then. Let's get started.'

'As you can see, we already did.' Hemmer met his eyes with a smile. 'Wasn't there supposed to be lunch, by the way?'

Hesk realized he'd completely forgotten to pick up the sandwiches he'd ordered. 'Odd. It should have been here twenty minutes ago,' he said, and glanced at his watch to make his lie more believable.

'Okay, because the thing is I have to be back at the docks in an hour to talk to the divers.' Hemmer pointed the remote at the overhead projector and an image appeared on the lowered screen. 'What I want to highlight—'

'Torben, all due respect, but I think that has to wait,' Hesk broke in, moving towards the screen. 'Because I have a few other things we need to—'

'I'm sorry, I'm in a hurry,' Hemmer cut him off. 'Like I said, I need to get going.'

'Right, but I'm telling you it has to wait until I'm—'

'Torben, how long do you need?' Julie Bernstorff broke in.

'Twenty minutes. Tops.'

'Then I suggest you do your thing now, and the rest of us can keep going when you leave. That works, right? What do you say, Morten?'

'I suggest we leave that to Jan, since he's in charge of the investigation.'

'But if you want me to have time to go over my things, I need to—'

'The only thing you need to do right now is turn off the projector, sit down, and listen,' Hesk broke in, with a calm that surprised even himself. 'Nothing else. Is that understood?'

Hemmer stood motionless with the remote in his hand. He glanced over at Bernstorff, who shrugged.

'I said, is that understood?'

After a long moment, Hemmer nodded, turned off the projector and sat down.

'There we go. Thank you.' Hesk looked around the room, meeting Hemmer's, Bernstorff's and Heinesen's eyes. 'As you all know, this is my first time leading an investigation, and I'll be the first to admit that I'm nervous and that I've spent the past few hours seriously doubting whether I'm the right man for this job.'

'Oh Jan, come on,' Heinesen said. 'Why wouldn't you be...'

Hesk held up a hand to silence him before continuing. 'I'd hoped our first case would be relatively straightforward. A chance for us to get to know each other and bond a little. To team build, simply put.' He went over to one of the glass walls and began to lower and angle the blinds, one after another. 'But when one of the victims turned out to be the Head of Operations for our intelligence service, I realized it would be anything but straightforward, and after swinging by Forensics earlier, I can only say that it's even worse than I thought.'

'I'm sorry, what have you found out?' Bernstorff said.

'I'll get to that. But first I need to make sure you trust me. If you don't, we'll never solve this.'

'What do you mean, trust?' Hemmer shrugged. 'We only just met, we barely know each other.'

'That's entirely correct. But nevertheless, I'm in charge of this investigation. So you either let me do my job, or you hand in your resignation.'

'No, that's fine. I'm on board.' Hemmer threw up his hands and sat down.

'And you two?' He turned to Bernstorff and Heinesen.

'Of course I trust you,' Heinesen said. 'I always have.'

'Me too,' Bernstorff agreed.

'Good. I'm glad.' He lowered the last blind with renewed vigour. 'Then I suggest we get to work.' He took over the remote and pushed the button to raise the screen. Then he went over to the whiteboard mounted on the wall behind it and turned on the lights. 'Right, there was one more thing. I would like to ask you to cancel any plans you might have for the rest of the week, as this will very likely require us all to put in extra hours.'

'Can I ask what makes this case so complicated?' Hemmer said.

'Two things, mainly. Firstly, as we've already touched on, one of the victims was the Head of Operations at DSIS. As soon as that information becomes public knowledge, all eyes will be on us. That is why I've said as little as possible and am holding off on the press conference for as long as I can.'

'So we're not going to make any of the information public?' Bernstorff asked.

'We will, but for now we're keeping it to a minimum. Secondly, it has become clear beyond a doubt that we're dealing with a third person. A person who not only drove the car off the pier but also murdered the woman, which means our theory about erotic asphyxiation and suicide is out the window.'

'Do we have any idea who it might be?' Bernstorff asked.

'No, but a number of factors point to it being the owner of this.' Hesk held up a transparent vacuum-sealed bag that contained the colourful handkerchief and then passed it to Hemmer.

'Where did you find this?' Hemmer studied it from various angles before handing it to Bernstorff. 'In her mouth?'

'I would probably call it her throat. It was pushed very far down.'

'It's a classic Paul Smith,' Bernstorff said. 'But what I don't understand is how this points to there being a third person.'

'Just let me be clear that by third person I mean someone in addition to the two victims. There could, of course, be more than one. Back to your question. I don't know how familiar you are with Mogens Klinge's sartorial style, but a Paul Smith handkerchief is probably as far from it as you can get.'

'But he was wearing a tuxedo?'

'Sure, but it was a rental from Amorin on Frederiksberg, and they don't carry Paul Smith handkerchiefs.'

'Julie has a point, though,' Hemmer said. 'It's hardly proof a third person was involved.'

'I agree. But I would claim this is.' Hesk passed around a

close-up of the female victim's nails, which clearly showed something dark underneath them. 'According to Trin Bladh, the woman's hands had been washed, but despite that, she found plenty of blood and tissue under her nails – she must have scratched her killer pretty good.' He passed around another picture, of the bent-back nail. 'The samples have been sent off for analysis, of course. But the thing is that there are no scratches on Klinge's body.'

Hesk let silence settle in the room and relished watching the others nod as they looked at the pictures. Maybe he could do this after all.

'Well, well, well. What have we here?'

Hesk turned around to see Kim Sleizner enter the room.

'Hi, Kim,' he said with a smile, even though Sleizner was the very last person he wanted to see just then. 'As you can see, we're in the middle of a meeting.' Of course he had to come in and try to take over. 'Was there something you needed?'

'Oh dear, getting your own office has sure made you cocky, I see.'

'I'm sorry, I didn't mean it like that. I was just wondering if there was something urgent you needed us to do right now...'

'No, no, no. Calm down. Everything's fine.' Sleizner held up his hands. 'Carry on, don't let me distract you. I mostly just wanted to see how you're doing.'

'We're only just getting started, but things are going well, actually.'

'That's great.' Sleizner nodded. 'Not that I would ever think otherwise. Not with you behind the wheel.'

'Thank you.'

'No, thank *you*. I really mean that. After all, this is a case that's going to draw quite a bit of media attention, so it's good to know it's in safe hands.' Sleizner turned to the others. 'And as for the rest of you, I want you to listen very carefully. Not to me, but to that man there.' He pointed to Hesk. 'Because he knows what he's talking about. And besides, I'm off to the dentist to fix a filling so I'll be gone for the rest of the day.'

Heinesen and the others nodded. Hesk made sure to keep a straight face, even though he didn't believe a word coming out of Sleizner's mouth.

'Okay, great. I'm done bothering you, then,' Sleizner continued, turning towards the door. 'Just one more thing.' He turned back to Hesk. 'When do you think you'll have something to present? I mean, apart from the fact that this Klinge seems to have stuck his hand a bit too deep into the cookie jar.'

'Well, like I said, we've only had this for a few hours. But we're working as quickly as we can.'

'Sounds terrific. Just make sure you keep me informed about your progress, though I hardly think it takes a rocket scientist to figure out what happened. Am I right?'

Hesk knew what he was supposed to say. But he said nothing. Maybe it was something in Sleizner's eyes or tone. He had no problem understanding that his boss was unsure if he'd be able to solve this case. He probably doubted it even more than he did himself.

But that didn't mean he was going to just give up and roll over. This was his investigation, his chance to show everyone that not only did he deserve his promotion, he was a force to be reckoned with. But to do that, he needed to keep Sleizner as far away from the case as possible.

'Okay, Jan, I get it,' Sleizner said at length. 'You're the captain of this ship, and you obviously have to turn over every stone before you make pronouncements. What I'm trying to tell you is that this isn't a case that should be drawn out unnecessarily.

This isn't the time to go interviewing everyone Klinge went to school with or analysing every last bin within several miles' radius of the crime scene. The sooner we can wrap this up, the better.'

'Of course. That's how we're approaching this, and the second we learn anything of interest, you'll be hearing from me,' Hesk replied, having carefully weighed each word.

8

THEY WERE SHOWN into the lift. Sonja, Matilda and him. And their lawyer, Jadwiga Komorovski. None of them spoke, and while the lift descended, silence reigned. Each of them in their own darkness. Their eyes focused on anything but each other: a smudge on the wall, a flickering light bulb, a cluster of swirling dust motes. Or nothing.

They were standing there because of him and his actions. There was no other way of looking at it. He was the one who had pushed Theodor to contact the Helsingør Police to give a witness statement, to tell the truth. His insistence had pushed his son to try to jump in front of a train in Pålsjö Forest. He'd only just managed to stop him at the very last second. And still he had refused to let up, and a few days later they'd gone over to Denmark together.

He'd tried to tell himself he couldn't have known they would arrest Theodor. That in his wildest dreams he would never have imagined the consequences. But it wasn't true. All the signs had been there. Every warning he'd needed to avert disaster.

The lift doors slid open, and they were received by a woman in a lab coat with her hair pulled back. With a simple nod, she led them through a hallway with a shiny floor and dirty walls. They passed hospital beds here and there. Most were empty, but on some, thin sheets concealed bodies.

This was clearly not a place intended for visitors. And they had been offered to see Theodor in one of Helsingør's funeral parlours, where there would be a more dignified space. But transporting the body there and setting everything up would have meant another day's delay, and if there was one thing Fabian couldn't do, it was wait more.

He needed to see Theodor, and he needed to see him now. If for no other reason than to squash the thought once and for all that maybe this was just a misunderstanding, so he could finally accept that the only thing left for him to do was grieve.

He had almost gone over to Helsingør on Tuesday. Without any real plan, intending simply to turn up at the detention facility unannounced, flash his police ID, and force them to let him in to see Theodor. But he had checked himself, for Sonja and Matilda's sake. His role was to provide calm and stability, and every day he'd tried to explain to them how different the rules were in Denmark, that they had no choice but to wait for the Danes to invite them.

But in his heart, he'd been furious and unable to understand what was taking so long. Without telling Sonja, he'd hassled Komorovski, who had hassled the Danes in turn, but no one had been able to provide any form of coherent explanation, other than that there was a lot of extra paperwork involved because he wasn't a Danish citizen, which sounded like an excuse.

The woman stopped in front of a door and knocked three times before swiping her card through a reader, punching in a four-digit code and leading them into a room where several candles, flowers in a vase, and sheets taped to the walls did their best to hide the fact that they were in a mortuary.

In front of him, Komorovski shook hands with a man in a white coat and a short, stocky man wearing glasses and a jacket with elbow patches. He could hear that they were saying things but couldn't make out the words. It didn't matter now anyway.

Because there, at the back of the room, lay the body. On a collapsible stretcher under a white sheet, it lay there, motionless, and with every step he took towards it, hope swelled inside him. Hope he knew was futile, which he did everything he could to ignore.

But now that he was here, it was impossible to fend off the notion that maybe this wasn't Theodor. That there was a chance, despite everything, a small chance. That his Swedish personal identification number had been mixed up with a Danish one. Or that this was a nightmare that would end the moment he grabbed the sheet, composed himself, and folded it back.

Theodor looked like he always had when he was sleeping. His closed eyes and that peaceful shimmer that made every last muscle in his face relax. That made Fabian want to wake him with a gentle kiss on the forehead. Like he'd wanted to do every day since he became a father. Never mind that colic had racked his son's tiny body, making every waking hour a struggle.

He wanted to wake him now too, and as though the motion had come from so deep inside his lizard brain he was powerless to stop it, he bent down over Theodor, who, just like when he was little, looked like sleep had freed him of pain.

After that, nothing was the same. The cold that met his lips spread through him and changed everything. Gone was any form of doubt and left was only the realization that his son, his darling son, no longer existed.

But no tears came. Try as he might to conjure them, it was as though his grief had seized up and was refusing him access. But Sonja and Matilda, they cried. He could see the tears glistening on their cheeks, and from far away he could hear it too. The grief that was overflowing.

He went over and wrapped his arms around them. Held them as tight as he could, to console them, but also to try to feel like them. But he couldn't. He wasn't there. He could feel that now. More clearly than ever. He needed to know. Like the detective he was, he needed to know exactly what had happened.

'And how did he die?' he said, letting go of Sonja and Matilda.

'Fabian, you already know that,' Komorovski said. 'I told you on the phone.'

'Yes. But I want to hear it from him.' He walked up to the doctor. 'Because you're the one who performed the autopsy, right?'

'Yes, that's correct. My name is Frank Bendt Nielsen, and I'm the coroner here.'

'And my very simple question is: how did Theodor die?'

'Fabian, is this really necessary?' Sonja said.

'Yes,' he replied. 'I'm afraid it is.' Then he turned back to the doctor.

'Your son hanged himself.'

'Where? Where did he hang himself?'

'Dad, please, stop.'

'Matilda, let me handle this. I said, where did my son hang himself?'

'In his cell,' the corpulent man replied, extending his hand. 'Flemming Friis. I'm in charge of the Helsingør Detention Facility, and I want to start by expressing my deepest condolences. What happened is in every way a terrible tragedy. Not just for you, but for all of us who work here.'

'So he hanged himself in his cell. And exactly how did it happen?'

'What do you mean?'

'I mean, how did he go about it? I assume you don't supply ropes or anything else that—'

'Fabian, please, stop,' Sonja cut in.

'Honey, I'm sorry, but I need to know what happened. How is it that a young man who was kept under watch as though he were already a convicted murderer managed to hang himself in his cell?'

'Fabian, it goes without saying that you will have all the answers.' Komorovski walked up to him. 'But this isn't the time. We're only here to—'

'Jadwiga, I know why we're here.'

'Pardon me.' Flemming Friis adjusted his glasses and took a step towards him. 'I understand that you feel a need to understand what happened here. You're a police officer and we will hold nothing back. The problem is that we're not done with our investigation.'

'You've kept us waiting for three days just to come and see him, an eternity in this kind of context, and you still don't know what happened?'

'What we do know for sure is that he ripped his bed sheet into long strips and plaited them into a rope.'

'Dear lord.' Sonja shook her head. 'Do we really have to listen to this?'

'Honey, you can wait for me outside if you want. Maybe that would be for the best. I'll be out as soon as I'm done here.' He turned back to Flemming Friis. 'Go on.'

'Then he tied the two ends together, picked up his bed, leaned it against the wall, and then—'

'Hold on. He picked up his bed? How is that possible? Isn't it bolted to the wall, like in every other jail?'

'That's correct, and it shouldn't have been possible. But

somehow, he must have had access to a wrench, though we don't know how yet.' Friis shrugged.

'And then? What did he do next?'

'Well, then he tied the sheet around the leg of the bed and his own neck. Then he sat down, and that's how we found him.'

Unreasonable as it sounded, it was, in fact, at least marginally plausible. And why wouldn't it be? What had he been thinking? That someone had something to hide? They were all aware Theodor hadn't been doing well. But that he'd been desperate enough to undertake all that preparation and in the end actually go through with it had come as a shock to everyone at the facility.

'Do you have any other questions?' Friis said.

Fabian shook his head. He was bursting with questions, but couldn't think of a single one, so he took Sonja and Matilda by the hand and turned to leave.

'And if there's anything else, we'll know more after the autopsy. That's just how it is. So it would really be best if we could wait for that.'

'Of course.' Komorovski shook hands with Friis. 'We'll talk about it then.'

It was possibly the fact that Flemming Friis's hand had begun to tremble, or the glance he'd exchanged with the doctor, the slightly anxious glance. Or maybe the barely noticeable shift in his tone of voice.

'Great, we'll talk to you then.'

Whatever it was, alarms had immediately started going off in Fabian's head, screaming at him to stop and turn around again.

'Darling, what's the matter?' Sonja said behind him. 'We're leaving now.'

But he couldn't pay her any heed. Not now. This was too

important. 'I'm sorry, he hasn't been autopsied? Like I said, it's been three days.'

'He has, but it was a clinical autopsy. In order to be completely sure, we need a forensic—'

'Okay,' Fabian cut in. 'But then I think I would prefer for that to be performed in Sweden. So I would suggest we take him with us.'

'I'm afraid that's out of the question.' Friis shook his head and adjusted his glasses again. 'He will need to be examined here, in...'

'No, you've had him for long enough.' Fabian walked back into the room. 'And I'm not just talking about the past few days, I'm talking about the past month. A month during which you've produced not one credible argument for why his trial was postponed. Am I right, Jadwiga?' He turned to Komorovski, who nodded.

'I understand, but that's up to the prosecutor. Not...'

'Excuse my language, but I don't give a shit about who it's up to. It's enough already. Do you hear me? Enough.' He started to walk towards the stretcher and heard Matilda burst into tears and Sonja comforting her. But even though it was too late, there was no other way to go now.

'Listen here,' Friis said, following him. 'The incident took place here in Denmark, and...'

'No, you listen to me.' Fabian rounded on Friis. 'My son came here voluntarily, as a witness. To help you convict a bunch of killers. You thanked him by arresting him and treating him like another suspect. Now it's time for him to come home with us.'

'I hear you, but it simply can't be done. We are required to keep him here until we've...'

'You can say whatever you want, I don't care. I'm not

leaving him here again. Do you understand me?' He grabbed the stretcher and disengaged the brakes.

'Fabian, listen to me.' Komorovski came up to him. 'You do understand that we can't obstruct their investigation.'

'I don't trust them. Something's not right here, and I'm going to find out what.'

'Come on, Matilda.' Sonja put her arm around their sobbing daughter. 'Let's go.' They disappeared into the hallway.

'Fabian, I'm begging you.' Komorovski put her hand on his shoulder. 'You have to calm down. This is pointless. You know that as well as I do.'

Fabian shook his head. He had no reason to calm down. No reason to back down. He could see that more clearly than ever. From their reactions, their nervous looks. That regardless of the rules and regulations, right was on his side.

9

THE ARTICLE HAD been published on *Ekstra Bladet*'s website just minutes before. And it was hardly above-the-fold stuff. If anything, it seemed to have been written with a shrug of the shoulders. As though it weren't really news, just an event they felt obliged to inform the public of.

Two bodies discovered outside the Refs Peninsula, the uninspired headline read. The body of the article said a woman kayaking with her boyfriend had discovered a dead woman and a dead man in a car at the bottom of the harbour in the early hours of the morning. The only picture had been taken from a considerable distance and showed a white van surrounded by the members of the investigation team.

Dunja had no problem understanding why *Ekstra Bladet* had instead led with an article about how to get through a camping holiday without filing for divorce. Two dead bodies in Copenhagen was about as remarkable as Himmelbjerget – one of Denmark's highest points at 482 feet above sea level.

And yet something about it made her prick up her ears. Something that made her read and reread the brief article several times and scrutinize the picture for further information. But the only thing she could wring from it was that one of the men in the picture looked like Jan Hesk and that they must have cordoned off an unusually large area.

It was the same on the other news sites. A grainy picture

taken from afar and two short paragraphs. It was almost as though the various outlets were competing to be the most terse.

In truth, it smelled of the police trying to keep the lid on, a tactic they used whenever an investigation was extra sensitive for whatever reason. But they didn't fool her. This was clearly the reason Sleizner had woken up so early and cancelled all his meetings.

'Okay, the subject is arriving,' Fareed said, his eyes glued to one of the screens, where a red dot was moving on a map.

'The subject.' Qiang shook his head. 'Why can't we just call him Sleizner?'

'Because that's not how it's done. Especially when there's more than one person. Then you have to label them subject 1, 2, 3, or, alternatively, A, B, C, so there's no confusion.'

'But we only have one.'

'How can you be sure? Most things point to there being at least two more, and why would it have to end there?'

'Right, so it's a good thing he has a name. Which is Sleizner.' Fareed sighed and shook his head.

'Fareed,' Dunja interjected. 'Why don't you just tell us where he is.'

'He has just parked his car on Amaliegade and is now travelling on foot across Sankt Paul Square towards Zeleste.'

'Alone or with someone?'

'It's hard to tell while he's on the move. The only thing we can triangulate to an exact location is his phone.'

'But he's not talking to anyone, for what that's worth,' Qiang put in, his headset in his ears. 'No additional subjects.' His eyes were on his screen, which was dark apart from a faint hint of light right at the top.

'Can I hear?' Dunja said.

'Sure. But this is as exciting as it gets.' Qiang turned up the volume, and a rustling sound from one of the speakers revealed that Sleizner's phone was in his pocket.

'He has entered the restaurant.' Fareed zoomed in on the map, on which the dot was still moving. 'And it looks like he's being shown to a table in the courtyard.'

'Great. Then maybe we can even dare to hope for some reception,' Qiang said.

'How's his battery life?' Dunja asked.

'It's at seventeen per cent, but how long that'll last is anyone's—'

'At least he has stopped moving now,' Fareed cut in.

'All right, so he's probably seated then,' Dunja said, looking back and forth between their screens.

The red dot on the map was no longer moving, and the glimpses of light at the top of Qiang's screen were gone. Even the rustling sound had subsided. In other words, nothing was happening, other than that the seconds were turning into minutes.

Since discovering Sleizner's reservation for three, Dunja had been looking forward to this. But only now did it occur to her that she had no earthly idea what to expect, other than that it should be something. Otherwise, why would he have labelled this a dentist appointment in his official work calendar?

'This isn't working,' she said after a few more minutes. 'We need to do something. Fareed, how precise is the positioning of the other phones around him?'

'Given that they don't have GPS trackers, unlike Sleizner's, my best guess is somewhere between thirty and sixty feet.'

'Okay, get me a list of everyone within fifty feet of the wanker.'

Fareed nodded and pushed his chair over to the next work area, where he booted up another computer.

'The wanker,' repeated Qiang, who had been working on adjusting the sound settings. 'Maybe that should be his code name.'

He pushed the volume up even higher, and now voices could be heard through the speakers. But only as a faint mumbling, the words impossible to make out.

Dunja went over to Qiang and leaned closer to the speaker. 'Can you hear what they're saying?'

Qiang shook his head.

'This is fucked. We have to make him take it out of his pocket before we miss the whole thing.'

'And how are we going to do that?' Fareed said, his eyes on the screen, where a map showing the area around Restaurant Zeleste was populated with numerous mobile phone numbers. 'Call him up and ask him to put his phone on the table? Hi Kim, it's Dunja. Would you mind…'

'I have an idea,' Qiang broke in, and he looked up at the screen above, which showed Sleizner's mobile desktop. He clicked his way into Contacts, found the name Viveca Sleizner and clicked the number, and the phone dialled.

'Are you sure about this?' Dunja said as they listened to the phone ring on the speakers.

'No,' Qiang said, shaking his head.

'*Yes, what do you want?*' Sleizner's ex-wife's weary voice said. Qiang put her on speakerphone. '*Hello?*' Viveca said. '*Kim, I know it's you, and you know I prefer to communicate through our lawyers.*'

'*Viveca, is that you?*' Sleizner's voice came through loud and clear. '*What do you want? I'm in the middle of—*'

'*What do I want? You called me.*'

'*I did? Sorry, I must have pocket dialled you. Bye now.*'

There was a click and the call ended.

The screen that had been completely dark now showed parts of the yellow half-timbered façades surrounding the courtyard and a shade sail blocking out the sun. And the sound of voices was finally coming through loud and clear.

'And the phone is on the table!' Qiang exclaimed, getting up to do a quick victory dance.

'Very nice,' Dunja said. 'Not the dance, obviously, the...'

Fareed shushed her and turned the volume up even higher.

'*I'm sorry, where were we?*' Sleizner said.

'*You were telling us you've put Jan Hesk on the case,*' a man's voice replied. '*And to be perfectly honest, I would have preferred if it were you leading...*' The sound began to skip and then cut out for several seconds.

'No, not now.' Dunja turned to Qiang. 'Do something, please.'

'His battery's down to seven per cent.'

'Seven? Didn't you just tell me seventeen?'

'Yes, but now it's seven.' Qiang opened the camera app. 'I'll try turning off the camera.'

The screen showing the yellow timber-framed façades and a patch of sky went black.

'*Last time was one time too many.*' Sleizner was speaking again. '*Trying to pull that again would constitute an unacceptable risk. It simply can't be done. That said, you have nothing to worry about. I have every faith in Hesk and I'm convinced he will handle this with aplomb.*'

'*How the hell do you expect me not to worry after—*'

'*Look, listen to me,*' Sleizner cut in. '*Whatever Klinge did or didn't do, it has nothing to do with us, okay? That's on him. I can promise you that as soon as this case is closed, everything will go back to normal again.*'

'Klinge,' Dunja said. 'Ring a bell, anyone?'

Fareed and Qiang shook their heads.

'*The problem is that all they have to do is scratch the surface ever so...*' a third voice continued before the sound began to skip again. '*... Mogens' close connections with not just the police, but every part of the legal system.*'

'Mogens. Mogens Klinge.' Fareed turned to the others. 'Isn't that the guy from DSIS?'

'That would explain why they're keeping a lid on this,' Dunja said.

'*At the end of the day, we're just hard-working law enforcement officers, tasked with finding out what happened,*' Sleizner said. '*And if you ask me, it's fairly obvious, and I can promise you it will be obvious to Hesk, too.*'

'*You promise a lot of things. Maybe too much sometimes. Just look at what's happened to—*'

'*Look, I know Hesk,*' Sleizner broke in. '*He's a good little simpleton who will do exactly what's expected of him. One plus one equals two. No more, no less. Trust me.*'

'*You keep saying that. Over and over, as though that would make it more convincing. But let me make one thing absolutely clear...*' The voice was once again chopped into indecipherability and drowned in digital white noise.

'Oh come on, can't you do something?' Dunja turned to Qiang. 'We're missing it.'

'What do you want me to do? The phone's out of juice. It's down to two per cent and could die any second.'

'I don't know. Try closing all other apps.'

'It won't help. It's just...'

'I don't care, do it anyway. Just do something.'

'*Jakob, I've saved your skin once, and I won't...*' Sleizner's voice suddenly returned, only to disappear again just as abruptly.

Dunja turned to Fareed. 'Is there a Jakob within fifty feet?'

Fareed searched the growing list of names and phone numbers.

'*He reports directly to me, so I'm completely in control, okay? Completely in control,*' Sleizner's voice cut through the hissing static. '*This'll blow over.*'

'Three, actually,' Fareed said. 'Jakob Larsen, Jakob Sand and Jakob Brønnum.'

'Jakob Sand, isn't that the obscenely rich entrepreneur?' Qiang said.

Dunja nodded. She wasn't surprised in the slightest to find Sleizner fraternizing with a nouveau-riche misogynist who had likened the women he'd left to a weak poker hand.

'*Just one more thing before we wrap this up.*' Sleizner's voice returned again.

'How much battery does he have left?'

'Still two per cent, so maybe it did help a little after all.'

'*That thing we talked about in our last meeting. Did you see to it?*' The voice disappeared again. But there was no static this time. Rather, a group seated somewhere nearby had burst into raucous laughter, dominating the soundscape. '*You know, the thing about going public with...*' Another round of laughter made it impossible to make out what he said.

'This is fucked.' Dunja took out her own phone and dialled.

'What are you doing?' Qiang said while Dunja waited. But she only had time to put a finger to her lips.

'*Welcome to Restaurant Zeleste,*' a woman's voice said on the other end. '*How can I help you?*'

'This is supposed to be a calm and exclusive restaurant. At least, that's what I expected coming here.'

'*I see, so you're here now?*'

'Where I am is hardly the point. The problem at hand is

the group sitting a few tables away from us in the courtyard. Considering how loud and inappropriate they're being, I must say I'm surprised you haven't already come out to inform them that this isn't some campsite at the Roskilde Festival.'

'*Of course, I'll be right out to have a word with them.*'

'Wonderful. Maybe I'll be able to hear myself think again.' Dunja ended the call and moments later the noise from the adjacent table subsided.

'*The thing is that all the paperwork has to be in order,*' said the voice they hadn't been able to identify. '*Because this directive you're asking me for is a big one.*' The question was how much – and more importantly, what – they had missed.

'*I would prefer for it to go out as soon as possible.*'

'*So I've gathered. But you're going to have to wait until midnight tomorrow. That's the earliest I can do. Everything has to be done by the book unless we want it to come back and bite us.*'

'*Of course. I'm just worried...*' And then the sound disappeared again.

Dunja sighed and turned to Qiang.

'Don't look at me. What the fuck do you want me to do?' Qiang said. 'The battery is...'

Dunja clapped a hand to his mouth.

'*... could become a far bigger problem than Klinge,*' Sleizner said, half-buried in static.

'*Kim, I've heard all of this a thousand times, and if you ask me, you're suffering from an unhealthy obsession. But that's your problem. It'll go out tomorrow at midnight. Neither sooner nor later.*'

The voice faded into static again.

Then the static died too.

Leaving only silence.

10

THE GRIEF WAS monumental. A dark abyss that devoured everything and made him so fragile the lightest of taps in the wrong place would be enough to shatter him. But above all, it was a dry grief. A grief disconnected from all the emotions that were expected of him. That should have been there.

He had tried to conjure them by thinking about all the wonderful moments he and Theodor had shared. Like when he learned to ride a bike or swim. Or when he used to crawl into their bed after having nightmares about Darth Vader. All the games they'd played and all the laughs they'd shared. Before everything went off the rails. But nothing helped.

Not even when he was sitting there in the Danish ambulance, with his hand on Theodor's cold chest and his eyes on the face that had been given all the best parts of him and Sonja. Not even then could he feel anything other than a burning desire to find out what had really happened in the Danish detention facility.

It wasn't that he didn't know it was wrong. That he should leave things be and spend his time looking after Sonja and Matilda. He was already fully aware of how much he would regret this. Once it was too late and what he still had left was lost too. But try as he might, this was the only thing he was capable of.

The ambulance pulled up outside a red-brick house.

'All right, this is it. Traktörsgatan 38.' The Danish driver peered through the windscreen at the residential street. 'But it doesn't look much like a hospital.'

'We just need to pick up the coroner first,' Fabian replied, and found his number.

After a protracted discussion peppered with threats about suing them all in Swedish court, he'd managed to convince the Danes to allow the forensic autopsy to be performed in Helsingborg rather than Helsingør.

'You've reached Einar Greide at Forensics,' Flätan's voicemail said on the other end. *'And yes, you got it right. I don't have time to talk to you right now. And no, I don't have time to listen to your message either.'*

Fabian climbed out of the ambulance and straightened up. A group of young men roughly Theodor's age were standing about twenty yards away with skateboards under their arms, looking from him to the Danish ambulance and back again. He nodded to them and went over to Flätan's house.

It was his second visit, and just like the first time, he was struck by how little he knew about his colleague. That he was an eccentric had been immediately obvious at their first meeting. The crocheted, candy-cane striped trousers and the plaits that each represented a victim in the ongoing investigation. That he was one of Sweden's absolute top forensic pathologists he'd discovered much later.

That was about all he knew, because what Einar 'Flätan' Greide prized more than anything else was his privacy. He kept his work life out of his private life like no one else. They were separate worlds and never the twain were allowed to meet. Which explained why he had no compunction about keeping his phone turned off the entire time he was on leave.

About thirty bicycles were parked inside the gate and on the driveway leading up to the garage. Everything from cargo bikes with peace-sign stickers to long recumbent bikes. He'd heard rumours that Flätan rode bikes in his free time, and that he'd once cycled all the way down to Düsseldorf to compete in a bike race, ten years ago. But it still seemed improbable that he would own that many different bikes.

He continued in through the gate and up the garden path to the front door, where he rang the bell. The sound of voices drifted through the dense foliage, and he wondered whether he should have waited until Flätan's guests had left and he was alone.

No sooner had the thought occurred to him than the door was opened by a topless man holding a colourful cocktail. Simultaneously, an electronic track with a thudding bassline rumbled through the vegetation and out into the neighbourhood. That it was only noon was apparently not a matter of concern.

'Flätan, is he home?' he said.

'What?' the man said in English.

'Flätan,' Fabian said again. 'Is he...'

'Just come in,' the man cut in, and he melted back into the crowd.

Fabian followed and looked around at the partying men and women, who ranged in age from twenty all the way to what looked like at least eighty. In another life, he might have found the scene exciting. Now, the overcrowding coupled with the heavy bass made him feel claustrophobic.

He pushed through a cluster of dancing people, past the bar where a man and a woman with identical haircuts were mixing drinks, dressed in onesies that were as tight as they were sequined. Here and there on sofas and on piles of large floor pillows, guests in bikinis and Speedos reclined, laughing, snogging or sleeping.

He couldn't understand how any of them were laughing. How they could allow themselves to find joy in anything. He wanted to locate the main power breaker and turn it off. Scream at them to take their bikes and get out of there, so he could find Flätan and do what needed to be done.

The electronic groove was loud in the garden too, pulsing out of concealed speakers. But the volume was slightly lower here and the air easier to breathe, even though the lawn was also full of guests.

Then he spotted Flätan. Dressed in a kaftan, wide bone-white harem trousers and sandals, with a pink feather boa around his neck, he was standing behind a DJ deck, whipping his shoulder-length grey hair, which was unplaited for once, back and forth.

Fabian moved towards him but before he could reach him, Flätan turned around to flip through his vinyl collection and noticed him.

'Fabian?' He froze mid-motion.

'Flätan, I know you're on...'

'Fabian, Fabian,' Flätan cut him off and his face broke into a smile. 'No worries. I don't recall inviting you, but if anyone from work is welcome here, it's you. So just relax, take off those clothes and have a drink.'

'Thanks, but... Flätan, I'm sorry, but I'm not here to...'

'You want to get in on this action. Is that it? A little battle? You're a music lover, right, or so I've heard. By the way, do you know this one?' He turned back to the deck and pushed the volume up further. '"2 Hearts" by Digitalism. Brilliant stuff.'

'Flätan.' Fabian went up to him. 'I'm here because I need your...'

'Hold on, I just have to...' Flätan angled his head so one of his ears was pressed against the headphones around his neck, while he expertly moved the needle into position and started Kraftwerk's 'Musique Non Stop'.

'You definitely know this one.' Flätan turned back to him. 'Did you know I'm mates with Ralf Hütter and one of the few outsiders to have been inside the Kling Klang studio?' He shook his head. 'Now that's a genius.'

'Flätan.' Fabian grabbed Flätan by the shoulders and looked him in the eye. 'I'm here because I need your help.'

Flätan's smile turned into a thin line. 'And why am I even surprised? The fact that I'm on summer leave is apparently neither here nor there, nor that I'm in the middle of hosting a party.'

'If I had any other options, I wouldn't ask. I hope you know that. Have you been drinking?'

'What, alcohol?' Flätan gave him a disgusted look. 'Are you out of your mind? Not since I was fourteen. Fabian, what is this about? Can't you just ask Arne Gruvesson? I mean, granted, he may not be the drummer with the sickest groove. But he's on call and I can promise you he's just waiting for something exciting to—'

'Flätan, I'm begging you,' Fabian cut in. 'It's not a new case. It's my son. Do you understand? My son.'

Flätan seemed completely taken aback and looked at Fabian as if to gauge whether he was having him on. Then he nodded sharply and pulled off the boa. 'Come on, let's go.'

11

Jan Hesk had never understood why virtually every Copenhagener had at some point in their life dreamed of living in Kartoffelrækkerne – a neighbourhood consisting of almost five hundred terraced houses in the middle of the city, originally built as basic accommodation for the labourers at a number of large potato farms, hence the name. These days, the privilege of living in one came with a hefty price tag, even though the rooms were cramped and the ceilings so low anyone over six feet had to hunch over.

That said, he had to admit there was a certain idyllic small-town feel to the place as he walked up Jens Juels Gade after parking his car around the corner. Some children were kicking a football in the middle of the street, while others played hopscotch. A large group of people were celebrating a birthday with cake and coffee at tables in the shade of large patio umbrellas.

The sense of community was what the neighbourhood was most known for. The way the residents thought of themselves as one big family made up of successful artists, media types, and general high-ups like Mogens Klinge.

He passed the birthday party, where the din died down as if on cue, to be replaced by worried eyes that followed him. Klinge had probably been invited to the party, and when he hadn't made an appearance, they'd begun to suspect that something was amiss. And who knows? One of them might have seen something suspicious. As soon as he was done with the house, he was going to make sure to interview every last one of them.

Klinge's wife had died of breast cancer five years earlier. He'd read that in one of the many interviews he'd come across. Klinge had told the local paper how lonely he'd felt in his grief, since he had neither children nor siblings, saying he would never have got through that difficult time without his amazing neighbours.

Lonely or not, at least he'd continued to tend the small garden patch in front of number 38. Unlike several of the neighbouring plots, where rickety outdoor furniture cried out for oiling and nature was reclaiming parts of the façade, it was swept and tidy. The tree in front of the house was neatly trimmed and the picket fence was gleamingly white.

After pulling on gloves, Hesk took out the keys Hemmer had found in the car, unlocked the front door and stepped inside. The air was fusty, so he left the door ajar and continued into the living room, which was a textbook example of why he could never live in Kartoffelrækkerne.

It was likely the biggest room in the house, but there were simply too many things crammed into too small a space. While it was charming and homely in a way, he couldn't shake the feeling of having stepped into a doll's house.

Morten Heinesen had offered to come with him, but this was something he'd wanted to do alone. Sure, they were supposed to be a team and help each other. He wished for nothing more. The thing was just that he basically hadn't succeeded at anything all day. What he needed was something to help him gain their trust.

He already had Heinesen's. But the other two, Hemmer and

Bernstorff, it didn't matter what they said and how much they nodded along. If he didn't manage to unearth an interesting clue or at least an angle of attack none of the others had thought of, it wouldn't be long before they stopped listening and started to make their own decisions behind his back.

The problem was that he was all out of ideas. He had no clue what to look for. Somehow, he'd hoped just stepping into the house would make answers jump out at him. Something to catch his interest and help him make the investigation progress as quickly as they all wished it would.

But scanning the room, nothing seemed significant. All he could see was a bookcase full of books, a few landscape paintings on the walls, a stack of newspapers, a dark-blue sofa, a well-worn armchair in front of the TV and potted plants in the window.

Maybe he was the problem. Maybe the room was positively littered with clues and leads, if only he'd had the ability to analyse what he was looking at.

Like the fact that the bookshelf consisted mainly of non-fiction and biographies, almost no novels. It was well known that women read more fiction than men. But was that a sign that Klinge had culled all of his wife's books? And did that in turn mean that he hadn't grieved as deeply for her as he had made out? Had he maybe even led a double life with other women? Or had his wife just happened to be uninterested in fiction? And above all, was any of it relevant to the investigation?

The answer was that he had no idea. That the whole thing was a jumble of information that only contributed to exacerbating his headache and stress levels.

In his heart of hearts, he'd known it ever since he joined the police, but it had never been as brutally clear as in this moment. That he – unlike, for instance, the Swedish detective Fabian Risk

– had not an ounce of that quality that made a person want to solve a case and make sure the perpetrator was arrested at any cost. It went without saying that he wanted to see criminals caught and punished. But that hadn't been his main focus all these years. Rather, he'd been busy trying not to mess up or step on anyone's toes so that, eventually, he'd be promoted.

In other words, he was a poser. A phoney who had managed to cheat his way through one investigation after the other. The only talent he'd developed was the ability to sit in a meeting and pretend to know what was going on and what he was talking about. A talent so refined he'd sometimes fooled even himself.

And now he was standing in the corner he'd painted himself into and, poser or no, he was the one who had to move this investigation forward. On his way back into the hallway, he tried to convince himself the case wasn't at a complete standstill.

Mogens Klinge had been identified and they'd found a number of clues suggesting that a third person, and possibly even several people, had been involved in the murders. They still didn't know who the woman was, but with her cross-shaped scar, it was only a matter of time before that was cleared up. And besides, they hadn't even been at it a full day yet. Granted, he'd hoped things would progress quickly. But that had been that morning. Now, he knew better and, unlike Sleizner, he was convinced this would take some time.

He opened one of the three doors leading off the upstairs landing and stepped into a bedroom furnished with a double bed flanked on either side by nightstands, some wardrobes and a wall-mounted TV.

There was nothing in the room to indicate that this might have been where Klinge had sex with the unknown woman before being forced to eat his own gun. No signs of blood spatter on the walls, the carpet or the bedspread.

Nor had he expected any. Kartoffelrækkerne, with its deep-rooted sense of community, wasn't a place you brought a prostitute home with you. Nor was it a place from which you could smuggle out two dead bodies unseen, even in the middle of the night. No, wherever the murders had taken place, it wasn't here.

He left the bedroom and opened the next door. Just like the other rooms, it was cluttered, but at the same time cosy, with an inviting reading chair and matching footstool. One wall was covered with books, which surrounded a workstation consisting of a worn old desk, empty apart from a jar full of pens and a magnet covered with paperclips.

As in the living room downstairs, the windowsill was lined with potted plants. Here, they were pink and red hibiscus, all in full bloom. Not the easiest plant to keep, and he was surprised to find Klinge had such green fingers.

But most people had sides they kept to themselves, and he himself had, in fact, always enjoyed plants of all shapes and sizes. He made a habit of splurging on a large bouquet for Lone once a month, ostensibly to show her his appreciation and to make her happy, which usually worked, though in truth he primarily bought them for himself.

He went over to the armchair and looked out of the window at the small back garden, which contained a covered grill, some outdoor furniture and a folded clothes-drying rack. The garden was separated from the ones on either side by a high brick wall. But a door in one corner made it possible to go straight into the neighbouring yard, and just to be sure, he decided to find out who that neighbour was.

But his real focus was not on the garden, but rather the

windowsill. Or to be even more specific, on the elongated piece of grey plastic sticking out from behind one of the flowerpots. It made him think of a shark's fin. As though the nondescript piece of plastic had triggered a memory he hadn't been aware he had.

He wasn't able to put it together until he pushed the plant aside and saw the old bright yellow Ericsson phone. Because the Ericsson 310S had been nicknamed 'the Shark Fin' in the early 2000s. He'd owned one himself for a few years and could still recall how much he'd liked it, despite the oversized antenna that made it impossible to fit it into a trouser pocket.

Just ten years ago, they had been technological marvels, with a battery time of over a week, and in another ten years they would in all likelihood be retro enough to be worth more than when they were new. But today, they were nothing more than ugly, unsmart hunks of plastic, and any that had escaped being binned long ago were most likely gathering dust in forgotten drawers. For that reason, it was noteworthy that Klinge had his out. Especially considering that there had been a new Samsung Galaxy in his pocket in the car.

He picked up the phone and noted that there was no dust on it. Then he tried to turn it on. The motion triggered his muscle memory. But as it happened, the phone was already on, and when the screen lit up, he could see from the battery life indicator in the top right corner that it had about twenty-five per cent charge. The four bars on the left indicated that it also had a functioning SIM card.

The 310S was from a time before passcodes, which meant he could simply start clicking through the menus.

Apart from various service numbers, there was only one name in the contact list, *Contact1*. He resisted the temptation to push the green button to see who might pick up and instead continued on to the call list, only to learn that unless it had been wiped, not so much as one call had ever been made. But a number of texts had been sent.

Test was the first message from Contact1. It had been sent on 16 April, at 11.23 a.m. Six minutes later, Klinge had replied *OK*.

Five and a half hours later, a cluster of messages had been received.

'Don't ask me,' a voice suddenly said in English downstairs. 'Maybe he just forgot to close it when he left.'

'People don't just forget to close and lock their front doors,' someone else replied.

Hesk looked around for an escape route. There was no balcony, and neither his knees nor his hips would survive the drop to the paved terrace below. He should just get out his police ID and go downstairs to ask who they were. But he was too scared. For the first time in living memory, he was worried about what a confrontation might lead to.

And before he had time to stop and consider his options, he was back in the bedroom, climbing into one of the wardrobes. He'd never done anything like it before, apart from playing hide and seek with his children, and it felt completely absurd. But he couldn't think of a better alternative.

He was unarmed, too. As usual, his gun was in the weapon safe at the station – the last time he'd used it was last winter, at the shooting range. In fact, he'd never once made use of it in the field. But now he wished he had it with him. Now that he was squatting in the dark under hangers full of shirts and trousers, listening to the men coming up the stairs.

'We should be very close now, very close,' one of them said.

'Let's hope you're right,' replied the other one as he stepped into the bedroom. 'It's already taken far too long.'

Hesk held his breath and pondered whether he should jump

out in an attempt to overwhelm the man in the room. He had the element of surprise on his side. But that was all he had. In every other respect, he was at a disadvantage. Strength, balance, speed. He had none of that. In other words, he didn't stand a chance.

That the man was moving closer did nothing to help matters. He was so close now he could hear the faint whistling sound from his nostrils when he inhaled. Moments later, when he opened the wardrobe door, he threw it open with some force, as though he were expecting someone to be sitting in it.

That it was the wardrobe next to the one Hesk was in didn't make much difference. In a few seconds, his door would be the one thrown open, and once that happened, the only thing he could do was jump out and hope for the best.

'In here,' the other man called out, which made the man in the bedroom leave. 'At least, according to the screen. It should be somewhere in this room.'

'So find it. Don't just stand there. Find it.'

He heard the desk drawers being pulled out and emptied next door. The armchair was moved and one of the potted plants crashed to the floor.

'Is it still supposed to be in here?'

'Yes. Look for yourself.'

'That's it, I'm calling it.'

'You sure?'

'Do you have a better idea? We're running out of time.'

Hesk's hands refused to obey him, shaking with terror. But eventually, he managed to pull the old Ericsson phone out of his pocket just as it lit up. Before it could emit any sound, he pushed the red button and held it until the screen went dark.

12

FLÄTAN HAD INTRODUCED himself to the ambulance driver in fluent Danish and guided him down to Forensics in Helsingborg. Once they'd arrived, he had signed a number of documents, and then they had moved the black body bag over to a Forensics stretcher together.

But Fabian's recollection of the past half-hour was patchy. He might have nodded off a few times in the ambulance. Or not. Something inside him had been turned off, blocking him from any form of contact with the outside world and, first and foremost, with himself.

When Flätan stopped in front of his colleague Arne Gruvesson, he could see that they were talking. But he'd only heard odd snatches, Gruvesson wondering what Flätan was doing there in the middle of his holiday.

'Just a little examination,' Flätan had replied with a smile. 'Nothing you need to worry about. You just carry on drinking your coffee and playing Murder Snails, or whatever it is you get up to.'

On a normal day, Fabian would have stepped in, well aware as he was that Flätan and Gruvesson were a disastrous combination. Now, all he could do was stand there and watch his colleagues as though he were slowly driving past the scene of a traffic accident.

He had no recollection of how they made it to the

examination room. Suddenly, they were just in the brightly lit space with its tiled floor dotted with drains, gleaming autopsy tables under powerful lights, and disinfected tools.

Only when he pushed his hands in under the body bag and felt the weight of Theodor's legs did reality manage to push through every layer.

His son was dead.

He really was dead, and nothing could ever bring him back.

In the mortuary in Helsingør, he'd been bursting with questions he wanted answered. He'd been sure something was fishy. Now, they had all evaporated. His son no longer existed. It was a full stop, not a comma or an evasive answer with room for follow-up questions.

This was where the story of Theodor ended.

'I'll let you get on with your work.' He was too fragile to stay and watch his son's autopsy. 'I'll wait outside.'

'Forget it. You're staying.' Flätan unzipped the body bag all the way down, exposing Theodor, who lay on his back with his eyes closed and his arms crossed. 'Normally, I'd have my assistant here to help me. But she's on holiday.' He held out a green surgical gown.

Fabian hesitated briefly but then put it on and helped to pull the body bag out from under Theodor as Flätan lifted him up.

He wasn't sure he was going to make it through the entire autopsy. But maybe this was exactly what he needed. In order to accept that it was no longer up to him. That there was nothing left for him to do but to go home and take care of the family he still had left.

Flätan was already busy cutting the clothes off the body with a large pair of scissors. First the shirt, then the trousers, one leg at a time, then finally socks and underpants.

Fabian would have done anything to take Theodor's place.

Anything to be the one lying on the cold metal table. Instead of standing next to it, taking his punishment with every breath.

If it hadn't been for the livid bruises covering Theodor's torso from the chest and all the way down to his hips, he would have apologized to Flätan and offered to pay for a taxi to take him back to his party. But something had been awakened inside him.

He already knew Theodor had been in fights; Komorovski had informed him of that. They'd told her his son had launched an unprovoked attack on another inmate in the canteen, adding assault to his other charges. But these greyish-blue contusions told a different story. One in which he had clearly taken a beating too.

He was about to ask Flätan about them. How old they were and how hard he thought the blows might have been. Whether he was able to tell if they'd been made by one or more assailants, if they'd kicked or maybe even used weapons. But Flätan was busy studying something on Theodor's right palm through a magnifying glass.

'Found something?'

The answer came in the form of an outstretched hand. 'Tweezers, please.'

Fabian went over to one of several collections of tools, all neatly lined up on a green cloth, picked up one of many pairs of tweezers, and handed it over.

'See this?' Flätan held the tweezers up in the air between them. 'See this thing?'

Fabian nodded and leaned closer to study it. It was a small metal pin, about five millimetres long. 'But what is it?'

'If you're okay with a best guess, I'd say it's from a thumbtack.'

'Thumbtack? Where would he have got that from?'

'That's exactly what I'm wondering – it's certainly peculiar,' Flätan replied, and he bent down to study the palm of Theodor's hand again. 'There's traces of blood around the wound, too, which would indicate that he was alive when it happened. But let's move on to the bruises.' He placed the metal pin in a small, sealable plastic bag.

Fabian nodded. 'They told us he... that he had assaulted someone. That's what they said. That he was the attacker. So I had words with him myself... told him he had to get it together if he wanted to stand a chance in court.'

'What else can a person do than what they think is right?'

'I just don't understand how nobody told me. Why didn't anyone tell me the truth? Not even him. I was over there several...'

'Hey...' Flätan put a hand on his shoulder. 'Maybe you should go home to your family, and I'll keep going here and let you know the second I'm done.'

'No, I'm staying. It's too late anyway, so I might as well stay, and I want you to tell me everything you see. Okay? Don't try to spare me. I want to hear it all.'

Flätan sighed a reluctant okay and began to study the bruises on Theodor's hips and chest. Then he grabbed the body with both hands and heaved it onto its side to examine the back, which was also covered in large contusions.

'As you can see, he was unquestionably the victim of assault. The most likely scenario is that he was lying on the floor, being both kicked and punched.'

'Any weapons?'

'Hard to say. There are some pretty significant haemorrhages here, but they could just as easily have come from steel-capped boots as anything else. What is remarkable is that there is no bruising on the lower arms or shins.'

'And why is that remarkable?'

'Well, imagine it. You're on the floor, people kicking and punching you. What do you do?'

'I try to protect myself.'

'Exactly. You curl up in the foetal position and make yourself as small as you can, which virtually always means injuries to the lower arms and shins. The problem for the attacker is that injuries like that are visible if the victim wears a short-sleeved shirt, like the inmates do at the Helsingør Detention Facility.'

'So there were several of them.'

'I would say at least three.'

'Two to hold his arms and legs and one to do the kicking.' Images flashed before him like flies refusing to give up their cadaver.

It must have been the other members of the Smiley Gang, who were also awaiting trial. They had strong motive to make Theodor withdraw his testimony against them, and from what he'd seen in the videos of them beating homeless people to death, this was their MO. The thing was that they were supposed to have been kept in different units for that very reason.

'And there's another thing.' Flätan pointed. 'See these brown marks up here? They're about two weeks old, and the yellow and green ones down here, a week.'

'So it happened more than once?'

Flätan nodded. 'The black and blue marks both here and there are from four or five days ago.'

Repeated assault, in other words. And yet no one had said anything. Not Komorovski, not the prosecutor, not the guards. Had they not known, or was this a cover-up?

'Did they say anything about how he hanged himself?' Flätan asked. He had moved on to examining the marks around Theodor's neck.

'Yes, apparently he managed to unscrew his cot from the wall, leaned it upright, and tied the noose around one of the upper legs.'

'And the noose itself, what did they say about it?'

'That he ripped his sheet into strips and plaited them into a rope.'

'A plaited rope?' Flätan turned towards Fabian, who nodded and shrugged. 'That's interesting,' he mumbled, and he resumed his examination, gently turning Theodor's head to the side so he could get closer to the marks with his magnifying glass. 'I'd be surprised to find out these were marks from plaited strips of a bed sheet. That much I can tell you.'

'That's what they said.'

'Of course, to know for sure, I'd have to examine the noose and see if it can be matched to the marks. But don't count on that happening.'

'You can really see that with just a magnifying glass?'

'Believe me. I can see enough, and plaits is something I'm a bit of an expert on. But let's say that's how it happened. That he ripped up his sheets and plaited the strips. That likely means he plaited three strips of bed sheet together, which would in no way be strong enough to hold his weight. Which would suggest that he made three such plaits and then plaited them together, and that would never leave a mark like this. Alternatively, he could have plaited all nine strips at once; that would have resulted in a more even surface. But unless your son was some sort of textile crafts nerd, I consider it unlikely.'

'So what did he use?'

'A proper rope or an electrical cord of some kind. Something with a fairly smooth and even surface.'

Had they deliberately lied to him, or had they just been casting about for a plausible explanation to have something to say so he would leave? He had yelled and demanded answers, so if they'd said something in the heat of the moment that wasn't entirely true, that was, perhaps, not entirely surprising.

He turned to Flätan, who was leaning over Theodor's head, pushing his dark curls aside to examine his scalp. Those unruly curls that had always been his son's trademark feature, no matter how much Sonja had tried to smooth them down when he was little. Nothing could keep them from living their own life. Not even death.

Suddenly, something fell to the white-tiled floor. Something that must have been stuck in Theodor's hair.

He walked over, squatted down to take a closer look, and saw it was a flake of paint about the size of a pound coin. He grabbed tweezers and transferred it to a transparent evidence bag, holding it up to the light to study it.

It was relatively thick, more than a millimetre, and dark green, which was noteworthy in itself. Not that he'd ever seen Theodor's cell, but he found it hard to believe that either the walls or the ceiling would be as dark as this. But somewhere, there was a room exactly this colour. A room Theodor had been taken to for some reason.

The buzzing sound from a hair trimmer made him turn back to Flätan, who was shaving off Theodor's curls. They silently fell to the floor, one after the other. He wanted to tell him to stop. Shout that it was enough. That he knew all he needed to know. That he should at least leave the curls untouched.

But most of them were already on the floor, like a dark, fluffy rug, and when he looked up, the pieces fell into place. Both the flake of dark-green paint stuck in his hair and the livid blue-and-yellow marks that covered large parts of his son's shaved scalp like some rare skin disease.

13

THE WHEELS OF Mikael Rønning's suitcase scraped against the pavement as he hurried past a couple of prostitutes and a group of bickering junkies outside the Mændenes Hjem homeless shelter on Istedgade. Moments later, he narrowly avoided stepping in a puddle of vomit.

In other words, life on Copenhagen's skid row was the same as usual. He'd lived there for over ten years and had long since lost count of how many times he'd been asked how he put up with seeing the squalor every time he stepped outside his building.

The truth was that he loved it. The neighbourhood formed a counterweight to all the new construction with gleaming façades and model citizens who dutifully paid their taxes and were never late for work. A counterweight that was necessary for everything else in Copenhagen to function. Without the seedy underbelly with its filth, smut and danger, no shiny front.

But that wasn't something he had time to think about now. He didn't even have time to be annoyed that Samsonite, Rimowa, and every other luggage manufacturer in the world had failed to create a suitcase capable of traversing the beautiful but uneven pavements relatively quietly.

He was stressed. He had been ever since deciding to help Dunja Hougaard put a tap on Kim Sleizner's mobile. That was a month ago, and ever since, the mood at work had been different. It was as though Sleizner suspected him of being in cahoots with Dunja. Well aware that they knew each other, his boss seemed unable to refrain from dropping her name into every conversation, as if to test his loyalty. And on top of that, he felt as though he were being watched day and night.

He was convinced someone had been in his flat. Nothing was missing, and everything was almost exactly where it should be. But only almost. It was the same thing with his phone. Even though he made a habit of resetting it to factory settings every day to make sure it hadn't been hacked, he could hear strange clicking sounds that had never been there before.

He had no idea how Dunja was doing. And he didn't care. Well, no, he did care. The truth was that he was trying hard not to. To cut all ties with her and relegate her to the realm of memories so vague they could only be brought back through hypnosis.

But it was hard. He'd tried to call her several times to make sure she was okay. But she never answered. Not once had she bothered to pick up to just say hi. Except when she needed his help.

And if anyone had been there for her, it was him. He'd broken so many rules and taken so many risks it made him frightened. But he'd considered her a friend, one of his closest, and for your closest friends, there was nothing you didn't do.

But that was then, and now he was paying the price.

Which was why he had decided to cease all contact with her. Never mind that she had tried to call him several times this afternoon. He was out. He'd had enough of her and her pathological hatred of Sleizner and was going to check out for at least two weeks and head over to Malmö to be with his new boyfriend, Balthazar. He'd brought his phone, true, but it was turned off and would remain so for the rest of his holiday.

And yet he couldn't shake the feeling of being followed. Of being watched. By someone who kept their distance just enough that they couldn't possibly be blamed for either.

Like a minute ago, when he'd looked back over his shoulder one last time before crossing Reventlowsgade and entering the central station through a side entrance where opera music was being blasted through the speakers to keep the junkies away.

Granted, he'd only caught the briefest of glimpses of the man with the pulled-up hood that left most of his face in shadow before he'd slipped out of sight behind the hot-dog stand outside the entrance. But he was sure it was the same short man who'd been loitering across the street when he exited his building.

After rushing through the concourse to the big information display, he discovered that the next train to Malmö was due to leave in just two minutes from platform five. After that, it was a twenty-six-minute wait for the next one.

He glanced back over his shoulder but didn't see the man with the hood or anyone else suspicious. This was his chance. This was his opportunity to shake off whoever was following him. Never mind trying to buy a ticket from one of the machines, he just had to make sure he got on that train.

Time would tell if it was the right decision. Either way, he ran, as fast as he could, over to the stairs and down, against the stream of travellers going in the other direction, and across the platform towards the train, whose doors were closing.

It was both stupid and forbidden, but he didn't hesitate before swinging his suitcase in between the doors, which squealed in protest as he pushed in between them. With his fellow passengers' annoyed looks burning holes in his back, he finally managed to pull the case free so the doors could close.

Let them stare. The important thing was that he was on

board and the train was pulling out of the station. If a conductor came through and asked him for his ticket, so be it. What was a fine compared to having to stand on the platform for almost half an hour, just waiting for that short bastard to find him again.

He wiped the sweat from his forehead, picked up his suitcase and gently pushed his way down the narrow aisle, past the bathroom towards the rows of seats, several of which were unoccupied.

From behind him came the sound of the toilet flushing and the bathroom door opening. But he didn't give it any thought until a hand grabbed his shoulder.

He barely had time to turn around before a second hand grabbed him and he was pulled into the cramped bathroom and pushed face first against the wall as the door behind him was closed and locked. Then the hands let go of him and he could turn around and face the short man. Who wasn't a man at all.

For a split second, the confusion was so overwhelming he had to find something to hold on to, to keep from falling down. Only after he'd made sure he wasn't seeing things, that his eyes weren't deceiving him, even though it just couldn't be true, did he trust himself to let go.

'Dunja?' he managed after a few more seconds. 'What the fuck? Are you the one who's been—?'

'Mikael,' she cut in, and put a finger to his lips. 'Not now. We don't have much time.' She pushed the hood back so he could see her face and her short silver hair. 'I promise I'll explain everything once this is over. But right now, I need your help, okay?'

'Help?' He chuckled nervously. 'Whenever it suits you, huh?' Of course it had been Dunja stalking him. 'Well, I have bad news for you. I'm done playing this game.' He shook his head. 'So if you don't mind stepping aside so I can get out of here. Public bathrooms have never been my scene, you know.'

He started to push past her but didn't stand a chance when she grabbed hold of him again and pushed him up against the mirror above the sink.

'This isn't a game.' She looked him in the eyes. 'This is serious, Mikael. Bloody fucking serious.'

He met her gaze and shook his head. 'You've been working out, and I'm sure that's good for both your posture and your self-esteem. But unless you let go of my freshly ironed shirt, I'm going to scream for help. And I promise you. If there's one thing I'm good at, it's screaming.'

Dunja hesitated, but eventually let go of him. 'I'm sorry. But we need to talk in private, and I saw no other way since you won't pick up when I call.'

'*You* need to talk to me. *We* don't need anything.'

'Mikael, I get that you're mad. I know I've been the world's worst friend over the past few months. But as soon as this is over, I promise I'll do everything I can to—'

'Dunja, I stopped being mad a long time ago,' he broke in. 'Right now, I'm just scared. Of losing my job. Of the fire you're playing with. Of how this is going to end. You should be too. So my advice to you is to drop this shit and go back to your life.'

'What life? There's nothing for me to go back to. Not while Sleizner walks free. It's him or me, don't you get that? The moment he finds me, it's over, for real.'

'Yes, we all know Sleizner isn't exactly an angel. But Dunja, you're exaggerating. You're obsessed with him. You're practically manic.'

Dunja shook her head. 'I don't have to exaggerate. That's the problem. Is he a liar? Yes. A groping, disgusting, rapist swine? I'll give you one guess. Fully fledged psychopath? Absolutely. But that's the tip of the iceberg. To really describe him, you need to invent new words. So no, I can't just give up and pretend everything's tickety-boo. Because this isn't going to stop with me. Forget it. That man will keep going until someone puts him away for life. Don't kid yourself.'

'So what do you have? What is it I've missed that's so incredibly sinister? And don't tell me he tried to rape you, threw you out, and did everything he could to sabotage your investigations, because I already—'

'Mikael,' Dunja cut in. 'What he has done to me is the least of my problems. I honestly couldn't care less. What I do care about is all the things we don't know about and all the things he hasn't done yet but will. For example, I know that as we're talking, he's cooking up something big, and that's where you come in.'

'Cooking up something big? Are you joking? This is what you're telling me? After a month of hacking his phone?'

'We've obviously found quite a lot of more concrete stuff, but—'

'Dunja,' he cut her off. 'Let's speak plainly for once. From what you're telling me, you don't have shit. You don't even have a theory about what it is he's doing that's supposedly so heinous he ought to be executed at dawn.'

'Fine, so he has been lying unusually low recently, I'm not denying it. But he's at it again now, and nothing has been the same since this morning. Just listen to this.' She held out her phone and played a number of edited audio files.

'*The thing is that all the paperwork has to be in order,*' a male voice said. '*Because this directive you're asking me for is a big one.*'

'*Of course. I'm just worried...*' Sleizner's voice replied. '*... could become a far bigger problem than Klinge,*'

'*Kim, I've heard all of this a thousand times, and if you ask me, you're suffering from an unhealthy obsession. But that's your problem. It'll go out tomorrow at midnight. Neither sooner nor later.*'

Dunja stopped the playback. 'In case you haven't heard, Mogens Klinge, the Head of Operations at DSIS, is one of the two victims found in that car in the harbour.'

'Okay,' he said, nodding.

'And from what we can gather, this is a big problem for these gentlemen. We don't know why yet, and that's not why I'm here.'

'So why are you here?'

'To find out what constitutes *a far bigger problem than Klinge*, and that's where you and that directive being published at midnight come in. It's likely already uploaded to the intranet, just waiting to be approved before being sent out.'

Rønning shrugged. 'It could be anywhere, and it's almost certainly encrypted.'

'The encryption isn't a problem. We'll take care of that. What we need your help with is getting past the firewalls, so we can send in our spiders, and once they've done their thing, we need someone on the inside to clean up after us.'

Rønning looked at Dunja and gently stroked her cheek. 'I don't think you know how much I love you. How important you have been and still are to me. And how hurt I was when you just vanished.'

'Mikael, I know all that, but right now...'

'No, *I'm* talking now, and I want you to listen, because you still don't seem to understand what this is bloody about.' He paused and rubbed his temples for a moment before continuing.

'Of course I want to help you. Of course I want to do anything for you. But the last thing you need right now is help to get past the firewalls of the Police Authority's intranet.'

'That's what you have to say to me?'

'Dunja. All of this, whatever it is you're doing, has gone too far.'

'After all these years. After everything we've been through.'

'Goddammit, can't you see what you're doing? Can't you see you need help before it's too late?'

'Okay, you've made yourself clear.' Dunja nodded grimly. 'Good, I know where you stand now, so let me just wish you an amazing fucking life with your new boyfriend in Malmö. I guess there's nothing else left to say.'

'I guess so.'

'Then leave. What are you waiting for? A hug? A don't-worry-about-it-let's-have-dinner-when-this-is-all-over?'

'No, I'm waiting for you to give me back the keys to my flat.'

Dunja stared at his outstretched hand, then looked him straight in the eye while she fished his keys out of her inside pocket and handed them to him with an attempt at a smile. 'And who's going to water your plants now when you're not home?'

Rønning didn't return the smile, just shook his head, pushed past her, unlocked the door and opened it. But on his way out, he stopped and turned around. 'I really hope you take my advice and get some help. But...' He trailed off, unsure whether to go on. 'Knowing you, you're more likely to go hunting for some young uniformed officer with a radio tomorrow night. Granted, that's Saturday, not Tuesday, but we all have to make sacrifices sometimes.'

14

Jan Hesk made sure not to drive all the way home. Instead, he parked one street down from his house and killed the engine at the eastern end of Uralvej out on Amager, south of Copenhagen. Then he sat behind the wheel and tried to slow his breathing to something close to a normal rhythm.

But he couldn't. There was too much adrenaline pumping through his body. He was wired, which made him both excited and anxious.

He was finally on to something. Him. Not them. Not the team in some kind of collective effort, just him. And that was exactly what he needed to show, not just Heinesen and the others, but more importantly Sleizner: that he deserved his promotion. That he was someone to be reckoned with.

At the same time, he'd never been so scared in his life as when he was sitting in that wardrobe with the turned-off phone in his hand, trying not to breathe.

He had no idea who the two men were who had searched Klinge's house. If he had to guess, he would have said some form of hired security. What was not in doubt was that it was the same two men who had barged in during the autopsy at Forensics to change the light bulbs.

On both occasions, they'd communicated in English, and one of them had a distinctive Eastern European accent. The other, who was clearly his superior, had spoken fluent Danish. But he had no idea who paid them.

Hiding had turned out to be the right choice at the time. Just a minute or two after he'd turned off the mobile, one of the two men had received a call and they'd left as suddenly as they'd arrived.

But hiding was no longer an option. They had likely already identified him as the lead investigator and, judging from their methods, it was only a matter of time before they dropped by for a visit.

The solution was to reverse course in terms of their investigative strategy. From now on, no more playing things close to the chest – they were going to make everything public. It was really the last thing he wanted to do, but the more people who knew about their findings and how the case was progressing, the more immune and uninteresting he would seem to the two men.

The first thing he was going to do was convene a press conference. He would gather all the newspaper, radio and TV outlets tomorrow morning and share most of what he knew.

He had already discussed the idea with Heinesen during the drive home, and as expected his colleague had insisted that they should inform Sleizner, who had expressly asked to be kept in the loop. Going against such a request would, according to Heinesen, be seen as an unambiguous refusal to follow a direct order.

He probably had a point, but Hesk had stood his ground. Giving Sleizner advance notice of the press conference was tantamount to letting him take it over. Which Heinesen obviously didn't mind. He'd never had any managerial ambitions and seemed to have no objection to staying permanently in the background.

But Hesk had no choice. If he let Sleizner overshadow him for so much as a moment, he would forever be relegated to the level of ineffectual middle manager with no mandate to think a single independent thought. That they would also lose control of who knew what was another argument for not involving Sleizner.

He took out the old Ericsson phone and weighed it in his hand. It was what the two men had been looking for, no question about it. They'd had access to sufficiently advanced equipment to pinpoint its location to the study, and less than ninety seconds after he turned off the phone, they'd known they'd lost contact with it.

The frustration in the next room had been palpable. At first, they'd assumed the problem was their own equipment, and the Danish-speaking man's criticism had been vicious. Then they'd moved on to the theory that the battery in the phone had run out, and they'd spent the next few minutes turning the study upside down before suddenly receiving a call and leaving the property.

He'd stayed in the wardrobe a full half-hour before daring to open the door and climb out. There had been no one there, inside or outside the house. Even the street had been deserted. No more playing children or celebrating adults.

He'd hurried back to his car, set his course south towards Amager, parked a block from his home, and now he'd been sitting there for over twenty minutes, trying to convince himself that going home was safe.

It was another five minutes before he finally climbed out of the car, locked it, and walked down Sumatravej to Japanvej, where, after a furtive glance over his shoulder, he entered his own garden and walked past the children's toys strewn across the lawn.

The front door was unlocked as usual, but to his relief neither Lone nor the children were in the hallway. It wasn't that he didn't want to see them. Quite the opposite. Just not yet. Lone would instantly know something was wrong and worry. So he closed and locked the door as quietly as he could and went down to the basement.

He took off his clothes in the bathroom; they were still damp with sweat. He sniffed them and thought he caught a whiff of his own panic, which made him shove the whole lot into a black bin bag.

In the shower, he felt a sense of serenity spread through his body for the first time that day. There was something about the water hitting his head and streaming down his body. It didn't just rinse off the sweat, it took with it some of the anxiety too, and once he'd dried off, brushed his teeth and put on soft loungewear, he was ready to go upstairs and see his family.

That was when he realized he hadn't heard them. Normally, they made enough noise to rival an entire nursery school, but there hadn't been so much as a peep since he got home. There could be any number of explanations for that, but fear that the two men had beaten him back made him race up the basement stairs and dash over to the closed kitchen door.

As soon as he saw them in the kitchen, he knew it was a sight he would carry with him forever. Like a photograph in an album that couldn't be burned, it would be the first thing he saw when he woke up for the rest of his life. Because there they were, all three of them, in what appeared to be perfect harmony.

Katrine was playing happily with Benjamin on the floor. That they were even in the same room without being at each other's throats was remarkable. Lone was standing with her back to the door, doing dishes.

In other words, everything was as it should be, and he was able to breathe a sigh of relief, walk into the kitchen, and wrap his arms around his wife from behind.

'Hello, my love,' he said, and kissed her earlobe.

'What are you doing?' she said, twisting free of his embrace.

'What? Is a little hug too much to ask after a long, hard day at work?'

'Maybe today isn't the day for it.' Lone pulled off her rubber gloves and went to hang up her apron. 'I didn't know when you'd be home, so we've already eaten, and unfortunately there were no leftovers.'

Oh right, she was pissed off. 'Okay, that's fine,' he said. He'd completely forgotten about that. 'Don't worry about me. I'll sort myself out.' It felt like a lifetime since they'd had to cancel their trip to Legoland, but it was still the same day.

'There's bread and things to make sandwiches. I'm going for a walk.'

'Sure, go ahead. No problem.'

'And just so you know,' she said on her way towards the front door, 'I think I'll be taking the long route, so it would be great if you could put Benjamin to bed.'

'Of course. Don't worry about it.' He went over to Benjamin and picked him up. 'Or what do you say, little man? That'll be great, right?'

'Not Daddy.' Benjamin shook his head.

'Oh, come on, Daddy promises it'll be fun.'

'Not Daddy,' Benjamin said again and hit him in the face. 'Not Daddy! Don't want to!'

'Great.' Katrine got up from the floor with a sigh. 'I just managed to calm him down.'

Forty-five minutes later, Benjamin was finally asleep so he

could shut himself in the bedroom and sit down at the secretary desk with the Ericsson phone.

What he really wanted to do was just turn it on and go through Mogens Klinge's communications with the phone's one contact over the past few days. But he didn't dare to. The risk of it connecting to nearby masts and seconds later appearing like a pulsing red dot on the two men's screen was far too great.

It was impossible to say how long it would be before they appeared outside his house. A few hours, a day, or just fifteen minutes? It didn't matter, sooner or later, they would come.

So instead, he unscrewed the two screws in the back, removed the battery cover, and pulled out the battery using the tiny rubber tag sticking out from under it. He remembered each step as though he'd performed it only yesterday and had no trouble pushing out the small metal holder, folding it out and pulling out the SIM card.

After putting the battery back, he pushed and held the red button until the screen lit up. Back in the day, he'd never thought twice about how long it took the phone to boot up. Now, it felt like an eternity before a message appeared on the screen.

NO SIM

He tried to get past the message, but no matter what buttons he pressed, it made no difference. Without a functioning SIM card, the phone refused to do anything. He extracted the battery again to get to the SIM card holder. This time, he inserted the card from his own phone instead.

The screen lit up again, and within seconds it made contact with the masts and was ready to be used. He started by opening the address book, but there wasn't a single contact in it. And nothing in the call log. Empty, as though someone had wiped the phone.

At Klinge's house, he'd seen a number of texts before he'd been forced to hide, and now they were suddenly gone. Something wasn't right, and unless he'd accidentally deleted things, the information should still be somewhere.

The question was where.

The answer came to him when he closed his eyes and cast his mind back to the days when he'd owned the same kind of phone, and it was as simple as it was discouraging. Just like all other mobiles from back when internal storage constituted the greater part of the cost of a phone, you could choose between saving information on the phone itself or on the SIM card. That was obviously where everything was.

For the third time, he extracted the battery, pulled out his own SIM card and put Klinge's back in. But before he slid the battery back into place, he unscrewed the two screws securing the shark-fin-like antenna, which could then be detached.

He had no idea if that made any difference. There was nothing to say the phone wouldn't connect to the nearest mast even without its fin. It could just be some kind of amplifier that improved reception.

He should really get in the car and drive away from his home before he started up the phone. But Lone still wasn't back, and he couldn't just leave the children home alone. His second-best option was the basement, in the furthest corner by the winter tyres, where he knew reception was extremely poor.

When the screen lit up once again, he was ready, eyes fixed on the flashing reception symbol and his thumb on the red button so he could turn the phone off immediately in case it looked like it was about to connect to the network. But once the message *No network* appeared on the screen, he relaxed and began to look through the menus.

Just like before, the first message from Contact1 contained the word *Test*. It had been sent at 11.23 on 16 April that year. Klinge had replied soon after with a succinct *OK*. Almost six hours later, Contact1 had sent five separate messages in quick succession.

Rule1: We contact you. Never the other way around.

Rule2: All communication will take place via text.

Rule3: The decisions of the presidium cannot be appealed.

Rule4: In case of rejection, all contact will cease, the phone will be destroyed.

Rule5: Assigned dates/times cannot be altered/changed.

The decisions of the presidium. It made no sense to him.

Six days later, on 22 April, there was another message from Contact1.

Thought I'd made myself clear. Never call. Rules1 & 2 broken.

The reply from Klinge had been sent less than a minute later.

Sorry. Just so curious to know how things are going.

Don't do it again. Will be in touch when there is news.

Then, not another word from Contact1 for almost three

months, until another cluster of messages was received on 4 July between 03.46 and 04.02 a.m.

The presidium has made its decision. Your membership has been approved. Congratulations.

What kind of people had meetings at four in the morning, and what kind of group had Klinge become a member of? The whole thing reeked of some kind of cult or secret order. Maybe a sex club. There were tons of them in Copenhagen, catering to every conceivable taste and predilection. And it figured. If you were relatively well known, you probably preferred closed social circles.

The next message read:

The initiation will take place on 28 July at 8 p.m.

That was Saturday, six days ago. So that was when something had gone so terribly wrong it had ended up with two dead bodies in a car in the harbour.

Dress code: Black tie.

It all made sense, and yet he couldn't shake the feeling he'd likely seen no more than the tip of the iceberg.

You will be picked up at 7.30 p.m. at 55.692378, 12.586963.

The only thing he felt reasonably certain of was that the person or people they were looking for lurked behind the moniker Contact1.

Rules for the ceremony: There are no rules.

He went back to the address book and clicked *Contact1* to see the number. Then he hurried over to the workbench and rooted around the toolbox until he found a pen so he could write down 26 58...

That was as far as he got before the phone died.

15

DUSK HAD DARKENED into night by the time Fabian paid the taxi driver, opened the passenger door, and climbed out on Pålsjögatan. It had begun to rain too, but just scattered drops with no real force behind them. The taxi did a U-turn and set off back towards the city centre. He just stood there, staring at their house.

As a boy, he'd always dreamed of living in these particular brick terraced houses. Now they'd resided here for just over two years, but it felt like twenty. Twenty nightmarish years where none of the things he'd hoped for when they packed up their lives in Stockholm had come to pass.

The idea had been to heal and come together as a family. Now here he was, lonelier and more isolated than ever. He could make out Sonja's profile through the living-room window. Watched her walk in from the kitchen, holding something in both hands, probably a tray with a teapot, honey and cups, only to disappear from view when she sat down on the sofa.

But when the three tealights were lit, she became visible once more, in the form of three flickering shadows on the ceiling. Sonja and Matilda, who was sitting next to her. The shadows were really too vague and flickering for a person to tell anything by them. But to Fabian, it couldn't be clearer that Sonja poured the tea, first into the large purple mug with no handle, then into Matilda's Moomin mug, and then raised her own mug to her lips with both hands.

He should cross the street, walk up the front steps and go through the door. Go be with his family, sit down on the sofa and keep them company. It was all they needed. It was all they wanted, and it was exactly what he wanted too.

But instead, he stood there, frozen on the pavement, with his eyes glued to the shadows on the ceiling, hoping the stray droplets would turn into a proper downpour. A deluge that turned the storm drains into fountains and swept away everything in its path. That washed the world clean and turned into hail. Big, fat balls of ice that left bruises, beat him to a pulp, and made him feel something. Pain. Grief. Anything, so long as it was something.

But instead, the droplets turned into nothing. The moment they landed on the warm asphalt, they evaporated, and in the end he watched himself cross the street, turn the key in the lock, and open the door.

Quiet music greeted him, piano, strings, and a muted trumpet. It was the last song on Tom Waits' album *Closing Time*, Sonja's favourite album of all time, and when 'Ol' 55' from the same album came on straight after, he knew it must have played on repeat all evening.

He took off his shoes, hung up his jacket on a free hanger and continued into the living room, where he stopped and let his eyes rest on Sonja and Matilda, who were sitting just the way he'd pictured, as close together as possible, surrounded by cushions, drinking their cups of steaming tea.

'Hi,' he said, raising his hand to wave.

'Hi,' Sonja replied, letting the unspoken question of where he'd been erect an invisible wall between them.

'I'm going to bed,' Matilda said, and she gave Sonja a long

hug before getting up off the sofa and starting to move towards him.

'Goodnight, you,' he said, ready to give her a hug. But he let his arms fall when she continued past him without a word or a look. Without anything at all.

He watched her disappear up the stairs. Of course he was the one she was mad at.

'Hey, I actually think I'm going to go to bed too,' he said after a while, and he started to turn around.

'You're not going anywhere.' Sonja topped up her mug. 'You're going to come over here and sit. There's tea if you'd like some.'

'Darling,' he said in the middle of a long exhale. 'I'm completely beat, and...'

'Sit down,' she hissed in an attempt to hide how upset she really was. 'You think you're the only one who's tired? That everything's about you and your needs? We're going to talk, you and me, and we're going to do it now.'

He nodded and went to sit in the armchair. She was right. Of course they needed to talk. It would probably take them hours to find their way back to each other. But that wasn't how this conversation was going to go. He'd known it as soon as he had seen the shadows dancing on the ceiling.

'I have no idea what you've been doing or where you've been all day,' she said, working hard to maintain her composure. 'But I know one thing, and that is that your behaviour today, when we went to see Theodor, is some of the—'

'Darling,' he broke in. 'I can explain. Just like I suspected, something's not—'

'No, I don't want to hear it.' She raised a hand as if to protect herself from him. 'I'm not interested in the slightest in your suspicions and explanations.'

'But Sonja, listen to me. This is about our—'

'No, it's time for you to listen and let me speak.'

He neither spoke nor nodded.

'Our son has taken his own life,' she went on. 'That's something no one should have to experience. It goes against everything and is impossible to accept as part of life. There are no tools, no methods to use to get through it. And it has only been a few days, so we're all in shock and probably reacting differently. But you and I are supposed to be the adults here. Regardless of how we choose to tackle things. We're supposed to find a way to get through this, so we can't be causing scenes like the one this morning. Do you understand? We can't. We have to stick together and support each other. It's the only way if we want to get through this. Everything else will have to wait.' She sought his eye for some kind of confirmation.

'The problem is that it can't wait,' he said when he was sure she was done. 'I understand it must have been awful for the two of you. But if I hadn't caused that scene, if I hadn't done exactly what I did, if anyone but Flätan had performed the autopsy, I would have had no way of confirming my suspicions. Do you understand? Because something's not right. Not least how long it took before we were allowed to see him.'

'Please. I don't want to hear it.'

'But, Sonja, they're lying to us. You were there, you heard them say he'd ripped up his sheet and plaited it into a rope. Right? But according to Flätan, the marks around his neck suggest that it was something smoother, like an electrical cord or something...'

'Are you not hearing me? I really don't want to.'

'But don't you see? They're covering something up.'

'No, you're the one who doesn't see. I don't want to hear about my son's autopsy. I don't want to hear that something's not right. I don't want this. Theodor is dead. Isn't that enough? Do you really need more than that?'

'I need to know what happened.'

'What happened. Okay.' Sonja nodded. 'And then what? What is that supposed to achieve? Is it going to bring him back to life, bring him back home? Huh? Is that what you think? That everything will go back to normal?'

'No, but...'

'So why keep digging? What is it you want?'

'To find out what really happened. To work through our grief together based on knowing the truth and not some made-up story that...'

'Truth?' Sonja closed her eyes and shook her head. 'Always with the goddam truth. It's all you talk about. Truth, truth, truth. Is it the only thing that matters to you? Is it more important than everything else?'

'No, but if we don't find out. If we don't know what really happened, all of this will remain an open wound for the rest of our...'

'But the truth is what bloody killed him! Or have you managed to forget that already? That you forced him to go to Denmark to turn himself in and testify. If it weren't for your obsession with the truth, he would have been sitting here with us right now.'

'Do you really believe that? That he would have been sitting here, drinking tea with us, pretending like what he went through was nothing? Have you even watched those videos? The ones where they torture homeless people to death in the most macabre and horrifying ways imaginable?'

'You make it sound like he participated. He stood lookout one time. Have you forgotten that? Because they forced him to.'

'No, I haven't forgotten, and I never will. Because I don't think things go away just because you don't talk about them and pretend they didn't happen. I don't think you can make things undone by just keeping mum for long enough. But apparently you do. Never mind that it would have meant the real perpetrators getting off scot-free so they could carry on with their sick games. Because that has nothing to do with us or Theodor.' He shook his head. 'Maybe that works for you, Sonja. Living a lie, putting on a smile, and hoping no one sees through it. But it doesn't for me. I can't just ignore that something doesn't make sense about Theodor's death. I can't let all the misconduct and abuses he was the victim of slide as though they never happened. I just can't.'

'You're right about one thing,' Sonja said, nodding. 'I would have done anything to still have him here with me. Absolutely anything. Even if it meant living a lie with a fake smile on my face, I would have done it.'

'And all the injustices he endured? You don't care about that. Lovely.'

Sonja looked him in the eye with a darkness that reminded him of the abyss that swallowed him in his dreams. 'Fabian, the greatest injustice our son endured was having you as his father.'

Then she stood up, carried her tea mug into the kitchen, and disappeared up the stairs.

16

'YES, THAT'S CORRECT,' Hesk replied to the direct question of whether he could confirm that it was DSIS Head of Operations Mogens Klinge who had been found dead in a car off the Refs Peninsula. 'But we're still working on identifying the woman who was found with him.'

He looked out at his large audience – all the big papers, news channels and radio stations – and realized he felt completely calm. He, who usually sweated and tugged nervously on his tie whenever Sleizner wanted him to be on stage with him. He couldn't help but feel pleased so many of them had turned up, despite invitations having been sent out just an hour before the press conference started.

The primary reason for the short notice was the two men who had stalked him the day before, looking for the phone. There were certain indications they had police connections, since they'd apparently known when and where Mogens Klinge's autopsy was taking place.

'Is it true he shot himself through the mouth?' someone in the back row asked.

'Klinge was found to have been shot, that's correct. The bullet entered through the mouth and exited through the back of his head. That's all we can tell you right now.'

'Does that mean you can confirm Mogens Klinge took his own life?'

'No, the only thing we can confirm at present is that he was shot.' He broke eye contact with the reporter and addressed the whole room. 'Generally speaking, we are still in the early stages of this investigation and want to avoid closing doors or jumping to conclusions.'

'What can you tell us about the woman?' another person asked.

'Not as much as we would like, unfortunately.'

'Was she a prostitute?'

'It's possible, but that's not something we can comment on at the moment, since she has not been identified as of yet.'

'Is she Danish?'

'If by that you mean a Danish citizen, it is possible. From her appearance, however, she was not ethnically Danish. But now we're in the realm of more or less educated guesswork. We hope some of these questions will be answered as soon as we know who she is. For that reason, we have decided to appeal to the public for help.'

Using a remote, he opened one of the many pictures Hemmer had taken of the young woman's face on the projection screen above him, and the room instantly filled with the sound of cameras snapping a barrage of pictures.

'Don't worry, this will be available for download in high resolution from our website,' he said, moving on to a picture of the woman's scar. 'As will this.'

'What is that?' someone in the front row wanted to know.

'A scar shaped like a cross on the inside of the woman's right thigh, and I would like to take this opportunity to urge anyone who thinks they might recognize her or this scar to contact the police so we can...' He trailed off when the cameras suddenly went off again. But this time, they weren't aimed at him, but at the side of the room.

Why that was became clear when he turned and saw Kim Sleizner climb the steps to the stage and walk up to the table, holding a bottle of mineral water and two glasses, flashing a much too wide smile at the gathered press.

'Hello, ladies and gents. Don't let me interrupt.'

This couldn't be happening. Hesk didn't know whether to laugh or cry, but felt he had no choice but to squeeze out a smile when Sleizner put the bottle of water and the two glasses down on the table and bent down towards him, one hand covering the microphones.

'Interesting,' he whispered in his ear. 'I give you an inch and you immediately go behind my back, thinking you're a ruler.'

'Kim, I can explain. As soon as I'm done here, I'll tell you more.'

'Don't worry.' Sleizner patted him on the shoulder. 'I'll hold your hand and make sure this goes okay. No one should have to sit up here alone.'

'Thank you,' he whispered back. 'But I still think it would be better if I just did this...'

'Kim,' a female reporter on one side of the room called out. 'What are your thoughts on Mogens Klinge's death?'

'Hi, Mette.' Sleizner raised a hand in greeting. 'Great question, but I can only tell you what I tell everyone. If you think I'm here to take over this press conference, you're mistaken.' Then he sat down in the chair next to Hesk's, opened the bottle, and filled both glasses with water. 'I'm just here to underscore that I have every confidence in Jan Hesk when it comes to leading this extremely important investigation. In fact, I would go so far as to say I don't know anyone better suited than Jan.'

'But how involved are you personally in the investigative work?'

'Like I just said, Jan is in charge. But given the gravity of the case, he is of course keeping me abreast of any and all developments. Anything else would be a dereliction of duty.' Sleizner turned to Hesk with a smile and sipped his water.

'But surely you have some thoughts?'

'Of course I have thoughts. Tons of them. But for the sake of you and everyone else in this room, I'm going to keep most of them to myself.'

Many of the reporters laughed at this, and Sleizner grinned in the spotlight as though he'd never been happier.

It was less fun for Hesk. His pulse was racing, and sweat was pushing through his skin, out into the palms of his hands, which were already so clammy the whole event risked slipping out of his grasp unless he got his act together and did something.

'But what do you think about Mogens Klinge?' someone shouted.

'Me?' Sleizner pointed to himself. 'What do I think about Klinge?'

'Yes. Did he kill himself?'

'I'd probably say it's been demonstrated beyond reasonable doubt that he was—'

'Excuse me, Kim,' Hesk broke in, even though the last thing he wanted was a public spat with Sleizner. 'But I think it would be better if I answered the questions.' He took a few gulps of his water and leaned closer to the microphones. 'We've already covered that. And like I told you, at present we can't confirm anything one way or another.'

'I'm not asking what you can confirm. I just want to know what the police think, and in this case specifically what Kim Sleizner thinks and believes to be most likely.'

'That's fine, but this is a police investigation and not a guessing game. So, what specific individuals within the organization happen to believe is not a matter for this press conference.'

'What Jan is trying to say,' Sleizner said, 'is that right now we are working with several parallel theories, and we don't want to chain ourselves to one scenario or another. But that said, we also can't deny that most signs point to Klinge being the one who pulled the trigger.'

'And what is the other theory?' one of the reporters asked. 'If it wasn't suicide?'

'That a third party or third parties were involved,' Hesk replied.

'What else could it be?' Sleizner spread his hands and chuckled. 'The thing is that, right now, not a lot points to that. I would almost go so far as to say, nothing at all. But we keep all doors open, just a crack.'

For once, there were no more questions, and apart from the sound of reporters scribbling in their notepads, the room was silent. How long the silence lasted was hard to say. But long enough for Sleizner to eventually lean over towards him.

'What do you say we wrap this up now?' he whispered. 'Since there isn't much else to say at present.'

Hesk turned to the gathered press, who thanks to the blinding spotlights looked like a dark mass of heads, indistinguishable from one another. Even so, he could see it clearer than ever.

He was at a crossroads.

Staying quiet and acquiescing to ending the press conference meant acquiescing to Sleizner informally taking charge of the investigation and thereby steering them away from the leads that suggested other people had been involved. The trail would eventually go cold and in the end, those leads would be dismissed.

The case would be wrapped up quickly, which would in turn likely mean that the two men who had been following him would give up and leave him alone, so he could go home and take his family to Legoland with another fake feather in his professional cap.

But could he live with it?

With himself?

And somewhere inside him, he found the answer. What was there even to think about?

'Unfortunately, that's not the case,' he heard himself say just as the first droplet of sweat trickled down his forehead.

'Pardon?' Sleizner turned to him. 'What was that?'

'I said that unfortunately, that's not the case,' he repeated loudly, wiping his forehead with his sleeve. 'On the contrary, quite a few things point to one or more unknown persons being involved in some capacity.' But the sweat kept pushing out of his pores.

'Like what?' one of the reporters called out.

'Several things, but most importantly, that we have found blood and tissue under the woman's nails that do not belong to her or Mogens Klinge.' His back was soaked through now. He downed the last of his water.

'Do you have a suspect?' another reporter shouted.

'That is not something we can comment on at...' He broke off, realizing he'd forgotten what they were talking about. 'I'm sorry, could you repeat your question?'

'Do you have a suspect? Do you think it may have been politically motivated?'

'No, all I'm saying is that we're working on a scenario in which...' He trailed off again. Maybe he should have wrapped things up. To get away, if nothing else. Away from the hot lights. From all the questions.

He saw Sleizner lean closer to the microphones and talk to the reporters, but the only sound he heard was a low droning.

He needed more water. A lot more. But both the glass and

the bottle on the table were empty. He tried to swallow, but his throat felt like sandpaper. He stood up, had to get away, but he'd moved slightly too quickly, his chair toppled over behind him.

Then everything went dark.

17

FABIAN COULD TELL the uniformed guard had made his decision before he'd even finished his sentence. That the man continued to nod along, smiling vaguely, changed nothing. His eyes spoke volumes. His pupils, contracting and instantly changing his mildly quizzical look to one that was hard and hostile.

He had no problem understanding his reaction. Of course his request to visit Theodor's cell was against the facility's rules, and of course he couldn't let just anyone in simply because they wanted him to. Especially not after the scene he'd caused at the mortuary the day before.

And eventually, what he'd been waiting for came – the inevitable shake of the head.

'No, I'm afraid that's out of the question.' The guard stroked his moustache and continued to shake his head. 'I'm sorry, but there's nothing I can do.'

The response was exactly what he'd been expecting, since he had neither charges nor an official investigation to lean on. Formally, no mistakes had been made.

Flätan had advised him to file a police report to try to force an investigation. But that would take months, under the best of circumstances, and meanwhile, the trail would go cold. Besides, he would never be allowed on the investigative team. Which was why he'd decided to leave his professional title at home and come as what he was. A father who had lost his son.

'I'm going to have to ask you to leave the premises now,' the guard continued.

In a way, it made him easier to dismiss. If it weren't for the fact that he had something more powerful than weapons, rules and signed warrants. His grief. If he could just tap into it, they wouldn't be able to turn him away.

He just didn't know how. It was as though he'd lost the key and thereby all access to that particular part of himself. Hard as he tried, it wasn't grief he was feeling, it was rage, which was anything but helpful to him right now.

'Please,' he said, closing his eyes in an attempt to work up some moisture in them. 'All I'm asking is to visit the room where my son was last alive. Is that so unreasonable? Ten minutes, it's all I need.'

'I'm sorry,' the guard said in his best Swedish. 'You can't. I have to ask you to leave now.'

'Can I ask you something?' He looked the guard in the eye. 'Do you have children?'

'I don't see what that has to do with...'

'Please, just answer my question. Do you have children? Huh? Do you?'

'Yes, I do,' the guard said after a pause, and he pulled on his moustache. 'Two boys.'

'Then you know what I'm talking about. Don't you?' He made sure not to break eye contact. 'Try to imagine if it were one of your children who had died in there and that you were being denied access. Try to...'

'Hey, Dennis, what's going on?' Another guard popped his head out of the staff room behind the counter.

'It's that Swedish detective, Fabian Risk. He wants to see the cell.'

'No, no, no. That's not it at all,' Fabian said. 'I'm not here as a detective. It's important that you understand that. This visit is completely private and just for me.'

'And what exactly is it that you want?' The second officer came up to the counter.

'I just want to sit in there for a minute. On the cot in the cell where he ended his life. That's all. Just ten minutes alone in there to say goodbye.'

The second guard turned to the first one. 'Ten minutes, fifteen, what difference does it make?'

'But the rules, we can't...'

'Oh, come off it. The man's grieving, as well he should be.' He turned to Fabian. 'You know what? I'm actually on my break, but whatever, follow me.'

'But Peter, we can't...'

'Dennis, it's cool. I'll deal with this.'

A few minutes later, he was shown into the empty cell.

'When you feel ready, just push this button here and I'll come get you.'

Fabian nodded, entered, and sat down on the cot.

It was his first time in Theodor's cell. All his previous visits had taken place in a visitation room.

This room was a lot smaller. A wall-mounted cot, a locker and a small desk, a chair, and a toilet with a sink. That was it, and there was no sign anywhere that this was where Theodor had spent the last few weeks of his life.

Was that why he couldn't feel anything? Because the cell had already been scrubbed of any trace of his son, it inevitably brought to mind a cheap hotel that used toxic cleaning products to keep the vermin at bay.

Not that he'd come here to find his feelings. That wasn't why he was sitting there trying to picture Theodor lying on this very cot in the early hours of Tuesday, alone with his anxiety, staring up at the ceiling until he made his decision.

It was for a completely different reason.

He pulled the small transparent evidence bag containing the flake of dark-green paint that had fallen out of Theodor's hair from the inner pocket of his jacket. He didn't even need to take it out and hold it up to the light-blue walls to know it hadn't come from there. Nor from the white ceiling.

He stood up and looked around but couldn't see any dark-green paint anywhere. It wasn't necessarily significant. The flake of paint could have got stuck in his hair in some other room, like the canteen, the gym, or anywhere, really. But another explanation was that this wasn't the room where he'd...

He quickly squashed that line of thought, dismissing it as utterly implausible. Of course this was where Theodor had taken his life. But like a stubborn mouse, the thought soon found a new way in and made him look up at the ceiling.

There was a light fixture up there, but no visible electrical cable. They probably used in-wall cables precisely to keep inmates from tearing them down just enough to stick their heads through and let go. But if Flätan was to be believed, Theodor had used an electrical cord, or a proper rope with a relatively smooth surface.

He went over to the intercom he was supposed to use when he was done in the cell, because in a way, he was done. There was nothing else for him to see there.

And yet he didn't call the guard.

The hallway outside was both wide and long, at least fifty feet from end to end, with cell doors lining either side. None of the doors were locked and the inmates were free to roam at will. Here and there, guards were talking to each other or one of the inmates. Things were calm and no one seemed to pay him any notice.

With no real plan or idea of where he was going, Fabian turned left and continued past the row of cells, which, despite being identical, looked like tiny worlds, each one different, a reflection of its occupant.

The hallway opened up into a common room full of sofas and armchairs, where inmates were playing cards, drinking coffee and reading newspapers. He thought about the teenage members of the so-called Smiley Gang, who were still awaiting trial. Would he even recognize them if they were sitting there, playing cards? And what would he do if he did?

On the other side of the room, a door opened and a man in white paint-spattered overalls with a mask dangling around his neck entered. He set two buckets of paint down next to some black bin bags that were lined up against the wall along with a mattress wrapped in plastic and a handful of paint trays coated with dark-green paint.

Maybe it meant nothing, maybe it was just coincidence. Maybe not. Either way, Fabian hurried over to the door the painter had come through, threw a quick glance over his shoulder, and opened it.

The smell of fresh paint was overpowering in what looked in the dim light like a storage room with empty shelves mounted along one wall. After closing the door behind him, Fabian fumbled around until he found the light switch and could turn on the lights.

The sight made him clutch his stomach as though he'd just received a hard punch to the gut. The plastic-covered mattress leaned up against the wall outside. The thick electrical cord running across the ceiling to the too-powerful light, and the wall-mounted shelves leading up to it. And the paint. The dark-green paint, on both walls and ceiling, which was freshly applied in places and whose strong smell was making it harder and harder to breathe.

Defying the fumes, he stayed in the room, desperately trying to process the fact that Theodor hadn't been kept in one of the cells, he'd been locked in here, in a stark, windowless room with bare, dark-green walls, with only a filthy mattress to keep him company. He didn't even seem to have had sheets. Nothing.

It was hard, and part of him resisted, casting about for alternative explanations while the rest of him had already realized there weren't any. That all the evidence he needed was right in front of him.

It was here, in this room, that Theodor had been broken down by what could almost be described as torture, hour after hour, day after day, until everything blended into a dark-green blur with no beginning, middle or end.

But why? What had his son done to deserve this? How was it even possible? When he was the victim of assault, not the other way around. When he was the victim. Who had come to tell the truth. To do what was right.

He didn't know if it was the powerful fumes that made him stumble and almost lose his balance. Nor did he know how long he stood there with a splitting headache and thoughts that were everywhere and nowhere all at once.

His eyes fixed on a patch of wall right in front of him. An area about halfway up where the green paint was a shade darker than the surrounding wall. He went up to it, touched it with his fingers and realized it was still wet. Then he tore off his jacket and wiped off as much of the paint as he could.

A number of patches of white filler were revealed. It was the last clue he needed to see it all play out before his inner eye. The wall, being repaired and smoothed out before a new layer of paint was added, which meant the wall had been damaged where the old paint had been chipped off.

Flake by flake.

Blow by blow.

Bruise by bruise.

He wanted to scream at the top of his lungs, and this time, he did. This time, he couldn't hold it back, so he just let it out, all at once, while he walked over to the wall-mounted shelves and started to climb up them. He didn't care when one of the many drawing pins that lay scattered across the second shelf from the top stabbed his hand.

This was how it must have happened. He could see it so clearly now. How Theodor had gone about it. There was no other explanation. He'd been locked up in this room. A storage room. He didn't understand why, but it all fitted. The beatings, the isolation, and the repeatedly delayed trial. All designed to break him down. To make him crack under the weight of his own darkness.

Suddenly, the pieces came together, one after the other, as he made his way, increasingly sweaty and out of breath, to where the electrical cord to the light ran across the ceiling.

All of his attention was on the area where the cord had been painted over with the new dark-green paint that hadn't quite dried yet, and just like it must have happened for Theodor, the cord came loose when he tugged on it. Within seconds, the loop was big enough for him to push his head through and let go of the shelves.

'Hey, what the fuck is going on in here?'

Fabian looked down and saw the two guards from the lobby come bursting in, accompanied by Flemming Friis. 'That's exactly what I want to know.' He jumped back down to the floor and went up to them. 'What the fuck is going on here? Huh? Answer me!' He stabbed a finger into Friis's chest. 'What was my son doing in here?'

'Let's calm down now.' Friis took a step back and adjusted his glasses.

'Calm down? Fuck that. I want answers, and I want them now.' Fabian stepped in even closer. 'Tell me what Theodor had done to deserve being locked in this storage room, when he was the one being assaulted!'

'Now, listen to me,' Friis said in Swedish, before switching back to Danish. 'I don't know where you got that idea, but your son was never here.' He spread his hands. 'Not ever.'

Fabian closed his eyes and heaved a heavy sigh as he shook his head. 'If there's one thing I can't take any more of, it's lies. So do me, and more importantly yourself, a favour and tell me why he was being kept in here.'

'Your son was never...'

'Oh, for fuck's sake!' Fabian took out the small evidence bag with the dark-green flake of paint. 'See this?' He held it up to Friis's face. 'Do you know where I found this? Huh? Do you?'

'No, how would I know...'

'In Theodor's hair. Would you like to know how it got there? I said, do you want to know how?'

Friis turned to the guards and nodded for them to step in.

'It happened because someone, maybe several people, assaulted him so brutally in this very room that you had to repair the wall afterwards.' Fabian pointed to the patches of filler. 'So now I demand to know who they were, and how it is that no one...' He broke off when the guards grabbed him by the arms and pulled him backwards.

'Fabian, I completely understand that you're upset.' Friis adjusted his glasses again. 'Believe me. But your son...'

'You completely understand?'

'What I mean is that...'

'Do you know what I think?' Fabian broke in, still restrained by the guards. 'I don't think you understand anything. Like the fact that this is on you. Everything that happened and everything that's happening right now. Every single lie will be on you.'

He wrenched free of the guards' grip, turned towards the door, and left the room.

18

HESK COULDN'T EXPLAIN how the compact darkness could so quickly be replaced by a light that was as powerful as it was headache-inducing. And even less could he explain where he was. It was as though he'd spent the past few hours – or were they days? – in a vacuum where time stood still.

He must have slept, because he was awake now, that was one thing he was sure of. And he was lying on his back, on something hard, he had gathered that much, and that a door had just closed somewhere nearby, or maybe opened. Someone had entered the room, he could hear that clearly, and the voice that accompanied the footsteps felt familiar.

'Jan? So this is where you're hiding?'

So familiar it was downright inexplicable that he couldn't place it. Defying the migraine, he opened his eyes and saw Kim Sleizner looking down at him.

'What the hell is this?' Sleizner spread his hands. 'Seriously? This was the best you could do?'

'What?' he finally managed to say, and he realized as his vision cleared that he was lying on a large table ringed by chairs.

'What do you mean, what?' Sleizner bent down and pretended to knock on his skull. 'Hello, is there anyone home? Do you even know what you're doing? Because I have no idea.'

There was a large, empty whiteboard on one wall, the curtains were closed and above his head hung a projector.

'I've backed you up and given you everything you've asked for. And this is the thanks I get.' Sleizner shook his head.

A conference room…? Hesk was utterly confounded.

'I thought I'd been clear that this investigation was too delicate to announce to the press. And what do you do? You hold a goddam press conference. And behind my back, too. Do you realize how that makes me look?'

Right, the press conference, which Sleizner had turned up to and taken over. He had no memories between that and now.

'Kim, I had no intention of making you look bad. I really didn't.' Despite the dizziness, he struggled into a sitting position. 'But quite a few things point to other people having been involved.' He must have passed out. It was the only explanation. It had been warm on stage, he remembered that now, that he'd sweated and downed the glass of water Sleizner had brought, and still been thirsty after.

'Okay?' Sleizner shrugged. 'And?'

Hesk tried to swallow away the dryness. 'All I'm saying is that we can't turn a blind eye to the clues and leads we…'

'Who the fuck told you to turn a blind eye? Not me. Are you saying I did?'

It wasn't the first time he'd passed out. In fact, it happened more often than he liked to admit. Sometimes, all it took was getting out of bed too quickly. But for it to happen in the middle of a press conference was a bit odd.

'Jan, I asked you a question,' Sleizner continued. 'Have I ever told you to turn a blind eye to what an investigation turns up? To hide the truth?'

'No, but…'

'No, exactly. What I have told you is that you are to keep me informed. To avoid disasters like this. Is that too much to ask?'

The thought felt completely forbidden, but there it was.

'Okay, you seem to have lost the ability to speak,' Sleizner went on. 'But let me lay it out for you. Personally, I don't give a toss if there's a third person, or a whole fucking platoon involved. The only thing I care about is that this is wrapped up as quickly as possible.'

'Kim, we're already working as fast as—'

'How about you just shut up and listen!'

Had he been drugged? Was that why he'd suddenly started to sweat and felt so thirsty?

'I'm the one who gave you this shot.' Sleizner raised his index finger. 'I'm the branch you're sitting on. For your own sake, don't you ever fucking forget it.'

Could it have been the water Sleizner had brought? No, it had been an unopened bottle. Or had he brought two bottles?

'Hello?' Sleizner grabbed his shoulders and shook him like a broken toy. 'What the fuck's wrong with you? You seem completely out of it.' He slapped him lightly on the cheek. 'Are you even listening to me?'

Hesk met Sleizner's eyes. 'There are people following me.'

'What do you mean, following? What are you talking about?'

'There's two of them. Two men. They speak English, but I think one of them is Danish.' He took out his phone and found the pictures Hemmer had sent him of the fisherman. 'That's one of them.'

Sleizner took the phone from him and stared at it as though it was taking him a minute to grasp what he was being told. 'Fuck...' He gave the phone back and zoned out for a moment. Then he nodded, as if to his own thoughts. 'This is exactly what I've been worried about. It must have been them. There's no other explanation. It must have been them.'

'So you know who they are?'

'I wouldn't say I know. The Head of Operations of our intelligence service is dead, possibly even murdered. You think they're just going to sit idly by, twiddling their thumbs, waiting for us to do our job?'

'So you're saying they're...'

'Who else could it possibly be?' Sleizner cut in. 'Which is exactly why wrapping this up quickly would have been preferable. They're clearly worried about what might bubble to the surface if we're in charge of the investigation. I just never thought they'd go this far.'

'What? What else have they done?'

Sleizner put his hand on Hesk's shoulder and swallowed. 'I'm not sure, but I suspect they may have drugged you. It may be why you passed out and only just woke up now.'

'But I don't understand? Why would they do something so... drastic?'

'I guess it was a way to silence you, I don't know.' Sleizner shrugged. 'All that talk about other people being involved. Or do you have another idea? Something you haven't told me? Regardless, your fisherman and another man came up on stage and took you away after you passed out.'

'I'm sorry, those two came up and carried me off stage?'

Sleizner nodded. 'I assumed they were regular security guards.'

'And then what? Then what did they do?'

'Carried you off. That's all I know. I had to stay up there and try to wrap things up as neatly as I could. I've been looking for you ever since.' Sleizner chuckled. 'I've tried to call you more times than an infatuated teenager.'

Hesk didn't know what to say. The whole thing sounded logical but was at the same time completely implausible.

'Can you stand up?' Sleizner continued, holding out a hand.

'I think so.' Aided by Sleizner, he gingerly got up from the table.

'All right. Good. Now I want you to go through your pockets.'

'But why...?'

'Please, just do as I say and make sure nothing's missing.'

Hesk started to go through his pockets, one by one. He'd already had his phone out.

'Your wallet,' Sleizner said. 'Do you have it?'

He nodded. The wallet was where it should be, in the left inside pocket of his jacket, and from what he could see, nothing was missing from it.

'And your keys?'

He patted his trouser pockets and finally found them in his left front pocket.

'Good. And all the keys are there?'

He checked, calmly and methodically, each key in turn, and finally nodded. They were all there.

The only thing that wasn't right was that he always carried his keys in his right front pocket.

Never ever in the left.

19

'ALL RIGHT, HERE'S *what I suggest we do*,' Sleizner's quiet voice said through one of the speakers next to the screen, which was black save for a glimpse of light in one corner. *'I'll contact DSIS and take their pulse. They've crossed a line and this isn't something we're going to just accept.'*

'Can you tell where they are?' Qiang turned to Fareed, who was studying the map with the red dot, which appeared to be at the Police HQ in Copenhagen.

'And what about me?' a weary-sounding Hesk replied. *'What am I supposed to do?'*

'I can't tell you which floor they're on.' Fareed looked over at the screen next to the one that showed the map and zoomed in on a virtual 3D model of the building. 'But unless they're standing in the middle of this hallway or they're in one of the bathrooms, they should be in conference room 44B on the second floor of the north wing.'

'The bathroom thing sounds exciting,' Qiang replied. 'But my money's on the conference room.'

'I'm wondering if you shouldn't just go home and rest,' Sleizner said. *'And given the state you're in, I'd prefer if you took a taxi. Work will pay, so don't worry about that.'*

'Is that Hesk and Sleizner?' Dunja asked as she stepped out of the bathroom, fresh from the shower and wrapped in a towel.

Qiang nodded. 'He just woke up.'

'*Thanks, Kim, but I'm fine. I feel better,*' they heard Hesk reply. '*Much better.*'

'Only just now?'

'Yep, the prick found him in one of the conference rooms on the second floor just as he was coming to.'

'But it's been almost two hours since he passed out.'

'Sleizner's wondering if he was drugged,' Fareed said.

'By whom?'

'DSIS.'

'This just keeps getting weirder and...' Dunja trailed off and leaned closer to the speaker from which Sleizner's voice was coming again.

'*Jan, listen to me. You just woke up after being out cold for two hours. Something's not right here, so I'm going to have to insist that you head on home and take it easy. Meanwhile, I'll try to find out more, and then we'll come at it again tomorrow.*'

'*Right, but I'm actually in charge of this investigation,*' Hesk replied. '*And I prefer to decide for myself if I need to go home.*'

'Wow, did you hear that?' Dunja turned to the others. 'He's not playing around.'

'*There's no need to get worked up, Jan. Of course it's up to you, and don't worry about the investigation. No one's going to take it away from you. I'm just here to help. Okay?*'

'*Okay.*'

'*The last thing I want is for you to burn out and not be able to come back for six months. All right? For me, that would be a disaster. It would put me in the shit and I'd have to go out and find myself a new star, and they don't exactly grow on trees, let me tell you. So I would prefer if you survived. At least until we can close this case.*' Sleizner let out a chuckle. '*Can't we at least agree on that? That you should stay alive a*' *while longer?'* He laughed again. *'Come here, let me give you a hug.'*

'That man.' Dunja shook her head. 'I don't know how Hesk can bear to even be in the same room as him. Have they said anything about the directive?'

'No, not a word,' Qiang replied.

'Odd. It's supposed to go out at midnight.'

'Or maybe not so odd.'

'And what is that supposed to mean?'

'I just mean that...' Qiang swallowed and exchanged a look with Fareed. 'That the question is whether... whether it's all that...'

'All that what? What are you trying to say?'

'If it really is all that interesting,' Fareed finished for him. 'Interesting enough to justify you going out tonight, with all the risks that entails, just so you can hook up with some police officer with a radio.'

'If you have a better idea, speak up. And why wouldn't the directive be interesting? You heard how hard Sleizner pushed to get whatever it is out as soon as possible. Why would he have done that at a secret lunch meeting unless it was important?'

'Fine, so what are you saying it is?' Qiang crossed his arms.

'No idea. That's what I plan to find out. But if I had to guess, it's something big enough to make everyone look the wrong way, and if that's true, then all we have to do is turn around. And the quicker we're able to do that, the better.'

'Dunja.' Fareed looked her in the eye. 'I know you think we're on to something since yesterday, and that the things that were said at that lunch meeting might be the key to something major. And maybe it is, what do I know. What I do know is that Qiang and I have gone over the entire recording, analysing it word for word, and I'm sorry to have to tell you, but there isn't much there.' He shook his head. 'The only concrete information is their concern about whether Hesk is the right man to lead the investigation, and judging by today's press conference, I at least have no trouble understanding that concern. This directive you're so fixated on is just something that came up in passing, and the question is if it's going to be anything of real interest.'

'It won't be, if Mikael Rønning's to be believed,' Qiang put in.

'What's he got to do with anything?' Dunja asked.

'Well, he's your best friend, and he would obviously have helped us with both firewalls and clean-up if he thought this was as interesting as you do.'

Dunja shook her head. 'The only thing Mikael wants is for me to drop this and go back to my regular life.'

'And it hasn't occurred to you that he might be right?' Fareed asked.

Dunja thought about that for a minute and then nodded. 'Of course it has.'

'But?' Qiang said.

'We're at war, in case you haven't noticed.' She looked back and forth between them. 'A war where there are only two options, and going back and pretending like nothing happened isn't one of them. It's us or Sleizner. And I can promise you that man isn't contemplating giving up and rolling over. He's working day and night to find and get at us, and right now he's terrified, panicking about us getting there before him, finding out whatever it is he's trying to sweep under the rug.'

Fareed sighed. 'Fine, he did deviate from his routine yesterday. I'll go as far as to admit that.'

'Me too,' Qiang said with a nod.

'But is that really so remarkable?' Fareed continued. 'After all, all eyes are on this investigation. And as far as the lunch meeting goes, I'd say Sleizner was the calmest of the three.'

'Me too,' Qiang said again.

'But I happen to be the one who knows him the best,' Dunja said. 'And from what I heard, that was a desperate Sleizner doing everything in his power to calm the other two down. I have no idea how Jakob Sand is connected to this. We'll find out. But what is beyond doubt is that Mogens Klinge's death is for whatever reason a blow to Sleizner in a very personal way, and our job is to find out why, though I have my own theories about that.'

'And how can you be so sure it's personal?' Fareed asked.

'Didn't you see how stressed out he was at the press conference?'

Fareed shrugged and shook his head.

'If you ask me, he seemed to be in a good mood and even relatively relaxed,' Qiang opined.

'But no one did ask you.' Dunja shook her head. 'No, what you saw was a Sleizner with a fake smile and try-hard jokes doing everything he could to seem at ease. In truth, he was fighting for his life.'

'I'd say Hesk was the one who seemed stressed out, sitting there sweating,' Fareed countered. 'And he was the one who passed out.'

'Yes, and that was weird too,' Dunja agreed with a nod. 'Hesk has always been sensitive, but I've never seen him quite that fragile. And he didn't start to feel poorly until after Sleizner joined him, which tells me those two are at odds at the moment. Plus, you just heard him talk back.'

'Doesn't that describe pretty much everyone's relationship with Sleizner, though?' Qiang said.

'Everyone's except Hesk's. He's always been Sleizner's good

little soldier and now all the arse-kissing has finally borne fruit and he's allowed to lead an investigation, he thanks his mentor by not even informing him about the fact that they're holding a press conference. So what happens? Well, the moment Sleizner is apprised of this little stunt, he hurries up on stage to tell the press what everyone is already assuming. Which is to say that Mogens Klinge took his own life after deliberately or accidentally strangling the woman during sex. The press conference could have ended right then, and no one would have so much as raised an eyebrow. But Hesk disagreed. I don't think I've ever heard Hesk disagree with Sleizner before. But he did today, and right in front of the cameras too, voicing a theory that contradicts Sleizner's, saying one or more people may have been involved. And knowing Hesk as I do, he wouldn't have said a peep unless he was sure.'

'And this other person?' Fareed said. 'Are you saying that's Sleizner?'

'Why not?' Dunja shrugged.

'And why would he have killed Klinge?'

'Good question, and I wouldn't be surprised if part of the answer is hidden between the lines of this directive.'

'Fine. But can I say something?' Qiang said, and he waited for Dunja and Fareed to turn to him before continuing. 'None of this changes the fact that for now, this is all speculation, more or less pulled out of thin air.'

'I know, we need concrete proof,' Dunja replied. 'But I wouldn't be surprised in the slightest if it turned out we're already sitting on it.'

'What, proof? What do you mean?'

'Over the past month, no one has kept a closer eye on him than us. We've collected data and mapped out his life, down to the smallest detail. We've watched his every step. Listened in on every phone conversation. Texts, emails, we've read them all, and it's all here.' Dunja gestured towards the jumble of computers, screens and hard drives. 'The problem is that we haven't known what to look for. It's like searching for a needle in a haystack without knowing that a needle is thin, pointy, made of metal, and no more than an inch or two long. But now we have both a name and an event, and come midnight, we'll hopefully know even more. So I would suggest spending the intervening hours going through everything we have one more time. And while you do that, I'll head out and see if I can't find myself a nice uniformed officer with a communication unit and make sure I have a front-row seat when this directive is sent out.'

20

FROM A DISTANCE and through the glass wall, he probably looked like he was in control, sitting in his chair behind his desk, staring out at his office. *There's a man who's done well for himself*, a person who saw him might think. *That Jan Hesk*. But nothing could be more wrong. In truth, he had his hands full trying to fight down the panic that was pumping out so much stomach acid he felt like he was corroding from the inside.

This wasn't what he'd pictured it would be like the first time he sat down to work in his new and completely private office with a view of the courtyard and room for both a sofa and armchairs. There was no hint of pleasure. No opportunity to lean back contentedly in his chair, put his feet up on the desk and relish the smell of finally having succeeded and being one of the people who could rightly call themselves successful.

He, who had even taken the time during his holiday to purchase a real leather office chair that cost half a month's salary. A chair that was, by the way, of the same exclusive brand as Sleizner's, only a slightly better model.

But this wasn't the time to pull the little lever under the seat and lean back. Or to gaze at the view or the books on the shelves, which Lone had sorted according to colour, or the framed Joan Miró posters on the opposite wall. All those things felt ridiculous now, and a part of him longed to be back in his cramped cubicle in the middle of the open-plan office with the rest of his colleagues.

The events of the past two days had knocked him completely off balance, and even though it had been a while since he woke up in the conference room, he still couldn't take in the fact that he'd actually been drugged and abducted in the middle of a press conference.

He'd been through some things during his years as a police officer, but he'd never been the victim of this kind of assault.

The good thing was that it had finally made him stand up to Sleizner, which had led to his boss treating him with something akin to respect for the very first time.

As far as the drugging went, Sleizner had concluded that DSIS was likely behind it, and he had no reason to question that. But exactly how it had been done was unclear. Which was why he'd decided to watch the recording of the press conference, which had already been posted online.

So far, he'd been unable to bring himself to click the white triangle and play the video, which was over an hour long. It felt like being forced to relive the trauma.

On the other hand, reliving the trauma was going to be impossible to avoid. The news of his collapse had exploded online, and the twelve-second clip of him slumping in his chair and falling to the floor had gone viral and already passed a hundred thousand views on YouTube.

He'd even watched it himself a few times. Because those weren't the seconds he dreaded, it was all the other ones. Something told him that was when the real violation had taken place.

He grabbed the mouse and moved the pointer to the triangle.

But he just couldn't. Something inside him was resisting and suddenly his index finger lacked the strength to left-click.

Instead, he took out his keys and studied them in the sunlight streaming in through the window behind him. He hadn't mentioned to Sleizner that they were in the wrong pocket. He'd still felt groggy after waking up and had figured maybe he'd put them in the wrong pocket after all.

But he hadn't, he was sure of that now. His keys had been moved from one pocket to the other while he was unconscious. They'd probably made copies, and it wouldn't be long before they began to use them.

They definitely hadn't been in his car. It was as chaotic as ever. They hadn't gone through his new office either. Not that it contained anything more exciting than his fancy chair.

His phone, which was lying on the desk, lit up and began to buzz. It was Lone. She'd obviously heard the news and seen the video. But she would have to wait and make do with a text: *No time to talk now, but I'm fine. Love, J.* That was when it hit him. The second after the swish sound confirmed that his text had begun its journey.

The mobile.

He'd completely forgotten. Of course that was what they were after.

The yellow shark fin.

He picked his phone back up and called Lone.

'*There you are,*' she said on the other end. '*How are you feeling? What happened?*'

'I'm fine. Everything's good,' he said, but he could hear how strained he sounded.

'*Fine? How can you tell me everything's fine when—?*'

'Darling. I'm going to have to tell you more about it later.

Everything's under control, I promise. That's not why I'm calling.'

'*No, but it's why I called, and I want you to tell me right now what—*'

'Lone, can it please wait until tonight? Right now, I just want you to listen and answer my questions. Okay?'

The silence on the other end spoke volumes.

'*I just watched my own husband collapse on live TV. And when I get worried and try to call, does he answer? No, not for hours.*'

'Darling, I know, and I can explain.'

'*No, I'm talking now, because I want to make one thing very clear to you. Just because you've gone and got yourself promoted doesn't mean you suddenly get to do whatever you want and start bossing me around.*'

'Of course not, I would never think that. But right now, I just need to know if anyone has come by the house,' he said, trying to ignore her mood.

'*Come by the house? No, who would that have been?*'

'And you've been home all day, right?'

He could hear Benjamin burst into tears in the background and her picking him up to try to calm him down. '*Jan, what are you doing?*'

'Please, just answer me. Have you been home all day or not?'

'*Where else would I have been? You're not here, and when I look around, I certainly don't see Legoland.*'

'Good, and you've been inside the whole time? I mean, you've been in the house?'

'*Seriously, what kind of interrogation is this?*'

'It's not an interrogation. I just want to know if you've been in all day. Or if at any point you've left the house and gone—'

'*Oh, for fuck's sake!*' she hissed.

'*Fuck*,' he heard Benjamin exclaim. '*You said fuck.*'

'*What do you think? Huh? It's twenty-seven degrees out. So yeah, of course I've been huddled up inside all day.*'

'Okay. Where did you go?'

'*Seriously, this is sick. You get that, right? Fucking mental.*'

'Lone, I'm begging you,' he said, in an attempt to calm her down. 'I understand this must sound strange and incomprehensible.' He wanted to just tell her the truth. 'But you have to trust me and tell me where or approximately how far from the house you went.' But she would freak out and once that happened, there would be no getting through to her. 'And if you remember when and for how long you were out, that would be even better.'

'*I went outside to hang laundry,*' she replied in a flat tone just as Morten Heinesen entered and looked around the new office. '*Your frayed old underpants included. It was at 9.58 and it took me twelve minutes and twenty-six seconds.*'

He signalled for Heinesen to get out and leave him alone. But his colleague shook his head and stayed where he was.

'*Then Benjamin and I went over to see Adam on the other side of the hedge at 1.07. Benjamin bounced on the trampoline.*'

'*Bounce, bounce...*'

'*And Adam and I had coffee in the sunshine, and it was a lovely two hours and three minutes, and then I came home to this delightful conversation.*'

Two hours. Plenty of time for them to search the house and find the phone.

'*At 2.42, Adam offered me a cigarette. Just so you know,*' Lone continued on the other end, while Heinesen took a seat on the sofa. '*And I said yes, because I felt I deserved it. But now, having talked to you, I'm realizing I should have had two.*'

She'd taken up smoking again. He'd suspected as much in the spring when he thought her coat smelled of smoke, but he'd dismissed it as paranoia. But it hadn't been. Despite everything they'd been through to help her quit. All his attempts to distract her from her nicotine addiction. All the times he'd met her foul mood with a hug and endless forbearance.

'Darling, I want you to go into our bedroom, to the desk.'

'*Darling,*' she mimicked mockingly. '*Do you even hear how pathetic that sounds?*'

'Please, just do as I ask.'

'*Fine, I'm here. What else do you want me to do? Jump up and down?*'

'I want you to open the desk, pull out the top-left drawer and see what you can find under the pile of envelopes.'

'*An ugly old yellow phone. Happy?*'

'Yes,' he said, breathing a sigh of relief. 'Very happy. Thank you, darling. See you tonight.'

There was a click and the call ended.

'I love you too,' he said into the silence, before putting his phone down and turning to Heinesen. 'What's the point of having your own office if people won't leave you alone?'

'I'm afraid this can't wait.' Heinesen got up. 'I've just been in touch with the other members of the team.'

'Okay? And?'

'The gun, the handkerchief, all the pictures and samples. They're all gone.'

21

JADWIGA KOMOROVSKI WAS sitting behind an antique walnut desk that held a banker's lamp with a brass stand and a green glass shade, a leather desk pad, a fountain pen, a lined notebook and nothing else.

It wasn't Fabian's first time in the comfortable visitor's chair, which was fully upholstered, including the armrests. But it was the first time he'd noticed what Theodor's defender and her swanky office with a view of Helsingborg harbour really looked like.

Almost every lawyer he'd had dealings with in his years as a detective had been hidden behind stacks of folders and documents, the centre of a swirl of dusty chaos in which no one but they stood a chance of finding the right folder.

By contrast, this place was gleamingly clean and there was a faint whiff of furniture polish in the air. Much like Komorovski herself, sitting there in her navy suit and cream secretary blouse, looking back at him with her reading glasses pushed up into her chestnut hair, which she wore down.

Was that why he'd hired her? Because of that air of control and exclusivity? He couldn't remember now. Anything further back than a few days had become hazy and impenetrable. She certainly was expensive, and maybe that had blinded him. The idea that everything would turn out all right if he just threw enough money at it.

'Fabian, this has become untenable,' she said, as though he'd been called into the headmistress's office. 'I hope you can see that.'

'Something's not right.' He was surprised at how calm he sounded. 'And they're covering it up.' Maybe he'd simply run out of energy.

Komorovski weighed her words carefully. 'I don't have children myself and I probably can't understand how difficult it must be to lose one. That's not what's supposed to happen. It goes against everything we believe in. But I do understand one thing, and that is that what you're doing now won't help you, Sonja or Matilda. On the contrary, it looks like it may make everything worse. Much worse. Sonja contacted me earlier today and told me that—'

'I know,' Fabian broke in. 'So you want me to just drop it and let them walk away unpunished? Is that what you're saying? That they should be allowed to just carry on like nothing happened?'

'Unpunished for what?'

'For having taken my son from me. For assaulting him and systematically breaking him down until in the end, he...' He broke off. The words still hurt too much.

'Fabian.' She leaned across her desk and handed him a tissue, which he accepted even though he had no need for it. 'I've been in contact with them, or, rather, they've been in contact with me after your unannounced visit earlier today, and believe me, they're not hiding anything.'

'Then why weren't we told he was in solitary?'

'We were, Fabian. I have it here in an email, in case you don't believe me.' She opened one of the desk drawers, took out a printed copy of an email and placed it in front of him. 'I received this on 27 June. It details the assault in the canteen and the decision to place him in solitary for a few days.'

'And why didn't you tell me?'

'I did. But you only wanted to talk about the assault. I could hear how angry and disappointed in him you were. As soon as I told you about it, you shut down and were incapable of taking anything else in. I still have the conversation if you don't believe me. As you know, I record everything.'

It was as though his memory had developed glaucoma. He couldn't remember any part of what she was telling him. In a way, he did want to listen to that conversation. Hear if he really had been so filled with fury he hadn't listened to what she was saying. But he couldn't, so he just shook his head. 'But what about Theodor? Why didn't he tell me when I visited him?'

'He didn't say much. Especially to people he didn't trust.'

Fabian looked up and met her gaze.

'I apologize; that sounded like criticism,' she went on. 'Which is not at all how I meant it. He didn't tell me, either.'

'But I'm his father. If he couldn't trust me, then who could he trust?'

'Is that what you're trying to do? Show him that he can trust you?'

'I just want to know what happened. I want the truth.'

Komorovski broke eye contact and was unable to contain a sigh.

'Sigh as much as you want. But I and one of Sweden's top forensic pathologists have studied the wounds and contusions on his body and head, and everything points to him being assaulted and trying to defend himself.'

'So you're saying they're lying to our faces?'

'It wouldn't be the first time.'

'But why? To what end? I mean, regardless, he did take his own life. And as far as the marks on his body go, surely it's conceivable that he took a few blows and kicks himself after jumping that other inmate? Or could they be self-inflicted? Could he have been banging his head against the wall until flakes of paint got stuck in his hair? Because self-harm behaviours aren't unusual in solitary.'

Fabian shook his head. 'If all their other claims had made sense, I might have believed that. But not now, not with all the smokescreens.'

'I don't understand what smokescreens you're referring to.'

'Like where he killed himself. They claim it was in his cell. But then how do we explain the thumbtack embedded in the palm of his hand? Or that Einar Greide confirmed that the marks around his neck couldn't have been made by a rope made of plaited strips of bed sheet? He believes an electrical cord was likely used. But there isn't one in his regular cell. One can be found, however, in the room where he was kept in solitary and where they have, by the way, touched up the green paint on the walls and along the cord, all the way to the light.'

Komorovski considered that for a minute before finally nodding. 'Yes, you may be right. Maybe he did commit suicide in solitary and not his cell.' She spread her hands.

'Which brings us to the questions,' Fabian said. 'Why would they lie about that?'

'Fabian, you may have forgotten, but I was there yesterday when you went to identify Theodor and suddenly began to interrogate the staff. I was there and I saw you push them, demanding to know exactly how he'd done it.'

'Yes, I did. And can you blame me?'

'Not at all. But maybe you weren't talking to the right people. Maybe you should have talked to someone who really knew what had happened and wasn't just reaching for the most likely scenario to try to calm you down.'

'Okay, say you're right about that. Then why not admit now that they gave me incorrect information and explain how it really happened, instead of clinging to the lie?'

'Fabian, I don't know. Maybe because you've been pushing so hard they don't feel like they have any other choice?'

'So it's my fault they're lying? It couldn't possibly be because they actually do want to cover up the fact that he wasn't even placed in a proper solitary cell, but rather a cleared-out storage room with wall-mounted shelves he could climb to reach the electrical cord on the ceiling. Is that what you're telling me? That they have nothing to hide and that I am, in fact, the problem here?'

He could see it in her eyes. The answer. Long before her lips began to move.

By the time the words came, he was already on his way out.

22

JAN HESK HAD never heard of anything like it. When technical evidence was lost or went missing it was usually a matter of erroneous labelling, and if you just took the time to look for it, you could usually find it, just on the wrong shelf.

This was something else entirely. This time, someone had broken into the Police HQ and Forensics, and more or less erased their entire collection of evidence.

The news had hit him like a kick in the face. But instead of rolling around on the floor, wallowing in self-pity, he'd been furious. He, who was always slow to anger, was suddenly filled with rage. Enough was enough. He'd had it up to here.

He slowed down and parked outside his house on Japanvej, killed the engine, and climbed out. There was no reason to park elsewhere or pretend he wasn't under surveillance any more. They knew where he lived.

The first thing he'd done was to gather the team and bring them up to date. This time, he hadn't left anything out, he'd told them everything, from the phone he'd found at Mogens Klinge's house to the two men who had stalked and maybe even drugged him.

It had been a daring move and given that, apart from Heinesen, he didn't know them well enough to know if they could be trusted, it could easily have blown up in his face. But he'd had no choice. He couldn't handle this on his own. He needed them, and as soon as he'd made them see that, the team spirit he'd been trying to foster all along finally kicked in.

Gone was the territorial pissing and constant questioning of his leadership. Suddenly, everyone knew their role, as though they'd always worked together.

Before walking up to the house, he glanced over his shoulder and noted a woman pushing a pram and an older man with a dachshund that was peeing on a lamp post.

They'd agreed that changing his locks would be enough, and that from now on they would conduct team meetings away from the station whenever possible. Heinesen had, after some mild pushback, made his flat in Christianshavn available and was now overseeing the work of moving the essentials over.

With regards to the stolen evidence, some was lost forever but some could be recreated. Any new evidence would be deliberately mislabelled according to an internal cipher and spread out and stored on the wrong shelves among evidence from closed investigations.

But above all, they put their hopes in the phone. The yellow shark fin.

As soon as they got it started again and were able to analyse the text conversation, they should have enough clues to set a course for their continued work.

Contact1's phone number was also of interest. So far, they only had the first four digits, 26 58. If they could get the last four, they would finally have a concrete lead.

He stepped into the hallway and locked the front door behind him, both the regular lock and the extra lock that required a key from the inside as well. That wouldn't stop them from entering with their own copied keys. But they were unlikely to break in while he and his family were at home. And the locksmith had promised to come within the hour.

On his way into the kitchen, he caught the scent of Bolognese simmering on the hob. He hadn't had anything to eat all day, and a big plate of pasta, meat and ketchup would be just the ticket.

'Hi,' he said to Lone, who was dumping the pasta into a colander. 'It smells lovely in here.'

'You're going to have to sort yourself out,' she said, pouring the pasta back into the pot. 'I had no idea when you'd be back.'

'Of course. How could you?' he said, noting that the table was set for three. 'It's no problem. Don't mind me. I'm not all that hungry anyway.'

'Great. Everyone's happy then.'

She always said that when she was sick of her life and, above all, him. *Great, we're all wonderfully happy. Lucky us,* she might exclaim with stinging sarcasm, and whatever he did and however hard he tried, a row inevitably followed.

But this time he wasn't going to walk up to her, give her a hug and ask what was wrong. Partly because he already knew and partly because he had neither the time nor the energy for a big fight.

Instead, he folded up the oilcloth tablecloth, grabbed the table, and pulled it across the floor so fast the glasses and plates clattered.

'My God, what are you doing?'

'Nothing. I just need to go up to the attic.'

'Now? But we're about to eat.'

'Yes, I gathered, but there's no reason you can't do that just as well right here,' he said, and he carried the chairs over before going to the cleaning cupboard to fetch the metal stick with a hook at one end.

'Jan, I want you to stop and explain to me what you're—'

'Not now, darling. No time. But later, when all of this is over, I promise I'll tell you everything, okay?'

'Okay, but—'

'I said later,' he cut her off. 'Not now.' He hooked the stick into the metal hoop on the ceiling hatch and pulled it open, and as usual when he hadn't been in the attic in a while, quite a bit of dirt and gravel rained down when he unfolded the ladder. 'Don't get worked up, I'll take care of it,' he said on his way up. 'I promise I'll clean up after myself.'

'You make a lot of promises these days,' Lone called out from below. 'Big ones. Like Legoland. Remember that? You promised that, too!'

But his focus was on the chaos surrounding him in the attic. Scattered everywhere were bin bags full of clothes they were never going to wear again, cardboard moving boxes, old tennis racquets, cross-country skis, piles of board games, and miscellaneous rubbish that came from he knew not where.

For years, he'd had a plan to spend a long weekend cleaning out the attic and getting it organized. He'd even considered renting a skip, getting rid of the lot, and starting over. The only thing that had stopped him was knowing what Lone's reaction would be.

In a way, it was thanks to her that he found the box he was looking for five minutes later. Because there it was. At the bottom of a stack of moving boxes, labelled *Office + Old Memories*.

He moved the other boxes aside, pulled it out into the empty space in the middle, and opened it.

There were two binders on top, labelled *Finances 1* and *2*, and underneath, a few rolls of unused fax paper, a collection of old pens, Post-it notes, and a locked red wooden box he'd made himself in woodworking class at school. But none of that was what he was looking for. What he wanted was the black cord sticking out from under a jumble of old pictures, floppy disks and other assorted cords. He pulled on it, gently so as not to break it, and fished out the charger to his old Ericsson phone.

'Well? Did you find whatever was so incredibly important it couldn't possibly wait?' Lone said as he folded the ladder back up.

'Yes, I did.' He held up the phone charger for her to see. 'Thanks to you, darling.' Then he walked over to her and kissed her on the cheek before continuing into the bedroom.

'And the floor?' she called after him. 'I thought you were cleaning up after yourself?'

'As soon as I'm done with this,' he called back, sitting down at the secretary desk, which was open.

He pulled out the drawer on the left and picked up the stack of envelopes, only to discover that there was no yellow shark fin there. Nothing but a handful of stamps, an eraser and a roll of foreign banknotes.

He should already be panicking. But he wasn't. Maybe Lone had accidentally put the phone back among the stacks of bills or why not behind the computer, for that matter. It was only after he'd searched every nook and cranny of the desk that panic started to assert itself.

'Lone,' he called, and he could hear the shrill edge of desperation in his voice. 'Lone! Where did you put the phone?' He frantically scanned the bedroom. 'I can't find it!'

Had they been here after all? He bent down and checked the floor underneath the desk and went through the clothes thrown on the office chair. Could they really have been here since he spoke to Lone on the phone? He rummaged through the overflowing bin and in the end turned it upside down. If that was the case, they must have tapped his phone and known exactly where to find it.

'Lone! Answer me, please!' he continued on his way back to the kitchen. 'Why aren't you answering me?'

'Answering what?' Lone put the ketchup bottle down on the table. 'What are you on about now?'

'The mobile phone, for fuck's sake!' he shouted. 'The one I called you about!'

'Hey, don't shout at me. Calm down.'

'You said it was in the desk!'

She turned away from him. 'Katrine and Benjamin! Time to eat! Tea's ready!'

'Well, it's definitely not there now, so my question is, where is it?'

'I don't know.' Lone shrugged. 'Don't ask me.'

'Who else am I supposed to bloody ask?'

'Katrine, Benjamin! Teatime!'

'Hello?' He grabbed her arm and turned her towards him. 'Who the hell am I supposed to ask if not you?'

'I don't know what you're doing.' She pulled her arm free. 'But unless you calm down right now, I'm taking the children and leaving, as soon as they have some food in them. As far as the house goes, my parents are guarantors and put up the down payment, so you can have until Monday to pack up your things. You've never been interested in the children anyway, so I reckon a few hours every other weekend should be enough.'

'Have you been over sneaking cigarettes with that Adam bloke again? Huh? Is that what you don't want to admit? And how long were you out this time? An hour? Two?'

Lone shook her head without breaking eye contact. 'I don't know if you understand how close to the edge you are right now. But no, I haven't been to see Adam. Benjamin and I went to the shops to buy things for tea and on the way home we stopped by the playground. Since we've been back, I've done laundry, cleaned the house, vacuumed, before you came and made everything filthy again, and cooked. And since we're interrogating each other, why don't you tell me why my underwear drawer has been turned upside down. Katrine, Benjamin! If you don't come here right now, I'm eating without you!'

'Darling, what do you mean, upside down?' There could be no doubt now. They had been here.

'Darling? Haven't we passed that stage several years ago?'

'Lone, I'm not trying to pick a fight.' They'd used the copied keys to get into the house and they'd taken the phone. It was gone. Their only chance to find some sort of clarity in this mess had slipped through their fingers.

'No? It's all you do every time you come home.'

Hesk pulled out one of the chairs, sat down, and poured himself a glass of water, which he downed in one. 'The only thing this is about is that phone, and while you were at the shops and the playground, they must have—' He broke off as Benjamin entered the kitchen. 'But...' The panic, the row, and the feeling of all hope being lost vanished instantly. '... there it is.'

'What?' Lone said.

'The phone, the one I've been looking for this whole time.'

'Oh, that. Benjamin hasn't let it out of his sight since you called and played Gestapo the first time. It's the only thing that keeps him quiet.'

'Oh, that's so great.' He chuckled and stood up. Benjamin had saved it. 'That's amazing.' If he hadn't taken it to the playground, it would in all likeliness have been gone by now.

'But now Daddy needs his phone back.' He walked over to Benjamin and held out his hand. 'Can Daddy have it?'

'No. Mine.' Benjamin put his hands behind his back.

'No, Benjamin, it's actually Daddy's.' He chuckled again and tried to stay calm.

'Not Daddy's. Just mine.' Benjamin shook his head and Hesk saw no other way than to grab his son's arm and wrench the phone from his hand.

'Don't take my phone! Not my phone. Daddy took my phone.' Benjamin burst into tears and ran over to Lone, who picked him up and tried to console him.

The best thing he could do was leave them alone, so he hurried back to the bedroom, closed the door behind him and moved the pile of clothes from the office chair so he could sit down with the phone. Then he pushed the charger into the power strip behind the computer, blew the sand off the phone and carefully inserted the slender plug into the port. Then he pushed the red button to turn the phone on.

At first, nothing happened.

Then, nothing kept happening.

The screen remained dark.

Even though he managed to blow away some more sand and double-checked that the cord was in one piece.

Even though he pushed the red button again and held it down for a full minute.

The phone was dead.

Doubt sank its claws into him. As though his firm determination to get to the bottom of this case had been nothing more than the thinnest of veneers, which cracked at the slightest sign of difficulty.

And then the screen finally lit up. As though it had just kept him on tenterhooks to see how long it would take to make him break down.

They would be able to go through and analyse all kinds of aspects of this phone, but right now, he just wanted one thing.

Contact1's phone number.

A few clicks later, he could add the last four numbers 89 32. Then he took out his own phone and called Morten Heinesen.

'*Hello*,' Heinesen said after just one ring. '*How are you getting on?*'

'Not too bad, after some minor trials and tribulations,' he said and just as he did, he heard the doorbell. 'Darling, could you get that?' he shouted in the direction of the kitchen. 'Sorry, it's the locksmith. And how are you getting on?'

'*We're just waiting for you. Torben has everything up and running and has just set up a VPN tunnel, so now all we need is that number.*'

'26 58 89 32.'

'26 58 89 32,' Heinesen repeated, and he could hear Hemmer repeating it again in the background. '*But look, there's something I've been thinking about*,' Heinesen went on, while the doorbell kept ringing. '*This whole thing. Is it really wise not to inform—?*'

'Darling!' he shouted again, but there was no response. 'Morten, I have to go. I'll call you back.'

'*Okay, understood. Don't worry about it. We'll talk as soon as you're done there.*'

Hesk ended the call and hurried out of the bedroom. 'Can't you hear that there's someone at the door?' he said on his way past the kitchen table, where Lone was having dinner with the children.

'I can, but as you see, we're eating, and none of us is expecting visitors.'

When he got to the hallway, he hurriedly unlocked both locks, opened the door, and froze mid-motion when he saw who it was.

'There you are. Took you long enough.' Sleizner flashed him one of his patented smiles. 'I hope this isn't a bad time.'

23

HEINESEN HAD JUST put his model version of the Star Wars ship *Slave 1* away in the bedroom when he heard Julie Bernstorff's voice from the living room.

'Torben, isn't this that bloke Bobby's helmet?'

He hurried back out to see her take the numbered helmet down from its shelf.

'What's his name again? Oh, Bobby Fett. Right?' She put the helmet on her head and turned to him. 'Hello, my name is Bobby, and I'm a robot.'

'Boba Fett,' he corrected her. 'And I would prefer if you put that back.'

'Oops. Sorry.' Bernstorff took the helmet off and handed it to Heinesen, who carefully put it back in its spot on the shelf. 'What, so it's worth a lot of money? Can I ask how much?'

'Enough, considering that it's still in one piece and has Jeremy Bulloch's autograph on the inside. Not Temuera Morrison, the original actor.'

Bernstorff nodded. 'So you don't take it with you to the woods when you go LARPing.'

'Coffee or tea?' he said to change the subject.

'Tea would be great. Thanks.'

'And I'd love a coffee, if it's no trouble,' piped up Hemmer, who was sitting on the sofa with a laptop in his lap.

'Absolutely. No problem.' Heinesen went into the kitchen,

where he turned on a pot of water and sat down at his table for one, waiting for it to boil.

They'd only arrived just over an hour ago, but he was already exhausted. But then, he could count on one hand the visitors he'd had in his almost thirty years in the small two-bed on Overgaden Oven Vandet in Christianshavn. Three times, his mother had stopped by unannounced, and on his fortieth birthday eight years ago, he'd had Anders, Frank and Lars over for dinner. And now, tonight, Torben and Julie.

Only a direct plea from Hesk had persuaded him to open the door to his colleagues. He didn't want to be obstructionist, and since the situation was undeniably extraordinary, what with the missing evidence and all the rest of it, perhaps it was no wonder they had to think outside the box.

But that didn't mean it felt good. He was a creature of habit and needed to stick strictly to his routines to function, and this went against everything he believed in. If it were up to him, they would at least have informed Sleizner of this newest development, if only to cover their own backsides, and he had suggested it more than once already. But Hesk had insisted on involving no one outside the team, and while Heinesen wasn't indifferent to the arguments about a possible internal leak, he couldn't help but see it as anything other than an unnecessary cockfight he wanted no part of.

In fact, he was increasingly worried Hesk was getting in over his head. There was no doubt he was prepared to do whatever it took to move the investigation forward, and he'd never seen Hesk as invested as he was now. But if he knew Sleizner right, none of this would go down well once the news reached him, as it inevitably would eventually. He could only hope and pray Hesk knew what he was doing.

But either way, the decision not to inform their superiors

was a clear breach of regulation. It didn't matter what you thought of the rules or how good your intentions were. In most cases, the rules were there for a reason, and bending, fudging or circumventing them might feel like a good idea in the moment, but in the end, it always spelled disaster.

Once the water was simmering a few degrees from boiling, he poured it into two cups, one with instant coffee and the other with a bag of Earl Grey, and returned to the living room, where Bernstorff had written the mobile number 26 58 89 32 in black marker at the top of a large notepad and was now busy drawing arrows to a number of boxes that said, among other things, *network provider, SIM card number, retailer, PAYG card* and *identity*.

Before getting stuck into that, she had apparently found time to fiddle with his collection of Star Wars figures, swapping Greedo and Bossk on the shelf. As though he wouldn't notice.

'Morten, what do you think of this?' she said with a satisfied smile as he put the cups down on the coffee table.

'You mean in case the number is no longer active?' he said, deciding to pretend like nothing had happened.

'Yes, because I really don't think we should count on that, so I reckon if we can just get the SIM number, the phone company should be able to help us narrow down where it—'

'That won't be necessary,' Hemmer broke in, looking up from his screen. 'Because not only is the number still active – the phone's turned on.'

24

'Pardon me, I didn't mean to interrupt your evening.' Sleizner stepped into the hallway. 'But I happened to be in the area and figured we should have a chat after everything that happened today.'

'Okay,' Hesk said, nodding. 'We were just sitting down to eat, but no worries. It can wait.'

'Wonderful.' Sleizner continued into the kitchen, where he waved to Lone and the children. 'Hello.'

'Hello,' Lone said, with her eyes fixed on her water glass.

'Mum, who's that?' Benjamin said.

'It's Daddy's boss.'

'What's a boss?'

'Why don't you focus on eating your food.'

'My name's Kim.' Sleizner bent down to the boy's eye level. 'But your mum's right. I'm your dad's boss, which means I'm in charge of him when he's at work. Like your mum is when he's at home.' He chuckled and turned to Hesk. 'Am I right, Jan? Do you have any say here at home, or is the missus wearing the trousers?'

'Ehm... I mean, we...'

'She certainly doesn't seem to think you deserve any dinner today.' Sleizner turned to Lone. 'Has the old man put on a few pounds? Is that why you have him on a diet?'

'You said you wanted to talk,' Hesk said.

Sleizner nodded, scanned the kitchen, and turned to Hesk. 'Preferably somewhere private.'

Hesk nodded and showed Sleizner deeper into the house.

'You have a lovely home.' Sleizner looked around and popped his head into the bedroom. 'Maybe a bit messy for my taste. But other than that, lovely. Or, how to put it? It has potential.'

'Why don't we have a seat in here.' He closed the living-room door behind Sleizner and sat down on the edge of the sofa, even though he normally preferred the armchair.

Sleizner looked around before sitting down in the armchair and drumming his fingers against the armrests as though it were his own.

'I actually don't think I've been here before,' he said at length, his eyes roving around the room. 'I guess you didn't have a moving-in party.'

'We did, but it was mostly our closest friends.'

'Of course.' Sleizner nodded. 'With a small house, you have to prioritize.'

Silence descended again. And again, it was unbearably uncomfortable.

'Can I offer you something to drink?' Hesk said, mostly to break it.

'Well, why not? Unless the missus minds?'

Hesk stood up and moved towards the door. 'What would you like?'

'A beer would be great. It's Saturday, after all.'

Hesk hurried out into the kitchen to fetch two beers. But they only had Tuborg Green, so he dashed out to the fridge in the garage. There was probably a good reason why he felt he couldn't just give him a regular Tuborg, or a glass of water with a lemon slice. But that analysis would have to wait.

When he got back, Sleizner was standing by the bookshelf, studying the rows of spines.

'Thanks.' Sleizner accepted the bottle and glanced at the label from Nørrebro Bryghus before taking a sip. 'Mm, I love a good lager. But tell me, have you read all of these?' He nodded towards the books.

'No, Lone's the reader in the family,' he replied, and tasted his beer.

'Same.' Sleizner took another sip. 'I don't understand how people find the time to get through several hundred pages, what with work, family, and all the other things a person has to see to. The last thing I read from cover to cover was the *Lord of the Rings* trilogy when I was a young man.'

'I didn't realize you like fantasy.'

'I don't. It took a whole summer, and I was never happier to go back to school than that year. What about you, have you read it?'

'No.'

'You're not missing out. I know they're supposed to be amazing and some of the best books ever written and all that. But if you ask me, I'd say they seemed... how to put it... written in a hurry. Just take the fact that you turn invisible when you put on the master ring.' Sleizner took a sip of his beer. 'I mean, come on. Not exactly the most creative. There's *The Invisible Man*, which must have been written sometime in the nineteenth century. Talk about being ahead of your time. And to this day, no one has been able to explain to me how anyone could be as stupid as Frodo, putting the ring on a second, third and fourth time, when he knows the black riders will be there within seconds. But never mind. That's not why I'm here. Cheers.' He raised his bottle and returned to the armchair.

Hesk sat back down on the sofa and noted that Sleizner's

painful attempt at joviality had now been replaced by seriousness.

'I heard about the technical evidence.' Sleizner looked up and fixed him intently. 'It sucks, but unfortunately, I can't say I'm surprised. That's how they operate.' He sighed and drank his beer.

'What is it they don't want us to find?' Hesk asked as his phone began to vibrate.

'Well, who knows.' Sleizner shrugged.

Seeing it was Heinesen, Hesk declined the call.

'But I do know one thing,' Sleizner went on. 'And that is that we're going to find out. Because if there's one thing that rubs me up the wrong way, it's when someone pisses on my turf.'

Hesk's phone lit up again and started to vibrate, but even though he was burning to take the call, it would have to wait.

'Do you understand what I'm saying, Jan?'

Hesk nodded, even though he wasn't quite following.

'What happened today was beyond the pale, and in a way, I feel complicit and want to apologize for horning in on your press conference and making everything worse. It really wasn't my intention.'

'Don't worry about it.'

'I do worry about it. But I think I should try to get used to the idea of you holding the tiller. But I didn't just come here to apologize. More importantly, I want to make sure you're not about to throw in the towel.'

'Why would I be?'

'You seemed pretty shaken up, and, how to put it, ambivalent about the whole thing when I found you in that conference room. And believe me, I have no problem understanding why. I would have felt exactly the same way. Powerful forces are at work here.'

'How do you want us to proceed?'

'Jan, it's your investigation. Not mine. But if it were me, I'd rather look over my shoulder one time too many than not often enough. And, speaking of which, have you seen any signs of them having been here, in your house?'

'No.' The answer came out before he had time to consider, and he had no choice but to follow up with a head shake. 'Nothing.'

'Okay, good. I don't know if they got away with all the evidence, or if you still have anything of value. But regardless, I think we should count on it happening again, unless we're careful. That's why I want you to have this.' Sleizner put a small brass-coloured key on the coffee table and pushed it towards Hesk. 'It's a key to the safe in my office. You know, the one built into the wall next to the filing cabinet.'

Hesk nodded.

'I'm afraid it's not refrigerated, so you can't use it for organic samples. But anything else that's not too big should fit in there.'

'And you and I are the only people with keys?'

'Of course. And you should feel free to come and go as...' Sleizner was interrupted by Hesk's phone as it lit up and began to vibrate for the third time. 'Maybe you should take that,' he said, and drank the last of his beer.

Hesk accepted the call and put the phone to his ear. 'Hi. Look, I'm busy right now. Can I call you back?'

'*No, sorry, this can't wait,*' Heinesen said.

'All right, what is this about?'

'*Hemmer did a search for that number, and as expected, it's anonymous. We may be able to find out where it was purchased and match it with a credit card, but that will take weeks. Anyway, he has triangulated the phone's location, and this is where it gets interesting, because it turns out the number's still active.*'

'Okay. So you have a location?'

'*Yes, and at first we assumed there must have been a mistake and so we redid the whole thing. That's why it took a while.*'

'Don't worry about it. Like I said, I'm busy right now anyway.'

'*But the thing is that we got the same location the second time, and the reason I'm calling is that we're hoping you can explain it.*'

'Me?'

'*Yes, because right now, the phone in question is at your house.*'

25

THE MAN UNDERNEATH Dunja was probably ten years younger than her. Maybe even more. But she didn't care in the slightest. At least not right now, when she was finally in control and making sure every tiny movement was for her pleasure.

He was muscular and had no problem flipping her into any position he liked. He'd demonstrated that more than amply at the start. First the missionary and then the spoon. Then he'd spun her around as though they were circus performers and taken her from behind before it was over.

The whole thing had been so typical of a young, porn-watching, testosterone-soaked man: rushing through as many positions as possible and then lacking the stamina to keep going for more than a few minutes and passing out the second he was done as though the power had suddenly been cut.

But he was well endowed. She had to give him that. If he hadn't been, she would have let him sleep, which would really have been better since they were minutes away from midnight.

In her previous life, she'd hit the town every Tuesday night, because the day she left Carsten had been a Tuesday. But over the past two months, she'd been forced to endure involuntary celibacy, unable even to take care of things herself without Fareed and Qiang noticing. And now, even though it was Saturday and the lover between her legs was terrible, something inside her had been awakened, and she promised herself to resume her Tuesday tradition as soon as possible.

On this particular night, she'd stepped right into the lion's den that was Byens Bodega, a stone's throw from the station, and just like back when she was a fresh-faced constable, this was where the youngest officers liked to meet for a pint after finishing their shifts. Nothing had changed. The brown wooden furniture, the smell of stale smoke, the small bar, the paintings on the walls. Nothing, except her.

At first, she'd felt overdressed in her jumpsuit and heels. The plan had been to draw as much attention as possible to locate a target as quickly as she could to minimize the risk of being recognized, just in case anyone knew Sleizner. To that end, she'd put on make-up, dressed up, and even pulled on a dark-brown bob-cut wig.

Her new look had worked better than expected. Before she'd even finished her first pint, the man whose name she could no longer remember, who had just started working as a traffic officer, had suggested heading back to his, and in the back seat of the taxi, a throwaway comment about police uniforms being a turn-on had been enough to make him swing by the station to pick up all of his equipment.

Once they got to his flat, she'd locked herself in the bathroom and told him she would only open the door to a real police officer, and within minutes he'd knocked, dressed in full uniform.

While he performed some kind of awkward striptease in the bathroom, she'd made him demonstrate the use of both the baton and the handcuffs, and most importantly, the handheld communication unit used for internal communication among police and emergency services. He'd even agreed to give her the password needed to turn it on.

Now, everything lay scattered across the bathroom floor, including her wig. Everything except the communication unit. That was what she was after. The rest was just a fringe benefit. Because it was there, in less than five minutes, that she would learn what Sleizner's next move was, which in a best-case scenario would give her enough information to hit him where it hurt the most.

It wasn't an active decision. Suddenly, her hand was just there, helping out while her hips kicked up the pace, thrusting deeper and deeper. Up until now, it had felt good. But it was as though her body had realized that if it wanted to feel really good, it needed to take charge, not just of the young man, but of her as well.

Nothing could stop it from pushing all the way to the finish line, sweatier, faster, harder, and once the fireworks exploded, she slumped over to catch her breath.

'Don't go anywhere,' he said, pulling out of her. 'I'll be right back.' He gently put her down on her side and left the bed.

'What if I fall asleep?' she said, pulling the duvet up. 'Then what will you do?'

'Then it'll be my turn to wake you up. Exactly how will be a surprise.' He disappeared into the bathroom.

As soon as the door shut behind him, she found the communication unit among the sheets, turned it on, typed in the password, and watched the clock in the corner of the screen go from *11.59 p.m.* to *12.00 a.m.*

Seconds later, a symbol came on, indicating there was a new unread message of highest priority, and the moment she opened it her heart skipped several beats before racing on at a pace that suggested it knew only one thing mattered now.

Survival.

The picture of her was no grainy screenshot from some

low-res CCTV footage. This was a crystal-clear portrait taken by a professional photographer in a real studio. She remembered it like it was yesterday: when it had been time to renew her police ID, she'd decided to spring for a proper photo.

The thing was, the photo had been manipulated. Gone were the blonde curls she'd never managed to tame. Instead, her hair was short and dyed silver and looked exactly like her current hairdo. Same thing with the hoop earrings and red lips. Even her cheeks had been altered to make her look thinner, like she did in reality.

NATIONAL APB

Former police officer Dunja Hougaard (36yo, 5'6") has been arrested in her absence on suspicion of intent to commit crimes against national security. She is believed to be in or around Copenhagen together with two men of foreign extraction. As she is known to be extremely violent, all precautions are to be taken in case of an arrest.

She breathed through her mouth, stressed, shallow breaths that were barely enough to oxygenate her blood. Her pulse was racing as though the accelerator and clutch had been pushed at the same time. She needed to get out of there. Right now.

Sleizner hadn't been trying to sweep traces of his involvement in Mogens Klinge's death under the rug. Instead, it had been about her. Of course it had. His seething hatred had reached a new level of insanity as he accused her of crimes against national security, a charge that was sufficiently vague to potentially include anything from leaking classified material to planning a terror attack. From now on, he wouldn't be the only one trying to catch her. Every police officer in Denmark had just joined the hunt.

She looked around. Her clothes were on the bathroom floor. With any luck, there would be something she could wear in the wardrobe. If not, she had no choice but to...

That train of thought ground to a screeching halt as the bathroom door opened and the man came back out, naked and with a hard-on pointing straight out. At her.

'As you can see, I'm ready for round three.' He humped the air before continuing towards the bed.

'Finally,' she said, pulling the duvet up over the communication device. 'I thought you were never coming back.

'But I'm here now.' He stepped up onto the bed, pushed her down onto her back and straddled her chest so that the engorged head of his cock pressed against her lips.

'Mm, lovely,' she said, and writhed out between his legs. 'But now it's your turn to wait.' She left the bed, hurried towards the bathroom, and locked the door behind her.

'Just don't take too long,' she heard him call from the bed.

'Just make sure you don't nod off,' she called back, while pulling on her knickers, which she found hanging on the bath tap.

There was no time for a bra. She needed to get out now, not in fifteen minutes or even five, right now. But getting the jumpsuit, which lay in a pile on the floor, back on proved to be slow work. First the legs were inside out, then the sleeves, and once it was finally on, she realized she was wearing it backwards.

But that couldn't be helped. She'd already stayed too long. The important thing was that he didn't get suspicious and react before she could get to the door. She'd have to carry her heels. She wouldn't be able to run with them on anyway.

She hurried over to the door and had just put her hand on the handle when it moved of its own volition. Fuck, she had time to think as she backed away from the door. Fuck, fuck, fuck.

'Hello? Would you mind unlocking the door?' she heard him say on the other side.

'Aren't you impatient,' she said, and flushed the toilet before walking over to the bath and turning on the shower.

'Hey! I want you to open this door!'

'What? I can't hear you.' When she got back to the toilet, she closed the lid, climbed up onto it and opened the small square window overlooking the courtyard.

'Open up! Right now!'

'I'm almost done. Hey, where might I find a clean towel?'

The window was too small to climb through. But it was her only option, so she started to squeeze through the tiny opening, arms first, without any idea of what awaited her on the other side.

Her shoulders were the biggest problem, and she could feel skin coming off on either side, as though someone had come at her with a grater. But the adrenaline rush took care of the pain, and the rest of her upper body came through fine.

The ground was further away than she'd thought. At least twenty feet. If she managed to avoid the bins and parked bikes and land on the little patch of grass a few feet from the wall, she might survive. But she would definitely be left crippled.

Her only option was the drainpipe that ran down the façade about three feet to the right of the window. If only she'd put her legs through first, she would have been able to hang from the windowsill and swing herself over to grab the pipe with her feet. Now she had to do the same manoeuvre upside down and could only hope her feet would be able to hold her weight.

But the other options were worse, and at the risk of having the slightest shift of her centre of gravity make her fall head first, she kept pushing herself further out until her entire upper body was hanging out of the window. At least the uneven brickwork offered plenty of handholds, which made it easier to drag herself towards the drainpipe, inch by inch.

Eventually, she was close enough to reach out to try to grab the pipe, and she might have made it, if not for the hands that suddenly grabbed her ankles and pulled her back inside. She tried to kick free, but he was too strong, and before she knew it, she was back in the bathroom, her head slamming into the toilet lid before she could catch herself on the tiled floor.

She tried to turn around, but he was already on top of her with the handcuffs, pushing one knee in between her shoulder blades.

'Good thing I had these with me.' He pulled down her left arm and snapped the cuff around her wrist, unaware that while he did so, she'd managed to grab the scales from underneath the sink with her right hand.

Without knowing exactly where he was, she swung the scales up over her head as hard as she could. The dull sound of the glass slab breaking, followed by a roar, suggested she'd hit her mark.

His knee was still on her back, but less firmly. With a quick twist, she managed to turn over onto her back. Only to discover that he was still naked and straddling her, busy prodding a bleeding cut under one eye.

She tried to wrench free of him, but even dazed as he was, he was too heavy and strong, so she grabbed his scrotum and twisted it so hard he rolled off her with a scream.

Once she was back on her feet, she quickly reviewed her escape routes. She could have gone around him via the overflowing bath where the shower was still running, but since he seemed somewhat out of it, she decided to jump over him instead.

'Forget it,' he said, as though he'd read her mind.

'Listen to me,' she said while he struggled back onto his feet. 'I know you're just a nice guy doing his job.' Just then, she caught a glimpse of a white shard of glass glinting in the cut underneath his eye. 'I could tell you that what you've just read about me isn't true. That it's all lies, made up by Kim Sleizner to frame me. But there's no point. You wouldn't believe me anyway. Which is why instead, I want to make it extremely clear to you that even though I've already hurt you more than enough, I won't hesitate to do even more damage.'

'Say what you want. But since you're wanted by the police, I suggest you tell it to a lawyer instead of me. Because no matter what you say, I'm arresting you.'

Dunja weighed her options before finally heaving a long sigh and turning around with her arms crossed behind her back. One heartbeat later, he was next to her, grabbing her left hand, which was already cuffed.

He was completely unprepared for her sudden movement. Just as he was about to grab her right hand, it disappeared as she spun around, threw herself anticlockwise, and appeared behind him. Two heartbeats later, she'd wrapped her arms around him, grabbed the loose end of the handcuffs with her right hand and pulled it tight around his throat. Then she kicked his legs hard.

That was all it took to knock him off balance and tip him backwards. His own mass did the rest, and she just had to take a half-step back and shift her centre of gravity and the handcuffs around his neck slightly to steer his fall towards the bath.

He flailed and kicked as he tried to free himself, but the laws of physics were on her side, and she soon had his head under water.

How many heartbeats passed after that, she didn't know.

Ten?

Fifteen?

She didn't pull him out until there were no more bubbles rising to the surface and his arms and legs had gone limp. Then she let him fall to the floor, coughing and gasping.

26

JUST OPENING HIS eyes and waking up was a punishment. A slap in the face, a reminder that starting now, his conscious mind was going to be in charge, tormenting him until he finally managed to force his eyes shut for a few more hours. Because it was only down there, at the bottom of the dreamless darkness, that he could find peace.

After his visit to Jadwiga Komorovski, he'd tried to numb his pain with alcohol. But it hadn't helped. Alcohol had never been his drug of choice. Instead of getting a break from himself, his thoughts and feelings had been amped up and twisted into something that hurt even more.

Then he'd thrown up like the dog he was.

After that, as he walked home because no taxi would take him, he'd considered other drugs, but had ultimately decided it was pointless. So long as you woke up at the end of it, sleep was only ever a temporary solution, and for the first time he'd seriously considered following Theodor's example.

'Are you there?' said a fragile girl's voice on the verge of tears. 'Hello? Can you hear me?'

Fabian turned towards the sheet hanging from the ceiling and realized he was lying on the basement floor, wrapped in a blanket.

'It's me, Matilda,' the voice on the other side of the sheet continued. 'I need to talk to you.'

'I'm here if you want to talk,' he said, while searching his memory for why he'd decided to sleep in the basement. But he found nothing so he concluded he must have avoided getting into bed next to Sonja out of sheer self-preservation.

'I need to ask if you could help me with something. Something really important.'

'Of course I'll help you, Matilda.' He sat up. 'There's nothing I wouldn't do for you.'

The greatest injustice Theodore had endured was having him as his father. Sonja had said those words without the slightest hint of hesitation in her voice. He'd cast about for arguments to prove her wrong and paint a different picture, but in the end, he'd been forced to admit she was right. It was all his fault, and there was nothing he could do now to change that.

But Matilda was still alive. He still had an unwritten future with her.

'You were right,' she said, and he wondered what she meant. 'You were right all along.' If there was one thing he hadn't been, it was right. 'And now I need to know if you're in contact with my brother?' she continued, and as she did, he suddenly put it together. 'His name's Theodor, but of course you already know that.'

The realization was painful, but it made perfect sense. Of course she hadn't turned to him for help; she'd gone in search of that spirit, Greta. That's who she went to for comfort.

'I miss him, and I need to talk to him. Do you understand?' Her voice sounded on the verge of breaking. 'I knew you were going to turn out to be right. But it can't end this way. It just can't be over. You have to help me to contact him.'

She was playing with the Ouija board again. The board that, whether you believed in its powers or not, had blinded his daughter and brought a darkness into their home.

'Could you ask him how he's doing? If he's okay? That's all I want to know. That he's doing all right. And tell him I love him. Please, tell him.'

Fabian defied the low pressure inside his skull, got up, and pulled the sheet aside. And there she was, his daughter and now only child, sitting on the floor, surrounded by tealights, with her finger on a pointer that was moving across a board full of letters and numbers.

'Matilda,' he said, sitting down in front of her. 'Can't you and I have a bit of a chat instead? We could go for a walk, if you want. Go out and get something to eat. Just you and me.'

'I would prefer to be left alone,' she said, without taking her finger off the pointer.

'And I would prefer if you stopped doing this.' He put his hand on hers to lift it off the pointer.

'Stop.' She pulled her hand away. 'You're going to break the contact.'

'Matilda, I know you're sad. We all are, and we each have our own way of dealing with the grief, but—'

'Greta, ignore him,' Matilda said. 'He'll leave in a minute.'

'Matilda, listen to me. I understand that you need someone to talk to.'

'No, you understand nothing. So please, just leave.'

'Hey. Why can't you talk to Mum or me, instead of those spirits, or whatever they're called? Or some other adult? I think we're all going to need counselling to get through this.'

'Her name is Greta, and I'll talk to her as much as I like. And I want you to leave now. Go upstairs and fight with Mum, or whatever. You're good at that.'

She knew exactly where his sore spots were. How to put him on the defensive and rile him until he lost control. But he wasn't falling for it this time. 'Matilda.' He leaned closer. 'That

Theodor chose to end his life has nothing to do with your imaginary friend.'

'You can call her whatever you want. But she told me someone in this family was going to die. She said it all along, but you refused to listen. Even though I told you several times, you—'

'I what?' he broke in. 'What are you saying I should have done with that information? Tell me. What should I have done differently?'

'Everything.'

It was the way she said it that hurt the most. Unflinchingly, with her eyes fixed on his.

'Matilda, I know I've made a lot of mistakes. Especially with Theodor. And I promise you, not a day goes by when I don't think about what I could have done differently to prevent what ended up happening. But that's not the same as saying I was actually able to do something.'

'All you had to do was leave him alone.'

'You're saying that would have saved him? That he would have been here, feeling great, if I had just not cared about any of it?'

'He would have been alive.'

'Would he? And for how long, do you think? And besides, that would have meant your friend Greta was wrong. I thought she knew everything and was always right.'

'She just said someone in our family. Not who.'

'So you're saying I should have died instead. Is that it?'

Matilda continued to stare him in the eye but made no reply.

'Well?' he said, but there was no reaction. 'Is that how it all fits together? I was supposed to die, and Theodor took my place?'

Matilda neither nodded nor shook her head. She just sat there, staring at him mutely.

'Was it him instead of me? Did she tell you that? That Greta person? That Theodor died instead of me? Or is that your own conclusion?' He waited for her to respond, but she said nothing. 'Matilda, please answer me when I talk to you. Hello?' He slammed his fist down on the old board, which broke into several pieces. 'Was I the one who was supposed to die?'

Matilda looked down at the broken board, stood up, turned her back on him, and left.

27

FRAME BY FRAME, Hesk was going through the press conference he would have preferred never to think about again. Sitting on the toilet with his laptop on his knees and Lone aggressively vacuuming outside, he'd steeled himself and was now reliving his public humiliation like a slow-motion walk down Via Dolorosa, with every still another insult from the clamouring mob. It hurt, but it might help him to find the answer to why he'd lost consciousness.

He hadn't slept all night. Sleizner's visit and his conversation with Heinesen about the fact that the phone Mogens Klinge had been texting was in his house at that very moment had left him no peace. Did this mean Sleizner was the third person? Had he killed the young woman in the car, and maybe Klinge as well?

That his boss was far from upstanding came as no surprise. That he bullied and degraded the people around him so he himself could climb the ladder and had no problem turning a blind eye to almost anything so long as it benefited him was general knowledge among Copenhagen's police officers. But there was a big difference between that and being a murderer. He had a hard time imagining it, even knowing what he knew about Kim Sleizner.

Instead, he'd tried to come up with alternative explanations, like how it might have been some kind of unfortunate coincidence, the mobile phone technology playing a trick on them at the exact moment Hemmer was doing his triangulation. But he hadn't even been able to convince himself, and in the end he'd been forced to accept that this particular puzzle piece fitted a little bit too well.

By now, he'd pushed through to the point where he could be seen turning towards the smiling Sleizner, who climbed up on stage holding a bottle of mineral water and two glasses, which he put down on the table in front of them. He kept clicking and saw Sleizner lean down towards him and whisper something in his ear with a hand on his shoulder.

From a distance, it could be interpreted as a friendly greeting between colleagues, but he remembered. Every last syllable. How they'd been delivered with a coldness that had knocked him completely off balance. In that moment, he hadn't been able to think about anything else.

Now, it was the water that interested him. The bottle of mineral water and the two glasses. He'd suspected it before but had dismissed it as silly. Or no, the truth was he'd been afraid to follow that line of thought through to the end because the consequences, if his suspicions turned out to be correct, would have been unimaginable.

They still were. The difference was that since Sleizner's visit, blissful ignorance was no longer an option.

Normally, there was always water and glasses on the table during press conferences. But not this time. Probably because so few people had known he was calling one that the water had simply been one of the things that fell by the wayside, which had made it seem natural when Sleizner brought some with him.

There was a knock on the door. 'Hello, have you fallen in?' Lone said on the other side. 'You're not the only one who needs to use the bathroom.'

'I'm almost done,' he called back.

'How almost?'

'Five minutes, tops.'

He heard her sigh and turn the vacuum back on. He'd reached the part of the video where Sleizner unscrewed the cap and filled both glasses, first his and then his own, and took a sip. In other words, the water was not what had poisoned him.

Could it have happened earlier? He cast his mind back to the hours leading up to the press conference. Where he'd been and who he'd seen, wondering if anyone had offered him anything to eat or drink at any point, but nothing came to mind.

For lack of a better idea, he played the video in reverse instead, frame by frame, watching as the mineral water retreated from Sleizner's glass and back into the bottle and, once it was empty, as he put it back on the table and grabbed his glass, and the water began to leave that glass too, streaming back into the bottle.

And that's when he realized how it must have happened. The part when Sleizner put his glass down and grabbed the cap to screw it back onto the bottle. In a single frame, the focus was on his glass. The glass that should have been empty. Dry as a bone, just like Sleizner's. But which had been anything but.

There, behind the table, in front of all the cameras, under the spotlights, he'd been too stressed out to notice. There, his only goal had been to get through the press conference in one piece, despite Sleizner's interference.

But now he could see it clearly. In the still, the transparent droplets on the inside of his glass and the pool of liquid at the bottom of it couldn't be missed. There wasn't a lot of it, no more than could have been caused by it having been washed recently, but certainly more than enough to put a grown man to sleep for hours.

28

HER SLEEP HAD been binary. From all in to all out. One to zero. So deep it had been anyone's guess if she'd ever wake up again. As though her body had got through the night by dimming its light to a spark so faint even a deep breath would have risked extinguishing it for good.

Now she filled her lungs with air and, listening to Fareed and Qiang's distant mumbling downstairs, she gingerly tried to take a deeper breath. She could do it, though her chest was sore from the blows she'd received. Then she lifted up the duvet and looked down at the countless bruises, welts and cuts.

It wasn't a pretty sight. But she felt like an upgraded version of herself, bursting with energy, and after making sure nothing was broken, she struggled out of bed, pulled on a pair of joggers and a T-shirt, and climbed down the narrow wooden stairs.

'My, my, looks like someone had a good time last night.' Qiang watched her limp towards them.

'More fun than I've had in a long time,' she replied.

'Are you okay?' Fareed asked, a steaming cup of tea in his hand.

'Far from it. But never mind that. How did you get on?'

Qiang and Fareed exchanged a look.

'Dunja.' Fareed put his cup down. 'You're wanted by the police.'

She sighed. 'I know. What I'm asking is if you found

something. Unless I'm misremembering, you were supposed to go over everything one more time while I was gone.'

'And we did. But, look, having an APB out for your arrest and being suspected of crimes against national security is no game. It's tantamount to a terrorism charge and we can't just pretend it's nothing.'

'What do you want me to do? Turn myself in?'

'That's your decision. The thing is that Qiang and I are mentioned too. Luckily not by name so far, just as *two men of*—'

'Fareed, I read it,' she cut in. 'I told you he was up to something. Not what I had expected, granted, but in hindsight, I can't say I'm particularly surprised. It's just like Sleizner to go way over the top. The question is how we proceed.'

'What I think Fareed is trying to say...' Qiang swallowed. 'Is that the real question is if we *should* proceed.'

'Okay, let me just make sure I'm understanding you.' Dunja looked back and forth between them. 'You're kidding, right?'

'I don't hear anyone laughing,' Fareed said, turning to Qiang. 'Do you?'

'No.'

'If you seriously think you can just pack up and get out—'

'Dunja, so far, all he knows is that we're of foreign extraction,' Fareed said. 'But it's only a matter of time before—'

'It's not a matter of time. He obviously already knows who you are. How else would he have found our old place? I promise you, he knows Qiang's left-handed and chews his cuticles when he gets excited. And that you hate rooibos and get pissy if anyone accidentally refers to it as tea.'

'But you're the one he's after,' Qiang said. 'Not us.'

'That's true, but if you think he's going to just leave you alone once he's done with me, you're crazy. You're on his blacklist, which means you're as deep in the shit as I am, just with a slight time delay.'

Fareed and Qiang exchanged another look.

'But let's reframe this,' she continued. 'At the end of the day, he's the one who's in the shit. Not us. Take this last move of his, for instance. To my mind, he couldn't have given us clearer proof that he feels cornered and under threat. He's desperate, and like I was saying yesterday, he's trying to direct everyone's attention away from himself. And why would he be doing that unless he had something to hide?' She paused to allow them room to object but went on when neither of them spoke. 'The best thing we can do now is to keep pushing him until he makes a mistake. Because he will, I'm sure of it, and that's when we strike.'

'So, what do you want us to do?'

'How about you start by telling me what you found.'

'We already did.'

'Are you saying you found nothing? You went over and analysed all the material again but didn't manage to dig up even the tiniest lead for us to follow up on?'

'I don't know if it's significant, but I might have something,' Qiang said after a long pause.

'What? You do?' Fareed turned to him. 'Why didn't you tell me?'

'Because I only thought of it last night, right before I fell asleep, and I'm sure it's nothing. But as you know, I've been tracking Sleizner's movements, and there's this one location I don't have a good explanation for.'

'What location is that?' Dunja asked.

'You know that garage by Østerbrogade?'

'You mean the one where he likes to park his car a few nights a week?'

'That's the one.'

'But we do have an explanation for that,' Fareed said. 'An explanation that lives across the street and goes by the name of Jenny Wet-Pussy Nielsen.'

'I know, but...' Qiang trailed off and shook his head.

'So you don't think he's there to see her?' Dunja said.

'I took a closer look at her this morning, and this is what she looks like these days.' Qiang opened a picture on one of his screens, showing a close-up of a woman whose face had been ruined by plastic surgery and whose hair was bleached to within an inch of falling out. 'I don't know about you, but I have a hard time believing this is what brings him there several nights a week.'

Dunja studied the picture, and even though she didn't think there were depths Sleizner wouldn't stoop to, she was inclined to agree. 'So you're saying it's a coincidence that his old favourite hooker happens to live right there?'

'Or maybe there's some other explanation for it. She moved there from Vesterbro at the end of the summer of 2010, which was shortly after her name had been linked to Sleizner in the papers, and she has reported no income whatsoever since then.'

'She'd hardly be the first prostitute not to pay taxes,' Fareed said, booting up one of his computers.

'Where else would she be getting money from?' Dunja said.

'Well, I wouldn't be surprised if there were some kind of connection to Sleizner,' Qiang replied.

'Could he be the owner of the building?'

'Why not?'

'I find it hard to believe he'd be able to afford an entire building in the city centre,' Fareed said, while typing in a few search commands. 'His salary's decent enough, but he's still just a wage slave.'

Dunja went over to the whiteboard, which was filled with pictures of Sleizner taken from a distance. One of them featured a tall, bleached-blonde woman in leather trousers and large sunglasses in the background. 'Couldn't this be her?' She pulled the picture down and compared it to the woman on the screen. 'Yes, look, that's her, right?' She handed the picture to Fareed. 'So they're clearly still in touch. Where was that taken?'

'Gunnar Nu Hansen Square. It's right above the garage.'

'And another thing,' Qiang said. 'For some reason, it seems his phone always stays in the car when he's there, and I don't see what possible reason he could have to hang out in a garage for hours on end, practically every other night.'

'Isn't it simply a matter of our GPS tracker losing reception underground?' Dunja asked.

'Sure, it disappears from our screens when he heads down there and only reappears when he comes back up to go home. But whether he's going to Jenny Nielsen's or some other place, he would have to leave the garage on foot, and that should bring the tracker back online.'

'Unless he leaves the phone in the car so he won't be disturbed, like that time when the Swedish police were trying to get hold of him.'

'All right, listen to this,' Fareed said. 'Since 1992, that building is owned by investment company Greener Grass Investment Limited.'

'And who is that a front for?' Dunja said.

Fareed took his eyes off the screen and turned to them. 'None other than Jakob Sand.'

'Isn't he the bloke who was at that lunch?' Qiang said and Fareed nodded.

'Finally,' Dunja said. 'This is what I've been telling you all along. What can you tell us about the building itself?'

Fareed kept clicking. 'It's a corner property with its front entrance on Østerbrogade 120. It consists of twenty-six flats spread over five floors, and two commercial spaces on the ground floor, which are leased to Sesam Låse and McDonald's.'

'That's it?'

Fareed scrolled through various documents. 'Well, and it underwent a major renovation in 2005, when the same investment company also purchased the garage on the other side of Østerbrogade.'

'Are we talking about the garage Sleizner parks in?'

'Looks that way.'

'Boom. There it is,' Qiang said.

'There's also an auto repair shop down there. Kronow Auto.'

'And that renovation,' Dunja said. 'Do you have any plans that show what they did?'

Fareed nodded and walked over to the printer, which had just woken up and was printing pages that he taped into two sets of four. 'This is the old one, and this was submitted along with the planning application.'

Dunja put the two blueprints down next to each other and could immediately see that a number of changes had been made. Flats had been merged and subdivided. The attic had been converted, and windows and doors had been updated. In fact, so many things had been done it was impossible to judge if any of them were of interest.

But that task was made significantly easier when she put the two plans on top of each other and held them up to the light.

'Have you found something?' Fareed came over, followed by Qiang.

'I don't know. Maybe.' She put the plans down on the floor side by side again. 'Look at this.' She ran a finger along the basement floor on one of the plans. 'See that? And now compare it to the other one.'

Fareed and Qiang studied the two plans more closely.

'But I don't understand.' Qiang turned to her. 'The one with the basement is the old one.'

'Exactly.' Dunja nodded. 'That's what's so strange. I mean, look at this lift.' She pointed to a lift shaft. 'Before the renovation, it went all the way down. Now, it stops at ground level.'

'That must have cost a fortune.' Fareed shook his head. 'I don't get it, who does something like that?'

Dunja didn't get it either. She didn't even have a working theory for why anyone would decide to simply get rid of an entire basement floor.

29

HESK DIDN'T KNOW how to handle the silence that had descended after he shared his suspicions about Sleizner. The first minute of it had been okay. If it turned out he was right, it would be a scandal bigger than anything any of them had experienced in their years working for the police, which was why he'd figured Heinesen, Hemmer and Bernstorff were, as he himself had been and still kind of was, in shock.

But now the silence had dragged on for another minute and a half, and he was starting to suspect it was because none of them believed him. Why else would they be sitting there on the worn leather sofa, awkwardly avoiding his eyes?

Or was he supposed to break the silence and open the floor for questions, instead of gormlessly staring at Heinesen's collection of Star Wars paraphernalia? He was in charge of this investigation, after all.

Both Bernstorff and Hemmer were relatively green. Neither of them had worked closely with Sleizner and would at most have heard some rumours about him. Heinesen was different. In his case, it was about so much more than rumours and a well-known face. He was one of the people who had worked with Sleizner the longest, and maybe that was why he was just sitting there, his face closed and impassive.

'How sure are you?' his old colleague finally said, breaking the silence.

'As sure as I can be without being one hundred per cent sure.' That was exactly how he felt. Confused, but not really. 'For now, these are suspicions based on circumstantial evidence. But I would say those suspicions are strong enough that we have to consider Sleizner our main suspect.'

'Okay, look, I just have to ask,' Bernstorff said, turning to him. 'Are you seriously saying we should go after one of the top brass based on a few circumstantial factors that, if you ask me, seem fairly vague?'

'Vague?' Hesk snorted derisively and shook his head, which made him realize he was annoyed. 'How are they vague?' So, he was annoyed. She was the one who was attacking him. 'What the fuck do you mean?'

'I think all Julie's trying to say is that it's not enough for us to act,' Hemmer piped up.

'And I think Julie can speak for herself,' Hesk snapped, turning to Heinesen. 'What do you think, Morten? Do you feel what we have is too vague to make Sleizner our main suspect?'

'Erm, well...' Heinesen shifted uncomfortably and swallowed hard, even though he'd had nothing to eat or drink. 'I don't know? Look, it's...'

'What do you mean, you don't know? Morten, come on.' What was with everyone today? Didn't they realize this was serious? 'Admit it, you've never liked him either and, like me, you've sensed this. Haven't you?'

'Well, sure, Sleizner's always been Sleizner, but—'

'Morten, this obviously comes as a shock. But are we really all that surprised, if we're being completely honest?'

Heinesen didn't seem to know what to say.

'That's exactly the problem, though,' Bernstorff said. 'How can we be sure it's not just because you happen to dislike him?'

'That was actually my thought exactly,' Hemmer said.

'I haven't even been on the job a week, but I already feel completely indoctrinated by how pretty much everyone who has worked here a few years seems to hate the man.'

'No one said anything about hating him,' Hesk said, trying hard to dial down his annoyance. 'But you're right in that he's hardly the most well-liked manager in the building, and I'm not going to deny that he and I have had our disagreements over the years. But if you think this is some kind of personal vendetta on my part, you couldn't be more wrong. Believe me, I wish for nothing more than our perpetrator being anyone but Sleizner.' He leaned forward in his armchair and looked Bernstorff in the eye. 'To be completely honest, I can't imagine a worse situation than the one we're in, and if it weren't for the fact that you're new and don't know me or Sleizner, I would have taken your objections as a personal attack.' He picked up his cup but was shaking so hard the coffee sloshed over the sides, even though he was using two hands. 'Goddammit...'

'Don't worry about it.' Heinesen was instantly on his feet. 'I'll fetch some paper towels.'

'I'm sorry, I didn't sleep a wink last night,' Hesk said while Heinesen wiped the armchair and the floor underneath.

'Maybe you should rectify that before we make a decision on how to proceed,' Bernstorff put in.

'And what the hell is that supposed to mean?' He put his cup down a little too quickly and splashed coffee onto the table. This time, he saw no reason to hide his irritation. It was justified, and the fact that Heinesen was immediately there with his bloody paper towels didn't help either. 'Are you saying I'm too tired to think clearly? That I don't know what I'm talking about?'

'All I'm saying is that making our own boss a serious

suspect isn't a decision you make without serious deliberation. Especially considering the state you seem to be in.'

'But this isn't about what bloody state I'm in, or how rested I happen to be. This is about the evidence pointing to Sleizner. So much so that I would argue it has to be him. Am I right, Morten?' He turned to Heinesen, who was coming back from the kitchen. 'Back me up here?'

'I suggest we start by going over everything we know for sure,' Heinesen said.

'Okay.' Bernstorff nodded. 'That sounds like a good idea.'

'I thought I'd already covered the most important parts. But okay. I don't mind doing it again,' Hesk said, straightening up. 'From 16 April of this year until the days before Mogens Klinge's death, Klinge was in contact with Sleizner via an old Ericsson phone. Through their messaging, he found out, among other things, that his membership of something had been approved. My guess would be some kind of gentleman's club. Then he was given information about an initiation ceremony that was to take place on 28 July, which matches the time of his death. He was also told the event was to be black tie, and that he was going to be picked up from a specific location at half past seven that night. I've written it down here. Torben, would you mind finding out where this is?' He handed a note with the coordinates to Hemmer.

'And how can we be sure it was Sleizner and not someone else on the other end of the line?' Bernstorff asked.

'Because Torben's triangulation put the phone at my house as Sleizner was knocking on my door.'

'But is it really that precise?' Bernstorff turned to Hemmer.

'No, but I would say down to thirty, forty feet.' Hemmer shrugged.

'Thirty or forty feet? That means the phone could have been

in a different house altogether, or why not in a car parked on the street outside?'

Hesk turned to Hemmer, who nodded agreement while he typed the numbers on the note into his laptop. 'True, but that would be an incredible coincidence. But sure, it's possible.'

'Have you checked its position now?' Heinesen said.

'Yes, right before we started this meeting, but it was turned off,' Hemmer replied. 'I'll keep checking periodically, but I don't think we should count on it being turned back on.'

'We'll have to wait and see,' Hesk said. 'Let's keep going. Because there's more, and the reason I'm only telling you about it now is that I only realized it myself about an hour ago, and I'm likely still in some kind of shock.'

'Jan, what happened?' Heinesen gave him a worried look.

'There are things that point to Sleizner being the one who drugged me at the press conference.'

'Are you serious?'

'Why wouldn't I be serious? He was the one who served me the water, and he was the one who found me in that conference room. Just as I was waking up, too.'

'And you're still convinced you were drugged?' Bernstorff said. 'I mean, that it wasn't just a sudden drop in blood pressure or something like that?'

'I was out for over two hours, so no, I don't think so.' He shook his head. 'Julie, it's not that I don't understand that all of this may feel overwhelming. It's how I feel, too. But I've watched the recording of the press conference, and you can clearly see there was something in my glass, the one Sleizner brought me, before he filled it with water. What's more, we're dealing with two men who have followed us and looked over our shoulders since we fished the car out. They've made copies of my keys, they've entered and searched my home, stolen most of our technical evidence, and broken into Klinge's house to recover the phone. All of these things are known facts. And if that's not enough, Sleizner stopped by my house last night to try to suss out if we have any evidence left or if they got everything. He even gave me a key to the safe in his office in case we wanted a truly secure place to put things to make sure they don't go missing. Taken together, these things tell me they're desperate to get their hands on that phone.'

'And where is it now?' Heinesen asked.

'At my house. I figured it was the safest option since they've just searched it. But as soon as we're done here, I want you to take a closer look at it, Torben. I'm sure there are things I missed.'

Hemmer nodded without looking up from his screen.

'Speaking of which, have you found out where he was supposed to be picked up?'

'Yes, Østerport Station, just outside the main entrance.'

'Which tells us absolutely nothing,' Bernstorff said. 'And I'm sorry to have to say it, but I still don't see why Sleizner would have to drug you and hire goons to stalk us and steal our technical evidence. It would have been so much easier to just put himself in charge of the investigation so he could run it as he saw fit. Then he would have had complete control.'

'It would also have been completely obvious,' Hesk retorted. 'Even for a person like Sleizner. Don't you think, Morten?'

'Me?'

'Yes, you. After all, you're the one who knows Sleizner the best.'

'I'm probably inclined to agree,' Heinesen said with a nod.

'Thank you,' Hesk said, and turned back to Bernstorff.

'I mean, with Julie,' Heinesen clarified. 'I guess I think the scenario you've painted is a bit convoluted and, how to put it, conspiratorial.'

'You do, do you?' Hesk was unable to stop a sigh from escaping. And his head from shaking. 'Well then. It almost sounds like he should have promoted you instead of me.'

'Jan, stop. That's not at all what—'

'No, I mean it. The whole reason he gave me a fancier office was that he assumed I would let myself be led by the nose. I didn't realize it at the time, but I do now. And with regards to this particular investigation, he was convinced I would accept the most obvious and simple solution. Which is to say that Mogens Klinge strangled the woman and then took his own life. If I had, everything would have been fine, and the case soon forgotten. But once he realized I wasn't going to do that, he had no choice but to act quickly in an attempt to take back control.' He shrugged. 'In hindsight, it seems so obvious.'

'No, Jan. It doesn't.' Heinesen shook his head. 'I would say it's anything but obvious. Besides, that kind of behaviour would indicate that there's more at stake here. Much more than the two of them happening to be members of the same gentleman's club.'

'Like a murder or two, you mean?'

'Yes, for instance, and at the moment we have nothing to suggest Sleizner was behind either murder.'

'Speaking of which, the results of the DNA analysis of the tissue from under the woman's nails came in a few hours ago.'

'And there were no matches?' Bernstorff said.

'The computer in the lab is working on it. Let me log in and see if it's found anything.'

'Well, if it's Sleizner, there'll be no match,' Heinesen said with a chuckle.

'No, but I wouldn't be surprised if it matched a sample from this.' Hesk opened his briefcase and pulled out a transparent evidence bag containing an empty beer bottle. 'He drank this at my house last night, so there should be plenty of material.'

'I'm not sure we're going to need it.' Hemmer looked up from his laptop.

'What, you have a match?' Hesk didn't know what to think.

Sleizner couldn't possibly be part of the police's DNA database of known and suspected criminals. Or could he? It wouldn't surprise him if Sleizner had done things none of them knew about. But he couldn't have been convicted of a crime, or even suspected. They would have heard. The only explanation was if he was in there for some other reason.

'Can I see?' he said, taking the laptop, and lo and behold, the DNA analysis had generated a match in the database. Not with Sleizner, but with one of Denmark's most famous entrepreneurs: Jakob Sand.

Hesk didn't understand.

Didn't understand at all.

30

A FEW STRATEGICALLY placed trees, a high wooden fence hiding a cluster of bins, and some dense shrubberies together provided such effective camouflage it was virtually impossible to find the entrance to the underground parking garage, even though it was located in the middle of Gunnar Nu Hansen Square – a bustling city square in the middle of Østerbro, packed with cafés and pedestrians.

But then, no one gave the unremarkable, slightly rusty grey van driving down the grooved concrete ramp and disappearing into the garage a second glance either.

Behind the closed curtains that separated the cab from the rest of the vehicle, Dunja was monitoring a number of small screens, each of which was connected to a wireless camera. Four were mounted on the outside of the van, one in each direction, concealed behind anti-rust paint. Another four had been integrated into Fareed and Qiang's baseball caps, front and back, and the last four were still awaiting final placement.

'Take a left,' she said into her headset to the group call between the three newly purchased burner phones.

Fareed turned at the auto repair shop and continued at a crawl through the garage, between rows of parked cars.

She could see on the screens that the garage was built in the shape of a large circle with the auto repair shop Kronow Auto located directly opposite the entrance ramp and parking bays lining the circumference of the circle.

'*There's an open spot on the right up there.*' Qiang leaned forward in the passenger seat so she could see it on one of her screens. '*Should we grab it?*'

'No, keep going. I want to see the whole garage before we park.'

When they'd completed a full lap, she was forced to admit it looked like a regular parking garage with a mix of private and public bays. Not even the auto repair shop piqued her interest, with the men in blue overalls leaning in under open bonnets.

But why was there a loading dock in a parking garage? As far as she knew, there were no supermarkets on the ground level, nor any other business that would require heavy goods to be delivered on pallets.

'I want you to start with those bins on the loading dock,' she said as soon as Fareed had killed the engine.

'*You check them out, I'll set up the cameras,*' Qiang said, then they both left the van.

While Qiang dashed about, installing the last four cameras, Fareed climbed the steel steps to the loading dock and opened the first of the three bins.

'It's too dark. Turn on your torch, I want to see too.'

'*There's nothing to see. It's empty,*' Fareed replied, and he shone a light down the bin, which was indeed empty.

'Okay, next one.'

Fareed opened the next bin, which was also empty. '*Not very exciting, is it? Maybe they were just emptied.*'

'Could be, but check the last one anyway,' she said, for lack of a better idea. 'Just to be safe.'

Fareed opened the last bin and shone his torch down it, and this one contained something.

'Can you see what it is?' she said.

'*It looks like clothes, tattered and filthy.*'

'What kind of clothes?'

'*I don't know. All kinds. A pair of trousers, a skirt, a few tops, knickers and socks.*'

A pile of discarded clothes could mean practically anything. But knowing that this was where Sleizner parked his car almost every other night, the images they conjured in Dunja's mind were less than pleasant. At the same time, the find energized her. This was the first sign they'd had that they might not be in a regular parking garage.

'*Would you like me to check if there's something underneath?*'

'No, we're good,' she said, turning to the feed from the camera at the back of Fareed's baseball cap instead. 'Am I seeing things, or is there a door behind you?'

Fareed closed the bin, turned around, and walked over to the metal door.

'Is it locked?'

'*Yep,*' Fareed said as she watched his hand try the handle at the lower edge of the frame.

'Qiang, get the lock pick and help him out. We need to know what's on the other side.'

'*Got it,*' replied Qiang, who had just finished installing the final camera and aimed it at the loading dock. Moments later, he joined Fareed on the loading dock, holding one of the backpacks from the van, and once he'd fished out the pick gun, selected an appropriate needle and inserted it into the cylinder, it wasn't long before he could turn the lock and open the door.

'*All right, we're going in,*' Fareed said, then the four screens showing their camera feeds went dark.

But a motion sensor almost immediately roused a series of

fluorescent lights, running the length of what turned out to be a long underground tunnel.

It was hard to judge from the view on the screens exactly how long, but Dunja estimated somewhere close to 150 feet, which corresponded reasonably well with the distance from the garage to the property on the other side of the street. So this was how they accessed their secret basement.

About twenty feet down the tunnel, another metal door appeared on their left. But this one had no keyhole. Instead, a keypad was mounted on the wall next to it.

'*What do you say? Should I give it a go?*' Qiang asked. '*I brought everything I need.*'

'No, hold off on that and keep going.'

'*You sure? Because I've fine-tuned the software even more. Like, I've added an option to test the possible combination in a random order. Clever, no?*'

'*Super clever. But no, let's go,*' replied Fareed, who was already walking down the tunnel to the other end where there was another door with the same type of keypad as the first one.

'Can you open it, Qiang?'

'*I guess we'll find out.*' Qiang had already pulled out a screwdriver and was busy unscrewing the screws on the keypad. Then he took off the cover and attached a number of wires to the circuit card with clamps. Finally, he plugged the cables into his laptop and booted up a program that immediately set to testing various number combinations.

'How long is it going to take?' Dunja said, her eyes on the screen, where the numbers changed so fast they blended together, forming flickering eights.

'*It depends. Like I said, in case you weren't listening, the programme tests the combinations randomly to make sure we don't have to wait forever in case the code happens to be 9999.*'

'How long? That's all I want to know.'

'*God, you're worse than a pregnant elephant cow with—*'

'*Count on about an hour,*' Fareed broke in.

'An hour?'

'*Well, more likely forty-five, fifty minutes,*' Qiang said. '*If we're unlucky, it may be as long as ninety, assuming the programme can get through 111 combinations a minute. How long did you think it was going to be?*'

'A few minutes. At most.'

She heard Fareed and Qiang chuckle.

'*She's seen too many films,*' Fareed said.

'*Just be happy it's not a six-digit code. If it had been, it could have taken as long as—*' Qiang broke off suddenly.

'Hello?' Dunja said. 'What's happening?'

'*Thanks to my new function, it looks like you were right.*'

'What, it's done already?'

'*7895, if the tech is to be believed.*' Qiang put the cover back on the keypad, packed up his equipment and punched in the four-digit code. The door clicked open. '*Voila.*'

A heavy drapery later, they found themselves in a room with wall-to-wall carpet, dim lighting, a purple plush sofa in the middle, and dark patterned wallpaper.

'How many doors, not counting the one you came in through?' Dunja asked.

'*Two, looks like,*' Fareed replied, and one of the screens showed him opening one of them and stepping into a room where the faint light from red bulbs was bright enough to clearly reveal what kind of room it was.

In the middle of it stood a table hewn from stone, surrounded by four pedestals topped with twelve-armed candelabra. Further in, chains with hand and ankle cuffs dangled from the wall, along with thick ropes and a collection of whips, embellished with everything from tiny iron balls to barbs.

Fareed and Qiang's silence spoke volumes. It was finally sinking in that her misgivings about Sleizner were based on more than a grudge.

Qiang's screens showed him walking up to a wooden cabinet filled with everything from blindfolds, leather hoods and gag balls to pliers, electrical cords and dentist's drills. In one drawer he found knives and scalpels. In another, pipettes and small brown glass bottles full of hydrochloric and sulphuric acid.

Another screen showed a white SUV with tinted windows rolling into the garage.

'Hey,' she said, watching the car turn left, just like they had. 'I think you should get out of there now.'

'*What?*' Fareed said. '*Why?*'

'Just get out. Like, right now.'

'*But why? What's happening?*' Qiang asked as the two of them hurried out into the dark hallway, past the plush sofa, and into the underground tunnel.

'You must have triggered an alarm or something. Either way, they're coming, so please hurry.'

There wasn't really anything suspicious about a car in a parking garage, not even one with tinted windows. But this one was driving so fast around the garage she could hear the tyres screeching against the concrete.

Fareed and Qiang stepped back out onto the loading dock just as the car passed the van's rear-facing camera.

'They're almost there,' she said, and watched them set off at a run towards the van. 'No, you won't make it back here.'

'*Then where are we supposed to bloody go?*' Qiang hissed. '*We can't just—*'

'Hide somewhere,' she broke in. 'Anywhere, just do it right now.'

They threw themselves down behind some parked cars just as the white SUV skidded to a stop in front of the loading dock. Both front doors opened as though they were synchronized, and two men wearing suits and earpieces hurried up the steel steps towards the loading dock.

Dunja zoomed in, adjusted the contrast, and took a few screenshots of the men's faces before one of them disappeared through the metal door, while the other stayed behind as a lookout.

'*Are they gone?*' said Qiang, who from what she could make out must have squeezed in under a car. '*I can't—*'

'Qiang, if there was ever a time for you to be quiet, this would be it,' she broke in. 'One of them is standing lookout, just a few feet away from where you are.'

The man turned around and cocked his head, then stuck his hand into his jacket and pulled out a gun.

'And he's armed and moving towards the bins.'

On the screen, she could see the man open and look down into the three bins, one after the other. Then he turned back towards the steel steps and began to walk down them while scanning the garage.

'He's really close now,' she said. 'He's right next to the loading dock.'

Suddenly, the man turned and stared straight at her, so intently she had to remind herself she was the one who could see him, not the other way around. But once he started to walk towards the van, she began to doubt whether she was right about that.

Had he spotted something, or had he reacted to her voice? How much of the sound actually leaked out through the metal?

The man reached the van and looked around as though searching for something, then leaned in towards the camera until his face and staring eyes filled so much of the screen she instinctively pulled back.

Then he backed up a few steps and instead turned his attention to the cab. Via one of the cameras Qiang had installed on the wall across the aisle, she watched him walk up and peer in through one of the windows. She tried to recall what Fareed and Qiang had left in the cab, which would now be in full view, and what kind of ideas seeing those things might give the man, who suddenly yanked at the passenger door handle, rocking the entire van.

At least they'd remembered to lock the doors. The man went around to the driver's side, and this time he pulled so hard on the door handle her half-filled coffee cup slid off the small worktable and fell.

Instinctively, she pushed back her chair, bent down and caught the cup just before it hit the floor. If she'd had time to think about it for even a second, she would have let it break. After all, that would have been a somewhat natural sound when you rocked a van, unlike the scraping sound her chair had made against the floor, reminiscent of some angry cousin of Chewbacca's.

The sound made the man let go of the door and move back along the van, and that was when it hit her.

The back doors.

Even though they'd smothered it with both grease and lubricant, the lock on the back doors stubbornly refused to cooperate with the central lock, which was why she now rushed over as quickly and silently as she could and pushed the red button manually.

The man outside tugged on the door. Not just once, but

again and again, as though he had decided it was time for a victory. She braced as hard as she could, but if he kept at it like this, the doors would eventually give up. So instead, she prepared to surprise him by suddenly throwing the doors open as hard as she could and jumping him.

But it never came to that, because someone started to honk and shout further down the garage. The sound made the man let go of the door handle and head back towards the car that was unable to get past their SUV, which they'd left parked at an angle.

'Okay, listen to me,' she said quietly into the headset. 'He's on his way back to his car, which is in your direction. On my signal, you're going to get out of there. Don't come this way, you'll run straight into him. Go the other way and come all the way around.' She waited until the man opened the door and climbed in behind the wheel. 'Okay, now.'

Fareed and Qiang crawled out of their hiding places and scurried away, crouching low behind the parked cars. The further away they got, the more they straightened up, which meant they could move faster.

If it hadn't been for the red Citroën, which, like an oversensitive pinball game, woke up and began to honk and flash when Qiang squeezed between its bonnet and the wall.

The man was instantly back out of the car. 'Hey! You!' he shouted, starting to run towards Qiang.

'*He's seen me. What do I do?*' Qiang said, not stopping. '*Fucking say something. What do I bloody do?*'

'The auto repair shop,' she said, not knowing whether it was a good or a bad idea. 'Maybe there's somewhere to hide in there. If not, at least there should be witnesses to stop him from doing anything.'

'*Okay.*' Qiang turned around and started running back in the direction he'd come, towards the auto repair shop, where he rushed inside and dashed between cars with no wheels, looking around for somewhere to go so frantically it was hard to make anything out on the screens until he entered a room with a reception counter at the far back and a row of visitors' chairs and a cooler along one wall. That was all she had time to see before a voice made Qiang turn around.

'*What can I do for you?*' The older mechanic, with grey, unruly hair and blue overalls, came in from the shop and continued past Qiang to the other side of the counter.

'*I have a car that needs servicing.*'

'*It's usually something along those lines.*' The mechanic's chuckle turned into a coughing fit as he started to flip through a calendar. '*What kind of car is it?*'

'*A... a Volkswagen.*'

'*Volkswagen have a lot of models.*'

'Okay, don't panic, but just so you know, he's heading into the waiting room,' Dunja said, her eyes on the feed from Qiang's rear-facing camera, which showed the man in the suit entering. 'Just keep talking like nothing's wrong, and whatever you do, don't turn around.'

'*It's a Golf,*' Qiang said. '*The model, I mean. A 2005 Golf. And sometimes the engine just dies, for no apparent reason.*'

'*Dies.*' The mechanic nodded. '*Yes, these things happen. Sometimes when you least expect it.*' With a wry smile, he bent down and disappeared behind the counter.

Dunja didn't understand what he was doing, until she saw on the other screen that the man had stopped a few feet behind Qiang and was reaching for his gun.

'Get down,' she said. 'He has a gun!'

Qiang threw himself on the floor just as the shot rang out,

and without knowing if he'd been hit or not, Dunja continued to give him instructions.

'Now kick his legs out from under him. Don't wait for him to get his bearings and take aim again. Just spin around and kick out as hard as you can.'

The only thing she could see was a patch of dirty linoleum, a few of the chairs along the wall, and the legs of a Michelin Man. No sign of the gunman. But she could hear him as he let out a grunt, fell to the floor and dropped the gun, which skittered into the frame.

Qiang's hand grabbed the gun, then he stood up and turned towards the exit.

'Not that way. Won't work,' she said as the second man hurried past the camera by the entrance to the garage and continued into the auto repair shop with his gun drawn. 'There are two of them. You wouldn't stand a chance. Take the door behind you instead. On the other side of the counter.'

Qiang turned around and hurried back. '*You stay down,*' he said, aiming the gun at the man on the floor as he rounded the counter, and then the feed became fragmented again as he looked back and forth between the man and the mechanic, who was still squatting behind the counter.

'*You, too. Just stay down,*' he told the mechanic, while he continued towards the door to the office. After a few quick movements on the screen, the front-facing camera showed the man in the suit getting up off the floor. '*I said stay down,*' Qiang yelled as he backed into the office.

But then he stopped abruptly, as though his feet were stuck, and when he looked down, she could see the mechanic was hanging on to one of his legs. Qiang's reaction was instantaneous, and even though the feed skipped, Dunja could tell he had struck the mechanic on the head with the butt of the gun.

Then the door was closed and locked, and Qiang turned around to survey what looked like a messy office with two overflowing desks and a number of wall-mounted shelves that sagged under the weight of countless binders.

Judging from his shallow breathing and the images on the two screens, which showed movements so quick and jerky the only thing she could make out were blurred patches of colour in shades of brown and beige, Qiang was panicking.

'*And now what? What the fuck do I do now?*' he yelled. '*You're the one who told me to come in here, so you'd better fucking tell me what to do now!*'

'Try to slow down your movements, so I can see where you are.'

'*You want me to calm down? That's easy for you to say, sitting there and—*'

'Qiang,' she cut in. 'Your greatest enemy right now is panic. I promise you, it's far more dangerous than the blokes outside. They know you have a gun and won't hesitate to use it.'

'*But I will. I've never shot anyone, and—*' There was a banging on the door, and then someone started tugging at it. '*See, they'll be in here any second. What the fuck do I do then? Huh? I can't just—*'

'Qiang, for fuck's sake! Listen to me. That guy was about to shoot you in the back. But you threw yourself onto the floor, kicked his legs out from under him, and took his gun. That'll earn you some respect. So pull yourself the fuck together.'

'*Okay,*' he replied, and she could tell he was nodding and forcing himself to take deep breaths as the violence against the door a few feet away from him increased in ferocity.

His movements slowed enough to allow her some idea of what the space he was in looked like. She could see a filing cabinet in one corner and a picture of Queen Margrethe surrounded by posters of pumped-up boobs and tanned crotches.

'Could you go over and have a closer look at that?' she said, noting that something was making one of the posters bulge out from the wall.

'*What?*'

'There's something behind that girl spreading her legs.'

'*Which one?*'

'The one on the trampoline.'

As Qiang began to move towards the poster, a shot suddenly rang out. '*Fuck*,' he exclaimed, his eyes on the door whose broken lock was about to give up.

'Fire the gun,' she said. 'Fire back at the door.'

Qiang fired two shots in quick succession, and the break-in attempts ceased.

'Good. Now we have the upper hand.' There was no time to worry about whether anyone had been hit on the other side. 'I want you to walk all the way up to the wall and have a look at what's under that poster.'

'*But I need to guard the door so they can't get in. If they do, I'm done for.*'

'Qiang, just do what I tell you.' She couldn't explain why, other than that there should be a connection to the first door they'd encountered in the underground tunnel.

The screen showed Qiang back away from the door, gun in hand, and move towards the poster-covered wall. When he reached it, he tore down the picture with the woman on the trampoline without taking his eyes off the door for a moment, and via his rear-facing camera, Dunja could see that with some luck, it might be exactly what they needed, but would never have dared to hope for.

'Turn around,' she said, but there was no reaction. 'Qiang! Wake up!'

Qiang finally turned towards the keypad on the wall. '*What the fuck is this?*' he said.

'Who cares, just punch in the code.'

'*But? There's no—*'

'Just do it, what are you waiting for? 7895.'

Qiang punched in the code with a trembling finger, and something clicked.

'Did you hear that?' she said, but there was no reply.

Qiang was already studying the back of the filing cabinet.

'Qiang, answer me? Did you hear that clicking sound?'

Without responding, Qiang put both hands on the filing cabinet and pushed it straight into the wall. He didn't even seem to have to try very hard, it was that easy, and in moments, the entire cabinet had disappeared, leaving a dark opening in its place.

She was about to tell him to go through it, but he was already in the dark and judging from the sound, the filing cabinet was sliding back into place. Both his screens were black now, but through the headset, she could hear him fumbling through the darkness.

It was impossible to say if it was a narrow corridor or a large room, but when light began to flow in through a growing crack, she knew he must have found a door. It was like a different world. No hint of the shabbiness of the auto repair shop in here. Gone was the harsh fluorescent light, chaos, and binders. Here, the walls were an austere shade of grey that went nicely with the blue carpet.

Qiang opened the door fully and stepped into a cramped room that housed as much advanced tech as their own HQ. A number of screens were mounted above what looked like a large control panel. One of them showed feeds from various CCTV cameras placed around the parking garage, at the loading dock, inside the underground tunnel, and the various parts of the auto repair shop.

She pondered what it might mean, but hadn't reached any conclusions when she saw another screen in the feed from Qiang's rear-facing camera. A screen that displayed the manipulated picture of her from the APB.

So this was Sleizner's command centre, from which he hunted them. The question was how much he had on them. Whether they had found him, or he had found them.

'Turn around and look at the computer behind you,' she said, but there was no reaction. 'The one with the picture of me.' Still no reaction. 'Hello? Qiang, can you hear me? Qiang?'

She took out her phone, realized the call had cut out and tried to call him back. While she waited, she watched Qiang turn towards another computer screen, which showed a number of CCTV screen grabs of various degress of sharpness. What they all had in common was that she was the focus. There were images from the central station, but also from all kinds of public places in Copenhagen, as well as Byens Bodega, and from when she...

Without warning, the screen disappeared from view, replaced by a table leg and the blue carpet it stood on. As though Qiang's baseball cap had fallen to the floor. Or maybe Qiang himself. Then both his screens went black.

31

HESK TURNED INTO the parking garage and almost imme—
diately found a free space. He decided to reverse in, but
inexplicably ended up at an angle relative to the concrete
pillars and was forced to go back and forth several times like
a nervous learner driver before he could finally kill the engine,
unbuckle, and climb out.

He, who was usually something of an expert at fitting
a car into a tight space and always had to take over from
Lone whenever precision parking was required. But he was
decidedly off-kilter today and even felt a bit shaky as he walked
through the garage, taking note of the cars he passed and their
registration numbers.

The simple explanation was that he was tired after going
almost twenty-four hours without sleep. And there was no
denying he was tired. Incredibly bloody tired. But that wasn't
the whole explanation.

The primary reason was that he felt lost. He'd gone from
having a set course, unclear as it may have been, to no longer
being able to tell left from right. It was as though anything
could happen, without warning, and he was standing in the
middle of it all, fighting to fit the pieces together while the
puzzle refused to take shape.

That was why he'd decided to head into Østerbro instead
of going home after the meeting at Heinesen's, to check

out the garage to which Hemmer had tracked Jakob Sand's mobile. He didn't know what he was looking for, or even if he should be looking. But he didn't mind. He'd come mostly for lack of anything better to do, and because if there was one thing he was too tired to face, it was going home to another awful fight with Lone. He infinitely preferred a speculative trip to this garage to try to regain some of his lost confidence.

He'd long since come to terms with the fact that he was far from the sharpest detective in the country, but he couldn't recall ever feeling so certain of something that had subsequently turned out to be completely wide of the mark. In hindsight, it was definitely one of the most embarrassing things he'd experienced as an officer of the law, including his collapse at the press conference.

Even Heinesen had questioned him. Heinesen, of all people. Who never questioned anyone or anything. That they'd turned out to be right hadn't exactly improved matters. From now on, they were going to disregard him.

He could hardly blame them. But that didn't mean he was going to take his defeat lying down, without even trying to do something about it. Maybe he was down for the count. But until the referee had counted to ten, he still had a chance to get up off the mat.

Setting aside his own predicament, the investigation had in fact taken a big step forward. As he'd told the team in an effort to smooth over the whole incident, they should be happy and relieved Sleizner wasn't behind the woman's murder. It would make their work significantly easier going forward. And they could feel good about having identified Jakob Sand so they could start preparing to make an arrest.

That said, Bernstorff had, like the truth-speaker she was,

been completely right when she'd insinuated that his suspicion of Sleizner had been based on more than just the facts. He hadn't wanted to admit it at the time, and didn't exactly relish doing it now either, but the simple truth was that he was disappointed. Terrible as it may sound, in his heart of hearts, he'd hoped it would be Sleizner.

It really would have seemed like just deserts if the approach his boss had honed to perfection – bending every rule to breaking point – had finally led to his own demise.

As far as the homicide unit and their work went, there was no doubt Sleizner was the root of the problem. With impressive determination, he'd made sure to spread his venom to every part of the organization. Hesk had ended up in the cross hairs himself on more than one occasion, and he'd seen others subjected to treatment that was so unacceptable he couldn't understand now why no one, himself included, had reacted and filed a complaint.

But that was then. Now, he had put his foot down, drawn a line with Sleizner in a way he would never have dared to before. It was as though recent events had helped him break through some kind of inhibition, and if it ever came to it, he would have no qualms about knocking on the door to his boss's swanky office, walking up to his desk, and calmly and politely informing him of the charges against him before cuffing him and taking him to a cell.

But Sleizner hadn't killed the woman, and he might not have been the one texting Mogens Klinge either. Maybe Bernstorff was right. Maybe it was just an unfortunate coincidence.

Instead, the perpetrator was very likely Jakob Sand. The successful entrepreneur all of Denmark loved to hate. It was a scandal and would make headlines. But then, that man made headlines just by getting out of bed in the morning. If it wasn't another tax evasion scandal, it was a new mistress, or yet another divorce.

But he bounced back every time, picked himself up, dusted himself off, and carried on like nothing had happened. Even that time six years ago, when he'd been suspected of murdering a prostitute by the name of Jana Helsing. That time, a DNA analysis had saved him. Now, a DNA analysis was going to get him sent down.

And there it was. His car. Or at least one of his cars. A cherry-red Mercedes-Benz with scissor doors and the option to take the top off. So Hemmer's triangulation had been accurate. But there was no sign of Sand himself, of course.

He bent down to look through the car's side window and cupped his hands around his face to see better. The interior was black and red and there was a box of Läckerol and a green bag of Fisherman's Friend on the passenger seat. Whatever that may signify, other than that the man cared about how his breath smelled. Hesk straightened up and decided the best thing he could do was to go home and get a few hours' sleep. He wouldn't find any answers down here; even if there were any to find, he was too tired to see them.

Just then, as he was about to squeeze past the concrete pillar, his phone buzzed in his jacket pocket. He took it out and saw it was a Swedish number he didn't recognize.

'Yes, hello? This is Jan Hesk.'

'*Hello, my name is Malin Rehnberg, from the Stockholm Police. I'm so sorry to be calling this late on a Sunday.*'

'What is this regarding?'

'*Okay, cutting straight to the chase.*' She chuckled. '*But that's great. Suits me just fine. I'm calling regarding the woman in the car you're trying to identify. The one with the cross-shaped scar on the inside of her thigh.*'

'Do you know who she is?'

'*I'm afraid not. But the thing is that we've had a murder here in Stockholm, too.*'

'Yes, sadly even Astrid Lindgren World isn't immune to these things.'

'*Right, and how would little-brother-Denmark like big-brother-Sweden to react? Would you like us to stick our tongues out at each other, or should we try to help each other out instead?*'

'I'm sorry. I'm just tired. I didn't mean to...' He trailed off, unable to remember what he'd planned to say. 'Never mind. Is this also a double murder of a man and a woman?'

'*No, this is just a woman.*'

'Was she a prostitute?'

'*Not as far as we know. In fact, from what I've seen of your investigation, there are no similarities in terms of victim or method.*'

'Okay, but then I have to ask, why...'

'*I'm calling?*'

'Exactly.'

'*Finally, we're on the same page. You see, the thing is that the only clue we have to the identity of our perpetrator is a similar scar to the one your woman had.*'

The perpetrator? Had he heard that right? Or had he misunderstood her Swedish?

The sound of a heavy door slamming shut somewhere in the garage drew his attention.

'*Hello? Are you still there?*'

It was followed by the sound of quick footsteps, as though someone were half-running across the concrete floor. He leaned out from behind the pillar and saw a man in a suit hurry up to a white SUV parked in front of a loading dock.

'I'm going to have to call you back,' he said, and ended the call.

He could have stayed hidden behind the pillar. Pretended not to see the man opening the boot and taking out a roll of black bin bags, duct tape, and a dark duffle bag the size of a hockey trunk. It would undoubtedly have been the easier option. What you couldn't bear to see, you simply hadn't seen. Thirty seconds, that was all it would take for the man to disappear so he could return to his car in blissful ignorance.

It was a feasible option. Just not for him. Not now. Not after everything he'd been through. The man who was climbing the steel steps to the loading dock was the same man who had been fishing off the pier, had changed the fluorescent lights at Forensics, and carried him off the stage at the press conference. There was no mistaking the missing ring finger on his right hand.

So there was a connection between the two men and Jakob Sand, and apparently that was what he'd come here to get to the bottom of, so he left his hiding place and started to walk towards the loading dock, where the man was now unlocking a door.

While he walked, he unbuttoned his jacket and chest holster to take out his gun, but on second thoughts pulled out his police ID instead, so as not to provoke unnecessary violence.

What happened next would take him about a minute to comprehend. When he lost his balance and fell face first onto the concrete floor, it was already too late. Someone had jumped him from behind, that much was clear. But the man who had parked the car ought to be in front of him. Not behind. On the other hand, there were two of them.

He tried to turn around, but his attacker was already on top of him, pushing his arms against the floor.

'This is when you stay calm and absolutely quiet,' a voice hissed in his ear.

A voice he couldn't place until the pressure on his arms eased, and he was able to roll over and see that it was Dunja Hougaard.

'What the hell are you doing here?' he said as he got back on his feet and drew his gun. 'You're wanted by the police.'

'And you're apparently deaf.'

Hesk didn't have time to react when Dunja took a step forward, wrested the gun from him, and followed up with a powerful elbow to his chin.

32

'WHY DID YOU come here?'

Jan Hesk had heard several versions of that same question. *Why are you here? What brought you here? How much do you know?* But they'd all sounded so muffled and distant he hadn't realized that they were addressed to him. He'd only figured that out after he'd regained enough consciousness to open his eyes and found Dunja leaning over him in what looked like the back of a van.

'Jan,' she continued. 'I need to know what brought you to this particular garage.'

'You're the one with an APB on you. Not me.' He sat up and looked around the cramped space, marvelling at the tangle of cables, jumble of devices with antennae, and rows of tiny screens. Apparently, the rumours he'd refused to take seriously were true.

'But I'm the one holding a gun. Not you.' Dunja held out his weapon.

'Since your first day on the unit, you've impressed me. I was even a bit jealous sometimes that you, unlike me, have what it takes to do exactly what I've always dreamed of doing. But I never liked you.'

'Swell. I was starting to feel embarrassed there for a second. But at least our feelings are mutual, then.'

'I remember when Sleizner let you cut in front of me and

take my place just because he thought you were young and hot. He had no idea how good you really were, and I wonder if even you did. You were too busy lapping up his praise and stepping on my toes, so long as it helped you to get ahead.' He stood up. 'But I find it hard to believe you'd use that against an old colleague, even if you're considered a threat to Denmark's national security at the moment.' He walked over to her, took the gun out of her hand, and put it back into his chest holster. 'So now you tell me, what are you doing? What reason did you have, other than personal dislike, for attacking me and knocking me unconscious?'

'I care about you.' Dunja handed him the magazine to his gun. 'It was the least I could do, considering what you did for me at that Christmas party in Sleizner's office. If you hadn't shown up, he would have raped me, and if it weren't for me just now, the man you were going up to would have offed you. Consider it a thank you.'

'That man happens to be one of the suspects in my investigation.' Hesk took out his gun again and inserted the magazine before sliding it back into the holster. 'Your so-called thank you stopped me from arresting him.'

Dunja shook his head. 'You have no idea what this is about, do you?'

'Well, I know that—'

'Jan, it's written all over your face,' Dunja broke in. 'How hard you're trying to convince everyone, including yourself, that you're in control, when in reality you have no idea what or who you're dealing with.'

'I'm in charge of the investigation into the double murder of Mogens Klinge and one other person. And yes, I'll be the first to admit that things are more complicated than they first appeared. More than once, I've wondered whether it's really worth it. But I'm not someone who just throws in the towel, and this is where the investigation has brought me. Which is why I can't accept that you—'

'Jan, believe me,' Dunja interrupted. 'You wouldn't have stood a chance. They've already taken a friend of mine.'

'A friend of yours? How many of you are there? And all of this?' He indicated the devices and screens. 'I'll ask you again. What are you up to?'

Dunja looked at him with eyes that seemed to be trying to delve through skin and bone, all the way into his thoughts. But just as she was about to reply, the door behind him opened.

He whipped around and pulled his gun on the dark-skinned man in the baseball cap who was climbing into the van backside first. 'And who are you?'

'Just a man of foreign extraction,' Fareed said, shutting the door.

'He's with me.' Dunja stepped up next to Hesk and pushed his arm down. 'How did it go?'

Fareed took off his baseball cap and shook his head.

Dunja nodded with a sigh and turned back to Hesk. 'I'm sorry, where were we?'

'You were about to tell me what you're up to.'

'I'm going after Sleizner.'

'And he's apparently going after you, too.'

'The difference is that he's up to no good. Don't ask me what, but from the little we've seen here today, it's unsavoury.'

'Unfortunately, I can assure you he's innocent.'

'Of what?'

'The murder of the woman and possibly also Mogens Klinge.'

'Hold on a minute.' Dunja turned to Fareed, who had sat

down with a laptop on his knees. 'Did you hear that? They suspected Sleizner of being behind the double murder.'

'Suspect is the wrong word.' Hesk shook his head. 'Until a few hours ago, I was convinced he did it.'

Dunja studied him in silence.

'I know exactly what you're thinking,' he went on. 'That I'm Sleizner's good little minion, and maybe I was. But not any more. Some things have happened since you disappeared.'

'What made you think he did it?'

'Several things, but primarily an anonymous mobile phone number Klinge was communicating with on a secret phone from April of this year until the day before he died. We managed to ping its position, and it turned out to be at my house just when Sleizner had stopped by for an unannounced visit.'

'So he has another phone?'

'That was my assumption, and probably still is.'

Dunja turned to Fareed. 'Why haven't we thought of that?'

'Good question.' Fareed shrugged. 'That would explain a lot.'

'Okay, but now you're saying it wasn't him.'

Hesk nodded. 'The DNA of the tissue found under the woman's nails didn't match Sleizner's, it was...'

'Jakob Sand's,' Dunja cut in.

'How did you know?'

'I didn't. It was just an educated guess. The two of them, and a third man we haven't been able to identify, had lunch together at Zeleste just a few days ago and at that lunch they not only made the decision to put me on the wanted list, they also discussed you and how well suited you are to lead the investigation.'

He wanted to ask where she had all her information from. If they'd listened in, and if so, how they'd managed to do that during an informal lunch at an intimate place like Zeleste. He wanted to know exactly what Sleizner had said about him. What tone he'd used. If he'd laughed or sounded serious. He wanted to know everything. But before he could begin to question Dunja, the man called Fareed turned to them.

'Dunja, check this out.' He pointed to one of the screens, which displayed various shades of white. 'See that? The camera's live again.'

'Which one?'

'The front-facing one in his baseball cap.'

Hesk went over too, and stared at the white screen, uncomprehending.

'Could it be that he's closer to us now, so the reception's better?' Dunja asked.

'No, because then the rear-facing camera would be online too.' Fareed pointed to the next screen over, which was black.

'So how do you explain that it's suddenly back on?'

'I don't, I have no idea.' Fareed leaned forward for a closer look. 'The question is if it's even on him. It almost doesn't look like it.'

'How can you tell? It's just a bunch of white.'

'It's not moving at all. See?' He pointed to the various shades. 'No movement.'

'But that means he's... that he's...' Dunja trailed off.

'See the slightly darker lines, here and here?' Fareed pointed to the screen and Dunja nodded. 'That could be a floor, right? A tiled floor.'

'So you're saying he's lying down.'

'I'm afraid it looks that way.'

None of them knew how long they sat there with their eyes glued to the screen. They were hypnotized by the shades of white and gave a start when Dunja broke the silence.

'Isn't something happening right now?' She pointed to the screen. 'Or am I the only one who thinks things are moving?'

'No, you're right.' Fareed's face brightened.

And it was true, the various fields of light were moving relative to each other and before long, the lines of the grid, which they had figured to be a floor, multiplied as each square shrank.

'Yes, look, he's getting up.'

'But why is the feed so fuzzy?' Hesk nodded towards the screen, where the camera seemed unable to focus, though they could still make out that they were looking at a white-tiled room.

Fareed tried to zoom in. 'It almost seems like the lens is fogged up.'

'Doesn't it look like a bathroom?' Dunja said.

Fareed nodded. 'See if you can call him and ask him to wipe the lens.'

Dunja pulled up the number on her phone and dialled while the image on the screen began to move jerkily back and forth. At regular intervals, they saw the overhead lights, which were so powerful the screen went white. On one occasion, something that might have been a sink swung by. Then a gleaming metal floor drain.

'No, it doesn't even connect.'

'No reception, probably. But...' Fareed leaned closer to the screen.

'But what?'

'I'm not sure, but it doesn't look like he's wearing the baseball cap on his head. The camera's too low down and seems to be swinging back and forth.'

'Maybe he's holding it in his hand?' Hesk said just as Dunja's phone lit up.

'Hold on, it's him.' She accepted the call and put it on speaker. 'Yes, hello? This is Dunja. How are you feeling?' She waited for a response, but the only sound was faint static. 'Qiang, can you hear me? Hello? Qiang? I can't hear you. Hold two fingers up to the camera if you can hear me.'

Fareed connected a cord to Dunja's phone, which made the static come out of two speakers instead. Then he adjusted various frequencies on an equalizer to try to bring out anything but the white noise.

While he worked, the blurred contour of a dark figure grew bigger as the camera moved closer. The shadow turned out to be a person kneeling on the floor with his hands behind his back and his head bowed. But it was only when a finger entered the frame and wiped the fog off the lens that they could see it was Qiang.

'Oh my God.' Dunja turned away from the screen.

'Is that your friend?' Hesk turned to Fareed, who nodded.

Another person entered the frame and went to stand right behind Qiang. All they could see of him were his boots and thick camouflage trousers.

'What the fuck's happening?' Dunja turned to Fareed. 'What are they doing?'

'No idea.'

'We have to do something. We can't just sit here and do nothing.'

The man's right hand appeared and grabbed a fistful of Qiang's hair, forcing him to look straight into the camera with eyes that shone with terror.

'But that's him.' Hesk pointed to the hand, which was missing a ring finger. 'That's the man I just saw out there.'

'Hello, what do you want?' Dunja shouted into her phone.

'This is Dunja Hougaard speaking. Tell me what the fuck it is you want!'

'*You have to listen to me,*' Qiang's frightened voice said between sobs. '*Okay? You have to listen carefully.*'

'We're listening,' Dunja said. 'Just tell us what to do and we'll do it. I promise everything will—'

'*Listen, okay, because these pricks mean business. You have to...*' Qiang broke down, sobbing.

'Qiang, we—'

'There's no point,' Fareed broke in. 'He can't hear you.'

'*You have to stop, okay?*' Qiang went on. '*All of it. The phone tapping, the pictures and videos. You have to delete the lot, okay? Otherwise they'll take us out, one by one. That's what they're saying. One by one.*'

'Of course we will. Qiang, we'll do anything they ask, so long as they let you go. Tell them that. Anything...'

That was as far as she got before the camo-clad man's left hand entered the frame so quickly they didn't realize he was holding a knife until he'd already stabbed it into Qiang's throat, where he left it, just above his Adam's apple, while blood pulsed out of the open wound and down onto his clothes and the white tiles.

Qiang tried to say something else but couldn't. The only things that came out of his mouth were blood and bubbles, and eventually he collapsed, twitching, and then the transmission was cut.

33

FABIAN APPLIED THE two-component adhesive along the thin wooden edges in the light from the work lamp in his basement office. Then he blew on the glue, pushed the piece into place and applied pressure as evenly as he could.

It was the last piece; the old Ouija board looked as good as new. Granted, the cracks from his fit of rage would always be visible at close inspection. But that was the extent of the consequences, unlike with some of his other mistakes.

He'd spent the past few hours going for a long walk. First down to Pålsjö Forest and the bridge over the tracks. Then he'd gone down to Pålsjö Beach with its gravelly sand, taken off his shoes, and continued north along the water's edge.

After about an hour, the sharp stones and the broken seashells had made his feet sore, and near Hittarp he'd cut one of them on a piece of glass. But he'd just kept going and an hour later, the pain in his feet had subsided.

Near Grå läge, he'd taken off his clothes and walked out into the water. The idea of just swimming straight out, into eternity, had occurred to him. But something had held him back, and once he was back on dry land, he'd sat down in the sand and let the sun dry him.

And sitting there, gazing out at the sea and the Danish lowlands that shimmered just above the horizon, he'd made the most difficult decision of his life, to cease his attempts at finding out what had really happened to his son.

It had felt like betraying Theodor yet again, and in a way he was running from a debt he owed. But right there and then, he'd decided to drop it. To accept that he would never know and that all the clues and signs pointing to something being fishy would be buried along with Theodor.

Sonja, Komorovksi and everyone else were right. It didn't matter how close to the truth he got, he could never turn back time. What had happened had happened, and some things were best left undisturbed.

For the second time that summer, he opened the middle drawer of his desk, took out an object wrapped in cloth, placed it in front of him next to the Ouija board, unwrapped it, and looked at the gun his son had brought home after that fateful night he'd spent in Helsingør with the Smiley Gang.

He'd tried to make Theodor tell him where he'd got it but had never managed to drag anything other than obviously made-up replies out of him. It was a Heckler & Koch USP Compact 9 mm, a model intended for close combat, common among the Danish police. He knew that much, but since the serial number had been scratched off, there was no way to do a search for it.

The plan had been to hand it over to the Danes and let them look into and analyse it. But sitting on the sun-warmed sand outside Grå läge, he'd changed his mind. No one was ever going to examine it. He was going to get rid of it. Make sure it disappeared forever, along with all the other unanswered questions.

He wrapped the gun back up, put it aside, and checked his repairs, then he took out the finest sandpaper he could find and began to carefully smooth down the glued edges. From now on, he was going to think about the future and be there for Sonja and Matilda. If they were still interested in having him in their lives.

Which was far from certain. The way they'd looked at him and the words that had come out of their mouths would echo between them for a long time. Maybe forever. But he was going to make an honest effort.

As soon as he was done with the board, he was going to take it up to Matilda and apologize to her. No excuses or caveats, just a sincere apology for his behaviour that morning. He was going to make it clear to her that she was free to go down to the basement as often as she wanted to talk to the spirit she called Greta. If Greta was something she believed in and needed to work through her grief, he wasn't going to stand in her way.

He had no idea what to do about Sonja. There was no apology he could make that would change anything between them. No healing 'I'm sorry'. In all likelihood, it made no difference what he said. She had made up her mind, and in a way, he could understand where she was coming from.

He'd done his best over the years, but he'd fallen tragically short. There were so many things she wanted that he could never give her. So many, in fact, that the question was if he wanted to keep trying.

He closed his eyes, ran a hand over the board, and noted that the surface was so smooth his fingers felt like they were hovering above the wood. True, he could feel the fault lines, but only like the vague traces of something that already felt distant and diffuse. As though the wood itself held a healing power.

When he opened his eyes, it was as though he saw the board for the first time. The craftsmanship, the veins in the wood

– it was beautiful, despite being so old and worn some of the letters and numbers were barely visible.

What if it was true?

What if Matilda was right?

The one thing that indicated she might be was an episode from about a month earlier. Which he had repressed, along with so many other things, in an attempt to convince himself it hadn't happened. But something *had* happened. In the middle of an ongoing investigation, something had spoken to him. Just as they'd made a number of arrests and had finally begun to make out a pattern in some of the cases, something had told him everything they knew was wrong. Which had made him tear up the entire investigation and start over, which had, in the end, led to the arrest of the Dice Killer.

He should say thank you. Whether he believed or not, it was the least he could do. So he stood up, carried the board to the other side of the sheet, and sat down on one of the cushions on the floor.

That was where Matilda and Esmaralda used to sit when they held their séances, and like them, he lit the tealights that were arranged in a circle around him. Then he placed the pointer on the board and made sure it was able to move unimpeded across the letters.

From what little he'd seen of Matilda's method, she'd rested her index finger on the pointer while she asked questions. It was pretty much exactly like the children's game 'the spirit of the glass', which some of his classmates in secondary school had been so fond of playing.

It felt like a betrayal of everything he believed in when he extended his right arm and lowered his forefinger towards the pointer. As though he were doing something forbidden. He couldn't sense any sort of magical power, and his thoughts revolved more around how embarrassing it would be if someone were to walk in on him doing this than what he thought would happen.

'Excuse me,' he said cautiously at length. 'But if there's someone there, on the other side, I just wanted to...' He trailed off. Just hearing his own voice break the silence made him cringe. Part of him tried to get up, while another made him stay seated. 'My name is Fabian, Fabian Risk,' he pushed on. 'I'm Theodor's father. And Matilda's.' He didn't know why he added the last part. This was about the assistance he'd been given with the investigation, nothing else.

And the pointer didn't move so much as a millimetre. Not surprising, given that the weight of his entire arm was pushing down on it. Maybe he was pushing too hard, maybe he should ease up a little?

'I don't know if anyone can hear me.' He tried to speak louder this time. 'Probably not. But I still want to thank whomever or whatever it was that helped me with the investigation by telling me everything we knew was wrong. It might have been someone called Greta, I don't know. But anyway, it did help us. That was all I wanted to...'

The sudden vibrations made him jump and snatch his hand away from the pointer, as though he'd been burned. But once he calmed down, he realized it was just the phone in his pocket receiving a text.

He pulled it out, opened the message, and read it.

It was signed by his former colleague Ingvar Molander, who was in detention, awaiting trial. It consisted of five sentences. No more, no less.

Five sentences that changed everything.

34

HESK PUSHED AND held the top button in the long column of posh surnames until the entry phone lit up and began to ring. Then he quickly smoothed down his hair, downed the last of the beer in his bottle, and put it behind his back so it couldn't be seen through the camera.

A few hours ago, he'd been on his way home. But once he'd climbed into his car, turned the key and exited the parking garage on Østerbro, the images of Qiang's execution had returned. Zoomed-in pictures of details no one should have to see.

Not that such things were new. Ever since video recording technology had become readily accessible to the public, people had been raped, assaulted and murdered on camera. Terrorists had made coming up with more and more heinous ways of killing people and spreading the footage online their calling card.

But this was different from some anonymous snuff film on the internet. Not that he knew the victim. He'd never met Dunja's friend, the man who'd been trussed up and forced to bleed out on the floor in what must have been indescribable pain.

No, what had got to him was that it had happened in real time, right in front of his eyes. This wasn't some pre-recorded murder that had taken place somewhere far away a long time ago. This was something that had happened right then and there, and the only thing they'd been able to do was to stand and watch as his life quite literally left his body.

The bastards had only stabbed him once. A single cut to make sure it wasn't over too quickly. So they'd really have time to see and understand who they were dealing with. What lay in wait for them.

Despite all the images and thoughts, he'd set his course for home, but on his way south towards Amager along H. C. Andersens Boulevard, he'd suddenly burst out crying at a red light outside Tivoli. It hadn't been silent, dignified crying either, with glistening eyes and the occasional tear trickling down his cheek; he'd been sobbing hysterically all the way over to Langebro, where he'd finally turned right so as not to risk losing control of the car.

There had been no helping that the road was for cyclists only, and after hitting a number of sharp kerbs, he'd managed to round the block and find an open parking spot outside Café Langebro. And then he'd just sat there, crying, while the knife was rammed into Qiang's throat again and again, whether his eyes were open or closed.

Once he was calm enough to get out of the car, he'd walked into the pub, sat down at the bar, and ordered a pint and a glass of Gammel Dansk. And with each pint he drank, the film running on a loop in his head had faded slightly, until he was only able to make out the bloody contours of it through the thickening fog.

The entry phone stopped ringing. He pushed the button again. It was the middle of the night, but he'd seen a row of lit windows on the top floor of Gemini Residence, one of the ugliest buildings on Islands Brygge, and he'd even noted a shadow moving inside, so he was going to keep ringing until he was let in.

When the bartender had eventually put down a large glass of water instead of yet another pint, he'd managed to coax one last bottle out of him, then he'd paid and wandered down to the pier, where the reflected lights from Danhostel's high-rise and Nykredit's glass cube on the opposite shore had danced across the dark water.

Down there, the fresh breeze had felt like a cool caress against his warm, puffy face, and it had made him continue west along Islands Brygge. But as his intoxication subsided, the images of Qiang's Adam's apple bobbing up and down as he struggled to suck in air instead of blood, had come back into focus. It got so bad he had to throw up, and afterwards he'd sat there on the pier, realizing how close he really was.

It hadn't been his intention to come this way. But once he'd turned around and looked up at the concave façade, lined with glass balconies, it had occurred to him that there might be a purpose to his wandering after all.

From there, a plan had formed. A plan that would have him prove to everyone, once and for all, that he was someone to be reckoned with and that it was too soon to write him off. The whole thing was a wild gamble, and it could go wrong in any number of ways. But if anyone could pull it off, it was him.

'*Jan? Is that you?*' a voice said through the speaker.

'Hi, Kim,' he said, squeezing out a smile for the camera. 'I thought we might have a little chat.'

'*Now? It's half one in the morning. Can't it wait until tomorrow? We can have breakfast if you don't want to meet at the station. I know a nice place on Vesterbro.*'

'No, I'd prefer if we could do it now.'

The silence that followed didn't last long, probably no more than a few seconds. But it confirmed that despite the late hour, he was on the right track.

'*Okay, but what is this about? What is it that can't wait a few hours?*'

'You told me to keep you informed of any developments. Didn't you?'

The next silence was longer, much longer, and when it was finally broken, it was by a clicking sound from the door.

He hadn't been there in years. Back in the day, Sleizner and his wife, Viveca, had hosted an annual *glögg* party on the first Saturday of December, and every November the question had been who at the office was going to receive one of the coveted invitations.

The inside of the building was much nicer than its exterior. The first time he'd stepped into the lobby, his jaw had dropped, he'd be the first to admit that. Like an enormous, cylindrical atrium, it rose all the way up to the domed skylight about a hundred feet above his head, and with the white walkways and stairs that seemed to hover weightless in the air, linking the different floors, it was like no other lobby.

But tonight, he didn't step into the lift with butterflies in his stomach and a feeling of being one of the chosen. He was here to get answers. To confront his boss and make him tell him what the hell this was all about. No more fumbling in the dark, gathering up crumbs, hat in hand. From now on, he was in charge, and his plan was as simple as it was brilliant.

Simple, because practically anyone could execute it. Brilliant, because no one, least of all Sleizner, would ever suspect him of being capable of doing anything remotely like it.

The lift doors slid open, and he walked towards Sleizner, who was waiting in the doorway, dressed in a robe.

'Wow, someone's been having a bit too much fun, I think. Come in.' Sleizner put his arm around his shoulders, led him inside and closed the door. 'I don't often have such illustrious visitors in the middle of the night.'

'Kim, I'm sorry to disturb you at this late hour, but I figured we might as well get something straight right away,' Hesk said, and he continued into the living room, where he slumped onto a curved, oversized sofa placed in the middle of the room in front of the largest TV he'd ever seen.

'Well, it *is* pretty late, but never mind that. The damage has been done on that front, so to speak, so I'll just have to take my overtime out of your pay cheque.' Sleizner chuckled. 'Calm down, I'm joking. Do you want a drink? You look like you're in need of some hair of the dog. How about a whisky? I have an amazing twenty-year-old Glenfiddich you just have to try.'

The last thing he needed now was more alcohol. But he nodded and accepted a tumbler with a bottom so thick you couldn't possibly knock it over, no matter how drunk you were. Then he sipped the whisky, or at least moistened his lips, and found that it was, in fact, amazingly good.

'Right? Not too shabby, eh?' Sleizner raised his glass in a toast and drank.

He followed suit, then put the glass down on a sideboard, cleared his throat even though he didn't need to, and tried to sit up straighter, even though that was a challenge in the deep sofa. But he needed to grab the reins and show Sleizner that he actually had an agenda for this meeting.

'When we pulled Mogens Klinge's car out of the harbour, I envisioned a fairly straightforward investigation,' he said, while Sleizner stood up and walked over to a wall-mounted shelf made of glass. 'An investigation that would be wrapped up quickly, just like you wanted.'

'Go on. I'm listening.' Sleizner picked up a remote.

'Now, three days later, it's clear I couldn't have been more wrong. Nothing has turned out the way I expected. On the contrary, we appear to have stumbled on something really—'

'Hold on, I just have to—' Sleizner broke in, aiming the remote at the other end of the room. 'I had these things installed a couple of months ago and you don't want to miss this sound. Trust me. Just listen to this.'

Yes started in on their 'Owner of a Lonely Heart' at such high volume that the sampled string beat could probably be heard all the way over at the police station across the water.

'Don't worry,' Sleizner shouted, turning the volume up even higher. 'I've had the entire flat soundproofed, so no one else gets to enjoy it. Admit that it's out of this world!'

Hesk nodded and decided to have another sip of whisky. He needed all the help he could get to stop just sitting there, letting Sleizner walk all over him.

'Feel that bass?' Sleizner went on, and began to play the air bass while performing a series of obviously rehearsed dance moves to the music. 'There's a subwoofer in the sofa! Pretty ridiculous, when you think about it, but bloody effective when I have ladies over!'

Hesk was about to laugh along, the way he always did when Sleizner cracked a bad joke. But this time, he looked down at his whisky instead, which finally made Sleizner lower the volume.

'Sorry, I just wanted you to hear it. Where were we? You said something about how you'd been wrong?'

Hesk nodded and tried to recall what he'd meant to say next, but then decided to come at it from a completely different angle instead. 'In the past twenty-four hours, some – how to put it – surprising and very serious things have come to light in this investigation.'

'Glad to hear something's happening. Honestly, I was starting to feel worried. But maybe I can even expect some results soon, then?'

Hesk nodded. 'In a way, that's why I'm here.'

'All right. Exciting. Tell me. What have you found?'

'Kim, I'm not here to tell you things, I'm here to see what you have to say.' There was a silence then, a choice that would set the course for the rest of this conversation, and he could tell just from looking at Sleizner, standing there in his robe, that he was thinking exactly the same thing.

'Huh? I'm not sure I follow.' Sleizner put a hand on his chest. 'Exactly what do you want from me?'

'I'd like you to shed a bit of light on a few things.'

Sleizner nodded and fired off a smile. 'I'm not exactly sitting on any kind of secret information, but if I can be of assistance, just say the word, of course.' He adjusted his robe, tightening the knot. 'So, lay it on me, I'm at your service, let's see what I can do for you.'

'Do you know Jakob Sand? The entrepreneur.'

Sleizner, who had been about to take a sip of his whisky, lowered his glass without drinking. 'No, other than that I know he's that eccentric businessman who won *Let's Dance* last year or the year before.'

'Or the eccentric businessman who was suspected of murdering a prostitute.'

'He was cleared though, wasn't he? It was so long ago, I don't remember the details.'

'He was. A DNA analysis saved him. It's a bit odd you can't remember, though, since you led the investigation.'

'Well, you know how it is. With so many investigations, they all tend to blend together. Cheers.' Sleizner raised his glass and drank.

Hesk said nothing, just sat there studying his boss, who was definitely acting like someone cornered.

'Or maybe you don't know, actually,' Sleizner went on. 'Since you haven't been involved in even half as many investigations as I have. But let's not dwell on that. How does this Sand come into it?'

'We have a DNA match.'

'Blimey, really? And where are the samples from?'

'Blood and skin from under the woman's nails.'

'Well, what do you know. Good job.' Sleizner nodded and his eyes seemed to turn inward. 'Very good.'

'But you don't know him?'

'No, not at all. Why would you think I do? I've never met the man.'

So Sleizner was lying to his face. Granted, lying was part of his nature, but it had never been as obvious as in this moment.

'And as far as DNA analysis goes, you should get one thing straight,' Sleizner went on. 'Contrary to what you might imagine, it doesn't guarantee a conviction.'

'If DNA could save him, it should be enough to convict him.'

'Sure, but you have to understand something. Just because his skin happens to have been found under this woman's nails, that doesn't mean he killed her. If she was a prostitute, she might have been with Sand before she met up with Klinge. And say things got a bit rough and she accidentally scratched him. I wouldn't be surprised if he's the kind of man who is turned on by things like that. It's actually more common than you might think for alpha males like him to want nothing more than to be dominated.'

'I would say she was the one who was dominated. Not Sand.'

Sleizner sighed. 'All I'm saying is that no matter how badly you might want it to be, DNA isn't the be-all and end-all of a case.'

'Sure, I guess we just have to cross that bridge when we get to it. For now, we'll bring him in for questioning and see what he has to say.'

'Sounds like a reasonable next step.' Sleizner nodded and took a sip of his whisky. 'Do you have any other questions I can answer for you, or are we almost done here?'

'Are you familiar with a parking garage near Østerbro Stadium?'

'No.' Sleizner shook his head. 'I'm not sure I understand the question. Why would I be?'

'It's on Østerbrogade, right across from the McDonald's there.'

'And I ask again. Why would I be familiar with it? There must be a million parking garages around there.'

'Because you were there just yesterday after stopping by my house,' Hesk said, well aware that he was throwing himself into the unknown with second-hand information from Dunja as his only lifeline.

'What do you mean, I was there? What are you talking about? Why would I have been there?'

'That was going to be my next question.'

'Okay, Jan, hold on. What is this? Some fucking interrogation, is that what you're doing? Am I under some kind of suspicion? Should I call my lawyer?'

'I don't know. That's what I'm trying to find out.'

'Then let me suggest that you try to stand up instead, and go home, before you make even more of a drunken fool of yourself.'

Sleizner was probably right. This was a conversation he should have been sober for. But there was nothing for it now.

He was sitting here, and the cat was out of the bag, and if he knew his boss, it would get stuffed right back in if he backed away now.

'We have information indicating that you've been parking in that garage pretty frequently in recent months.'

'Excuse me? I'm sorry, I really don't know what you're driving at.'

'We also have information indicating that you had lunch with Jakob Sand and another person at Zeleste on Friday.'

Sleizner looked at Hesk and shook his head. 'Okay, at first I thought this was a joke, or maybe that I'd misunderstood something. But apparently I haven't. You seriously suspect me of something. I'm not sure what, but you're certain enough to throw away your entire career. But yes, I did have lunch at Zeleste on Friday. And yes, maybe this Sand bloke was there. But not at my table. Because I don't know that man. How hard is that to bloody understand?'

'I'm just trying to do my job.'

'Job?' Sleizner sneered and pulled the belt of his robe even tighter before taking out his phone, dialling a number and putting it to his ear. 'I would call it trespassing. Yes, hello… That's correct… Hesk. Jan Hesk. Perfect, thank you.' He ended the call, went over to the sofa and squatted down so he was at eye level with Hesk. 'Jan, listen to me. You're drunk and you don't know what you're doing.'

He didn't feel drunk. Tipsy, maybe. But the reality of his situation probably didn't have a lot to do with how he felt, and regardless, he'd definitely had too much to drink to be sitting there, trying to pull off his plan with Sleizner as his opponent.

'But it's okay,' Sleizner went on. 'We all stumble into that ditch from time to time. And don't worry. I'm going to pretend this never happened, and tomorrow, everything will be back to normal. I hope you didn't drive here.'

'I did, but my car is parked over by Café Langebro, and I don't mind if it stays there.'

'Great, then just come with me, I'll help you get down to the taxi.' Sleizner straightened up and extended a hand. 'Jan. Come on, before this gets out of hand.'

'Thanks, but I think I can make it on my own.' He crossed his arms and realized the alcohol was actually helping him. 'As soon as you've answered my questions.' If not for the alcohol, he would never have had the guts to do what he should have done a long time ago.

'Your questions?' Sleizner shook his head. 'So you want answers? Huh? Are you sure you want to hear what I have to say? My answer to you is that right now, you're digging your own grave. Do you understand that? Your career will be over if you continue down this road.'

'Then let it be over. But that doesn't change that I want to know why you're in contact with Jakob Sand and why you keep parking in the same garage—'

'For fuck's sake, Jan! What the hell's wrong with you? What is it you don't understand?' Sleizner broke in. 'I'm not in contact with Sand. I've never even met the man! And that garage you're on about.' Sleizner spread his hands. 'I don't bloody know. Maybe that was where I had my tyres changed and my car repaired. Maybe it wasn't. If there's even an auto repair shop there, which I'm sure you know better than I do. But it doesn't matter. None of this matters, because you're leaving. Right now. Am I making myself clear? You're going to get up on those wobbly legs and walk out of here.' Sleizner pointed towards the front door with his arm extended.

'But there's one thing I don't get.' Hesk made no move to

stand up. 'If it's true what you say, that you don't know Sand and have never even met him...' Instead, he reached for his whisky glass and took a big gulp to keep himself from chickening out. 'Then how is that the two of you discussed whether I'm the right man to lead this investigation over lunch at Zeleste? Please explain to me why Sand, an eccentric businessman and winner of *Let's Dance*, would be interested in that at all. And I would prefer an explanation that isn't spelled DNA.'

Sleizner stared at Hesk with a look on his face that suggested it had only just dawned on him that he had fundamentally misjudged his colleague. 'So you've been tracking my phone? Huh? Is that what you've been doing behind my back? Tracking it, tapping it? And here I've been nothing but supportive, making sure you enjoy a career you would never have come close to if it weren't for me. Fucking answer me!'

'Yes, that's correct,' Hesk said. 'We've taken certain measures.'

'And why the fuck is that, if you don't mind me asking?'

'I can't comment on an ongoing investigation. But the best thing for you to do now would be to come with me to the station and spend the night in a cell, and then we can get everything cleared up tomorrow in a proper interview.'

'A cell? Are you out of your mind, you useless fucking cunt? Who the fuck do you think you are? Huh?'

'Kim, this is as hard for me as it is for you.'

'You come knocking on my door in the middle of the night, barge in here and think you can boss me around.'

'Please, I'm begging you, don't make this harder than it already is.'

'Hard? You won't be able to spell hard once I'm done with you. I'm going to make your life so miserable you're going to wish your mother never spread her legs for your father.'

Well aware that his threats were anything but idle, Hesk steeled himself and knocked back the rest of his whisky before he spoke. 'Kim, this is the situation. We know you're in contact with Sand. We know you have frequented the parking garage on Østerbrogade, and we know you have another phone, probably an older model, with which you communicated via text with Mogens Klinge about his initiation ceremony at 8 p.m. on 28 July, which was the night he died. We already know this. I just wanted to give you a chance to explain yourself. But clearly, you can't.'

Sleizner blanched and swallowed several times, as though his stomach was about to turn itself inside out. 'Okay,' he said finally, running a hand through his fine hair. 'You're right. I'm sorry. I haven't told you the whole truth. I admit it. And now you're obviously wondering why not, if I have nothing to hide. And the simple explanation is that I hoped and believed it wouldn't be necessary. That everything would work out so long as I let you lead the investigation and made sure I gave it an appropriately wide berth. That was wrong, of course. I can see that now. Incredibly bloody wrong. But there's nothing to be done about it. And that's all there is to it.'

'Kim, this is a murder investigation.'

'You wanted an explanation, so you'd better bloody listen. Yes, I was in contact with Mogens while he was being considered for membership of our club.'

'Club?'

'We're a group of gentlemen who run a club where we do things together.'

'Like what?'

Sleizner thought about that for a moment before answering. 'Various things, but to answer your question, we do sometimes have sex with female escorts. And I want to stress that that's legal in this country, which, by the way, is true of everything we do.'

'Strangling a woman to death is, as far as I know, still illegal.'

'I was referring to our other activities. What happened in this particular case was, needless to say, deeply unfortunate.'

'Maybe you should tell me what happened.'

Sleizner nodded, then went to fetch the whisky bottle, topped up his own glass, and mutely offered it to Hesk. Hesk held out his glass, let him fill it up, and then they drank without exchanging either words or looks. Once their glasses were empty, Sleizner pulled up a chair and sat down across from Hesk.

'How long have you and I known each other, worked together?'

'Twelve years.'

'Thirteen come September. I remember the day I hired you as though it were yesterday. I could see straight away that you were talented, despite your relative youth. There was no question about it. But that wasn't why I gave you the job. Truth is, you were far from the best applicant. But what you had, which none of the others even came close to, was a hunger for advancement. It was written all over you that you were willing to do whatever it took to climb the ladder.' Sleizner chuckled and shook his head. 'A lot of people frown at that, but I saw something of myself in you, and if you ask me, there's no better motivator. It makes a person ambitious and thorough, and above all loyal to the people who can help them get a leg up.' He poured himself another glass and held the bottle out to Hesk.

'I'm good, thanks.' Hesk raised his hand to decline.

'Just let me know if you change your mind.' Sleizner knocked back his glass. 'I know I can be harsh, and that you and I have had our disagreements. But I never doubted your ability to lead an investigation, or your loyalty. I could always count on you, and you have, in fact, always been able to count on me. A symbiotic relationship I hope can continue even after I tell you something I never thought I would have to tell another soul.'

'Kim, I'm in charge of a murder investigation, so if it turns out you've done something that—'

'Jan, please,' Sleizner broke in. 'If you want me to tell you, then please let me do that. My way. All you have to do is listen and wait until I'm done. Okay?'

Hesk nodded.

'After being in contact with Mogens via text for a number of months, I picked him up on the evening of 28 July, outside Østerport Station,' Sleizner said. 'Once he was in the car, I blindfolded him and drove him to our clubhouse.'

'This clubhouse,' Hesk said, even though he had promised not to interrupt. 'Is it by any chance accessed through the parking garage we've talked about?'

'I'm afraid I can't tell you that, since I'd be in breach of our precepts. This is a secret society and not something to blab about to outsiders.'

'Kim, this is—'

'An interrogation?' Sleizner broke in and shook his head. 'No, it's not. I don't see any recording equipment or a lawyer by my side. The only thing I see is two drunk co-workers having a chat. All right, so the initiation ceremony begins as planned, and one of the rites is that you're given an escort with whom you can basically do whatever you want. Within the boundaries of the laws of the land, of course. We've never had a problem, but this time, everything went wrong. The rest of us were out in the Crystal Room, waiting for him to finish, when we suddenly hear a shot ring out.' Sleizner spread his hands.

'None of us understands what's going on, and Jakob Sand runs over to see what happened. It turns out Mogens, idiot that he was, had brought one of his guns and this girl must have got her hands on it. For whatever reason, she shot him through the mouth. Execution style. According to Sand, the girl was out of her mind and attacked him. Those are his words, but I have no reason to doubt him. Either way, in an act of self-defence, he eventually managed to grab her by the throat and tried to subdue her. But she acted like a rabid tiger, clawing and scratching any part she could reach, until she, I'm given to understand, collapsed lifeless on the bed. Just like that. It happened in the blink of an eye. Sand hurried out and fetched me, and I checked her pulse and breathing, and determined that the girl had passed away.'

'So he strangled her?'

'Yes.' Sleizner nodded. 'But it was self-defence. I want to stress that. Indisputable self-defence.'

'And why didn't you report this to the police?'

'We obviously should have.' Sleizner poured himself another whisky and downed it. 'But that's easy to say after the fact. At the time, everyone panicked. Started to shout at each other. In the end, I had to take charge in an attempt to make the best of the situation. The big problem with reporting it was that it would violate some of our most fundamental precepts. Among others, the one that guarantees everyone's right to complete anonymity.'

'So you'd rather break the law than—'

'Jan, I know exactly what you're going to say.' Sleizner sighed. 'And no, of course we're not above the law. Maybe it's hard for an outsider to understand, but our precepts are deeply ingrained in all of our members, and I mean really deeply, and I can promise you these aren't just any men.'

'In my world, everyone's equal before the law.' Hesk held out his glass.

'In mine, too,' Sleizner said, topping him up. 'I'm explaining this to help you understand why I acted the way I did.'

'What I hear you saying is that you had nothing to do with the murders.'

'Yes, that's correct. Not the murders themselves. But I was the one who invited and brought Mogens, and of course I should have made sure he wasn't armed, and I didn't. I was also the one who transported both him and the girl out of there.'

'But they were found in Mogens' car. I thought you said you picked him up in your car.'

'I never said it was my car, but it was. So the first thing I did was drive over to his house and fetch his car. Then I did everything I could to make it look like they'd been having BDSM sex in it and that he'd killed himself. You're wondering now how I could have been so stupid, and the only answer I have is that my only focus, wrong as that may be, was to get rid of the problem as quickly as possible.' Sleizner paused briefly and shook his head. 'And I have to say we were extremely unlucky to have that bloody canoe lady overturn herself in that exact spot and discover the car. I'd hoped it would take a few months at least. And the fact that you and your new team were a lot sharper than I'd thought you'd be didn't help matters, though in a way, it makes me proud.'

Hesk studied his boss as he poured himself another glass with a trembling hand and downed it. There was every reason to assume he was being less than one hundred per cent truthful. If there was ever a person who could improvise his way to a reasonably plausible explanation, it was Sleizner.

But this wasn't one of those times. Something told him that

this time, his boss had told him the whole truth. He obviously couldn't know for sure, but Sleizner had confessed to too many things, without reservation, for it to feel like a lie.

What this sudden openness was in aid of, however, was beyond him. Maybe he'd finally realized his situation was unsustainable. That the longer he withheld the truth and laid out smokescreens, the harder his fall would be. Or perhaps he'd simply given up and wanted to make the process as short as possible now.

The thing was, though, that Sleizner wasn't the type to suddenly just give up and roll over. He was the badger who hung on until it heard bones break, which made him think there was likely an ulterior motive to laying his cards on the table.

Be that as it may, his plan had worked, and the investigation was practically closed. He'd recorded the entire conversation on his phone. Sleizner's explanation and, most importantly, his confession, which would doubtless result in a lengthy prison sentence. The only thing left to do was to inform Heinesen and the rest of the team and wrap the whole thing up.

'Jan, I hope you're aware that I didn't have to tell you any of this,' Sleizner continued after a brief pause. 'I could have served up a much simpler story that would have fitted seamlessly with the evidence you have and got me off the hook completely. But I didn't, and do you want to know why?'

Hesk didn't even get a chance to consider it before Sleizner went on.

'Because I trust you. Our mutual sense of loyalty is the only reason I let you in. You wouldn't have come anywhere near leading this investigation without it. But now here we are, drinking the best whisky I've ever tasted, and for the first time in our almost thirteen-year friendship, it's your turn to do something for me.'

'Kim, if you're implying you want me to sweep all of this under the—'

'If you don't mind,' Sleizner cut him off. 'I'd be eternally grateful if you would let me finish before you start raising objections. Could you maybe do that for me?'

Hesk nodded.

'Thank you. And don't worry, it won't take long. I'm pretty much done. The only thing I'm asking you to do is to keep going like you have been and to do your very best to bring this investigation to a close so everyone can feel happy and satisfied. That's all.' For the first time in a while, Sleizner allowed himself a smile.

'I'm not sure I understand. If I keep going like I have been, that would entail arresting—'

'Jan, do exactly what you were planning to do before you came here. Bring Jakob Sand in for questioning and confront him. Do it. He's going to say something along the lines that he met the woman and had sex with her at some point in the afternoon of 28 July. Then he's going to explain that things got a bit wild and that during the climax, she accidentally scratched his neck. What she did after that, who she saw, and what happened to her, he won't be able to tell you anything about, since he has no idea.'

'And then what? What happens after that?'

'You thank him for his cooperation and let him go. Then, you have a choice to make. Either you continue to pursue him, to look for evidence to convict him, which will lead you from dead end to dead end, or you steer the investigation back towards the initial theory you formulated when you first saw the two bodies in the car. That Mogens Klinge strangled the woman during a sexual act and then took his own life. In other words, no third party as far as the eye can see.'

'But that's not what happened.'

'That's correct. It's not the exact truth. But it's similar to it, a useful version of it, like when you round 9.5 up to an even 10, and above all, it's the only scenario that allows you to close the case and move on. You can chase the truth from here to Sunday. But you'll never be able to prove it. Not with circumstantial evidence, or technical evidence, most of which you've managed to lose.'

'Not Klinge's phone. We still have that. The one he used to communicate with you.'

Sleizner nodded and smiled. 'That's true. If it weren't for that old thing, we probably wouldn't be sitting here like this. The question is how you're going to prove who he was in contact with? You don't seriously think I'm dumb enough to still be in possession of that phone, or that number, do you?' He leaned in closer. 'Jan, why not try to view this as an opportunity instead of resisting and beating your head against the wall?'

'An opportunity?' Hesk sneered. 'What's that supposed to mean?'

'How would you like to climb a few more rungs on that ladder and take over after me?'

Hesk looked at Sleizner to try to gauge whether he was serious.

'You heard me right,' Sleizner continued. 'And in all honesty, isn't that what you've secretly wanted all along?'

'But I don't understand? What about you? What are you—?'

'To be completely frank with you, I'm starting to get sick of it.' Sleizner took a sip of his whisky. 'No, starting's not the right word. I *am* sick of it. I feel I'm done with the Police Authority and simply put, I want to move on.'

'To what?'

'Time will tell, but DSIS wouldn't be half bad. They have

an open position there, after all, and I'm convinced I'd be able to do a lot of good in that kind of job. So, what do you say?' Sleizner spread his hands. 'Isn't this offer too good to ignore?'

Everything he needed was recorded on his phone. More than he needed. The only thing left to do was to stand up and walk away. But something inside him hesitated and made him stay seated, wondering if this was really happening, or if it was just a dream he was having, lying in a bush somewhere on Islands Brygge, sleeping it off.

'The promotion that had you so excited just a few weeks ago is nothing compared to this,' Sleizner went on. 'In terms of career trajectory, you'll go from snail's pace to warp speed. You'll be able to do entirely different kinds of work, set the long-term course of the department. You'll put teams together and you don't have to go to crime scenes all the time or sit through tedious meetings to analyse the significance of a tiny hair. And since we're being honest here, that stuff was never your forte anyway. Nor mine, for that matter. Other people, people who report to you, can take care of that. If they do well, you get the credit. If they don't, just blame them. Easy as pie.'

Hesk caught himself nodding along and grabbed hold of his chin to make it stop. But Sleizner was right. It wasn't easy to admit, but he'd always wanted to be senior management. It didn't really matter to him what field it was in, so long as he was someone to be reckoned with. That he'd ended up working for the police was mostly happenstance.

'Take your salary, for example, which I just raised, by the way,' Sleizner went on, speaking faster now. 'It's going to double in size, as is your office, once you take over mine. Or no, hold on, I think mine's three times larger than yours. We're talking total game changer, on every level.'

Hesk nodded again, and this time he did nothing to stop himself. He didn't care if it was the alcohol. Like Sleizner had emphasized, this was an offer he simply couldn't dismiss out of hand, and to help bolster his conviction, he held out his glass and was instantly topped up.

'From now on, you'll be free in a way you've never even imagined before,' Sleizner said, clinking his glass against Hesk's. 'Take Lone, for instance. Not to pry into how the two of you are getting along, but if you ask me, you didn't exactly seem infatuated the other night when I stopped by. And there can be any number of reasons for that. But to me, she looked a bit... how to put it... tired. In your new life, she wouldn't have to work any more. You would bring home the bacon and she could spend her days going to the gym and losing those extra pounds she's put on.'

Sleizner raised his glass again, and Hesk followed suit, unsure whether he was celebrating or trying to numb himself.

'I mean, since we're speaking candidly, it can't exactly be great to have to go to bed with all that flab billowing about like a stormy sea. In the end, you can't even tell if you're squeezing her tits or some bulge.' Sleizner laughed and drank again.

But despite the buzz, things were growing clearer.

'And if that's not enough to sway you, I actually have another ace up my sleeve. The best thing of all, if you ask me. Which is membership in our little club.' Sleizner fell silent, nodding while he let that sink in. 'Unfortunately, I can't tell you who the other members are until you've been approved and initiated. But it doesn't matter, you wouldn't believe me anyway. We're talking the crème de la crème. The upper echelons. It's where it's at. The real decisions are made in our little club. Which is, simply put, where you belong.' Sleizner extended his hand to shake Hesk's. 'So, what do you say?'

Hesk looked down at Sleizner's outstretched hand and then back up to meet Sleizner's eyes. 'I think I should be going now.'

'But you can't just leave? Not now when we're celebrating and everything.'

Hesk put his glass down and stood up, parrying his blood alcohol level. 'You can have until eight o'clock to think about what you want to do,' he said. He could feel the whisky making his throat thick.

'No, wait, hold on, Jan. Just take a minute and really think about what you're saying before it's too late.'

'Either you turn yourself in by 8 p.m. sharp, or I will issue a warrant for your arrest.'

'No.' Sleizner shook his head. 'No, no, no, tell me you're joking, Jan. That's unreasonable.'

'It's the only reasonable course of action, and you know that as well as I do.'

'Not after everything I've done for you over the years. Not after all of that. Your wagon's hitched to mine, whether you like it or not. But hey,' Sleizner held up his hands, 'I understand if you can't say yes straight away. It's fine. Sleep on it, and we'll talk again tomorrow, when we're sober. How about it? Tomorrow. I'll buy you a fancy lunch and we can go over all the details together. Doesn't that sound good?'

Hesk just stood there, looking down at his boss, and for the first time he realized how pathetic he really was, sitting there in his robe, which kept falling open. He didn't know what to say again, but this time, he didn't mind. Everything had already been said. All the words had been spoken and now risked being watered down if they were repeated.

'Okay, so, let's meet up tomorrow?' Sleizner said. 'We'll meet up tomorrow and talk, and if you have any questions, you can just ask them. Whatever they may be. Doesn't matter.

I'm begging you.' Sleizner slipped off his chair, fell to his knees in front of Hesk, and folded his hands. 'See? I'm on my knees. If you don't want to join our club, that's fine, I get it, it's not for everyone, though I'm convinced you'd love it. But maybe there's something else you want? Anything. Just point and I'll get it for you. Anything.'

Hesk pondered whether to say anything, to decline the offer or try to explain his position, but decided to simply turn his back on Sleizner and start walking towards the door. Behind him, he thought he heard Sleizner heave a heavy sigh and stand up, then two hands suddenly grabbed his ankles and yanked his legs back so forcefully he fell face first, too intoxicated to catch himself.

'I'm sorry, Jan. I'm sorry, I didn't mean to,' he heard Sleizner say while he rolled over onto his back and struggled into a sitting position, dazed and with a taste of blood in his mouth. 'But I can't just let you leave. You see that, right? Not after telling you everything.'

'That's exactly what you're going to do,' Hesk replied, wiping the worst of the nosebleed on the back of his hand while he braced himself to get back up. 'You're going to let me go and you're going to give some thought to what you want to do. You have until eight.'

'But I can't.' Sleizner grabbed his jacket to keep him down. 'How hard is that to understand? Jan. We have to be able to talk about this. Like grown men. Don't you think? We can't just—'

'Kim, let go of me,' he said, trying to sound calm. 'There's nothing more to talk about. Not here.'

'But there is. There's all kinds of things to—'

'I witnessed the execution today,' he blurted out, even though he'd decided to hold that back until the official interview.

'I watched with my own eyes while they plunged a knife in right beneath his chin and just let the blood pour out until it was over.'

'Execution? I don't know what you're talking about.'

'No? That's odd, since it was the same men who carried me off stage. Which is to say, your men.'

Sleizner froze and his pupils contracted into two black pinpricks. 'Dunja... You've talked to Dunja.' He let go of Hesk's jacket. 'That's the only explanation. You've been in contact with Dunja.'

Hesk could see panic spread like wildfire through Sleizner, whose face blanched as his breathing grew shallow and rapid, as though he were about to pass out.

But instead, it was Hesk's world that went dark, and when he opened his eyes, he realized he was on the floor again. This time with a dislocated jaw and Sleizner straddling his chest with his knees pressed so hard against his arms he couldn't move.

'Kim,' he managed, despite the pain. 'What are you doing?'

'Me? This is all on you.' Sleizner unbuttoned Hesk's jacket. 'This isn't what I wanted. Not even close,' he continued as he loosened Hesk's tie and tugged on both ends until they were the same length. 'I did everything I could to make sure we didn't end up here.' Then he tied a knot and pulled hard on both ends. 'I did, didn't I?'

Hesk tried to respond but couldn't get a word out.

'I did, right?'

He could still breathe, but the tie was so tight now his vocal cords weren't functioning.

'But you gave me no choice.' Sleizner pulled the tie even tighter. 'You see that, don't you? You held the brush and painted yourself into this fucking corner. Do you even understand that, you goddam fucking idiot?'

The pain wasn't the worst of it. Nor was the lack of blood that made both his head and the veins in his neck feel like they were about to burst at any moment. The worst part was the pressure against his windpipe and the feeling of being back in second grade, in the schoolyard, unable to kick the football back because someone had stolen his inhaler.

'I've never killed anyone. Not once in all these years.' Sleizner pulled the tie so tight Hesk not only felt but also heard the cartilage around his windpipe being crushed. 'This is the first time. Do you understand that? The first time. And it's your fault, Jan. Your fucking fault! If you'd just accepted my offer, none of this would've had to happen. But you just couldn't help yourself, could you? You had to go all the way, even though I warned you. Even though I did everything to make you understand, giving you one chance after another. Despite everything I've done for you, you had to keep coming after me, didn't you? So you're the one who drove me to this. You, no one else! Isn't that right, Jan? I said, isn't that right!'

But Hesk couldn't reply.

He couldn't even try.

PART II

The end or not the end. The eternal question.

Nothing lasts forever. Not even the universe. For my part, the question has always been what comes after. What lurks beyond infinity. Maybe it's only the end of the beginning.

The only thing I know for sure is that I've run out of words. The will to explain. To tell anyone.

When that happens, the only thing left to do is to put down one's pen and stand up. Leave one's desk and go from word to action.

35

'*I* CAN'T TAKE *your call right now, so please leave a message, or, even better, send me a text, and I'll get back to you as soon as I can.*'

Morten Heinesen ended the call, put his phone down on the table, and met Hemmer's and Bernstorff's enquiring eyes.

'Maybe he just overslept.' Hemmer shrugged. 'He did seem tired yesterday, to say the least.'

'I don't care how tired he is.' Heinesen shook his head. 'Jan's not the type to oversleep.'

'Maybe he's just feeling a bit low and needs some time to himself,' Bernstorff suggested.

'Low?'

'Yeah, after the meeting yesterday when his suspicions against Sleizner fell apart. He'd clearly put all his eggs in that basket, so when we got a match for Jakob Sand instead, it was like he just deflated. You didn't notice?'

Hemmer nodded. 'Wasn't that whole thing just a bit odd? I mean, sure, Kim Sleizner is clearly not the coolest cat in the building. But that he of all people would be behind these murders, would appoint a colleague to lead the investigation, and then when things don't go to plan would launch this whole clean-up operation, with all the risk that entails.' He shook his head. 'No, it's like most conspiracy theories. The motive just doesn't hold up.'

Bernstorff nodded. 'The question is if he's even going to be able to carry on working in this unit. I know I wouldn't feel comfortable if I were him.'

'Maybe that's why he's not here. I mean, after all, Sleizner's the one who called us here to give him an update on how the case is progressing.'

'No, sure,' Heinesen said. 'It's hardly something he would be looking forward to, but he would never just not show like this. Not in a million years.'

'Fine, but for whatever reason, he's not here,' Bernstorff said, glancing at her watch. 'So what say you we start this meeting without him? Because I have quite a few things I'd like to run by you before Sleizner gets here.'

'You're referring to Jakob Sand,' Hemmer said.

'Yes, the thing is that we don't have all day if we want to bring him in for questioning. From what little I know about him, there's a considerable risk he might suddenly decide to get on one of his private jets and leave the country. Wouldn't you agree, Morten?' She turned to Heinesen. 'Shouldn't we act quickly?'

He wasn't prepared for that question. Much less that it was up to him to decide. He, who had spent his career being the little grey mouse no one noticed. Now, he was suddenly the most experienced detective in the room.

What he wanted was for Hesk to turn up, so they could agree on a strategy before Sleizner joined them. Now, the strategic decisions were suddenly his call, just because Hesk had missed his alarm, or whatever it was that had prevented him from coming to the meeting. He, who had never strived to lead an investigation, or climb the ladder for that matter. Who had always been content with his position and had a hard, not to say impossible, time envisioning himself in the driver's seat.

'Okay,' he said, and he nodded in an attempt to temporarily shoulder the responsibility as best he could. 'Let's get going.'

Bernstorff stood up and walked over to the whiteboard, where she picked up a marker and drew a number of lines. 'As you know, his home has been under surveillance since last night, and I'm told Sand came home at half past two this morning, so it's not too outlandish to assume he's still asleep, which, if you ask me, provides us with a terrific opportunity to go nick him.'

Heinesen nodded again. There was no doubt they had reason not to dawdle. Sand should be interviewed as soon as possible. With luck, they'd be able to press him enough to get a confession, and then the case would be virtually closed.

But he was distracted. For Hesk not to turn up was worrying, and he had a hard time believing his colleague had simply overslept because his phone had died. Hesk would never allow that to happen. On the other hand, he hadn't been himself the past few days.

From the first day of this investigation, he'd seemed unusually nervous and under pressure. So under pressure that he'd been on the verge of mania the day before. And today, he was nowhere to be found.

'Okay.' Bernstorff drew one last line on the whiteboard. 'As you can see, art was not my forte in school, but just imagine that this is the building where Jakob Sand lives. It's on the corner of Frydendalsvej and Jacobys Allé on Frederiksberg. There are four entrances, one on each side, and a fire escape that runs from the top floor to the roof of the parking garage. Now, I really don't think he's going to make a run for it when we ring the entry phone. But just to be on the safe side, I think we should have at least six...' She was interrupted by Heinesen's phone, which began to vibrate on the table. 'Is it Hesk?'

Heinesen picked up his phone, saw a number he didn't recognize, and answered. 'Yes, this is Morten.'

'*Morten Heinesen?*' A woman's voice said.

'Yes, that's correct. Who am I speaking to?'

'*And you're one of Jan Hesk's colleagues. Is that right?*'

'Yes, that's right. We've worked together quite a bit.'

'*Good. I wasn't sure I had the right number.*'

'I'm sorry, who am I speaking to?'

'*My name's Lone. Lone Hesk, Jan's wife.*'

'Oh, hi. I'm glad you called. We were starting to wonder where he might be. We were supposed to meet here half an hour ago.'

'*Oh my God...*' He heard her gasp and fight back tears. '*So you don't know where he is?*'

'No, we figured he'd overslept and assumed he'd be here any minute.'

'*I could sense it. I could. I knew something was wrong, even yesterday. I'd made dinner, roast chicken that I know he likes and rhubarb pie with custard for dessert. I'd even put one of his favourite wines in the fridge to cool. Things have been a bit, how should I put it, rocky lately, you see. Though really it's mostly because I've been angry with him, and I wanted to try to—*'

'Lone,' he broke in, and waited until she had stopped talking. 'Jan didn't come home last night?'

'*No, and he always calls if he's working late. Always. But he didn't last night. Not a word, and I didn't want to call because I know you're in the middle of a murder investigation and don't want to be disturbed. But then I did anyway, and it was really late by then, but he still didn't pick up. It's the same thing now. I've tried several times, but it just keeps going straight to voicemail.*'

The door opened and Sleizner entered. 'Good morning, everyone.'

'*What am I supposed to do?*' Lone asked on the other end. '*What if something happened to him?*'

Sleizner closed the door behind him and looked around the room. 'Has everyone had a good night's sleep?'

Hemmer and Bernstorff nodded.

'That's great. I heard you were working late, and we all know that can slow us down the next day.'

'We're okay,' Bernstorff said. 'I think we're going to crack this.'

'Good to hear. I obviously don't want to disturb your work, I'm just here for a little update on how things are going and how the case is coming along.'

'Lone,' Heinesen said. 'I'm sure he's fine. But can I call you back in twenty minutes or so? Because I'm in the middle of something here.'

'*But what if something happened to him? It didn't, did it?*'

'Not that I know of, and I'm sure I would have heard if it were anything serious. But I'm going to call you back in a bit and we can talk more. Okay?'

'*Okay. I'm here, you can call any time. Preferably as soon as possible.*'

Heinesen ended the call and turned to Sleizner and the others. 'That was Jan's wife. She's worried something might have happened to him.'

'I was just about to ask where he is.' Sleizner looked around the room. 'I figured he'd be holding court in here.'

'We actually don't know where he is. I've tried to call him, but there's no answer, and according to his wife, Lone, he never came home last night.'

'Oh dear.' Sleizner looked back at them. 'That doesn't sound good. Not good at all. When did you last see him?'

'At the meeting last night,' Hemmer replied.

Sleizner nodded and stroked his chin. 'Do you think it might have something to do with the investigation?'

Heinesen shrugged. 'I honestly have no idea. We had the results of the DNA analysis of the skin samples taken from under the woman's nails back yesterday, and it turned out they were a match with Jakob Sand.'

'Jakob Sand?' Sleizner looked like he couldn't believe his ears.

'Yes, you know, the entrepreneur, who—'

'I know who Jakob Sand is. But surely you're not saying he's our perpetrator?'

'Certain things suggest it,' Heinesen replied.

'Speaking of which, I don't think we should hold off much longer on bringing him in and interviewing him,' Bernstorff said.

'No, certainly not.' Sleizner shook his head. 'If you have a DNA match for him, you clearly have to just get to it as soon as possible.'

Bernstorff nodded and stood up.

'But make sure it's done discreetly, if you don't mind,' Sleizner added. 'Given how famous he is, we'll have to try and keep this on the down-low. At least until we know for sure. Because there could be some other explanation.'

'Of course. We'll send plain-clothes officers to ring his entry phone,' Bernstorff said, and she left the conference room.

'And what about Hesk?' Heinesen held up his phone. 'I promised to call his wife back.'

'Lone, you mean,' Sleizner said. 'I'll deal with it. Don't worry. We've met several times, at dinners back in the day when I was still married, so I know her fairly well. But I have to say the whole thing feels ominous.' His eyes stared into the distance. 'What did she say when you spoke to her?'

'That he hadn't called or come home last night, and that they've been going through a rough patch recently. She'd been angry with him and seemed to feel guilty about it.'

'Maybe that's our explanation,' Hemmer said. 'Maybe he just checked into a hotel to get away from the fighting.'

'You wouldn't say that if you knew Hesk.' Sleizner shook his head. 'This really isn't like him. He's neatness personified and would never just drop off the radar in the middle of an investigation, which he is in charge of, no less. Have you turned up anything else, apart from the DNA samples? Something Hesk was dealing with, perhaps, that might have somehow made him...' Sleizner spread his hands and sighed. 'Well, I don't know. Get into some kind of trouble. Whatever that might be?'

'The leads in this case point in all kinds of directions,' Heinesen said. 'Like that old phone he found at Klinge's house, with a number of text messages that suggested he'd been admitted to some form of secret society.'

'Secret society.' Sleizner chuckled. 'Well, why not? It wouldn't surprise me, with Klinge or Sand, if I'm being totally honest.' He shook his head. 'And that old phone. Where do you keep it?'

'It's at Hesk's house. Since we've been burgled and lost some of our evidence.'

'Yes, I heard about that. Completely absurd. But if that phone turns out to be significant, I'm sure it'll turn up. Like Hesk himself will before long, I hope. By the way, have you pinged Sand's phone?'

'Yes, we did that yesterday, as soon as we had a DNA match,' Hemmer said.

'And where was he then?'

'In a parking garage on Østerbrogade, and the strange thing is that he seems to have been there the past few nights.'

'What's so strange about that? Doesn't he just park his car there like everyone else?'

'And his phone, too, then, since it never leaves the garage until he drives away, often hours later.'

Sleizner nodded and stroked his chin again. 'Well, I can't deny that sounds a bit odd.' He turned to Heinesen. 'What do you think, Morten? Maybe you should head over there and take a look. Who knows? There's a chance Hesk swung by on his way home last night. If we're lucky, there are CCTV cameras in the garage that might give us some answers.'

Heinesen nodded and stood up, relieved in a way that someone else had taken charge, but also concerned. Not just about Hesk, but maybe most of all because of a vague feeling that had grown stronger in the minutes since Sleizner had taken over the meeting.

36

FABIAN HANDED OVER his keys, wallet and phone, and was searched and scanned before being led down one of the many hallways of the detention facility. A few locked doors and gates later, he entered a visiting room, which, in addition to a table for four, a sofa and a cot, had been tarted up with plastic flowers in the barred window and a handful of watercolours of clowns in pastel shades on the walls.

He thought about the message he'd received from Ingvar Molander back in the basement at home and realized he could recall it almost verbatim, down to the smallest comma.

Hi Fabian,

Heard about your son Theodor and wanted to offer my condolences. Rumours abound, and I'm hearing things here in the nick. Things I imagine would be of interest to you. If you want to know more, just stop by. I have, as you know, all the time in the world.

Best,
Ingvar Molander

The message had turned everything inside him upside down. Having made a decision to stop digging into his son's death and instead focus all his energy on Sonja and Matilda and the upcoming funeral, he was now doing the complete opposite.

He pulled out one of the chairs, sat down at the table, and nodded to the guard who had accompanied him to let him know he could leave. He was glad he was the first one there. That Molander would be coming to him and not the other way around.

Five weeks. That was how long it had been since he'd arrested the Helsingborg Police's own crime technician down in the North Harbour. At the time, it had been all he could think about. His first and only priority had been to dig up enough binding evidence to have Molander convicted. To make sure he was never let out.

Since then, he hadn't given it so much as a second's thought. Just like that, Molander and the many murders he'd committed had been erased from his memory, transformed into something he might have read about in the paper. That his former colleague was awaiting trial – a trial no one, least of all Molander himself, doubted would result in lifetime imprisonment – just a few hundred yards from the police station made no difference.

Fabian hadn't been worried in the slightest. Not until now, sitting there, waiting reluctantly. Did Molander have something up his sleeve? Was this meeting a part of something bigger that would throw a spanner in the prosecution's case down the line?

There was no way of knowing. There never was with Molander.

That was why he'd always found it difficult to feel relaxed and comfortable around his colleague. Even though they'd solved some of the country's most complex murders together, he'd always had the feeling that anything could happen whenever they were in the same room. That Molander was the last person in the world he'd want to turn his back on.

He didn't know if the other people on their team had felt the same way. Many of them had likely been taken in by his competence. That he always had a glint in his eye had probably helped, too. Molander had, like no one else, known how to keep spirits high, no matter how gruesome the case they were working.

It was natural to assume it was something he'd done for the team. Fabian had thought of it that way himself until he began to suspect him. But for Molander, it had always simply been about the investigation they were working on. The more horrifying and cruel the perpetrator had been to his or her victims, the happier Molander had seemed. But then, they were the people he had drawn inspiration from.

Rumours abound, he'd written in the message, referring to Theodor's suicide. That was all it had taken to make Fabian call back to find out more. But no one had picked up, and in the end, he'd been forced to accept that he would have to go and meet him in person.

'Well, if it isn't the man himself,' Molander exclaimed as he entered the room, accompanied by a guard. 'The man, the myth, the legend, not to mention my favourite former colleague. It's good to see you. And let me think. Is espresso still your drink?'

Fabian nodded and wondered if he should get up and shake Molander's hand, but in the end remained seated.

'I've had to get used to filter coffee with a pH value high enough to be the undoing of any digestive system,' continued Molander, who was clearly in a terrific mood. 'But maybe we could make an exception and ask for two frothy cappuccinos, since we have such fancy company?' He turned to the guard standing in the doorway and folded his hands. 'Please?'

'All right. I'll take care of it,' the guard said, turning to leave.

'Oh, I'm eternally grateful to you. And if it's not too much to ask, I'd love a dusting of cinnamon and sugar on top,' Molander called after him, before taking a seat across from Fabian. 'You know, they have a proper espresso machine in the staff room, probably just to annoy us regular mortals. But they didn't even know how to use it before I came.' He shook his head, paused, and looked Fabian in the eyes. 'It's good to see you. I wasn't sure you'd come, given as how I, as I'm sure you understand, wasn't able to send that text from my own phone.'

'From what I understand, you shouldn't be able to send texts, period.'

'No, that's true.' Molander chuckled. 'It's about as forbidden as a cup of quality espresso. But either way, you're here, and it sure has been a while, huh?'

'Thirty-nine days,' Fabian said, his face impassive. He refused to pretend he was enjoying the reunion.

'So you're counting, too. Interesting.' Molander nodded. 'It's as though our lives will be forever defined by that date, 28 June 2012. Who knows?' He shrugged. 'Maybe one day we'll write a book about it together.'

'I haven't been counting. I looked it up before I came. Apart from that, I don't think about you at all.'

Molander replied with a smile. 'Do you remember the first time we met? You'd just moved here and were supposed to be on leave, and I'd finally been given a murder scene that offered a bit of a challenge, in the woodworking room at the Fredriksdal school. A case that turned out to be far from conventional or unimaginative. I was immediately struck by your ability to see what everyone else missed. And yet I underestimated you.' He chuckled again and shook his head. 'It's not that I didn't realize you were conducting a secret little investigation of me. I knew that straight away. In fact, I considered that a—'

'You said something about rumours about my son's death,' Fabian broke in.

'Why in such a rush?'

'Because I don't have all day.'

'I hardly think there's any need for me to remind you, but I actually do.' Molander turned to the guard, who had returned with two cappuccinos on a tray. 'Wow, Bengt, I think you've outdone yourself today. If I could, I'd give you a sizeable tip.' He pushed one of the cups towards Fabian and raised the other to his lips. 'Mmm... perfection. I've even persuaded them to buy proper beans and a good-quality grinder. Try it, you'll see.'

'Ingvar, I'm not here to sit around and reminisce. I'm here because you sent me a message that said—'

'Do you know that you're the first visitor I've had?' Molander cut in, and he sipped his coffee. 'No one from the team has stopped by, even though we're practically neighbours. Not even Gertrud has deigned to come. I mean, isn't that just a bit lazy?'

'I don't know. Don't forget that she's still in the hospital.'

'From what I hear, she's up and about again, with her rehab in full swing, so walking over here would probably only do her good.'

'And you don't think the fact that you tried to kill her might dampen her enthusiasm? You did, after all, lock her in a root cellar and just leave her there.'

'I don't know about trying to kill her.' Molander shrugged. 'Believe me. If I'd wanted her dead, rehab isn't where she'd be. Besides, she was only down there a few days. Which is to say no time at all compared to how long we were married. Almost thirty-five years. Which is more than you and Sonja are going to manage, mark my words.'

'Let's talk about the rumours instead. What have you heard?'

'You know how it is. People talk in places like this. I'd wager the only place with more gossip flying around is the women's detention centre.' Molander chuckled. 'Anyone who believes even half of it is probably too dumb to survive more than a year. If you believe a tenth, you're just naive.' He shook his head. 'But when I heard what was being said about Theodor, there was no doubt in my mind. I have, as I'm sure you're aware, been keeping an eye on both you and your family since last spring, and unfortunately I can't say I'm very surprised, considering how poorly that boy seemed to be doing.'

'The rumour,' Fabian said, working hard not to let his emotions take over. 'Why don't you tell me about the rumour instead.' Because that was exactly what Molander wanted. 'You can discuss all the other things with your therapist or whoever can bear to listen.' To toy with him and push him around until things reached a boiling point.

'Why would I be seeing a therapist?' Molander sipped his coffee again. 'It wasn't my son who killed himself. I'm not the one who thought everything else was more important than being there for him when he needed me the most.'

'You don't know what you're talking about.'

'No, that's true. Who am I to be sitting here, thinking I know how you're feeling? You always succeeded at whatever you put your mind to. Like arresting both me and the Dice Killer. In a way, you can feel good about yourself. Never mind that it cost your son his life. We all have our priorities, don't we?'

Fabian stood up, intensely focused on making the movement appear calm and collected. 'I think I should leave now.'

'So soon? You haven't even tried your coffee.'

'I'm not big on sugar and cinnamon.' He started to walk towards the door with calm, controlled steps. It shouldn't come as a surprise that Molander just wanted to jerk him around. First one foot, then the other. He obviously felt a need to get back at him, to poke him where it hurt.

'Preben's his name,' Molander said as Fabian put his hand on the door handle. 'The guy who was transferred here after doing a few months in Helsingør.'

He wanted to open the door, walk through it, and leave all of this behind. Lock the door and throw away the key. But he was already turning around.

'What do you think?' Molander went on, taking another sip of his coffee. 'Did his family have a sense of humour, or were they just having a bad day when they decided it made total sense to name their son Preben, of all things? I wonder what the Swedish equivalent would be? What do you reckon? Sven perhaps, or maybe even Fabian?'

Fabian made no reply, just stood there staring blankly at his former colleague.

'Well, it doesn't matter. What I'm getting at is that when he found out you and I used to work together, he told me an order had been passed around to the Danish guards. An order from the top brass, saying they were to use every available method to break down your son until he... well, until he was broken, simply put.' Molander chuckled again. It couldn't have sounded more out of place. 'Maybe you think those are my words, but they're not. That was what they actually said. *Until he was broken.* As though he were a porcelain doll you could just crush under your boot.'

Fabian remained quiet.

On the outside.

37

ALL NIGHT, DUNJA had had the feeling she was hanging by her fingertips. The moment she couldn't hold on any longer and lost her grip on the edge, she'd fall, and everything would fall with her, down into the bottomless abyss. Down into eternal darkness. That the sun was high in the cloudless sky outside made no difference. Everything would be over.

Fareed was probably struggling with the same thing she was. Trying to process and understand the images of Qiang's execution, him sitting there on his knees, waiting for something to happen. The shock when the knife was plunged into his throat had been overwhelming. For her, Hesk and Fareed, but it was nothing compared to what it must have been like for Qiang.

She'd seen it in his eyes. The horrible pain, but above all a question about what had happened. How he'd ended up there. And just like his unsuspecting heart had continued to pump blood out of his mouth and throat, she could only hope he hadn't had time to understand before it was over.

She and Fareed hadn't talked about it yet. They hadn't spoken at all. She'd made a handful of attempts to start a conversation but had been shut down every time. Instead, there had been silence, and within that silence they'd improvised some kind of agreement that had at least helped them get through the night in one piece.

They'd slept in shifts, an hour at a time, while the other kept an eye on the area around the van through the cameras or made sure the vehicle was in motion to recharge the batteries and avoid curious eyes.

They'd been back in town for two hours now, watching the chess house from a parking bay on Vester Søgade on the other side of Sankt Jørgen's Lake, to make sure there were no uninvited guests inside. What Qiang had endured before the camera was turned on was something they'd never know. If the two men had made him reveal where their lair was and how much they knew. There was no helping it. Even if they risked running right into an ambush, they couldn't simply abandon the building. It was where they kept most of their equipment, and, even more importantly, their evidence. They both lowered their binoculars at the same time and exchanged a look.

'What do you say?' she said. 'Should we risk it?'

Fareed nodded, so they climbed out of the van and began walking along the lake in the shade underneath the trees, past Tycho Brahe's planetarium, on the lookout for unnatural movements or passers-by. Like the couple sitting on a bench, heads together, speaking softly, or the old man feeding the ducks by the water's edge, or the panting joggers, their faces red and sweaty.

But everything and everyone seemed normal, and before long they had squeezed through the dense hedge in the back and were walking up to the building, where they paused for a minute before rounding the corner to get to the front door.

Once they were inside, they looked around for signs of someone having been there. But everything looked exactly as they'd left it the previous day. The empty coffee cup next to the open bag of liquorice. The multicoloured snarls of wires connecting the various machines. The unmade beds on the floor, and the stuffy, slightly sweaty smell. Everything was the same as ever.

'Maybe he didn't talk after all,' she said, shaking the last few pieces of liquorice out of the bag.

'Maybe not.' Fareed walked up to his workstation, turned one of the computers around, unplugged it, and pulled off the cover.

'Maybe before we start we should talk about where we go from here? If we should stay or move someplace new. And if so, what to bring.'

'You go ahead and talk,' Fareed said, disconnecting the motherboard. 'You're good at that. I'm just here for my stuff. Then I'm out.'

'What? Seriously, you're out? What did I miss? You can't just up and leave me here with all of this?'

'I certainly can, and I intend to,' Fareed replied, continuing to disconnect circuit boards and other small units and stuff them into his backpack.

'Right, okay. And where are you planning to go, if I may ask? Back home to your little flat? Good luck, that's all I'm going to say.'

Fareed sighed before slowly turning to her. 'From now on, I think it would be better if we knew as little about each other as possible.'

'Hold on, let me make sure I have this straight. Just a few days ago, you were about to give up because you felt we didn't have anything on Sleizner. That we were out of ideas, that the whole thing was just a figment of my imagination. And now you're running away because the exact opposite is true?'

'I don't care how you put it. Whatever way makes you feel better. I don't care. Either way, I'm not staying a second longer than I have to.'

'So I've gathered. But what I don't get is what you're bloody thinking. Are you seriously telling me you're going to let them get away with this? That you're going to let them kill, no, execute, your best friend right in front of you? Is that what you're saying? That the only thing you care about is collecting your damn circuit boards?'

Fareed turned to her again. 'This is your war. Yours, not mine.'

'It might have been mine. But not any more. Not after this. Now if ever, it should be ours.'

'A lot of things should be what they're not. For example, Qiang and I should have left this sinking ship a long time ago. And do you want to know why we didn't? Huh? Do you? Because you paid us. I'm sure you'd like to think it was something else. But your severance package was the only reason we stayed. And I'll let you take a guess at whether it was worth it for Qiang. So yes, I'm going to collect my circuit boards, but more importantly, I'm going to try to survive.'

'Right, so you seriously think you can just walk out of here and it's all over for you?'

'You're the one he's after, not me.'

'Right now, sure. But as soon as he's done with me, you're going to be one of the next names on his list. Because that's how he functions. This is exactly the kind of thing that gets him revved up, and for him, this will never be over. He's going to keep going until someone stops him.'

'I have no doubt you're right,' Fareed said as he put the last few things in his backpack. 'And that's exactly why I'm going to make sure he can't find me.'

Dunja sighed. She wanted to say something. Something to make him change his mind, but everything had already been said. 'Okay,' she said finally, nodding. There were no more words. 'I guess that's it then.' She spread her hands, mostly because she didn't know what else to do with them. 'Stay safe, wherever you're going.'

Fareed nodded and zipped up his backpack. 'And speaking of salary, you still owe me for July.'

'Absolutely. No problem. I'll take care of it.'

'Okay.' Fareed kept nodding as though he didn't know what to do either. Then he turned around and slung the backpack over his shoulder. He pulled his phone out of his pocket and put it on the table along with the keys to the house and the van. 'I guess I'll be going, then.' He waved awkwardly and started to walk towards the door.

Dunja watched him leave. She wanted to shout at him to come back. Threaten him with a gun – not that she had one – and force him to come to his senses. But that was exactly what Fareed had done. She could see that now. There was nothing for him to come back to. No plan. No path forward. Nothing, other than the realization that they'd lost.

And yet he stopped and turned to her. Not because he'd forgotten something or changed his mind, but because of the voices. The voices speaking English right outside.

There was no time to think or weigh their options. There were no options. The men were already trying to break through the door, which wouldn't hold for long. An exchanged look, that was all they needed to reach a decision.

The sound of the door being kicked in reached them on the way up the stairs to Dunja's sleeping loft, where they were going to hide and hope the men would be more interested in the equipment downstairs and what might be stored inside it than in looking for them.

At least it didn't sound like either of them were on their way up the stairs. It didn't even sound like they were looking around. Instead, something was set down on the floor, something hard, possibly metal, while the two of them talked, or more like mumbled, to each other. Soon after, she thought she heard the sound of water being poured, as though they were filling up the coffee machine, or something like that. But that couldn't be right. Were they really feeling so relaxed they were taking the time to make coffee?

Then there was silence. Complete silence. She couldn't even hear mumbling any more.

She exchanged a look with Fareed and saw that he, just like herself, was too scared to do anything but wait for the men to leave. The silence dragged on, as though it, too, were waiting for something to happen.

In the end, it was the smell that convinced her the men must have left the building. The acrid smell of smoke.

'Come on,' she said, hurrying down the stairs. 'Before it spreads too far.'

But once she reached the ground floor, she could see that most of their equipment was already ablaze and the billowing black smoke from the fire was filling the room.

'I'll fetch the extinguisher,' Fareed shouted, hurrying over towards the kitchenette.

But the fire was already burning so hot it was impossible for them to get close enough to put it out.

'It's too late,' she called out to Fareed. 'It's too far gone already!' She couldn't understand how it could have happened so quickly. Not until she saw the flames spread across the floor on either side of her, encircling her with a wall of fire. It hadn't been water she'd heard. It had been petrol.

'Dunja, we have to get out,' Fareed called from over by the front door. 'We have to—'

That was as far as he got before the hallway exploded in

a sea of flames that set off a pressure wave so powerful it knocked her over.

No, not Fareed, was her first thought when she came to and couldn't hear his voice. Not him too. 'Fareed,' she shouted, struggling back onto her feet. 'Fareed!' But the sound of the raging fire that was eating everything in its path drowned her out.

Everything was burning now, and when a searing pain in her legs made her look down and realize the fire had spread from the floorboards to her trousers, she pulled her shirt up over her head and hurled herself through the fire and out of the house, where she collapsed with flames still licking her legs, though she could no longer feel them.

What she did feel was the petrol. The still-cold petrol being poured over her. So they'd waited outside. The two men. They'd stood here, waiting for her to come out.

The only thing that was wrong was the smell. Or, rather, the absence of any smell. It was explained when a pair of hands pulled off her shirt and gently opened her eyes so she could see it was Fareed.

That was all she needed to understand.

No words.

Just a look.

From now on, it was their war.

38

LONE HESK SHOULD really be sitting out on the terrace. The sun was shining, and it was bound to be lovely out there. But she couldn't bear to be seen by the neighbours, who were probably starting to sense that everything was not as it should be. Because that's how it worked out here in the suburbs. If anyone so much as sprained their pinkie toe, people talked.

Which was why she preferred to sit under the kitchen fan with the curtains drawn, filling her lungs with soothing smoke while she let the new cigarette kiss the old one just long enough to light it. Then she stubbed the old one out and sucked down another lungful, even though it didn't taste particularly good any more.

But she needed it. She had to busy herself with something that at least gave the illusion of calmness to keep from cracking under the pressure. And what else was she supposed to do, other than sit there in the kitchen, waiting for absolutely nothing to happen?

She took another drag, breathing in as deeply as she could, with her eyes on the kitchen fan that roared overhead. As though it made any real difference. The carbon filter hadn't been changed in years, so all it did now was disseminate the cooking smells, or in this case the reek of cigarettes, to every corner of the house. That they still hadn't fixed the vents to make sure the fan exhaust was pushed all the way to the outside was nothing short of unfathomable.

At least Benjamin had gone down for his nap and Katrine and one of her friends had taken their bikes over to the beach in Amager Strand Park. She hadn't told the children anything yet, but Benjamin had sensed something was wrong and cried at the drop of a hat. And last night, when they were watching the news, Katrine had asked if they were getting divorced. Just like that, out of the blue. She'd reacted all wrong; she'd raised her voice, sounded angry, the only effect of which had been to demonstrate to her daughter what a sore point it was.

But the truth was that right now, she missed Jan more than she had in years. Suddenly, she couldn't recall a single one of the million things that normally irked her.

All she could think about now was how kind and thoughtful he was. How loyal and reliable. And good-looking. That struck her every time she took out her phone to look at a picture of him. Unlike so many men his age, he'd held on to his hair and he had no wrinkles or bags under his eyes.

And yet she'd been so angry and frustrated she'd complained no matter what he did. In the end, his mere presence had been enough to set her off.

Until this morning, she'd been convinced he must have decided to take the bull by the horns and finally leave her, in an act of sheer self-preservation. That the thing that had been hers, the thing she'd been considering for so many years but had never dared to face the consequences of, had now become his. As though he'd stolen her idea and was now one step ahead in starting his new life.

It was only after plucking up the courage to call his work that she'd become worried in earnest, and by now she was convinced something terrible had happened, which made her absolutely petrified.

How was she supposed to get by? Take her shop, for example; it didn't even make enough to cover the rent. She would have to close it down, and maybe that was just as well, though the thought of going back to her old job behind the till at the supermarket gave her heartburn. She would have to sell the house, and they would have to move into some cramped rented flat far from the...

The harsh sound of the doorbell made her drop her cigarette, which drowned with a hiss in her coffee cup. She stood up, went out into the hallway and unlocked the front door.

It was probably Adam. He was at home, looking after the children while his wife worked, and they'd been helping each other to pass the time. If she didn't pop over to his, he knocked on her door.

They hadn't done anything yet, but they flirted and every time they were together, the air hummed with something that had nothing to do with love. It was unsustainable; sooner or later, they would take it too far, they both knew it. And once that happened, it would be over. Which was why she'd tried to drag it out, to relish their forbidden game for as long as possible. But not today. Today, she just wanted to be left alone to sit under the kitchen fan.

She opened the door and was just about to say that she wasn't feeling well when she saw that it wasn't Adam, it was Jan's boss, Kim Sleizner.

'Hi, Lone,' Sleizner said, smiling. 'Can I come in?'

She wanted to tell him no and ask him to leave. Ever since that time several years earlier when they'd been over for dinner with Sleizner and his wife, she'd felt dirty every time he looked at her. And yet she nodded and stepped aside to let him in.

'I mostly wanted to stop by to see how you're holding up,' he said on his way to the kitchen, where he stopped and turned to her. 'So, how are you doing?'

'Eh, well... I'm not really sure.' She shrugged, just wanting him to leave. 'It's, I don't know how to put it, hard not to know. To just walk around here at home, wondering. You haven't heard anything, have you?'

Sleizner shook his head. 'Not yet. But we will, soon, I promise. I've made every resource available to make sure this doesn't drag on. So whatever's happened, we'll know soon.'

'It almost sounds like you already know something *has* happened,' she said, and she felt tears welling up in her eyes. 'Something serious.'

'No, no, no.' Sleizner chuckled and shook his head again. 'We don't know anything right now. I promise, there's no need to worry. The moment we have news, you'll be the first to hear it.'

She looked him in the eye and felt like she could see right through his attempt to hide that he already knew, or at least suspected, and just wanted to give her time to prepare herself.

'Hey...' he said, and went up to her. 'That's just how I am. A consequence of the work I do. After all my years with the police, I've developed a habit of assuming the worst. Most of the time, it turns out much less dire. But in the rare event that it doesn't, I just don't want to be caught with my pants down. Do you know what I mean? Because I've never been good with surprises.'

Lone nodded, even though it was just words. Words that sounded good but meant nothing to her.

'Lone,' he went on, putting his arms around her in an embrace. 'I know how hard this must be, but I'm sure it will turn out okay, you'll see.' He held her close and let one hand roam up and down her spine. 'I'll do everything in my power to find out what happened. *If* something happened. Who knows, there could be some other explanation. Regardless, I'm going to find out.'

She couldn't even hear his words any more. They blended together, forming a thick carpet of sound. It was his arms that meant something. The warmth of his body and the deep thudding of his heart just an inch or two from her ear.

She didn't like it, the hug or the back-stroking. It made her feel as dirty and gross as she had after that dinner that had started with him playing footsie with her right in front of both Jan and his own wife, Viveca. But she still didn't want it to end.

Just a few minutes ago, she would have said over her dead body. But no matter how dirty it made her feel, it was exactly what she needed. A hug and some closeness. Apparently, it didn't matter who from.

Later, after dinner, he'd poured Jan a big glass of whisky and led her off to look at a painting by Jens Jørgen Thorsen he'd just acquired. It had been called something to do with Disneyland and a horny Mickey Mouse. To her eyes, it just looked like a mess of colours, and she had told him as much. But Kim had just laughed and led her on through the large flat and into a bathroom.

'Hey...' he said, his arms still around her. 'I was thinking about this case Jan is working on. I was wondering whether it has anything to do with his disappearance. He didn't talk to you about it, did he?'

'No, not a word,' she said, noting that the hand stroking her back had awakened something in her. 'He's always been very secretive about his work and almost never tells me anything. But he was stressed, I can say that much. I could tell from the way he acted.'

'I see.' Sleizner let his hand slide all the way down to her behind, where the slightest touch made her tremble. 'And he didn't bring anything back to the house?'

'Not that I know of,' she said, self-loathing mounting inside her. 'Like what?'

'Who knows. Some clue he was working on or anything, really. It might help us figure out what happened to him. Like an old mobile phone, for example.'

'Phone?' She suddenly remembered and looked up at him. 'An old yellow Ericsson phone?'

'Why not?' Sleizner's face broke into a smile, and he pushed her hair behind her ear. 'Why don't you go get it and we'll see.'

39

AFTER FIFTEEN MINUTES spent driving in circles, Morten Heinesen finally found the entrance to the underground parking garage on Østerbrogade. He paid, put the ticket on the dashboard, and started to look around.

The only reason they were interested in the garage was that if Hemmer's triangulations were anything to go by, Jakob Sand had a habit of parking there at night. Often for hours at a time. Which perhaps wasn't so very strange in itself. What was strange was the fact that Sand himself didn't seem to leave the garage during that time, unless he left his phone in the car, which would also be odd.

According to Hemmer, Sand had been in the garage last night. Whether that could have been enough to make Hesk decide to come here after their meeting was hard to say. Hesk wasn't a natural risk-taker or prone to going off on daring solo missions. If driving down into a public parking garage could be considered daring. Even if Sand had been down here, and not just his phone, he was, after all, not some kind of psychotic serial killer.

Heinesen, for his part, had always felt uneasy about parking garages, and particularly public ones where anyone could get in and proceed to lurk in the shadows. Anyone, whether they had business there or not. It was also frighteningly easy for a potential perpetrator to make his or her escape.

He felt the same way about petrol stations located next to motorways in the middle of nowhere. Especially ones on the continent, located where several motorways met. Kidnapping a child waiting in the car while the parents were paying at the till would be the easiest thing in the world. Then you just had to disappear in any direction.

Not that anything had ever happened to him. But he hadn't hesitated to pay extra for an American-style lock on his car, for which one push on the fob unlocked just the driver's door, so no one could get in on the passenger side and pull a knife on him the moment he unlocked the central lock and climbed in behind the wheel.

But in this particular garage, he didn't feel too perturbed. The presence of an auto repair shop with two men in blue overalls working inside was reassuring, and just as Sleizner had suspected, there were a number of CCTV cameras. One by the entrance and exit, two by the auto repair shop, and a fourth one next to a small loading dock.

'Excuse me,' he said, after driving a full lap around the garage. 'Pardon me.' He waved, even though one of the mechanics was leaning in under an open bonnet and the other had just rolled in under a car. 'You wouldn't happen to know who's in charge of the CCTV cameras in this garage?'

Neither of the men reacted. Instead, welding sparks began to fly out from under the floor of the car.

'Hello? Excuse me?' he said again as loudly as he could without shouting, which made the man underneath the bonnet pop his head out. 'I'm from the police and I need to know who...'

'Policja?' The man turned to his colleague underneath he car. 'Krzysztof!'

The man whose name was apparently Krzysztof rolled

out from under the car, stood up, and wiped his hands on his overalls.

'I'm from the police and I would like to know who's in charge of the CCTV cameras in this garage,' Heinesen said again, in English this time.

But the man made no reply, just turned to his colleague and said something in what sounded like Polish. The colleague answered in the same language. At that point, Heinesen pulled out his police ID and held it out to give his words more weight. 'Like I said, I'm from the police, and—'

'Not me,' the man across from him cut him off. 'My boss.' He nodded towards a door at the back of the shop. 'Talk to boss.'

'Okay, thank you.' Heinesen walked past them and felt their eyes on his back all the way to the door, which was labelled *Reception*.

There was no one in there, but the surface of the water in the blue cooler was rippling as though someone had just filled one of the plastic cups. He continued up to the unmanned counter and rang a small bell, whose harsh ding made him realize just how quiet the room was.

He counted the seconds it took for the sound to subside, but it was so many he lost count before silence fell once more. He would certainly never bring his car to be repaired here, that was for sure. He considered ringing the bell again, this time even harder, but stopped himself when he spotted a jagged hole, an inch or two across, in the door behind the counter and noticed something blue moving about on the other side, in what appeared to be an office.

He leaned over the counter for a better look, and yes, he could clearly see a pair of legs in blue overalls underneath an overflowing desk. Talk about terrible customer service. 'Hello?'

he called, sounding deliberately annoyed. 'Please come out? I've been waiting for a while now.'

After a few more moments, the door was opened by an older mechanic with a phone pressed to his ear.

'Dobrze. Dobrze,' the man said before ending the call and meeting Heinesen's eyes. 'What can I do for you?'

'It's about the CCTV cameras in the garage. I need to know who's in charge of them.'

'And who are you?'

'My name is Morten Heinesen, I'm with the Copenhagen Police.'

'ID. I want to see some ID.'

Heinesen took out his ID and had just put it on the counter when the door behind him opened. He turned around and saw that there was a man in a suit behind him now, standing with his arms crossed as though he'd been made to wait for far too long. He smiled at the man to let him know he knew the feeling but got no response.

The older mechanic studied his ID, as though he were memorizing his personal identity number, then put it back down on the counter, looked past Heinesen, and nodded to the man in the suit.

Heinesen turned to the man, who was walking towards him. 'I'm sorry, but I don't think we're quite done here, are we? We're not, right?' He turned back, only to discover that the older man was squatting down behind the counter. 'I'm sorry, what are you doing?' He leaned over the counter. 'Hello, would you mind answering me? I'm talking to you. Who's in charge of the CCTV cameras out there? Who do I need to contact to get access to the footage from the past—?' He broke off when the man behind him tapped him on the shoulder. 'Like I said, I'm not done,' he hissed, and brushed the man's hand away.

'How hard is that to understand? Or maybe you don't speak Danish, either?'

The man said nothing, just held out his hand, offering him a USB stick.

'And what is this?'

'The footage you were asking for,' said the older man, who had straightened back up and was now holding pen and paper. 'Name, phone number, and a signature here, please.'

40

SONJA HAD A hard time hiding her surprise when Fabian appeared outside the funeral home on the corner of Pålsjögatan and Föreningsgatan several minutes early. She probably hadn't expected him to come at all.

'Hi,' she said, suppressing the reflex to ask where he'd been all morning.

Fabian said hi back but didn't mention that he'd been to see Molander, who'd told him that the abusive environment their son had endured had apparently been the result of an order from the most senior managers of the Danish detention facility. 'Shall we?' he said instead, and took her hand.

She nodded but let go almost immediately to hold open the door. An ugly aluminium door that brought to mind some dilapidated school from the seventies where no one had ever been happy.

Once they were inside, he tried to take her hand again, but she was already following the undertaker, who'd introduced himself as Tjälve and offered his condolences in a manner that seemed so obviously rehearsed and phoney, it couldn't possibly have been clearer how little he cared.

They were shown into a meeting room with off-white walls hung with bland art prints, the only furniture a well-worn conference table big enough to accommodate a large group of loved ones. The ceiling light with its six white glass arms held the worst kind of low-energy bulbs, of which two had gone out. It was uninspired, shabby, and above all undignified.

'Of course, I will see to it. So just have a seat and relax.' Tjälve gestured towards the table. 'And help yourselves to cinnamon buns. They're fresh, from Börjes on Tågagatan. Best buns in town, if you ask me, and worth every calorie.'

The undertaker disappeared, and they pulled out chairs and sat down. First him and seconds later her, with an empty chair between them. Whether that was deliberate or not was hard to say, but they were now too far apart for him to try to hold her hand.

He turned towards her and noticed that she was staring straight ahead. He'd always thought she was beautiful. But in profile, she was simply stunning, with her slender neck, which was on display now that her hair was cut short. She always had been and still was, despite everything they'd been through, in a league of her own. Even now when she was sad and staring into space, doing everything she could to stay in control of herself.

He handed her the box of tissues, and she took one and gingerly dabbed her eyes while Tjälve returned with three cups, two coffee, one tea, a small jug of milk and a bowl of sugar cubes on a tray. How had he known Sonja preferred tea after lunch? Had she told him that while he was showing them in?

'Budget?' Sonja turned to him. 'I'm not really sure if we've talked about that?'

'I don't know,' he said, and smiled at her. 'I haven't actually had time to give that much thought. But I suppose money isn't the main priority, we'll figure that out. The important thing for me is that you get what you want.'

The only one smiling now was Tjälve. He was clearly hoping to be able to sell them his most expensive coffin and extra everything for the wake afterwards. Sonja, on the other hand, remained expressionless. He'd only meant to show his support by giving her free rein.

But to her, it had come off as something else entirely. He could tell. What she'd heard was that he was abdicating all responsibility, saddling her with every decision and consideration. And in a way, she was right. He couldn't care less about the lining in the coffin, or how many types of biscuits they served their guests. If it were up to him, he would have picked the cheapest and least lavish option. Theodor was dead, and no gilded curlicue letters on cream invitations could change that.

The only reason he was here was Sonja. She was the one who thought this was important. This was her way of processing her grief. Not his.

He was still busy thinking about his meeting with Molander and the supposed rumour about foul play being behind Theodor's death. What he'd told him tracked so well with his own suspicions it couldn't be completely made up. There had to be a grain of truth in there somewhere, and that was the real problem. That grain would never let him turn his back on this and move on. It would be there, chafing him bloody until he found out the truth about what had happened, once and for all.

Sonja and the undertaker suddenly stood up as one and went over to a display room filled with different types of coffins. He followed them and saw the man point to one of the paler coffins, made of white-painted wood with chrome handles. Sonja nodded, and she might have said something too. Or not. Either way, the man made a note in his folder.

It didn't look like the cheapest model, but not the most expensive one either. It certainly wasn't nice-looking. Not that he knew what counted as nice-looking when it came to coffins. But whatever it was, this coffin was the opposite of everything Theodor had stood for. He'd hated white and would definitely have picked a black one, preferably with leather and studs, if he'd had a say.

There was more talking, nodding and note-taking, then they returned to the conference room, where even more words were exchanged. Then there was handshaking and more nodding, and on the way out he suddenly remembered the cinnamon buns neither of them had eaten and realized how hungry he was.

'You might as well go now,' Sonja said as they stood on the pavement outside the entrance, and he'd just made up his mind to ask her to come with him to some nice place and have a bite to eat.

'Go? Where am I going?' he said, wondering what he'd missed this time.

'I don't know.' She shrugged. 'But you're not here anyway, so maybe you should just leave and go chase whatever's tormenting you.'

He nodded, figuring he understood.

'But this is the last time,' she went on. 'If you leave me now, it's the last time.'

He'd promised himself never to let it happen. To do everything in his power to find another solution, convinced that somewhere down the line, things would seem brighter, even for the two of them.

But in the past few years, the decision had been there, lurking in the background, biding its time. Even though it was forbidden, he'd toyed with it, imagined it, like different versions of the same scene, being played out just for him. He'd heard the dialogue, his own arguments. Sonja's. Had heard them fight, cry and scream, only to then eventually calm down and agree to the inevitable.

But none of the versions had ever been this terse and composed.

But then, there was nothing left to say. Everything had already been said too many times, and the only thing left to do was to nod and walk away.

For the last time.

41

SHE DIDN'T KNOW if things were over with the boyfriend in
Malmö. From the name alone, Balthazar sounded like a man
right up Mikael Rønning's alley, and when Fareed had also
managed to find pictures of the Swede, she'd been unable to
imagine a scenario in which Rønning would willingly have left
someone as fit as him after only three days, when the plan had
been for him to stay for two whole weeks.

Granted, Balthazar could have been the one who got bored.
But Rønning wasn't the kind of man you got bored of. If
anyone got bored, it was him. Always, always him.

The third and, according to herself, most likely explanation
was that he'd changed his mind following their conversation on
the train. Not that pricks of conscience had ever been his thing,
but he was, after all, a relatively rational being, and the APB
alone, in which she was accused of being a threat to Denmark's
national security, should have been more than enough to make
him see that Sleizner had to be stopped at any cost.

Whatever the reason, he was back in Copenhagen, and that
had raised her spirits. Despite the setbacks and adversity, despite
the state of her lower legs, which after repeated application
of cooling ointments and hours of rest with icepacks taped
to them still burned, even despite Qiang's horrifying fate, she
once more felt like they might have a chance.

Rønning had returned to his flat on Lille Istedgade a few

hours earlier. Fareed had discovered it when he'd randomly pinged his phone. They'd agreed to make another attempt at contacting him. Having someone on the inside who could keep a watchful eye on Sleizner and his actions would make all the difference.

Which was why she'd just sunk into a squat on the pavement outside the Mændenes Hjem homeless shelter and started frantically scratching her forearm while rocking back and forth with her hood up, indistinguishable from the rest of the junkies on the block. All so that Rønning wouldn't spot her when he stepped out of the building across the street and, as usual, scanned his surroundings before moving on.

Five minutes earlier, she'd just made it through the cluster of equal parts deprivation and wheeling and dealing on the corner with Istedgade. Her plan had been simple: she was going to walk up, knock on his door, and have a nice calm chat with him. Tell him about all the things he didn't know. But just as she was about to cross the street in front of his building, Fareed had informed her via her headset that it looked like Rønning was about to leave his flat.

They'd had to rethink their approach on the fly and improvise. This wasn't the kind of conversation you could rush. They needed peace and quiet, and above all, they needed time.

'*From what I can see on my screen, he's walking towards Halmtorvet. Is that correct?*' Fareed said from the van, which was parked about a hundred yards away, outside Øksnehallen in Kødbyen, the meat-packing district.

'Yes,' she replied, her eyes on Rønning.

'*Do you think he's on his way to the station?*'

'Well, he's not heading over to DGI Byen for a spot of bowling. I suggest we nab him on Stoltenbergsgade.' She straightened up the moment Rønning disappeared around the corner, on his way towards the roundabout where, just a few years earlier, prostitutes used to jostle for the best spots. Now, the scouring pad of gentrification had scrubbed the kerb clean and forced the prostitutes down to the eastern end of Istedgade, or the hard end, as the blocks closer to the central station were known colloquially.

It was hardly a bold guess that Rønning was on his way to work. He almost always was when he crossed Halmtorvet Square, unless he was going to his favourite Indian, Tandoori Masala.

That suggested he intended to come back from leave early, which was exactly what she'd planned to suggest he do. Because it was there, in the back hallways of the sixth floor of the police station, that he could do the most good.

'*I'm passing him now,*' Fareed said. '*And I don't think he's out for a balti chicken palak.*'

'All right, see you on Stoltenberg.' Dunja broke into a run towards Istedgade and then down towards the central station. It was the long way round, but there was no helping it. Luckily, despite the pain from the burns, she'd never been in better shape, unlike Rønning, who'd always stubbornly refused to so much as slip on a pair of running shoes.

Stoltenbergsgade was just two blocks from the police station, which was to say much too close for them to pick him up. The problem was that his route cut through some of Copenhagen's busiest areas. Especially at this time of day.

On Tietgensgade, which took him across the train tracks, the pavement was nearly as crowded with people as the arrivals hall, and she had to zigzag to avoid collisions. Then he was going to continue down towards the south-west corner of Tivoli, where there would be even more people milling about.

Things wouldn't calm down until he turned right down Bernstorffsgade, and once he reached Stoltenbergsgade, the street should be deserted enough that no one would have time to react to what was happening.

'*All right, I'm in position,*' Fareed said as she squeezed herself out through the east entrance to the arrivals hall and cut across the street between cars that were about to go since the light had just turned green.

'Don't park right on the corner, he might notice the van.'

Once she reached the Tivoli side, the pavement was so crowded she was forced into the cycle lane, where she was able to run at top speed all the way to the next intersection, ignoring the cyclists racing in the opposite direction, furiously ringing their bells at her.

'Okay, I see him,' she said, watching Rønning as she paused to catch her breath. 'He's crossing Bernstorffsgade.'

'*Good, then he should be here any minute.*'

Dunja prepared to cross the street the moment Rønning turned right onto Stoltenbergsgade. But instead, he continued straight ahead. 'Okay, we have a problem,' she said. 'He's walking down towards H. C. Andersen.'

'*Why? Did he spot you?*'

'No, he hasn't so much as looked in my direction. I'm going after him.'

With Rønning at a safe distance in the corner of her eye, she continued down towards H. C. Andersens Boulevard and then onto Stormgade while she and Fareed tried to figure out where he might be going. But they had no idea. This wasn't Rønning's part of town at all. Especially down by Frederiksholm Kanal, which he'd always claimed was so picturesque and charming that he was overcome with acute Tourette's every time he happened to pass by.

This time, however, he didn't seem to be happening to pass by. On the contrary, he was striding ahead with ever increasing determination, constantly checking his watch as though he were late. A few hundred yards later, along the cobblestoned Gammel Strand, he sat down at a free table in the outdoor serving area of Café Diamanten.

What the fuck? Dunja stopped and stared at him. Diamanten was her place. It was where she would go and hide among the tourists when she needed to be alone. A real local would never even consider coming here.

Just her.

And apparently Rønning now, too.

This was where she'd asked him to meet her the last time he'd helped them. That had been about a month ago. He'd eventually been able to bring them Sleizner's phone, which Fareed and Qiang had then hacked and attached a GPS tracker to. While they did, she and Rønning had managed to exchange a few words. But there had only been enough time for her to say that she'd been forced to disappear and she'd left him with most of his questions unanswered.

When she realized what was going on, she had to laugh.

'*What's so funny?*' Fareed asked.

'I'm going over there,' she said, and started to cover the last fifty feet. 'I'm going to go talk to him.'

He was obviously messing with her. Prick. It was so like him to take it all the way, too. How could she not have seen it before now? He'd obviously been fully aware she was going to follow him before he even left his flat, and what better place to meet than here? She was going to get him back so hard when all of this was over.

Three steps later, everything changed.

From colour to black and white.

White to black.

The synapses in her brain were unable to keep up, and she had to focus every ounce of her attention on keeping her feet moving so she could veer away from the café somewhat inconspicuously and not risk just standing there, drawing attention.

Within a fraction of a second of spotting him, her brain had begun casting about for an alternative explanation. But to no avail. There wasn't one.

This wasn't an unfortunate coincidence.

It was Sleizner.

Like a ghost in broad daylight, he'd come strolling towards the café from the opposite direction. There had been less than fifteen feet between them when they passed each other. The only good news was that his eyes had been on something else, behind her.

That was when the pieces had started to fall into place. One after the other. But it couldn't be true. It just couldn't. As though new evidence suddenly indicated the Earth was flat, she refused to accept it. Not even when she finally dared to stop, turn around, and watch him shake hands with Rønning and sit down across from him. Not even then could she believe it.

'*Dunja, are you still there?*' Fareed said after a while. '*What's going on?*'

'Sleizner's what's going on, Fareed. Kim fucking Sleizner.'

'*But I don't get it? What the hell does he have to do with—*'

'There's no point trying to understand. Just turn on the microphone on his phone and connect it to my headset so I can—'

'*But just so I'm sure I've got this right. Are you seriously telling me Rønning and—?*'

'Fareed, for fuck's sake,' she hissed. 'Just do as I say.'

'*I am. It just takes a second. At least it looks like he's put the phone down on the—*' Fareed's voice was cut off by loud static, followed by a distorted, choppy soundscape, and then, finally, she could make out voices.

'*Camilla Krystchoff?*' one of them said, probably Rønning. '*With a C, H, and double F?*'

'*Exactemento,*' Sleizner replied as the waiter poured a glass of mineral water right next to the phone.

'*Just give me her personal identity number and I'll take care of it. No problem.*'

'*Great,*' Sleizner said, and sipped his water. '*And as I'm sure you understand, this is something we should, at least for now, keep on the down-low.*'

'*Of course. So long as—*'

'*No, no, no, don't worry about that. There's no malfeasance here. None at all. It's about helping her. That's all I want, and as you yourself know, she's currently not just a danger to herself, but to the entire... Well, you know what I mean.*'

'*I'm actually not sure. Not entirely.*'

'*Mikael, what I'm trying to say is that if this leaks out too soon, all hell's going to break loose, and the only one who loses in that scenario is her. Are you with me?*'

'*Yes, I understand. Is there anything else I need to know?*'

'*Not at the moment. You'll have more details in due course. But before I give you more, I need to know I can trust you completely.*'

'*Of course you can trust me.*'

'*Yes, so you've said, and that's great. Really great.*' Sleizner paused for a moment before speaking again. '*Well, so, if you don't have anything else, I suggest we wrap things up here.*'

'*Okay. Or actually, hold on, there was one thing,*' Rønning said.

'Go for it.'

'You might recall that I ran a security update on your mobile about a month ago.'

'Sure, absolutely. Does it need another?'

'No, there shouldn't be any need for that. But given everything that has happened, and since we're here, I figured I might check to make sure everything's in order, as it should be.'

'All right, no worries. Be my guest. Here.'

She heard the phone being picked up and handed over. Then followed the sound of Sleizner drinking, pouring more mineral water into his glass, and drinking again.

'Oh my,' Rønning said after a while. 'When did you last leave this unattended?'

'Why, have you found something?'

'Quite a bit, actually. Look at this, for example, and this. See?'

'Fuck me... Is it her? Huh? Is it? Is it her?'

'It's possible. But don't worry, it should be relatively easy to...' Rønning's voice vanished, replaced by static for a few seconds before that went silent, too.

42

'OKAY, IT'S ALREADY late, so let's keep it snappy,' Sleizner said on his way into the conference room. 'No tedious tangents or irrelevant details, it's full steam ahead now and I'm the captain. Any questions?'

Heinesen had a lot of questions but said nothing, just shook his head like Hemmer and Bernstorff. He didn't want to stick out and risk drawing Sleizner's ire.

'Okay, good,' Sleizner said after a brief pause. 'Because we have a lot to get through and the fat lady's about to sing.' He closed the door behind him and went over to the far end of the oval table. 'As you all know, it's during the first few hours after a disappearance that the trail will be hot and our chances of finding Hesk relatively good. Very soon, that curve is going to take a nosedive, and once that happens, it'll become virtually impossible to find out what happened.'

'Can I say something?' Hemmer raised a hand.

'No. Not unless it's about your interview with Jakob Sand. Because what I want right now is a quick summary of how that went before we move on to more important things.' Sleizner turned to Bernstorff.

'Well, there's not much to say.' Bernstorff shrugged. 'He came along quietly and we conducted the interview as planned.'

'And he was cooperative and answered all your questions?'

'Yes, he was very calm and collected and actually didn't seem rattled in the slightest.'

'I suppose he feels he has nothing to hide.'

'How did he explain the fact that his skin was found under the woman's fingernails?' Hemmer asked.

'He admitted to having been with her on Saturday 28 July, which is to say the day she was murdered, but during the afternoon, four or five hours before Mogens Klinge's initiation ceremony, which was at eight in the evening.'

'What initiation ceremony?' Sleizner asked.

'We don't know exactly, but judging by the fact that the woman was a prostitute and from the text conversation on Klinge's old Ericsson phone, it could be some kind of sex club.'

'All right. So a proper deviant, in other words.' Sleizner shook his head. 'Anyway. Back to Jakob Sand. Was he able to help us identify her?'

'No, sadly. He picked her up on Istedgade, on the corner of Viktoriagade, and drove over to one of his properties out in Valby. Apparently, things got a bit rough, but as he pointed out, he was the one left bleeding, not her.'

Hemmer nodded. 'And why didn't he come forward of his own accord? It's been several days since we made pictures of her and her strange scar public.'

'If he is to be believed, he hasn't been following the reporting on the case and had no idea it was the same woman.'

'What did he have to say about the pocket square we found in her throat?'

'That it was a handsome one and he had one just like it himself.'

'Which is irrelevant anyway, since it's vanished from our collections,' Sleizner said. 'I assume you had no choice but to let him go. But what do you think, having talked to him? Is he our man?'

'Yes and no. On the one hand, he was far too calm, given how well known he is and that he's under serious suspicion. It was as though he knew exactly what I was going to ask him and had answers ready for me. On the other hand, I have to admit his answers were both logical and plausible.'

'All right.' Sleizner took the picture of Jakob Sand off the whiteboard and put it on the table. 'We're not dismissing him entirely, but we're going to put a pin in this and move on to Hesk's disappearance.'

'I'm sorry, but just because we put a pin in Sand doesn't necessarily mean we put the entire investigation on hold, does it?' Heinesen said.

'Who said anything about putting the investigation on hold?' Sleizner looked at him as though he were a bag of kitchen refuse that had been left sitting out in the sun for too long. 'I certainly didn't.'

'I thought you said we were going to move on to Hesk's disappearance,' he said, making an effort not to break eye contact. 'And I'm just saying that there are enough of us here to work on both things simultaneously. There are quite a few loose ends related to Sand that we should look into.'

'Of course there are,' Sleizner said. 'The question is just whether that's so much more important than the disappearance of our colleague. It's about priorities, Morten. Priorities. And right now, I want us to put all our eggs on Hesk. What you want to do is a matter for your memoirs.'

'Is there anything in particular you would want us to look into straight away?' Bernstorff asked Heinesen.

'Yes. For example, that corner of Istedgade and Viktoriagade. If it's true Sand picked her up there, there's a chance one of the other girls soliciting there might know who she was and can help us identify her.'

Bernstorff nodded and turned back to Sleizner, who nodded.

'That's an excellent idea, great, and of course we'll get to that. Absolutely. But not right this second, okay? It's simply going to have to wait for a day or two.'

'Why?' Heinesen said.

'Because there's no bloody rush! What's so hard to understand?' Sleizner stared at Heinesen. 'What needs seeing to quickly is the disappearance of our colleague. Every second counts.' He looked at each of them in turn. 'Jan Hesk might not mean as much to you as he does to me. Fair enough. But I'm asking you to get your priorities straight so that we can pull together to find out what happened to our colleague instead of wasting this short window of time by discussing a bunch of things that can easily wait.'

Bernstorff and Hemmer nodded, and Heinesen realized he had to as well, unless he wanted to start a full-scale war with Sleizner.

'Good. Then let's get to it.' Sleizner clapped his hands. 'I don't know if some of you have already heard, but this afternoon, Hesk's car was found in a car park by Islands Brygge, right outside Café Langebro.'

'Who found it?' Bernstorff asked.

'Some parking attendant writing a ticket. I'd flagged the registration number, so it must have come up on his screen or whatever. Either way, I've dispatched a diving team that should already be busy dragging the bottom along the pier.'

'So you're saying he fell into the water?' Hemmer said.

'No, I'm not saying anything. But the fact is that all it takes is one drink too many at that inn by Langebro and then straying too close to the edge.' Sleizner shrugged. 'Personally, I can't think of anything less like Hesk than that. But from what I hear, he's been a bit off-kilter these past few days. And I've promised his wife Lone to turn over every stone, and that's a promise I intend to keep.'

Once again, Heinesen followed the others' example and nodded, even though he didn't know what to think. He had so many questions, but no time to ask any of them. Sleizner wasn't there to turn over every stone. He clearly already had. And in no time at all.

'Hello, this is Houston. Houston to Morten.'

Heinesen turned to Sleizner, who brightened.

'Well, what do you know. There he is. Where did you go?'

Heinesen started to say something.

'Never mind,' Sleizner went on. 'Though you seemed to prefer it to being here.'

'I'm sorry, I was just wondering how—'

'Don't worry about it. We all need to zone out and take a break now and then. It's been a long day, and we're all tired. But before we say nighty-night, I want to know if you turned up anything in that parking garage. Did they have CCTV?'

Heinesen nodded and put the USB stick on the table. 'I was given this.'

'Great. Let's see if there's anything of interest on that, then.' Sleizner turned to Hemmer. 'Can you set it up?'

'What, you mean right now?' Hemmer picked up the USB stick and studied it. 'Because I could go over it tonight and edit together the interesting parts for tomorrow. That way, we could spend the time we have now—'

'Why wait, said the boy to the girl,' Sleizner broke in with a chuckle before suddenly slamming his fist down on the table. 'What the fuck's wrong with you lot? If you're not asleep in your chairs, you're pushing things until tomorrow. This is our colleague we're talking about, not some fucking nobody we can't even identify. This is about hours and minutes, if we want to have a chance. Not days.'

'Sorry, it was just a suggestion.' Hemmer plugged the USB stick into his laptop and connected the projector, which after a few commands began to play the recording from the four CCTV cameras in the garage on the screen Sleizner pulled down.

The picture was divided into four equal squares, each showing a different angle. Apparently, the cameras were equipped with motion sensors because there was either a car or a person passing by one or several of the four cameras. In the top-left corner, a timestamp said *3.00 p.m., 05.08.12*.

'Three in the afternoon's a bit early, don't you think,' Sleizner said as a maroon Volvo rolled down the ramp. 'When was your meeting over last night?'

Heinesen and the others exchanged looks.

'I think somewhere around eight or half past eight,' Bernstorff replied.

'All right, skip forward to eight o'clock. Like I said, we don't have all night.'

Hemmer nodded and fast-forwarded until the timestamp in the corner said *7.55 p.m., 05.08.12*.

A silver Lexus could be seen entering the garage and turning into an open bay, and then a woman with blonde hair in a bun, leather trousers and high heels climbed out of it and disappeared out of the shot. After that nothing happened and the cameras must have turned off, because the next clip began at *8.48 p.m., 05.08.12*, when a blue Peugeot came down the ramp.

'Correct me if I'm wrong,' Sleizner said as it reversed in and out of a parking spot a few times before finding the right angle. 'But isn't that Jan's old Peugeot?'

Heinesen nodded. That was Hesk's car and that was Hesk himself passing one of the other cameras shortly thereafter, his eyes intent on the two rows of parked cars.

Sleizner shook his head. 'I can't begin to imagine why he doesn't trade up to something peppier. With the salary he's on now, he could lease a Ferrari, no problem.'

So Hesk had gone to the garage on his own initiative. As Sleizner had suggested, he must have had a thought on his way home and decided to swing by to see if Jakob Sand or his car were there. And evidently he'd found what he was looking for, because now the bottom right square showed Hesk stopping next to a shiny red sports car and disappearing from view as he squeezed between it and a concrete pillar.

The next clip was from a few minutes later, as Hesk peeked out from behind the pillar with his phone pressed to his ear. His mouth moved as though he were talking, then he slipped his phone into his jacket pocket and started to walk towards the camera.

'Torben, could you check who that was he was talking to on the phone?' Heinesen turned to Hemmer, who nodded.

'Good idea, Morten,' Sleizner said, giving him a thumbs up.

They couldn't see what Hesk had spotted. But it was something, something that made him slip his right hand into his jacket, as though he were about to pull out his gun. But then he must have changed his mind and instead took out his police ID.

Had he confronted someone? Someone off camera? Yes, Heinesen could see him now. A third person, blocked from view by Hesk himself, only visible as a shadow on the concrete floor. Was this where things had gone off the rails?

'Am I seeing things, or is there someone standing right behind him?' Hemmer said.

'There is? Where?' Sleizner took a step closer to the screen.

'There.' Hemmer pointed. 'See that shadow on the floor?'

Before Sleizner could respond, the shadow launched itself at Hesk, who fell face first with a man on top of him. A man who once he got back up turned out to be a woman.

'What the fuck?' Sleizner turned to the others while Hesk struggled back onto his feet and once again blocked the woman from view. 'Did you see who that was? Huh? Did you?'

But they only recognized her when Hesk fell to the ground once more, this time unconscious and with his gun in his hand.

'That's Dunja Hougaard,' Sleizner said, while Dunja bent over Hesk, took the gun out of his hand, grabbed both his hands and dragged him across the concrete floor, out of the frame. 'Of all the bastards out there, she's the one who's taken him.'

Heinesen was speechless. Dunja Hougaard. Was this really happening?

That Sleizner hated her above everything else had escaped no one, and when he'd put out an APB on her, most people had agreed he'd taken his personal vendetta a step too far. But apparently, he hadn't. Instead, it now looked as though he'd been a step ahead of the rest of them.

'Could we see that again, please?' he said finally, and when the images flickered past again, he could confirm that it really was her, knocking Hesk unconscious with a single elbow and then dragging him away across the floor. In the next clip, ninety minutes later, two men in camouflage could be seen passing a camera, carrying something that couldn't be anything other than a human body, wrapped in bin bags and duct tape.

'Wait, hold on a second.' Bernstorff turned to the others. 'This Dunja you all apparently know, what has she got to do with our investigation?'

'That's a good question.' Sleizner turned to her. 'A very good question. She was a member of this unit for a few years, and those of you who know me know I never liked her. The list of acts of misconduct and outright criminality she's guilty of is longer than a bog roll. I'm not surprised she's dangerous and a potential threat. That's exactly why we have an APB out for her. But I do have to say this really takes the cake.'

'And what does she have against Hesk?' Hemmer said.

'Another good question.' Sleizner shrugged just as Hesk's blue Peugeot appeared in the top-left frame, driving back up the ramp to the exit. 'The only thing I know is that they had some disagreements back when she was new and they were working the same case. And for what it's worth, Jan has always been loyal to me, and that might obviously rankle with someone who—' He was interrupted by his own phone. 'Yes, this is Kim Sleizner... I see... Okay...' He heaved a deep sigh and started rubbing his forehead with his free hand. 'No, there's no point. You might as well stop and pack it up... Bye.' He ended the call, put his phone down, swallowed, wiped first one eye then the other, before turning to the others. 'They've found his body.'

43

FINDING THE HOME address of Flemming Friis, the director of the Helsingør Detention Facility, had required no more than a few clicks on his phone during the ferry ride across the sound to Denmark. Koldingvej 6, just south of Helsingør, a red-brick house that reminded him of the one his grandmother had lived in before she was moved to a nursing home against her will, after which she'd shrivelled into nothing in less than six months.

Fabian had already met Friis twice. But neither time had he felt he'd been given an honest account of the details of Theodor's suicide. He'd been met with excuses and contrived justifications.

Which was why he wasn't seeking him out at work this time, but at home, in the evening. Because this wasn't work, it was personal. Which was also why he hadn't brought his gun.

He parked on the street right outside the house. He wasn't about to waste time searching the sleepy residential neighbourhood for a secluded spot to leave his car in. He wasn't the one who had something to hide.

Then he opened the glovebox, pulled out the cloth parcel containing the gun Theodor had come home with and unwrapped it. Once he'd loaded the magazine up with ammunition and pushed it into the butt, he stuck the unmarked pistol into his chest holster and climbed out of the car.

Like several of the other houses on the street, Friis's house was encircled by a six-foot fence that completely hid it from view. Granted, there was both a garage door and a locked gate with an entry phone, but Fabian opted to climb over the fence and drop down on the other side instead. After all, this wasn't a visit, more like a visitation.

Gardening clearly wasn't high on Friis's list of hobbies. Granted, the lawn was mown, but so dry and brown a ray of sunlight through a pair of glasses might easily set it on fire. Here and there were old currant bushes that had long since given up on producing any berries, and in the middle of the garden, next to some outdoor furniture, stood a drying rack full of underwear. Judging from the garments on it, the Friis family consisted of Flemming himself, his wife and their two children, of which one was a daughter in her early teens and the other a son of about ten.

In the corner on his right, there was a swing set and a sandbox that nature was well on its way to reclaiming. And next to that, a trampoline, on the edge of which sat the son, staring at him. Fabian raised one hand and waved with a smile. As though it were perfectly natural for a complete stranger to come climbing over the fence.

'Who are you?' the boy asked in Danish, and he stood up on the trampoline.

'My name's Fabian,' Fabian replied, continuing to wave. 'Fabian Risk.'

But the boy didn't wave back. Instead, he looked over at the house and back several times before speaking. 'I know what you did, and you're not supposed to do that.'

'No, you're right,' Fabian said, starting to walk towards the trampoline. 'But sometimes people do things anyway. Right? Have you never done that? Something you weren't supposed to?'

The boy shook his head.

'Are you sure? I mean, sometimes you have no choice.'

'You always have a choice. At least, that's what my dad says.'

Fabian nodded. 'That's exactly what I used to tell my son, too.'

'You have a son? How old is he? Is he as big as me?'

Fabian laughed and nodded. 'Sixteen. He would have been seventeen come spring.'

The boy looked at him, full of questions. But he didn't ask any of them, just walked over and sat back down on the edge of the trampoline. 'My mum, she's from Sweden, too.'

'Is that right. So you speak both Danish and Swedish. Impressive.'

'I've never lived in Sweden, but Granny and Grandpa live there. And my uncle, and my cousins. Though I took an ice lolly from the freezer without asking today.' The boy turned to Fabian and looked him straight in the eye. 'I just did it, even though I'm not supposed to. But I didn't tell anyone.'

'I won't tell on you, if you promise not to tell anyone what I just did.'

Another long pause.

'Are you one of the good guys or one of the people my dad locks up?'

'I've tried to do the right thing my entire life, tried to be one of the good guys, but things didn't turn out too well, and now...' Fabian shrugged. 'Now I honestly don't know any more.'

'Well, you seem pretty nice. If you want, I could tell my dad not to lock you up.'

'That's nice of you, but it—'

'Hey!' someone shouted from inside the house.

Fabian turned around and saw Flemming Friis in an open window with no shirt on.

'What the fuck are you doing here?' he continued. 'Get out! This is private property!'

'His name's Fabian Risk and he's from Sweden,' the boy shouted back.

Even though there was at least thirty feet between them, Fabian could see Friis's face go rigid.

'Anton! Come inside, right now!'

'Why?'

'Because I say so! You're coming inside, and that's that!'

'But I don't want to.'

'Anton! Listen to your father and do what he says,' shouted a woman standing in the next window, waving for him to hurry.

'Maybe you'd better do what they tell you.' Fabian tousled the boy's hair. 'So I can have a chat with your dad.'

The boy sighed and let him lift him down from the trampoline. 'But promise you won't tell him about the ice lolly. Promise.'

'I promise.'

They shook hands and then the boy ran off across the lawn and up towards the house. Moments later, Flemming Friis came striding towards him, pulling a shirt down over his stomach.

'I don't know what you think you're doing,' he said, pointing straight at him. 'But unless you get off my property right now, the way you came, I'm going to have to call the police.'

'Your son's nice,' Fabian said, making no move to leave. 'A proper delight, actually.'

'Get out of here. Do you hear me? Out!'

'It must be nice to come home to a family where no one's missing. For your sake, I hope you have the time to enjoy it. Because you never know how long it'll last.'

'Okay, I'm calling the police, and they can come pick you up.' Friis pulled out his phone and unlocked it.

'I have a suggestion. How about we skip the phone thing?' In two strides, Fabian was there, snatching the phone out of Friis's hand and hurling it across the lawn. 'They emit all kinds of carcinogenic radiation anyway.'

The closed fist hit his face full force. But he didn't feel it. Just heard something break inside his nose, which began to bleed.

'Get out of here, you fucking prick!' Friis roared, pulling out a gun with trembling hands. 'And yes, I will shoot. I swear. I'll shoot unless you leave right now.'

'That makes two of us.' Fabian pulled out his gun, disengaged the safety, and aimed it at Friis. 'The question now is who has more to lose. You or me?' In one smooth motion, he grabbed the barrel of Friis's gun with his left hand and pushed it aside while at the same time kicking his legs out from under him.

The whole thing happened so quickly Friis had no time to react before he was on his back on the ground with Fabian straddling him and the muzzle of a gun pressed to either temple.

'I don't have a family any more,' Fabian continued, as dark-red droplets from his nose landed on Friis's face. 'You've already had a hand in taking my son from me. The rest of my family left me today. So without knowing too much about your life, I'd wager you have more to lose. Quite a bit more, from what little I've seen.'

'What do you want?' Friis was shaking uncontrollably, well on his way towards a breakdown. 'What the fuck is it you want?'

'I want to get out of here,' Fabian said, the blood from his nose spattering Friis's face. 'I want nothing more than to leave you, your wife, your daughter, and above all your lovely son alone. But in order to get up and climb over that fence, I need to hear from you what really happened to my son. Why he was repeatedly subjected to serious beatings in your detention facility. Why he was put in solitary in a storage room where everything he needed once he couldn't take it any more was already to hand.'

'I've already told you. I told you he—'

Fabian struck him with the gun. A blow so hard blood began to pump out of the resulting cut just below one of his eyes. 'Now we're both bleeding. It's up to you if you want it to stop.'

'I don't fucking know. I can't tell you any more than I already—'

The next blow landed in the exact same spot as the first, making the cut so deep it would forever remain a part of him.

'Apparently not.' Fabian studied Friis battling the pain. 'Which puts us at a bit of an impasse. You can't tell me more than you already have, and I can't leave until I have an answer. So the question becomes, what do we do now? Because there's this rumour making the rounds that the abuse my son endured was ordered by the senior management. Which is to say, by you.'

'No.' Friis shook his head. 'No, that's not right.'

'I would be very, very careful if I were you.' Using one hand and the end of the barrel, Fabian forced Friis's mouth open, despite the man's resistance and protests. 'You see, I've already crossed so many lines. Lines I wouldn't have strayed anywhere near just a few days ago.' Then he pushed the gun in as far as it would go. 'So for your own sake, don't make me cross another.'

Friis tried to say something, but Fabian couldn't make out the words. Probably more excuses. Excuses that would make him pull the trigger if he had to listen to them.

He'd reached the end of the road. His options had narrowed

to an either/or situation. Keep going or end it. The temptation to do the latter had never been greater. As though it weren't really up to him. As though he'd always gravitated towards this. Like Matilda had said. Towards a final decision. As though everything were preordained.

He lowered his eyes and pulled the barrel of the gun out of Friis's mouth. Sweaty and bloody, Friis coughed and started to talk.

'It wasn't me, Fabian. You have to believe me. It wasn't me,' Friis panted as Fabian got up. 'I was just following orders from Copenhagen. You know? From Kim. Do you know who he is? Kim Sleizner?'

44

THEY'D PARKED THE van just feet away from the old remodelled silo on the top floor of which Sleizner lived. It wasn't an inconspicuous spot, exactly; they were sitting in the middle of a cycle lane on Islands Brygge. A cycle lane that was an extension of Bryggebron, which in turned led to Vesterbro, and was consequently relatively heavily trafficked.

She'd suggested they park in one of the many open spots on the street behind the silo, so as not to be in full view of every last person passing by. But Fareed had insisted, claiming this was the least bad option. Sleizner's flat overlooked the water, and if they wanted to connect to the cameras once he was inside, they couldn't have the bulk of the building between them and the van.

At least they'd found a manhole cover to open up and cone off, and to improve their cover even more, they'd dropped a few loose cables down the hole. Now, Dunja could only hope their preparations in Sleizner's flat wouldn't take too long.

There had been no room for hope when it came to Mikael Rønning. The shock of learning that he was colluding with Sleizner was so overwhelming she wasn't sure she'd ever recover from it. That he almost certainly had only the best intentions, thinking it was for her own good, didn't change the fact that it was the deepest betrayal she'd ever experienced.

That, coupled with the fire and Qiang's murder, had changed

everything. Any game plan they'd had was gone, any rule book thrown out. No more lurking in the shadows, keeping their distance, trying to collect enough evidence to convict Sleizner in a court of law. From now on, she couldn't care less about the law or keeping things above board.

Instead, they'd worked out a new plan that would make Sleizner confess immediately. A plan that was as simple and effective as it was forbidden.

'*All right, I'm in the lobby,*' Fareed's voice said through the speakers, and on the screen showing the feed from his front-facing camera, Dunja could see him put the pick gun back in its case and walk further into the building.

'Take the lift,' she said. 'Less risk of running into anyone.'

'*But I'll lose contact with you until I'm back out.*'

'Then let's cross our fingers we're not too far apart once you're up there.'

On one screen, she watched Fareed walk towards the lift. On the other, she was the eyes in the back of his head. But the moment the lift doors slid shut, the images began to freeze and skip and then both screens went black.

At the same time, an alarm went off to tell her it was nine o'clock, and she hurriedly clicked her way to the police's website and the link to the live press conference Sleizner had advertised. No one knew exactly what it was going to be about, and the media had speculated about everything from a big break in the ongoing murder investigation to him announcing his resignation.

She didn't really care all that much. The only thing that mattered to her was that Sleizner definitely wasn't home. That they would be able to complete their preparations undisturbed. For that reason, she felt less than good about the fact that the podium in front of all the cameras and microphones was still empty, despite it being several minutes past nine now.

Granted, it was hardly out of the ordinary for a press conference to start late, especially if Sleizner was involved. He loved making people wait. But this particular time, it was worrying. Was this entire spectacle intended as bait, to lure them into a trap?

The feeds from Fareed's cameras flickered back to life, revealing that he'd stepped out of the lift and was heading towards the front door with a sign that read *K. Sleizner* on it.

'Hey,' she said, adjusting her headset. 'I'm wondering whether we should hold off.'

'*Why?*' Fareed replied. '*This is our chance.*'

'The thing is that the press conference still hasn't started. The stage is empty, and what if the whole thing is a—'

'*Okay, I get it,*' Fareed cut in, and the screens showed him looking around for a place to hide.

'I think you'd better come back here,' she said, without taking her eyes off the screen that showed the empty podium. 'As soon as possible, before you— Or actually, hold on, something's happening now,' she interrupted herself. 'Yes, here he comes, finally.' She'd never been happier to see Sleizner. 'We're good. Carry on.'

On the TV screen, Sleizner took a seat on the stage, poured himself a glass of water and took a few sips. At the same time, the other screens showed Fareed back at the door, busy examining the code lock.

For being alone on a stage, the centre of everyone's attention, Sleizner seemed unusually reserved. '*I'd like to begin by thanking you all for coming to this press conference. I also want to take this opportunity to apologize for making you wait.*' He trailed off and took another sip of his water.

Dunja felt confused. She couldn't remember Sleizner ever apologizing before.

'*As some of you might know, my name is Kim Sleizner,*' he went on. '*I'm the head of the homicide unit here in Copenhagen, and this morning, I was informed that one of my colleagues, Jan Hesk, had been missing since last night.*' He broke off and swallowed a few times before continuing. '*Following an intensive search, this afternoon my fears were confirmed.*' He paused again and emptied his glass. '*Today at 2.25, our diving team found Jan Hesk's body in the water off Islands Brygge.*'

Jan Hesk was dead. Dunja caught herself staring blindly into space, shaking her head. Hesk, who'd always been part of the homicide unit and who always would be, like a law of nature. They hadn't exactly got along while they were working together. She'd found him slow and overly conservative, and he'd been irked when she, a rookie, had stepped on his toes. But even so, he'd always been there when she needed him.

'Jan Hesk is dead,' she told Fareed, who was disassembling the code lock. 'That's what the press conference is about.'

'*Dead? But...? How? We saw him just last night when—*'

'I know. But apparently, they found him right here, off Islands Brygge, this afternoon.'

'*Jan Hesk wasn't just one of my most competent colleagues,*' Sleizner continued, his voice catching. '*He was also one of my very closest friends. Which is why it's extremely painful for me to have to tell you that the autopsy showed that his death was not an accident. Jan Hesk was murdered.*'

She hadn't seen him in years, and then they'd run into each other just a few hours before he died. Before he was murdered. Was it a coincidence, or just another move from the man behind the podium?

The question hung in the air unanswered because on one of the four screens, which showed the immediate area around the van, she noticed a parking attendant approaching the cones around the manhole. This was exactly what she'd feared, but there was nothing she could do about it. If the parking attendant wanted to slap a ticket on the van, let him. It was really the least of their problems.

'*The murder of an officer of the law is, as I'm sure you understand, something we take very seriously, which is why an investigation has already been launched,*' she heard Sleizner continue.

'*Okay, I'm in,*' Fareed said just as the parking attendant stepped past their cones and shone his torch down the open manhole, before taking out his phone and photographing everything from the manhole and the cones to their van.

'*And how are you getting on?*'

'You mean apart from the fact that someone killed Hesk and that some overzealous parking attendant is standing outside, taking pictures?'

'*What kind of pictures?*'

'Of the hole and the van and—'

'*You have to go out there and talk to him.*'

'About what? There's not that much to—'

'*Make something up, anything, so long as he buys it.*'

'Okay.' She got up and stepped out via the back door. 'Excuse me,' she said as she walked up to the parking attendant, who turned to her. 'Is there a problem?'

'You can't park here. You're in the middle of the cycle lane.'

'We're aware of that, but this cable work needs to be done.'

'What cable work? I don't see anything about this in our system.'

'You don't?'

'No, so I'm going to have to ask you to pack up your things and free up this cycle lane as soon as possible.'

'I'm afraid I can't do that. As you can see, we're in the middle of this and we can't move until—'

'That's your problem. Not mine,' the parking attendant broke in. 'I'll give you five minutes. Then I have to file a report.'

'Okay, hold on. How is it our problem that you can't see this in your system? I realize that sucks for you, but I honestly don't know what I'm supposed to do about it.'

'You're supposed to pack up and move the van, since you don't have a permit for—'

'Who said we don't have a permit, just because you can't see it on your screen? I don't know.' She shrugged. 'You probably have a new IT system or something.'

'Granted, we do, but these things don't normally glitch. It's almost always the location and timestamp of tickets that won't—'

'Look, I'm sorry.' Dunja held up her hands. 'But I don't have time for this. We have some fibreoptic cables that need fixing, and we've been cleared since this morning. What is or isn't showing up on your screen is between you and your IT department. And now I'm going to have to ask you to move back behind the cordon. It's an insurance issue. Otherwise, I'm going to have to file a report.'

The parking attendant backed up to the other side of the cones and stood there for a minute, looking from his handheld computer to the van to the open manhole and back before finally turning away and moving on.

Dunja climbed back into the van, closed the doors, and sat down to report that the problem was solved. But what she saw made her freeze mid-movement with her eyes on one of the screens, which, like a mirror, showed her own face. It was several seconds before she could bring herself to turn the volume back up.

'*Dunja Hougaard used to work for me,*' Sleizner said. '*Even back then, she had several disputes with Jan Hesk, and two years ago, after, among other things, falsifying my signature, I had no choice but to fire her.*'

'Hello? Dunja, are you there?' said Fareed, who seemed to be exploring the luxury flat.

'Yes, I'm here, Fareed. But Sleizner, he... he's accusing me.'

'*Little did I know that just a couple of years later, I'd have to send out an internal APB for her, which I did no more than two days ago,*' Sleizner went on. '*And now this.*' He fell silent and shook his head.

'Dunja, here it is.' Fareed was in a windowless room in front of a multigym with cables, weights, and various handles to pull on. '*But there's not enough room in here to fit a camera and everything.*'

'Fareed, he's saying I killed him,' she said. 'Do you understand? I'm the one he—'

'*But this should work. Right? There's even a fan in here.*' Fareed entered a kitchen with a wide hob underneath an equally oversized kitchen fan. '*All we need to do is move this table aside,*' he went on. '*Hello? Dunja? You can see that I'm in the kitchen, right? Or have you lost the camera feeds?*'

'*And how do you know Dunja Hougaard is behind this murder?*' asked one of the reporters on the screen.

'No, I can both hear and see you,' Dunja said into her headset. 'But can you hear me?'

'*Thanks for asking that question,*' Sleizner replied. '*I was just getting to that.*'

'*Loud and clear,*' Fareed replied as he started to pull the chairs out from around the dining table. '*A bit choppy and delayed, but no biggie.*'

'*This footage is from late last night,*' Sleizner continued. '*It's from a CCTV camera in a parking garage in inner-city Copenhagen.*'

Not even a day had passed since it happened. Yet somehow, she had managed to suppress any memory of it. But it all came flooding back now. Now that she was watching the CCTV footage in which Hesk was standing with his back towards the camera with a gun in his hand.

She could hear the sound of a distant helicopter in the background. She hadn't noticed it when she was standing down there in the garage, right behind him. Then, her focus had been on stopping him from walking right into the lion's den. But now, seeing him collapse after she struck him, she almost couldn't take in that she was the one who'd done that.

The sound of the helicopter kept growing louder, even though the clip was over and Sleizner was back on the screen, and only now did she realize the sound wasn't coming from the press conference.

'*We can set up the camera here and put the gym there.*' On the screen, Fareed was looking around the kitchen, where the dining table had now been pushed into a corner. '*But it's too heavy for me to move on my own.*'

'*Right now, our focus is on apprehending her, and we're grateful for any information the public can give us.*'

'Fareed, you have to listen to me,' she said as she watched herself take the gun out of Hesk's hand, stick it into her waistband, and drag him away across the concrete floor. 'They've—'

'*But with your help, it shouldn't be a problem.*'

'Fareed, for fuck's sake,' she broke in as their van appeared on the screen.

'*We have good reason to suspect that they're travelling in this van, registration number DH 48 895. All patrols have already been informed...*'

'*But that's the only way if we want to get the gym into—*'

'Would you just shut up and listen?'

'*Hello? Dunja, did you say something?*'

The sound of the helicopter was now so loud she could easily pick out the clatter of the rotor blades from the sound of the engine.

'Yes, I did. I'm wanted for Hesk's murder,' she said, trying to see on the screens where the helicopter was coming in to land. But she couldn't see it through the front, back or side cameras.

'*I can barely hear you. Try speaking into the headset.*'

'I am! But there's a helicopter flying around here.'

'*Yes, I can hear it too. Maybe they're still dragging the water.*'

'No, they already have a perpetrator in mind, and it's me!'

'*Seriously?*'

'Yes, the prick was just on live TV, showing footage from the garage of me knocking Hesk out and dragging him to the van. They're circulating the registration number of the—'

'*Okay, I'm on my way. Pack up the stuff and we'll go.*'

Dunja stood up and was just about to move towards the back doors when a loud thud made the whole van rock. She turned back to the screen but still couldn't see anyone outside. She didn't put it together until there was another thud and the metal roof above her sagged.

'They're already here.' With her eyes on the roof, she shuffled backwards towards the driver's seat. 'I can't wait for you. See you at the rendezvous point instead.' She slid in behind the wheel and put the key in the ignition as the sound of approaching sirens cut through the roar of the helicopter.

But before she could turn the key, a man in dark clothes from the special intervention unit came sliding down the windscreen from the roof and landed on the ground by the driver's door. A few blows with the butt of his automatic rifle were enough to break the window so he could open the door.

Dunja was moving towards the back doors as quickly as she was able when they were thrown open by yet another dark-clad man wearing a bulletproof vest and a helmet. She tried to back up to get out via the side door, but strong hands had already grabbed her ankles and were pulling her out of the van and down onto the ground, where she was flipped onto her stomach and had her hands cuffed behind her back.

'Are you Camilla Krystchoff?' a voice said, and when she didn't respond, a hand pulled her head up while another blinded her with a powerful torch. 'Yes, it's her.'

Then she was pulled onto her feet and dragged towards one of the flashing police cars that skidded to a stop in front of them. A door was opened, and she was pushed into the back seat, buckled in and driven off, past the parking attendant who was standing next to two uniformed officers, watching her.

45

Lone Hesk sucked in the smoke as though she were trying
to set a new record for longest drag. Right now, it was the
only thing that worked. The nicotine made her blood vessels
contract and drove her heart rate up. Never mind that her
old cough was back. Tobacco kept her nerves in check. She
took another marathon drag, and the cigarette grew so hot it
burned her fingers.

'Lone... never let it burn past the line.' Sleizner shook his
head as he turned onto Frederik V's Vej by Rigshospitalet.
'Take my word for it. It's a slippery slope. Once you cross that
line, everything else in life eventually starts going downhill
too. Before you know it, you've stopped making your bed and
pulling up your blinds, and the only thing you have the energy
to do while you shovel down cold ravioli straight from the tin
is to dig through the ashtray for butts.'

She wanted to tell him to shut his know-it-all mouth and
keep his advice to himself. But it was his car. Even though he
was one of Copenhagen's busiest men right now, he'd driven
all the way out to Amager to pick her up, and now he was
letting her sit there, saturating his upholstery with cigarette
smoke. No, now that she thought about it, she was the one
who should shut up. His intentions were good, she knew that.

In fact, Sleizner had been very attentive since Jan disappeared.
He hadn't just stopped by, he'd called several times too, to

make sure she was okay. As okay as someone in her position could be. But he was nice, he was. Just driving her over to Forensics like this, to identify the body, was going above and beyond.

They turned into an open parking spot in the gravel under the trees that, together with the dense shrubberies, formed a green wall of leaves that blocked the view of Fælled Park on the other side. 'Here. Have a new one instead.' Sleizner held out a full packet of Prince Red.

'I never took you for a smoker.' She rolled down her window and dropped the smouldering butt.

'I'm not.' Sleizner flicked the underside of the packet with his middle finger, pushing a few of the cigarettes up a little. 'These are for you. I figured you might need them, given what lies ahead.'

She tried to smile while she pulled out another and let him light it, but it turned into a grimace.

'Just take your time,' he continued, patting her thigh. 'I've let them know we're here and asked them to make sure the department's empty while we're in there, so there's no rush.'

'Thank you,' she said, nodding. 'Thank you.' She didn't know what else to say. He probably already knew she couldn't have done any of this without him.

At least she'd grabbed the bull by the horns and told Katrine the night before. At first, she'd planned to wait until after the identification today. But like her mother and sister, Sleizner had insisted – and they were obviously right – that even if her daughter didn't watch the news or read the paper, there was nothing to say her friends or their parents didn't.

She'd tried to prepare herself by giving a lot of thought to how best to put it. But once they were sitting on the sofa, her mind had gone blank, and she'd heard herself say *Daddy's dead.* She'd sounded like a news reader on P1. *They found him a few hours ago in the water off Islands Brygge and there is an investigation into potential wrongdoing.*

The silence that followed had made the living room implode. Katrine had just sat there, shaking her head with her hands over her ears. Then she'd got to her feet and screamed at her that she was lying and making things up so she could have sole custody now that her dad had finally done the right thing and left her. And she'd just sat there and taken it, all her accusations, whether fair or not, until she'd heard Katrine's door slam shut as she locked herself in her room.

Since then, it had been impossible to get through to her. Every attempt at starting something akin to a conversation had been met with immutable silence on the other side of the door. When Sleizner had called in the middle of it, to check in on her, she'd fallen apart. He'd offered to come over, and even though she had explicitly declined, just like she had refused to have her mother or sister or even Adam over, he'd jumped in his car and driven out to support her.

And for some reason, Katrine had listened to him. He'd even managed to make her come out of her room and sit next to her on the sofa so they could give each other a much-needed hug and a shoulder to cry on. Then he'd made a pot of tea, which he'd served with honey and a few crisp rolls he'd found in the pantry, before taking his leave so they could be alone. And now here she was, wasting both her own and his time while her cigarette burned ever closer to her fingers.

She was in no way ready to go into that mortuary and look at him. But when was she ever going to be? When was she going to be strong enough to accept that he'd left her and not the other way around? That she was the one left standing all alone, with a mortgage she couldn't afford and a shop that should be shuttered as quickly as possible. Probably never, so she might as well get this over with.

A quick nod. He understood and climbed out of the car, and before she had unbuckled, he'd opened the passenger door and rolled up the window.

'Let me help you out. There's a puddle right here.'

She took Sleizner's hand and stepped over the brown puddle, where her cigarette butt bobbed like a tiny boat, with a smoking chimney and everything.

They were greeted in the lobby of Forensics by a man and a woman in white coats, who were waiting to take them to the mortuary.

The further into the building they got, the heavier it felt. As though she were walking straight into her own guilty conscience. As though all the things she'd tried to suppress were coming out of the shadows.

Her complaining and constant disapproval must in the end have made him take unnecessary risks in his eagerness to show her he wasn't as useless as she always claimed.

The man in the white coat punched in a code and held open a door. The woman showed them into a cool room with square metal doors in three rows along two of the walls. It smelled clean.

Together, the man and the woman in white opened one of the compartments in the middle row, pulled out a covered body and stepped aside.

'I would prefer if you left the room and waited outside until we're done,' Sleizner said.

'But we need to be present to verify that...'

'No, you don't. I'm a police officer and I will verify whatever it is you need.' He walked over to them and took the folders they were holding out of their hands. 'We'll be out when we're done.'

The man and the woman exchanged a look before nodding reluctantly and stepping out. Sleizner turned to her.

'Come on, let's get this over with,' he said, taking her hand.

Skin against skin, just like that. It crossed a line, but it felt good. The whole thing was confusing, and her feelings were racing in every direction, but once she looked up at the tray on which she could make out the contours of her husband's body under the white sheet, she realized she had no choice but to get it over with.

'Lone, you take your time now.' Sleizner had turned to her. 'Like I said, there's no rush, and if you want to be alone, I can wait outside too, and you just come out when you're done.'

'I'd like you to stay,' she said, and made sure she didn't let go of his hand. If it weren't for him, she would have collapsed.

'Okay, are you ready?'

'How do I know if I'm ready?'

'You'll be fine.' He pinched a corner of the sheet and turned it aside.

She was unprepared for the sobs that began to rack her body the moment she saw his face. His peaceful face, whose closed eyes showed that nothing could ever trouble him again. Unlike her, who was standing there, shaking as though something deep inside her had broken.

They had a perpetrator, she knew that much. A woman called Dunja Hougaard. But why and how she had killed Jan was unclear to her. Sleizner had asked how much detail she wanted, and she had replied as little as possible. But now, she wanted to know. Now, she wanted to know exactly what that woman had done to her husband.

'The first thing we have to do is make sure this really is Jan.'

Sleizner turned to her. 'So the question is if you need to see more of him to clearly identify him.'

'What did she do to him?'

'Pardon?'

'This Dunja. What did she do to my Jan? I want you to tell me everything you know.'

'Oh, Lone...' Sleizner sighed and shook his head. 'Do you really want to go down that road now?'

'I need to know. Can't you understand that? That's my Jan lying there. My husband who suddenly... just doesn't exist any more.'

'Of course I understand.' Sleizner nodded and put his arms around her. 'I absolutely understand.' He held her so tight she could smell his deodorant. It was the same one Jan had always worn, Dior Sauvage; she'd bought it for him for Christmas after that dinner on Islands Brygge. 'But we'll know so much more in a few days, and I think you'll be more ready then, too,' he continued, lightly touching her back.

She'd considered whether to wear some kind of coat or jacket before finally deciding it was too warm out. So now, she was standing there in her thin summer dress that was cut far too low in the back and she could feel his hands moving up and down her spine.

'But you'll be glad to hear she has been arrested,' he went on as his hands continued to explore her back. 'We haven't made that public, though, so you have to promise to keep it to yourself for now.'

She nodded, even though all her attention was on his caressing hand. She wanted to slap it away and scream at him to stop. But she didn't have the strength; all she could muster was a shake of the head.

'There, there. It's okay, Lone. It's okay.' He stroked her hair with one hand while he let the other one slip in underneath her dress.

'Kim. I don't want to.'

He shushed her and continued his light caresses. 'I know it's hard. But it's going to be okay. I promise. So long as we can trust each other, everything will be okay. That's the most important thing right now. Do you know what I mean?' His hands stopped and he tried to catch her eye.

'I don't know.'

'What I'm trying to say is that you're not alone in this. Maybe it feels like you are, but you're not. I'm here for you, and I'm going to do everything and then some to find out exactly what happened and make sure this Dunja is punished, not just once but several times over. So don't worry about that part. I promise. There's no need to worry. Are you with me?'

She didn't know but nodded anyway.

The kiss was a complete surprise; she didn't see it coming. Suddenly, his lips were pressed to hers and she could feel the tip of his tongue looking for a way in. She tried to pull away and push him back. Then she intended to accept his earlier offer of leaving her alone and go over to the sink and rinse out her mouth.

But she didn't succeed. She was so exhausted she didn't have it in her to resist, and even though there was only the tiniest of cracks between her lips, his tongue managed to push inside and fill her mouth. In order not to suffocate, she let her own tongue fight back in what became a dance between the two of them. A dance she'd only danced once before, in his bathroom at that horrid, filthy dinner. And just like then, it was both a game and a fight, like two tigers on their hind legs, both aware which one of them would be left standing once the dust settled.

The slap was involuntary, and she could feel her palm throb

after it landed. 'I think you should leave now,' she heard herself say. She'd hit him. But apparently that was what it took to make him stop and understand how wrong it was. On just how many levels this was fucked up.

She'd been prepared for a reaction. But even so, she had a hard time computing what happened after the blow, other than that she felt whiplashed. Dazed, she tried to push him off her, but he was too strong.

What followed was something she would attempt to suppress the memory of with pills, alcohol, and endless broken relationships for the rest of her life.

46

AT A SMALL round table at the back of the café, Morten
Heinesen forced himself to swallow another bite of a dry salami
and Brie sandwich that didn't have enough butter, salami or,
above all, Brie in it. He'd had to buy something other than a
coffee to justify occupying a table while he worked.

He'd told Hemmer and Bernstorff he was going to skip
lunch and go for a walk instead, and to avoid running into
either of them, or anyone else he knew for that matter, he'd
opted to go to one of the countless cafés around Strøget.

It was all very unlike him. But over the past few days, things
had been happening so fast. Decisions and progress had been
made, and he'd barely been able to keep up with the twists
and turns.

What he needed now was to slow down and reflect, think
clearly, and that wasn't possible while sitting at a desk where
everyone insisted on constantly bombarding him with their
opinions.

The sandwich grew like spray foam in his mouth, and after
making sure no one was looking, he surreptitiously spat the
ball of saggy dough into a napkin, which he then buried under
even more napkins. His laptop was open on the table in front
of him. All he needed to do was insert the USB stick so he could
go over the CCTV footage from the parking garage again at
his own pace.

That Hesk was not just missing but confirmed dead, and that his killer was Dunja Hougaard, felt like the plot of a film that was too bad to run on anything but some obscure cable channel in the middle of the night. But they'd all seen it happen with their own eyes; she'd knocked him out and dragged him off like a sack of potatoes.

He'd had his fair share of dealings with Dunja during her time on the homicide unit. But he wouldn't say he knew her. He'd thought of her as competent and dedicated, and she'd joined the team with unusual verve and energy.

At the same time, there had been something ruthless about her, as though she would have gone to any lengths to get what she wanted. He didn't know if that was what had annoyed Hesk.

Hesk had been the one with all the experience, who was finally going to reap the rewards of his years of dedicated service when Dunja came in out of left field and stole the spotlight. In a matter of months, their dynamic had turned toxic, and before long they'd had trouble even being in the same room.

Which was why it was more or less incomprehensible that the two of them had been in contact again, and that was one of the big question marks surrounding his colleague's death. Had they agreed to meet in the garage? And if so, what role did Dunja play in their investigation?

The questions were confounding in themselves, since there had never been many question marks surrounding Hesk before. A more open book than him was hard to imagine. Pretty much everything he'd done, he'd done in concert with the team. Unlike Dunja, who'd had a habit of taking off on her own, Hesk had always advocated for teamwork and clear, open communication.

But apparently not this time, since he'd decided to fly solo, without informing him or Hemmer and Bernstorff, much less Sleizner. The most likely reason for that was the defeat he'd suffered at the meeting in his flat, after he'd revealed that he was convinced the whole thing was a big conspiracy aimed at him and their investigation.

None of them, himself included, had taken Hesk entirely seriously. With regards to that or his misgivings about Sleizner. They hadn't even let him explain himself properly, almost as though it had been too much for them to take in, and it didn't take a university degree to see how frustrating that must have been.

That said, most things pointed to Jakob Sand being the one who'd killed the woman in the car, not Sleizner. But that didn't change the fact that something wasn't right with their boss. Something was simmering behind his smiling façade. It was especially obvious in his handling of Hesk's disappearance.

Heinesen had reacted to it right away, in that first meeting. Not only had everything happened too fast but, more importantly, events had unfolded too smoothly. It was almost as though Sleizner had known Hesk had gone to that garage and been caught on camera with Dunja, but also that it would look better if another member of the team, rather than he himself, went to retrieve the USB stick. Even the way it had been handed over to him had felt unnatural.

That they'd found the body just hours later was also remarkable. It could, of course, simply be down to solid police work in combination with a big portion of luck. Sleizner had always possessed an intuitive ability to steer investigations in the right direction, and they'd never had a higher clearance rate than with him at the helm. He didn't want to even consider the alternative. Not until he had conclusive proof.

The first thing he was going to do was find out who Hesk had been on the phone with when he peeked out from behind the concrete pillar. Hemmer had managed to find the number, which was Swedish, and while the signals crossed the border, Heinesen prepared to revive the rusty Swedish his father had once taught him.

'*Yes, hello, this is Malin Rehnberg.*'

'Hello, my name is Morten Heinesen. I'm calling from the Copenhagen Police.'

'*Okay,*' she said after a brief pause. '*Right.*'

He could hear her sit down. 'Excuse me, but can I ask who I'm talking to?'

'*It would seem we're Scandinavian colleagues.*'

'I see. And speaking of colleagues, am I right in thinking you spoke to Jan Hesk on the phone late Sunday night?'

'*Yes. I called him.*' She sighed. '*I saw the news about his death yesterday. Just horrible.*'

'Yes, we're still in shock down here.'

'*No wonder. What I don't understand, though, is how Dunja Hougaard could possibly be behind it.*'

'What makes you say that?' he said, trying to keep his tone neutral.

'*Well, I wouldn't say I know her. But from what little I've seen when I've met her, I would be inclined to consider it extremely unlikely.*'

'I suppose I can tell you you're not the only one to think that, and that's why I'd like to know what you and Jan talked about last Sunday.'

'*It was something completely unrelated.*'

'Okay, but was it a police matter?'

'*My goodness, yes. I didn't know him. It was about a murder case I'm working on here in Stockholm. At that point, we had one victim, and now… Honestly, I still don't know where this is going to end.'*

'And what help were you hoping for from Jan?'

'The problem was that he didn't have time to talk to me. He promised to call me back, but, well, things happened.' She sighed again. *'It was about the scar on one of the victims in the case he was working on. Because it turns out our perpetrators have similar scars.'*

'Perpetrators? You mean victims?'

'Well, I should say both, really. Perpetrators because they're guilty of several murders. Victims because they are victims of trafficking by a network of people active in Copenhagen and Denmark more broadly. I don't have time to give you a full briefing, because I'm running from one thing to another. But to take one example, we've found a document that suggests your victim was purchased from Sweden, and that the Danish buyers were unhappy about paying full price when they saw the scar.'

'Wait, hold on a second.' Heinesen smiled at the waitress who, with poorly concealed revulsion, relieved him of the plate with the half-chewed ball of bread. 'Just to make sure I'm understanding you correctly. You've identified her?'

'Yes, her name is Elaya Goodluck.'

'Goodluck?'

'Yes, apparently it's a common surname in her native Nigeria.'

'And this document you've found. What is it?'

'A printout of a message with a picture of her scar, sent from an anonymous Danish number. I can send it over to you if you'd like.'

'That would be great. And if you don't mind, I'd love that Danish number too.'

'Sure. No problem. But all right, then. I have to go. Impressive Swedish, by the way.'

Before Heinesen could say thank you, she'd ended the call, and when he put his phone down, it was with a feeling of having barely scraped the surface of something he wasn't close to understanding. That the woman in the car was a victim of trafficking was hardly surprising. Nor that she'd been brought in from Sweden, or some other country. That was how those people operated. They sent their victims across one border after the other to keep the police from tracking them.

But the fact that there were other women with similar scars, whom the Swedish detective had referred to as *perpetrators*, was news to him. Did that mean Elaya Goodluck might in fact have killed Mogens Klinge? Or had he misunderstood her? He wasn't used to speaking Swedish, after all.

He was going to have to call the Swedish detective back. Maybe they could help each other. But not right now. Instead, he woke up his laptop and played the CCTV footage from the start.

Just like when they'd watched the video together yesterday, the timestamp in the top-left corner showed *3.00 p.m., 05.08.12* when a maroon Volvo came down the ramp and found a free space. In the next clip, eighteen minutes later, a man in jeans and an unbuttoned shirt over a T-shirt walked towards an Opel.

And so on until *8.48 p.m.*, when Jan Hesk's blue Peugeot entered and inched its way to a free space, where it struggled to squeeze in. To make sure he didn't miss anything, Heinesen slowed the playback and watched Hesk walk around, studying the parked cars, until he found and began to examine Jakob Sand's red sports car, only to be knocked unconscious a few minutes later by Dunja.

But he couldn't see anything suspicious. It really was Dunja, and she really did knock him out. The light, the shadows, everything looked genuine. The body wrapped in plastic that the two men in camouflage carried past one of the cameras in a later clip could, granted, be anyone, but the images he'd seen from the recovery operation at Islands Brygge showed that Hesk had been wrapped up exactly like it.

Others might have felt disappointed. Heinesen for his part was mostly relieved. He hadn't been hoping to find anything untoward. But he'd feared he might and that he would be forced to face the consequences of that. But that fear had proved unfounded. As far as he could see, none of the sequences was manipulated, which meant he'd done his due diligence and could relax with an easy conscience.

But even so, he pulled the marker all the way back to the beginning to play the video one more time. He couldn't explain why, other than that it felt like the right thing to do. *Felt...* He shook his head at himself. He, who had always preferred hard facts, evidence and logic over walking around 'feeling' things. Now here he was, a feeling his only argument.

He found the explanation for his gut instinct in the very first clip, the one of the Volvo entering the garage. But this time, the Volvo wasn't what interested him. He wasn't even watching that camera, his eyes were on one of the other three, where nothing at all was happening.

Suddenly, it was so obvious he couldn't understand how he and the other members of the team had missed it. It was probably because things had happened so fast. Sleizner had goaded them on, ordering Hemmer to skip to when Hesk turned up.

But it wasn't what he could see that was interesting about this first clip. It was what he couldn't.

More specifically, Jakob Sand's gleamingly red sports car.

In the bottom-right frame, a parking space gaped empty while the Volvo drove through the top-left frame. The same thing was true in the following five clips, which showed cars entering or leaving the garage. But then, as a silver Lexus drove down the ramp, the open bay was suddenly occupied by Sand's sports car.

The timestamp at that point said *7.55 p.m.* Sixteen minutes after the previous clip, which meant Sand must have arrived sometime between twenty to and five to eight that night.

One explanation could be that the motion sensors hadn't been triggered by Sand entering the garage and climbing out of his sports car, leaving the cameras in sleep mode. Another one was that someone had made sure to remove that particular clip.

47

KIM SLEIZNER...

Fabian repeated the name as he crossed the courtyard to the main entrance of the Copenhagen Police HQ.

Kim Sleizner...

It was one thing that the head of the homicide unit hated him and had done everything in his power to hinder him in his work. He'd long since figured that out. But driving his son to suicide was taking that hatred to a completely new level.

Kim Sleizner...

For him, one of the most senior members of the Danish Police Authority, to have ordered the abuse of Theodor, the mental torture and the isolation, should have been unthinkable. Isolation in a room where he was able to climb up to a sufficiently strong and easily accessible electrical cord. But to anyone who knew anything about Sleizner, it made perfect sense.

'Hi, my name is Fabian Risk,' he said after passing through the sliding doors, walking up to the man behind the reception desk and showing him his Swedish police ID. 'I'm from the Helsingborg Police and I'm hoping to speak to Kim Sleizner. Is he in?'

'Kim Sleizner. Let me find out.' The man typed the name into his computer. 'Yes, he should be in. Would you like me to call him?'

'That would be great, but could you hold off for one minute? I just need to visit a bathroom first.'

'There's a bathroom at the other end of this hallway, on your right.' The man pointed down the hallway.

Once he'd closed the bathroom door behind him, Fabian took off his jacket and shirt, hung them on a hook on the wall and washed his armpits and face.

After arriving in the Danish capital the night before, he'd driven out to Langelinie, where sheer exhaustion had finally made him nod off, parked with a view of The Little Mermaid. He hadn't woken up until half past nine in the morning, when a coach packed with Asian tourists, armed with cameras and selfie sticks, had forced him from the no-parking zone.

He patted himself dry with a paper towel and took a few deep breaths in an attempt to compose himself while he buttoned his shirt and pulled his jacket back on. But his heart stubbornly continued to hammer away like an alarm during a nuclear meltdown. It probably wasn't going to slow down until he was done. Completely done.

He left the bathroom and followed a woman with a swipe card into one of the lifts and rode it up to the homicide unit on the sixth floor.

On his last visit, he'd come to see Dunja Hougaard, who had been helping him with a case. That had been just over two years ago, and now her face was on the front page of every newspaper under the headline POLICE MURDERER.

'Excuse me, where are you going?' someone said behind him.

He turned around and showed the bespectacled man with the poorly dyed hair his police ID. 'My name is Fabian Risk, and I'm here for a meeting with Kim Sleizner.'

'Do you have an appointment? Because I haven't seen him all day. And without an appointment, you'll have to—'

'He's supposed to be in. I already spoke to the front desk, so I don't see what the problem would be. But perhaps you could show me to his office?'

The man pondered that for a second, then eventually nodded. 'Okay, follow me.' A few bewilderingly similar hallways later, the man stopped outside a door with Sleizner's name on a sign on the wall above a small light that was glowing red. 'As you can see, he's busy,' the man said, pushing his glasses up.

'No problem. I'm eight minutes early anyway,' Fabian replied, consulting his watch. 'You don't want to be late to an appointment, you know.' He smiled at the man. 'I'll just have a seat and wait.'

The man eyed him suspiciously as he walked over and sat down on a chair. Then he took out his phone and started clicking around at random until the man ran out of patience and moved on.

Once he was back at the closed office door, Fabian grabbed the handle and pushed it all the way down. As expected, the door was locked, which was why, after making sure he was alone in the hallway, he took a step back and gave it a hard kick.

The office was one of the biggest he'd seen within the policing world. Not even Sweden's National Commissioner could boast of that kind of square footage. But there was no one behind the desk. Or on the sofa, or in the armchairs. The light by the door might be red, but Sleizner was nowhere to be seen. Fabian closed the door as best he could behind him and continued across the creaking hardwood floor to the desk, which was placed symmetrically between two windows flanked by curtains.

Apart from a large computer screen and a keyboard, a few pens and a notepad, there were two tall stacks of documents, which Fabian flipped through.

Some of the documents seemed to be about Jan Hesk's sudden death. There were reports from Forensics, pictures showing the body, wrapped in plastic, being hoisted out of the water, and a series of handwritten timestamps with accompanying notes, such as *keep* and *cut*. There were also quite a few pictures of Dunja Hougaard. Pictures taken from a considerable distance, in the dark, printed-out screen grabs from various CCTV cameras.

But none of it caught his interest, so he moved on to one of the desk drawers, pulled it out, emptied it onto the desk and searched through the pile of erasers, throat lozenges, and even more documents with hastily scribbled notes such as *M. Rønning resets log, make sure to turn up the heat* and *b-cameras interview room 4*. There was also a list of *Missing persons* on which the name *Camilla Krystchoff* had been circled.

None of it meant anything to him, but after upending the other desk drawer, he finally spotted something. A red folder with the initials *T. R.* written on the front in black marker.

The sight made him stagger, and to make sure he didn't fall over, he sat down in the office chair before undoing the elastic around the folder and opening it.

The first document was entitled *Arguments for delaying trial.* The document was a report from a psychologist and used words like *depression, closed-off* and *suicidal.* Then followed a number of printed-out pictures of isolation cells, accompanied by a short note.

Hi Kim,

If you consider these too 'nice and cosy', we also have another room that doesn't meet the official standards for an isolation cell, but which has all the features you requested.

Best,
F. Friis

48

THE METAL BRACKETS holding the table in place had been secured to the concrete floor with massive bolts that couldn't be loosened without special tools. Each bracket was also connected to a table leg. The handcuffs around Dunja's wrists were fastened to a steel restraint ring attached to the rectangular tabletop.

She was wearing oversized tracksuit bottoms and a hoodie, both grey. There was no clock in the room, but she'd been counting the seconds and was up to five thousand, two hundred and forty-three, which meant she'd been waiting for almost an hour and a half.

Without water or food.

Without anything at all since she'd been brought to the detention facility through a back door she hadn't even known existed.

They were probably sitting on the other side of the one-way glass, waiting for her to crack after staring herself blind at the water cooler on the far side of the room. For her to give up and become easy prey in the upcoming interrogation. But giving up was the last thing she was going to do. Even though she wanted nothing more than to lean forward, put her head down on her arms and close her eyes, if only for a few minutes, she continued to sit up ramrod straight and wide awake, determined to not so much as graze the back of the chair.

The goal was to turn the tables and instead make sure her opponents were the ones to blink first. The ones who were biding their time. Waiting for her. For the collapse. The moment they gave up and came in, victory would be hers.

At five thousand, five hundred and nine, the door suddenly opened, much sooner than the ten-thousand mark she'd been holding out for.

'Well, well, well,' said the all too familiar voice before she could even look up. 'If it isn't the esteemed Dunja Hougaard.'

Every muscle in her body wanted to lunge at him. But she managed to redirect her energy, away from the humiliation of being tied down, into keeping her face impassive. 'Hi, Kim.'

'Is that all you have to say, after all this time?' Sleizner closed the door behind him and took a few steps into the room. '"Hi, Kim."' He sneered and shook his head. 'I certainly hope you haven't grown boring in your old age. We used to have a lot of fun together. Right? You and me?'

'We never did and there will never be a you and me.'

Sleizner smiled and continued to move towards her. 'I don't think you understand how much I've been looking forward to this. How I've longed for this exact moment. It's been the light at the end of my tunnel that one day I'd see you again. The one and only Dunja.' Sleizner spread his hands.

'Sorry to disappoint.'

'Who said anything about being disappointed? As far as I'm concerned, we couldn't be off to a better start. Well, maybe that "Hi, Kim" thing. You could have done better than that, come up with something snappier. But you'll get there. We have all day. All night, if need be.'

'I have a right to a lawyer.'

'Lawyer?' Sleizner laughed. 'I told you this was going to be fun. First off, this isn't the kind of interview where you need some ill-fitting suit by your side, holding your hand. There's nothing you can tell me that I don't already know. Secondly, you don't have a right to anything at all.' He bent down until his mouth was right next to her ear. 'Because this is my turf, and in here, I make the rules.' He stuck his tongue out, poked the tip of it all the way into her ear, and then licked up towards her temple and forehead. 'You see, we still haven't announced your arrest. Granted, last night, we arrested a woman who looked a lot like you. But her name turned out to be Camilla Krystchoff and not Dunja Bitch Cunt Hougaard.' He shrugged.

So this was what he and Rønning had been talking about during their meeting at Diamanten. *Krystchoff* and *we should keep this on the down-low for her sake.* Hard as she tried, she couldn't take it in. She was well aware that Sleizner was capable of virtually anything, but Mikael Rønning, whom she'd considered her best friend just six months ago? He probably didn't know any better, or maybe Sleizner had something on him.

'So unfortunately, no one knows you're here,' Sleizner went on. 'In fact, no one even knows I'm here. You might think there's someone behind that glass, watching, but there isn't. And those cameras.' He pointed to the two CCTV cameras in the corners. 'Don't ask me why, but apparently they're both on the blink.' He spread his hands. 'Unlucky. For you. Not for me. Because now, I can do whatever I feel like.'

Without warning, he struck her so hard she was thrown backwards, blood spraying from her nose. If she hadn't been cuffed to the table, she would have fallen off her chair.

'Like that, for instance,' he continued. 'I just felt like doing that. And it was really gratifying, actually.' He touched his hand, caressing his bloody knuckles. 'So gratifying, in fact, I think I'm going to do it again.' He struck her again. In the same spot with the same fist, but even harder. 'Oh dear. I think I broke your nose. It certainly looks crooked anyway. And it was always such a pretty nose. Poor Dunja, with her pretty little nose. Poof, and she's gone.' He put his finger on her broken nose and pushed. 'Instead, what we have here is a Camilla with this crooked, bloody nose.'

Sleizner pulled out one of the chairs, took a seat across from her and leaned forward. 'Though I do have to say I like your new look. Losing that baby fat and acquiring some proper grit suits you.' He reached out with his right hand and started squeezing her breasts, first one, then the other. 'But you really should do something about these. They were never exactly large, were they, but this is just pathetic.' He pulled up her hoodie and studied them. 'When did you last look in a mirror? You've been working out too much. You look like you've breastfed half the Third World. Do you even have any sensation left in them?' He pinched one of her nipples between his thumb and forefinger. 'Just think of it as a regular mammogram and let me know when it starts to hurt.'

The pain intensified as Sleizner squeezed harder, and after a while it was so overwhelming Dunja broke into a sweat. But she said nothing. Not a peep. Every ounce of her focus was on enduring in silence, and when he finally gave up, she was close to passing out.

'As I suspected,' he said, leaning back in his chair. 'Too much exercise and not enough sex. Hey, by the way, are you thirsty?'

She made no reply, just looked him levelly in the eyes. Those tiny, hideous green eyes that never stopped probing for weaknesses. She made it to one hundred and forty-two before he gave up the struggle with a smile.

'I know exactly what you're thinking,' he said, and he started to pick his nails. 'I have throughout this little cat-and-mouse game of ours. That's why I've always been one step ahead, in case you were wondering.' He chuckled. 'Like right now, for instance, you're thinking that if you just stay quiet, I'll eventually get tired of this, and it'll be over. But as with so many other things, you're mistaken about that. Because the thing is, for you, this will never be over. You might think that's bluster, and I suppose it's good to keep believing the sun will have to come out from behind the clouds eventually. But the truth is that it won't for you. So make sure you enjoy this.' He stood up. 'Are you sure you don't want a drink? I did ask them to turn up the heat, but I wonder if they weren't a bit overzealous?' He went over to the cooler, pulled out a plastic cup, filled it with water, and drank. 'Mmm, sometimes, there's nothing better than a few sips of ice-cold, crystal-clear water.' He filled the cup again and drank. 'Just let me know if you change your mind.' He filled it up a third time before returning and setting the cup down on the table in front of her. 'It'll be here, waiting for you.'

'Forty-eight hours. That's how long you can keep me before you have to press charges,' she said.

'That's absolutely correct.' Sleizner was unable to hide his delight at the sign of life from her. 'Or at least, it could have been correct.' He sat down on the edge of the table and leaned down towards her. 'But the thing is that there are never going to be any charges or a trial for you. Bizarre, no?' He spread his hands. 'The way I heard it, you were so good at going underground we never did find you, and in the end, we had no choice but to call off the hounds. So, congratulations, I guess.' He clapped a few times. 'Unfortunately, Camilla Krystchoff won't be so lucky. Granted, she's going to be signed out and get to leave detention tonight. But sadly, there won't be much in the way of freedom to speak of for her. Unless she considers a cave in an unknown location freedom. She can forget about daylight, which will probably be tough at first. But after enough time has passed, she's going to forget what it looked like, and her only wish will be for it all to be over. For her existence to end so the worms can do their job.' He laughed. 'For a while, I actually had a plan that involved gutting her. You know, to just slice and dice her with my little karambit.' He pulled out the fighting knife with the characteristically curved edge with a practised motion and pressed it against her throat. 'And that would have been delightful and ever so satisfying in the moment. You know, kind of like a premature ejaculation. But on second thoughts, I've decided to drag it out for as long as I possibly can instead and give her a proper, how to put it, tantric death.' He slid the knife back into its sheath. 'You'd have to agree that's better. I mean, since she *is* a little whore, I should have my fun with her first. At least in the first five to ten years. Then I'll bet she'll be too hideous and revolting as she slowly shrivels up. Because I obviously assume she's going to try to go on a hunger strike. But in my world, I decide how much or how little she eats. So she'll be force-fed with a funnel.' He shrugged. 'Maybe not the daintiest solution, but it works. And sometimes, when she least expects it, there will be something in her food that shouldn't be. You know, it could be anything from a tiny bit of rat poison to disinfectant. Not a lot, just enough to make her health deteriorate. Her hair will be one of the first things to go. But that's virtually pain-free. It'll be a different story when her nails fall off. Crikey. Not to mention when her internal organs start to fail. But that's years down the line, and at least then she'll be rid of me, because I will long since have lost interest in her. I'll probably just log in and have a look at her via the web camera whenever I need cheering up.'

He drank the last of the water in the cup. 'Mmm, this water. I know I'm banging on about it, but sometimes water is just so flavourful it beats everything else. Am I right? I don't know what it is. Maybe the different minerals, or just that it's so hot and stuffy in here anything would taste—'

'Fine, give me a cup, then,' Dunja broke in with a sigh.

'Wow, really? I almost thought you'd given up there for a minute. But of course you can have a cup.' With a smile, Sleizner unzipped his trousers, took out his penis, pulled back the foreskin, pushed the head into the cup and started relieving himself. 'Ah... sometimes pissing is just as great as drinking. If not greater. Oops, that filled up quick,' he said and strangled the flow. 'We don't want it to overflow.' He put the cup down in front of her, still with his cock hanging out. Then he wiped it on her hoodie, pushed it back in, and zipped himself back up. 'Please, go ahead.'

Dunja looked at the cup, which was filled to the brim with bright-yellow urine.

'What are you waiting for? Drink. You said you were thirsty. Oh, right, how silly of me. You need help, don't you? Aren't you lucky, then, because I don't mind helping you, not one bit.' He picked the cup up again and brought it to her lips. 'By the way, you do know urine is completely sterile, don't you? No bacteria or anything. There's even reason to think it's good for you. Look at Madonna, she cured her athlete's foot with her own urine, so drink up now.' With his free hand, he forced her head back and pinched her broken nose shut.

The pain was unbearable, but after just a minute or so, it began to pale in comparison to the lack of oxygen.

'Just do as the doctor ordered and open wide.'

In the end, she had no choice but to give up and open her mouth to breathe.

49

Just a few hours ago, Heinesen had been convinced that what he was about to do was a great idea. Now he was having second thoughts because no matter how good the plan itself was, he was relatively certain he was the last person in the world who could pull it off.

He, who'd been given the moniker Good Cop because he'd made it his virtue always to seek peace and consensus, was now being forced to do the exact opposite.

Jakob Sand's house on Frydendalsvej was huge. So huge it would take several fortunes to buy it, and that wasn't even counting the annual property tax and all the fancy cars parked outside.

Heinesen had never given his vote to Enhedslisten or any other party on the far left, but the idea that someone could be so obscenely wealthy he could afford a property like this in the middle of Copenhagen made him give it serious consideration.

Just the fact that the entry phone had three buttons, all with the same name on them, made him righteously furious and made him push all three at once. If you could afford all of this, you were probably guilty of all kinds of things.

'*Who is it?*' said a voice that sounded distinctly drowsy, even though afternoon was turning into evening.

'My name is Morten Heinesen,' he said, and he cleared his throat to sound more authoritative. 'I'm from the homicide unit of the Copenhagen Police and I have some questions I would like answered.'

'*I already answered all your questions.*'

'You answered some, but far from all.'

'*And if I refuse?*'

'That's your prerogative, of course, but it will only lead to me coming back with a Special Intervention Unit, and those boys don't ring the doorbell and wait quietly until you deign to open. Moreover, it'll be added to your file, and if we do choose to press charges down the line, a refusal to cooperate with an interviewer is unlikely to play well for you.'

He stopped talking and took a step back, both impressed and frightened by his own ability to force so many lies into a single sentence without even having to think about it. And apparently, it was effective, because there was a sigh on the other end, then the door was opened by a barefoot Jakob Sand, dressed in white linen trousers and a half-buttoned pale linen shirt.

'Make it quick.' Sand ran a hand through his slicked-back hair and nodded for Heinesen to enter. 'I'm on my way to a meeting. If this takes too long, we'll have to arrange a meeting at another time.'

'Hopefully, one question will suffice.' Heinesen stepped into a spacious hallway with chest-high wainscoting, greenish-brown paintings of birds, and a staircase with an impressive banister you could slide down if you wanted. 'Is there anywhere we can sit down and speak privately?'

'If that was your one question, the answer is no. This will do just fine.'

'We have a visitor?' said a much-too-skinny woman, also dressed in linen, who was looking down at them from the first floor.

'Hi,' he said, waving. 'Morten Heinesen from Copenhagen's homicide unit.'

'Homicide unit? What do you mean, homicide unit?' The woman turned to Sand. 'What's going on? Did someone die?'

'Not that I know of,' Sand said, spreading his hands. 'But you go back to your yoga and let me handle this, and hopefully I can explain later.' He turned his back on her as if to signal that she should leave them alone.

'Did you kill this woman?' Heinesen said, loudly enough for the woman upstairs to hear, and he held out a picture of Elaya Goodluck.

'Oh my God, Jakob. The police think you've killed someone?'

'No.' Sand shook his head and sighed. 'Of course not.'

'Actually, we do.' Heinesen looked up at the woman. 'In fact, quite a few things point to him—'

'Hey,' Sand broke in. 'You just took me off the suspect list.'

'Took you off?' the woman said. 'Jakob, when were you even—'

'All right, I think you should go do your bloody sun salutations, and I'm going to straighten out this misunderstanding. Okay?'

The woman lingered, looking back and forth between Sand and Heinesen, before finally turning around with a sneer and vanishing.

'And what was the point of dragging her into this, if I may ask?'

'No point whatsoever,' Heinesen lied. 'Like I said, I would have preferred to speak privately.'

'Yes, and there are many things I would have preferred.' Sand pushed his hair back behind his ear. 'But why don't you get to it. Like I said, I'm expected elsewhere.'

Heinesen shrugged. 'Right now, I'm the one doing the expecting.'

'Seriously, what the fuck is this?' Sand looked like he was ready to break something.

'I'm expecting an answer from you.'

'An answer to what?'

'To whether or not you killed this woman.' Heinesen held up the picture again.

Sand rolled his eyes. 'No, I didn't, which I made clear during my interview yesterday.' He took a step closer to Heinesen and lowered his voice. 'But I did see her earlier that day, and that was when she did this to me.' He pulled down the collar of his shirt, exposing red scratches on his neck. 'So, you've had your answer. Again. Are we done here?'

'Where did you meet her?'

Sand sighed and turned away. 'Come with me.'

Heinesen followed Sand into an adjacent study with an inviting sofa and armchairs in one corner.

'Don't even think about sitting down.' Sand closed the door. 'We won't be here long.'

'Let me be the judge of that.'

Sand sneered and rolled his eyes. 'How do you think I made my business one of the most profitable in this country? Huh? How is it, do you think, that I can afford to live like this?' He spread his arms wide. 'Do you think it's because I'm an idiot? Is that what you think? That I don't get that you don't have shit on me? Well, then you're incredibly fucking mistaken, because I can end this little exercise and throw you out whenever I bloody please. All I have to do is snap my fingers, and you're on your arse on the pavement, wondering what happened.'

'Should I take that as a threat?'

'Take it whatever way you bloody want.' Sand took a deep breath. 'My point is that the only reason I let you into my home at all is that I am eager to cooperate with the investigation. I want nothing more than for you to apprehend the perpetrator. So to answer your question, I picked her up on Istedgade at the corner of Viktoriagade. Then we drove out to one of my office buildings in Valby.'

'Does that building have an address?'

'Gammel Køge Landevej 65.'

'And what route did you take?'

'I don't know.' Sand shrugged. 'The usual one.'

'South or north of Vestre Kirkegård? They take about the same time, one is two minutes longer than the other.'

'Then I assume I took the faster one.'

'So, the one via Vigerslev Allé.'

'That's right. Yes.'

'Interesting.' Heinesen allowed himself a nod. 'But then how do you explain that we haven't seen any of your cars in any of the footage from the traffic cameras at the intersection of Vigerslev Allé and Enghavevej?'

'What traffic cameras?'

'You're not the only one. They're easily missed. But back to my question. Why haven't we been able to find one of your cars in the footage?'

'Because I wasn't driving one of my cars.'

'That's not what you said in your interview. According to the transcript, you explicitly said you were driving—'

'I don't know how many cars you have. But I own—'

'Thirteen. With Danish plates. And then you also have—'

'Okay, fine, I misspoke! Big deal.'

'It is, actually. So, which car were you driving?'

Sand was about to say something but changed his mind. Maybe he'd planned to say his wife's car, or one of his many company vehicles, but he probably realized none of them had been caught on camera either. 'That's right, hold on. It was a taxi,' he said at length and squeezed out a smile. 'That's how it was, right. I took a taxi. I completely forgot about that. My bad. Sorry.'

'Which company?'

'I'm afraid I don't recall.'

'Do you have a receipt?'

'No.'

'But maybe a bank statement showing the transaction?'

'I waved it down on H. C. Andersen by Rådhuspladsen and paid cash.'

Heinesen nodded. 'Well, that makes it hard to prove one way or another.'

'Yes, I'm afraid so. Was that it, or did you have any other questions?'

'No, that's it. For now. If anything else comes up, we know where to find you.'

'I'd appreciate if you'd call first next time. If you do, I might even be able to have some coffee ready.'

'That sounds lovely, but I prefer to come unannounced. You know how it is when a person's not prepared. Their words say one thing while their body language and eyes say something else entirely. Have a good evening.'

Heinesen left the study and continued through the hallway towards the front door. He couldn't hear Sand following him. Whether that was a sign of strength and confidence, however, remained to be seen. Either way, he was pleased with his own performance.

Once he was back in his car, which he'd parked two blocks away, he plugged in his headset and called Hemmer.

'*How did it go?*' Hemmer asked.

'Good, I think. How are you getting on?'

'*Yeah, I'm on it, I'm keeping an eye on both his official mobile and his wife's, their landline, and two additional anonymous pay-as-you-go numbers that are in the vicinity. Hold on, one of them is waking up.'*

'Which one?'

'One of the pay-as-you-go numbers.'

'Can you see who's being called?'

'Soon, hopefully, if everything works as it should.' He heard fingers tapping on a keyboard. *'I have the number here, but sadly, no match. It's likely another burner phone.'*

'Can you patch me in?'

'Absolutely,' Hemmer said as the sound of a phone ringing reached him.

'Hey. Look, this is a bad time,' a familiar voice suddenly said. *'I'll call you back as soon as I'm done here.'*

'You said it was over. That the situation was under control.' Sand sounded exactly as angry as he'd hoped.

'Calm down, Jakob. What happened?'

'One of your minions just stopped by to harass me.'

'Who?'

'He said his name was Morten Heinesen and he asked all kinds of questions about which route I drove and which car I was in with that girl. Apparently, the camera on Vigerslev Allé didn't register any of my cars.'

'What camera?'

'Some traffic camera, I don't know. I don't bloody care. I sorted it out by saying I actually took a taxi and paid cash. The thing is, if this continues, we're fucked, do you get that? They're going to sniff us out.'

'Okay, look, I think we should end this call and talk when we meet up tonight instead.'

There was a click and the call ended. A call that had confirmed in exceedingly clear terms what they had suspected.

Hemmer had obviously recorded it, but since they didn't have a warrant to tap his phone, they'd never be able to use it as evidence in a future trial.

But that hadn't been the aim anyway. For Heinesen, knowing that Sleizner was the person Sand had called was enough.

50

KIM SLEIZNER PUT the old Nokia phone back in his blazer pocket and turned to Dunja, who was sitting at the table with her straight back, cuffed hands, and battered face. 'I'm sorry, where were we?'

Dunja said nothing and made sure to keep her eyes fixed on a vague point in front of her. Just like he'd said, she was trapped in his world, and there was nothing she could do to change that. Whatever she said, his course was set; he was going to keep on humiliating and hurting her, do whatever took his fancy, really. The only thing he was never going to be able to do was break her. Whatever he did to her, she was going to keep the flame burning.

'Fine, you play your little game. Go ahead. At least you're not thirsty any more, so you'll be okay.' He walked up to her, but then kept moving, stepping in right behind her.

She wasn't going to look over her shoulder. Instead, she just sat there, waiting for something to happen. She already knew it would hurt. That it would cause another injury that would need time and care to heal.

Which was why she was surprised by the hands on her shoulders. The hands that began to gently massage her with calm, even movements. First her shoulders, then moving slowly in towards her neck, and all the stiffness that screamed out to be softened.

'Do you recall if I ever gave you a back rub back when we were friends and colleagues? You know, back when I was helping you, making sure you were given every opportunity to have an outstanding career.' Sleizner waited for her to reply without pausing the massage. But he waited in vain. 'I probably didn't; you would have remembered,' he continued instead. 'Because if there's one thing I'm known for, it's my perfect massages. My speciality is actually feet, but the shoulders and neck come a close second. You have to admit this feels good.'

Dunja made no reply. But that didn't mean he wasn't right. In another reality, in which those hands belonged to someone else, it might have felt good, great even. Now, it only made her feel sick, even though his fingers had an uncanny ability to find all the sore spots that had longed to be touched for years. So sick she was on the verge of throwing up from the revulsion of it being Sleizner standing behind her.

'I have to say, you're very stiff,' he said, as he continued to work her shoulders and neck. 'Have you been looking after yourself? I can tell you work out, obviously, but do you make sure to stretch and soften your muscles every once in a while? Like here, and here. Feel those knots?' He pushed a thumb into each knot and held them there until the knots began to dissolve, then he moved down her spine, in between her shoulder blades.

'Imagine how good we could have it, you and me,' Sleizner went on behind her. 'Don't worry, I know how much we hate each other, and that it can never happen. But let's, just for kicks, throw all this nonsense on the rubbish heap and entertain the thought that we were meant for each other.'

He was clearly trying to lull her into a false sense of security so she'd relax and begin to regain a measure of hope of making it through after all.

'I mean, imagine it, what a power couple we'd be. We'd complement each other like yin and yang. You can't deny it. You, with your stubborn refusal to give up once your mind's set on something, and me with my contacts and creativity. We could work wonders, you and I, mark my words.'

It was the MO of a classic psychopath. Start out mean and break your victim down. Then apologize and ask for forgiveness and assure them you love them. Then you strike again just when they're starting to believe things are going to be okay. The whole thing was just a game to draw things out for as long as possible, as Sleizner himself had explicitly told her.

'I'd rub your back every night.' Sleizner worked ever deeper into her muscle tissue. 'And you, you could...'

It took her a good long while to react to Sleizner's silence and open her eyes. She'd been prepared for anything, for the very worst, for everything except what she saw in front of her.

'Excuse me,' said a bearded man in a suit who was entering the room. 'But is this Camilla Krystchoff?'

'Eh...? Yes, that's right,' Sleizner finally managed, and he took his hands off her. 'And who are you, if I may ask?'

'Her lawyer.'

'But? I'm not sure I follow?' Sleizner cleared his throat. 'How is it that—'

'I guess we're both confused, then,' the man cut him off and closed the door behind him. 'Because it looks to me like you've already started the interview with my client, which goes against all—'

'No, no, no, I haven't started any interviews.' Sleizner took a step away from Dunja. 'Not at all. I just stopped by to see how she's doing and to make sure everything is as it should be. I'm not even the one who's going to interview her. But maybe you don't know who I am.'

'Oh yes, I know exactly who you are, and that certainly does nothing to help matters.' The man moved closer to Sleizner. 'Are you responsible for these injuries too?'

'No, no, that's all her. She's what you might call self-destructive, which was one of the reasons I wanted to check on her.'

The man was now standing right in front of him with a syringe in his hand, which he flicked to get rid of any air bubbles.

'And what is this about?' Sleizner said.

The answer came in the form of a needle straight through his jacket and all the way into his chest, which made him collapse onto the floor.

'Fareed, how the hell did you get in here?' she said.

'We'll have to save playing twenty questions for later.' Fareed hurried back to the door. 'Right now, you're just going to do as we tell you and keep your fingers crossed.'

'We? What do you mean, we?'

Fareed opened the door and Mikael Rønning entered. Dressed in a police uniform.

'Mikael? But—'

'Put these on,' Rønning said, cutting her off, and he put a full set of clothes down on the table in front of her while Fareed unlocked her handcuffs. 'Everything else is going to have to wait.'

She nodded, swallowed all her questions, and let them do their work in silence.

Moments later, she was free, the blood had been wiped from her face, and she could pull the white trousers and lab coat on over her other clothes.

As a final touch, she hung a stethoscope around her neck and wiped up the worst of the blood on the floor while Fareed and Rønning heaved the unconscious Sleizner onto a stretcher, placed him in the recovery position, hooked him up to a pulse oximeter and pulled a bag valve mask over his face. Then they all rushed out.

51

'SLEIZNER?' DIRECTOR OF Public Prosecutions Mads Jensen was sitting behind his desk, dressed in a crisp shirt and black-and-white striped braces with a matching tie, looking like he'd just been told a terrible joke. 'Seriously, Sleizner as in Kim Sleizner?'

Across from him in the visitor's chair, Morten Heinesen nodded while trying desperately to swallow. But the lump in his throat was too large, or maybe the tie he'd put on was too tight.

'And just to make sure I'm understanding this right,' Jensen continued. 'You're in all seriousness contending that Sleizner was in one way or another involved in the murder of Mogens Klinge and that girl?'

Heinesen nodded again. He'd never had a meeting with the Director of Public Prosecutions before. At least, not one on one. Normally, Sleizner or someone else far more senior than him handled things like this. Now, there was no one else. And the matter was grave enough and, more importantly, sensitive enough that if he approached a prosecutor on his level, it would immediately be run up the ladder and land on Jensen's desk anyway.

'But that sounds...' Jensen trailed off and shook his head. 'I don't know what to say. It sounds insane.'

'I know. I had a hard time believing it myself.' He

finally managed to swallow down some of his nerves. 'But unfortunately, a lot of things point to it.'

Jensen nodded, ran his fingers though his neat moustache, and made as if to speak. But instead, he just sat there, nodding, while the lump in Heinesen's throat began to grow again.

He'd expected to be questioned about what he'd based his suspicions and accusations on. What had made him come to such a dramatic conclusion. Instead, he was met with a silent, suspicious look that felt more oppressive each time he tried and failed to swallow.

'This is a summary,' he said at length, putting down the document in which he'd outlined in bullet-point format everything that pointed to Sleizner being involved.

It laid out in some detail Hesk's suspicions about Sleizner drugging him at the press conference and being the one who had been in touch with Mogens Klinge via an anonymous mobile number. It also explained his own thoughts about how his boss had seemed to know that Hesk had gone to the parking garage and been caught on CCTV as he was attacked, and that he was most likely the person who had made sure to cut the part showing Jakob Sand arriving in his sports car, along with other sequences.

Jensen read the list with a concerned frown on his face, and all Heinesen could do was wait until he was done and looked up again.

'But this is just a list of vague statements.' Jensen put the document down. 'As far as I can make out, you don't have a single piece of concrete evidence to back up your claims.'

'That's correct. There's no evidence. But the way I see it, none of those statements is vague. On the contrary, I'd say each is highly relevant and concrete. That, coupled with the sheer number of coincidences, makes this impossible to disregard.

In other words, there's too much smoke here for there to be no fire.'

'Be that as it may. In my line of work, smoke isn't enough. I need fire to act, and in this kind of case, we're talking a full-on forest fire.'

Heinesen nodded and allowed himself a smile. 'That's exactly why I'm only coming to you now. Because about an hour ago, the flames finally became clearly visible.'

He put his phone down on the table, pressed play, and studied Jensen while the audio file played.

'*Calm down, Jakob. What happened?*' Sleizner's voice said, and Jensen looked exactly as confused as Heinesen had hoped.

'So you're saying that's Sleizner?' Jensen asked. Heinesen nodded.

'*One of your minions just stopped by to harass me.*'

'And that's Jakob Sand.'

'*Who?*' Sleizner demanded.

'*He said his name was Morten Heinesen and he asked all kinds of questions about which route I drove and which car I was in with that girl. Apparently, the camera on Vigerslev Allé didn't register any of my cars.*'

Jensen was clearly in shock. His face had drained of colour, and his mouth was hanging open as though his jaw muscles had lost their hold on his skull.

'*What camera?*' Sleizner again.

'*Some traffic camera, I don't know. I don't bloody care. I sorted it out by saying I actually took a taxi and paid cash. The thing is, if this continues, we're fucked, do you get that? They're going to sniff us out.*'

'*Okay, look, I think we should end this call and talk when we meet up tonight instead.*'

Heinesen picked up his phone, locked it, slipped it back

into his pocket, and waited. This time, the silence didn't bother him. On the contrary, it made him feel calm. Of course Jensen needed a few minutes to process it all and consider the consequences before he spoke.

'This phone tap,' he said after a moment. 'Who approved it?'

'No one,' Heinesen said. 'Other than myself.'

'But then it can't be used.'

'No, but that was never the point.'

'I have to ask, then: what was the point?'

'To get the all-clear to proceed.'

'And how do you propose to proceed?'

'I want to bring both Sleizner and Sand in for questioning. Go through their phones and computers and search their homes and offices. Cordon off that garage and do a thorough search to find out what's hidden there. And preferably as soon as possible, before they can cover their tracks. It's the only straight play.'

'Yes, so you say.' Jensen nodded. 'And I might be inclined to agree, I might.' He continued to nod as though at his own thoughts. 'But I'm still going to have to reject your request.'

'Reject?' Heinesen straightened up. 'I don't understand. Why?'

'Kim Sleizner is one of our best and most successful leaders.'

'But we can do it under the radar. We just have to keep it internal until we know more.'

'And then what? What do you think happens after that?'

'Well, either we find that he's guilty, or it turns out that—'

'He's innocent,' Jensen cut in. 'But even if that's the case, this will cause a scandal that in the end does far more harm to the Police Authority than good.'

Heinesen couldn't believe what he was hearing. 'So you're saying he just gets to walk away scot-free?'

'I'm sorry, what's your name again?'

'Morten. Morten Heinesen.'

'Morten, we all know Kim and what he's like. But that he would have done… Well, whatever it is you're suggesting he did together with this Jakob Sand, who, from what I understand, has been taken off the suspect list, is what I would call completely unthinkable.'

'Unthinkable? So, what is it they're going to talk more about when they meet tonight?'

'I don't know.' Jensen shrugged. 'It could be anything. Just because they don't want it to get out doesn't mean it's illegal. You know how it can be when there's a scandal brewing and the heat is on. Everything and everyone is scrutinized, and it can be the downfall of the best of us, even when there's been no wrongdoing.'

Heinesen got up. There was nothing more to add. The conversation was over. The only thing he had left to do was to turn towards the door and start walking. To stay calm and composed until he could put his hand on the door handle, open the door, and leave the room.

On the way out, he felt his phone buzz in his pocket. But he didn't pull it out until the door was safely closed behind him. It was a text from the Swedish detective he'd spoken to earlier, Malin Rehnberg. He opened it and saw a picture of the document she'd described and promised to send him. It was a photograph that showed the cross-shaped scar on the inside of their female victim's thigh, accompanied by a note that said the price was too high, considering the goods were damaged.

But that wasn't what made Heinesen stop in the middle of the hallway and zoom in to get a better look. It was the hand at the edge of the picture, which was parting the woman's legs. Granted, it was blurred and only partly visible, but even so, it was enough for him to identify the watch around the wrist. A Rolex Day-Date, which, as Sleizner liked to tell anyone who would listen, was the same model as the one Tony Soprano wore.

It didn't get more concrete than that. Sleizner was not just in close contact with a suspected murderer. He was so deeply entangled himself it was no longer a question of serious suspicion, but about where this would end.

He should turn around, head back into Jensen's office, and present this new piece of evidence, which the Director of Public Prosecutions wouldn't be able to dismiss, no matter how much he might want to. But something told him that would be the absolute worst thing he could do.

52

IT WAS STILL unseasonably warm out, bordering on tropical. But signs that summer was almost over abounded. Like the richness of the air. It had stood still for so long it was high time to stir it up with a big storm, or at least some heavy rain. The shadows were another sign. They now grew to three or four times the length of their physical counterparts in the afternoon.

But above all, it was how early evening fell. Not long ago, nights had never been fully dark; now the sun dipped below the horizon soon after nine o'clock, and ten minutes later, it was dark.

Granted, it was beautiful. The view from his hotel room on the eighteenth floor of the SAS Radisson in the middle of Copenhagen was spectacular. The light from the hundreds of thousands of lamps below would be enough to make anyone wonder if there was something divine out there, beyond the realm of human perception.

But Fabian hadn't picked a room that far up to stare out into the universe and let himself be filled with other-worldly insights. He'd just wanted to get away from it all, if only for a few hours. As far away as possible, but without leaving Copenhagen. A brief respite. He was by no means done. Altitude had been his best option, and his finances had set the limit to the eighteenth floor.

The first thing he'd done was go to bed. Exhaustion had

overwhelmed him almost immediately, plunging him into five hours of dreamless sleep.

He'd shut down completely, as though the power had gone out inside him, and maybe that was why the swirl of rage and panic was still there when he regained consciousness and realized where he was. What had happened and who had turned out to be behind it.

He'd gone into the bathroom and drawn a hot bath, which he'd filled with all the bath oil the tiny bottles had to offer. He was still soaking with his eyes on the ceiling and his ears below the waterline.

He'd gone through the folder marked *T. R.* He'd read every little note, not just once but many times, and in the end he'd concluded there could be no doubt. There was no room for misunderstandings or misinterpretations. No loopholes or possible alternative scenarios.

Theodor hadn't been doing well. In fact, he'd been doing so poorly he'd taken his own life. But the dark thoughts and suicide attempts were one thing. The final act was something else entirely.

Sleizner was behind that.

He was the one who'd blocked all escape routes and made sure Theodor was pushed ever closer to the brink. He was the one who'd prepared and orchestrated the whole thing so that in the end, all it had taken was a gentle nudge, if that, to end it.

Not that he was free of blame. Far from it. Having pushed his son to choose the truth over a lie, he carried guilt that could never be exonerated. As Sonja and Matilda had rightly said, everything would have been different today if he'd chosen to act differently. Far from good, but at least better than this.

Whatever *this* was.

A full stop or a comma.

Was there more, or had he reached the end? The end of the line, lying in a bath on the eighteenth floor of a hotel in Copenhagen with nothing left to lose?

53

AFTER COMBING SLEIZNER'S flat for clues and finding fingerprints, bloodstains and hair, Dunja and Fareed had moved on to the real preparations.

The multigym had been moved from the windowless box room to the adjacent kitchen and placed in front of the hob. They'd set up the camera, fully charged and crisply focused, on a tripod in front of the gym. They'd tested and adjusted the sound to make sure every syllable could be heard, no matter how quietly he might mumble.

They had then sat the unconscious Sleizner on the gym's bench, and used straps to tie his feet together underneath. His arms they'd tied to the bar intended for back and arm exercises, which was suspended from a wire connected to a stack of weights that kept Sleizner upright. He looked like he was being crucified, and in a sense that wasn't too far from the truth.

While Fareed tested how much weight he needed to add to raise Sleizner off the bench, Dunja studied the CD collection in the living room. It took up several square feet of one of the walls and yet she was unable to find a single album she liked.

It was all eighties stuff. Eighties, eighties, eighties. A decade that in her opinion ought to be erased from music history. And this was the very worst of it too, so in the end, she randomly pushed *Diesel and Dust* by Midnight Oil into the Bang &

Olufsen player that was now poised to play with just one click of the remote, should they have need for it later on.

Back in the kitchen, she exchanged a look with Fareed, who with a curt nod indicated that he was ready. All that was left to do was wait for Sleizner to open his eyes.

'What do you think?' She squatted down in front of Sleizner. 'Should we wake him?'

'Don't be impatient. He can have a few more minutes.' Fareed walked over to the camera and turned it on.

But she was impatient. This was what they'd been fighting for over the past few weeks. Nothing had gone to plan, true, and just a few hours ago she'd given up on her revenge, dismissing it as a naive fantasy that could never be realized.

It would have been true, too, if not for Mikael Rønning. It had taken her a while to comprehend it, but she had him to thank for everything. Fareed had been involved, too, of course. But unlike him, Rønning had everything to lose from helping, and, more importantly, he'd been the brains behind her escape.

Apparently, Sleizner had been harrying him for weeks, fishing for information about her, well aware that they at least used to be friends. When Rønning saw the internal APB, which called her a terrorist, he'd decided to stake everything on gaining Sleizner's trust.

That had been the aim of their meeting at Diamanten. That was where he'd managed to persuade Sleizner to let him make sure her potential arrest stayed under the radar. If not for that, she would still have been in that cell, or on her way to some root cellar somewhere.

That he'd also managed to get in touch with Fareed, made sure all information about the arrest of Camilla Krystchoff had been deleted, provided clothes and equipment, and made a detailed plan for how to get them out of the detention facility without too many questions being asked, did nothing to lessen her debt of gratitude. And on top of all that, he'd arranged for an ambulance to be waiting for them with its lights flashing, to further underline to the guards that it was an emergency.

After a few miles, he'd pulled over and left them in the ambulance, saying the less he knew the better. She hadn't even had time to thank him or give him a hug before he'd hurried off into the night.

She hadn't told him any of the things she'd been thinking. Of course he needed to get as far away from her as possible. Not only because of what had just happened, but because of what was coming next.

When Sleizner finally gave a sign of waking up, it was a faint, almost inaudible groan; then he seemed to drift off again. It was all happening far too slowly for her taste, and in the end, unable to keep her fingers from the remote, she aimed it at the living room and pressed play.

The three opening chords, that was as far into 'Beds are Burning' as Midnight Oil made it on full blast through the kitchen speakers before Sleizner opened his eyes.

'What do you know. If it isn't the esteemed Kim fucking Sleizner,' she said while Peter Robert Garrett sang that the time had come. 'I hope you had a nice nap.'

Sleizner looked around, watchful yet half dazed, as though he simply couldn't believe he was tied up in his own kitchen, being filmed, dressed only in his underpants and with Dunja standing in front of him.

'What the fuck have you done?' he said once the realization began to sink in. 'Huh? What the fuck have you done, you fucking little bitch cunt?' He strained and tugged at the straps but succeeded only in turning slightly from side to side.

'You let us know when you're done, so we can get started.'

She turned the chair next to the camera around and sat down with the chair back between her legs.

'Get started with what? And how the hell did you get out of the nick?'

'My answer to question A is: your confession. As far as question B goes, though, I think a better person to ask would be Camilla Krystchoff. Wasn't that her name?'

Sleizner sneered. 'I'm going to give you one chance. One chance to untie me and tidy up in here. The gym's going back where you found it, and—'

'Or else what?' Dunja cut in, leaning forward against the chair back.

Sleizner sighed. 'You're even dumber than I thought. There is no "or else". You will die either way. The only thing that's up to you is how.'

'You're pretty cocky for a person who is now in my world, although I will admit this does look a lot like your kitchen.'

Sleizner shook his head. 'You're so naive I almost feel sorry for you. Yes, this is my kitchen. But so is everything else. Everything outside this room belongs to me as well, everything outside this flat, everything on the other side of the harbour. Amager, or whatever. Everything is my world. Every step you and that curry-infused Indian take is on my turf.'

'I must say, I'm impressed.' She nodded and turned to Fareed. 'Aren't you? He has no idea what he's in for. He is still banging on as though he has a say in this.'

'I actually think it's kind of cute,' Fareed replied.

'Cute? Hm, maybe.' She turned back to Sleizner and looked him in the eye. 'If it weren't for the fact that I know who he is.'

'Speaking of what people are in for,' Sleizner said. 'Do you seriously think you're going to be able to pull this off and walk away afterwards? I mean, seriously. Help me understand how a naive little slut like you thinks.'

'There's no point even trying. You'd never understand.'

'Your only chance is to untie me. Not now or in five minutes, half a bloody hour ago. I have friends and contacts. I have men working for me around the clock, and if I'm ever away for more than two hours without typing in my security code, they'll come looking for me. I don't know what time it is, but I'm sure they're already on their way. So I'd say you're out of luck. So incredibly fucking out of luck.'

'You're almost starting to sound a bit desperate. He does, right?' She turned to Fareed, who nodded. 'Oh well. I guess time will tell which one of us is out of luck. Let's get cracking, unless you have any other questions. If you do, we might as well get them out of the way now.' Dunja waited, but Sleizner said nothing. 'All right, so everything's clear. Great. Then I suggest we move on to my questions.' She turned the music off just as the band was about to launch into the chorus and nodded for Fareed to start the camera. 'Let's start with the garage and the basement on Østerbrogade. What kind of racket are you and Jakob Sand running down there?'

Sleizner shrugged. 'I don't know what basement you're talking about. But a garage, that sounds like a place to park cars.'

'Funny. But I was referring to the premises behind the garage.'

'Refer as much as you like. That doesn't change the fact that I have no idea what you're talking about.'

'I'm talking about the secret basement where you ordered your goons to murder Qiang Who.'

'Qiang who?' Sleizner quipped, chuckling.

'Hilarious. But now I'd like you to answer my questions,

and if you haven't figured it out by now, we already have evidence to back most of this up. Like, for instance, that you have spent quite a lot of time in the basement where Qiang was murdered. We are in possession of recorded phone calls and pictures proving your connection with Jakob Sand, who is the owner of the property, by the way. And we also know that you, Jakob and Mogens Klinge were there the night Klinge died. Or was murdered, I should say.'

'If I could clap, I would,' Sleizner said. 'It almost sounds credible. As though you have all kinds of evidence, when in reality you have nothing, since there's nothing to have.'

'Oh no? And what makes you so sure? Is it the fire you ordered? Were you counting on that to destroy everything? Sure, we did lose some stuff, I don't mind admitting it, but luckily, it wasn't anything pivotal.'

'You're bluffing.' Sleizner looked her in the eye and smiled. 'I'm not even slightly surprised. What does surprise me is how bad you are at it. Your eyes, your tone of voice, your whole body language. You're pretty much making all the classic mistakes.'

No one had made lying as central to their personality as Sleizner. If there was one thing he knew how to do, it was to serve up a lie without blinking. And now he seemed to be seeing straight through her, reading her mind as though he were listening to an audiobook.

'Let's talk about Jan Hesk,' she said after a while. 'Your little trick, using that CCTV footage of me attacking him to pin his murder on me, was pretty impressive. Both elegant and efficiently executed, though we both know it had nothing to do with the truth.'

'It didn't?'

'At first, I thought you were just out to get me. Which in a way, I understand. But it still seemed odd that it happened so quickly. Your so-called investigation, the finding of the body, the accusations against me. Unbelievably quickly, actually. I think we're talking hours, which must be some kind of record. In hindsight, I obviously realized you already had all the facts, and just had to dispatch the divers to where you knew they'd find Hesk.'

Sleizner shook his head. 'You should write crime novels. Not that there's much need for yet another ex-copper with subpar prose and an overly active imagination. But just like crappy plastic toys and ugly souvenirs in tourist hotspots, I'm sure it would sell.'

'So how do you explain that we've found Hesk's fingerprints here in your flat? And not just in one place, but in several, like on one of your whisky tumblers.'

Sleizner made no reply, just sat there staring at her intently, trying to read her.

'In case you're wondering, we also found some hairs that might be his, on the living room rug. But that remains to be seen. It usually takes a few days for results to come back.'

Sleizner nodded, his Adam's apple bobbing up and down, and Dunja could almost feel a decision taking shape inside him. But instead of speaking, he cleared his throat, not just once but several times, until he had enough phlegm in his mouth to hawk a big gob of spit, right at the camera. Whether it was skill or luck, the thick beige gloop landed in the middle of the lens.

'I'll take that to mean you're not going to confess or tell us anything whatsoever.'

'Maybe you're not so dumb after all.'

'All right.' She sighed and turned to Fareed. 'Let's not waste memory.'

Fareed turned off the camera and pulled out a tissue to wipe the lens clean. While he worked on that, Dunja stood up, went over to Sleizner, and squatted down so their eyes were level. Until now, nothing about his behaviour had surprised her. She'd never counted on him just confessing right away.

So far, it had all been about warming him up, making him understand what was expected of him. Now, they were going to get down to brass tacks.

'Remember that feeling the first time you're on a roller coaster?' she said, and she waited for a reaction that never came. 'You know, when you're going up that first long climb, slowly, slowly, towards the top. You're scared shitless and regret ever getting in the queue, and you just want to get out. At the same time, there's something thrilling about it. Something inside you looks forward to what's going to happen when you pass the peak and start plummeting back down. When you allow yourself to lose control and just go along for the ride. That's what this is like for me.'

'I was never into roller coasters,' Sleizner said. 'But I'm happy for you.'

'We'll see how I feel I am in a minute. Because I was never into torture. Not even as a kid, being forced to go to the cinema to see some horror film. I don't know about you, but I always looked away when the fingers were being severed and the eyes gouged out. I always thought those particular scenes were gratuitous and sensationalist; even though I shut my eyes, I never seemed to miss any pivotal part of the plot. And I'm still like that. But I'll make an exception for you. I'd obviously hoped you'd confess and that there was still a chance for me to get off this ride before it was too late. But a small part of me is nevertheless looking forward to what's going to happen when we pass that peak and start plummeting down.'

Sleizner didn't even seem to need a second to ponder how to react; a second gob of spit hit her forehead and slowly slid down her swollen nose. Fareed was there in an instant, handing her a tissue so she could wipe it off. But the damage had already been done. Even though she was the one moving about freely, Sleizner had the upper hand.

Maybe he was right about her being a terrible liar. Either way, he'd seen through her bluff, and all she could do now was pretend that nothing had happened and raise the stakes by giving Fareed the signal he'd been waiting for.

Without a word, he picked up a 45-pound kettlebell and placed it on top of the stack of weights behind the multigym. The stack was pushed down and Sleizner was hoisted up, dangling almost a foot above the bench.

'May I ask what you're going to do?' Sleizner tried to look over his shoulder to see what Fareed was up to.

'I'm the one asking the questions,' she said, going over to the kitchen counter to fetch something. 'In your shoes, I'm sorry, pants, I would focus more on answering.' She returned with an adult nappy, the sides of which had been cut open, and pulled Sleizner's underpants down to his knees. 'On providing, for instance, a complete account of your involvement in the murder of Mogens Klinge and the woman in his car.'

Somehow, she must have known it was going to come to this. Seeing him strung up there, exposed and helpless, made her realize it. She'd even prepared a snarky comment about how small it was. How it reminded her of a bullied baby turtle that had crawled into its shell to hide.

Unfortunately, it wasn't hiding. On the contrary, it was hanging there, ponderous and half erect. Something must be wrong, was her first thought. He must have misunderstood something. Or had he taken Viagra?

'It's a beauty, isn't it?' he said with a smile.

Viagra or no Viagra. The prick got off on this. Probably because he assumed her threats were idle. But still. Even though he was right, she had to admit his confidence was impressive.

'You have nothing because there is nothing. My only involvement has been to launch an investigation to find out who is behind the murders.'

'Let's talk about that lunch last Friday instead,' she said, catching the bottle of lighter fluid Fareed tossed her. 'You know, the one you had with Jakob Sand at Zeleste.' Then she calmly and thoroughly soaked the adult nappy with lighter fluid. 'Who was the third person?'

'I don't know what lunch you're talking about.'

'No? You know, the one where you were supposed to be at the dentist? I'm sorry, this might feel cold.' She put the nappy in his underpants and pulled them all the way back up. 'But only at first.' She nodded to Fareed, who turned the kitchen fan on full blast. 'Mads Jensen, isn't that his name? The Director of Public Prosecutions.'

'I don't know what you're talking about.'

'No?' She pulled out a gas lighter and lit it with a push of the button. 'Because his phone happened to be there at the exact same time as you and Jakob, and unless I'm mistaken, you've been friends since you were both wearing nappies.'

'It would be far from the first time you were mistaken.' Sleizner looked back and forth between her and the yellow flame at the tip of the lighter, and judging by the look in his eyes, something had changed. As though it had only just now occurred to him that she might not be bluffing after all. 'But then you're nothing but a stinking little bitch cunt who has no idea what she's got herself into,' he said after a pause, and smiled.

His words had long since lost their meaning. His eyes were a different matter, though. Those penetrating eyes were calling her bluff, throwing down a challenge that painted her into a corner. She didn't know if that was why she had lowered the flame towards his crotch. All she knew was that she'd lost control and was ready to go along for the ride.

'Dunja, what are you doing?' Fareed said. 'What the fuck are you doing? We were just going to—'

'There's a lot of things we were just going to,' she cut in without taking her eyes off Sleizner. 'Isn't that right, Kim? Not to mention all the things we never thought we were going to do.'

His self-satisfied smirk was gone. His ironclad conviction that even now, he was going to come out on top. Because he always did. Whatever the issue, he invariably ended up the winner.

There was none of that left now, and like a giant toddler being told for the first time that he couldn't have candy, his eyes shone with disappointment. A disappointment that morphed into uncertainty as the flame licked his underpants.

'You wouldn't dare,' he said and shook his head. 'You would never—'

'Did you kill Hesk?' she broke in, as the fire spread across the red and white stripes of the fabric. 'Because he was on to you?' First in a small brown patch, then in an ever expanding circle.

'Dunja, for fuck's sake,' Fareed shouted. 'This isn't what we agreed.'

'What, am I burning?' Sleizner turned to Fareed. 'Did she set me on fire?' Finally, there was concern in his eyes. 'Huh? Did you? Did you set me on fire?' Concern that quickly turned into fear.

'Did you kill Hesk?' she said as the flames spread through his underpants. 'Did you? Answer me! Did you order Qiang's murder?'

As though the pain suddenly went from zero to a hundred, Sleizner roared. 'Okay, I confess,' he screamed, panting hard. 'Just put it out and I'll confess.'

'Confess to what?' she said as the stench of burnt hair and flesh spread through the kitchen.

'Everything,' he howled, snot running down his face. 'I promise! I'll tell you everything!'

54

It was with a measure of melancholy that Morten Heinesen opened his desk drawer. During the course of a normal workday, he probably performed that very action upwards of fifteen times, to get out a pen or something of that kind. Which meant he must have opened the drawer over fifty thousand times in his years as a detective on the homicide unit. Fifty thousand times without ever giving it a second's thought. This time was different.

His notebooks took up most of the drawer, and since he was keen to save those, he placed them in the cardboard box sitting in the middle of the desk. He packed up the pens that still worked and the wristwatch he'd stopped wearing since he got his first mobile. He couldn't throw away the collection of scented erasers in the shape of various Star Wars figures Frank had given him either. But everything else went in the bin. Even the used-up batteries that should really have been recycled.

There was no time.

The fact that it hurt and felt like he was throwing away a part of himself was irrelevant. He couldn't allow himself to drag this out. Not because he'd been fired or given an order he had no choice but to obey. No, this was entirely for his own sake. He was doing it to make sure he was ready to take this all the way and be prepared to face the consequences. To make himself realize there was no way back.

The sound of footsteps in the hallway outside, followed by the creaking of the door, made him look up at Julie Bernstorff and Torben Hemmer, who were walking towards him through the office landscape, their eyes full of questions.

'There you are. Good,' he said, taking the last of the books off his shelf. 'I'm just about done here.'

'What are you doing?' Bernstorff said. 'You're not quitting, are you?'

'Not yet. But time will tell how this turns out.' He tossed the last few things in the bin and turned off his desk lamp. 'But don't worry. This is entirely on me. All you're doing is obeying a senior officer.'

'Maybe you could tell us what happened?' Hemmer said.

'Let me put it this way,' he said, lowering his voice and looking around the room, where a few other people were still working. 'Quite a bit has happened. I can't say much more until we're out of this building.' He picked up the cardboard box and started to walk towards the exit.

'But Morten. Hold on.' Bernstorff and Hemmer hurried after him.

'There's no time to lose.'

'You haven't even told us where we're going.'

'We're leaving, going into the hallway.' He stopped in front of the door and turned around. 'Would one of you mind opening the door?'

Hemmer held the door open so he could walk through it with his box.

'Okay, and now what?' Bernstorff said, rushing to catch up. 'What happens now?'

'Now, we continue towards the lifts,' he said without stopping.

'Morten, I have no idea what you're doing,' Hemmer said when they reached the lifts. 'But if you think Julie and I are just going to follow orders and come with you blindfolded, you're—'

He was interrupted when the door of one of the lifts opened and two uniformed officers stepped out and continued past them.

'So either you tell us what this is all about,' he continued quietly as soon as the uniforms were out of earshot and they themselves were stepping into the lift. 'Or—'

'Julie, would you mind pushing the button for the garage?' Heinesen cut in.

Bernstorff pushed the bottom button as Hemmer heaved an exasperated sigh and started to say something else. He stopped himself when Heinesen looked him in the eye and then glanced up at the CCTV camera in the corner.

'Julie, you come with me in my car,' he continued once the lift had reached the garage and they were walking past rows of patrol cars and unmarked vehicles. 'And Torben, you grab the van with your equipment and make sure you stay right behind me.'

'And you're still not going to tell us what this is all about?' Hemmer said as they approached the members of a Special Intervention Unit, fully equipped with bulletproof vests, helmets and automatic rifles, who were crowding into a black police van.

'Hey, Magnus. Are you ready?' Heinesen said to the commanding officer, who was just climbing into the passenger seat.

'Yep, we're going to head out and wait in the agreed-upon location.' He slammed the door shut and the van set off towards the exit.

'Okay, so they know where they're going, but we don't.' Hemmer shook his head.

Heinesen stopped and turned towards them. Then he looked over his shoulders, first one, then the other, before meeting their eyes again. 'Magnus has been here as long as I have, and I'm sorry to have to say it, but you still have some way to go.'

'And what's that supposed to mean?' Bernstorff exclaimed. 'That you don't trust us?'

'It means that once I bring you inside, you, unlike him, are going to ask me questions, and right now, there's no time to—'

Just then, his phone went off. He pulled it out and saw that it was Sleizner calling.

'Yes, hello. This is Morten Heinesen.'

'Don't pretend you don't know who this is,' Sleizner slurred on the other end. *'So fucking pathetic.'*

'Kim, is that you? I almost didn't recognize your voice.'

'You don't think I know what you're doing? Huh? You don't think I've figured it out?' He could hear him pause to drink something. *'Fucking dyke bitch...'* He hiccoughed and had another drink. *'But just so you know, I already confessed. Someone else beat you to it, so once you get here...'* He drank again. *'It'll be too late.'*

There was a click, and the call ended.

55

FABIAN HAD LEFT the SAS Radisson half an hour earlier and walked south, past Tivoli, all the way down to the harbour, where he'd turned right and continued down the wooden promenade along the water until he could turn left onto a pedestrian bridge across the water to Islands Brygge.

The building looked exactly the way he'd expected a building Sleizner lived in to look. Grotesque and repulsive, but also intriguing. As though despite the gently curving façade and the balconies overlooking the water, it was closing in on itself, turning away from everything. From the world. As though it didn't belong among the other buildings surrounding it but rather came from a civilization vastly different from our own, and had just happened to land here.

The illuminated entrance was located in the back, and he pushed the button next to the engraved name *K. Sleizner* with his other hand over the camera lens.

The speaker beeped loudly six or seven times, then fell silent again. Maybe he wasn't home, or maybe he was sleeping. It was, after all, the middle of the night. He rang again and counted five beeps before silence fell once more.

'Hello?' he said after a while. 'Is there anyone there?'

'*Morten, is that you?*' said a voice that might be Sleizner's. '*Heinesen, I know it's you.*' But it sounded slurred and intoxicated.

'Yes, it's me,' he replied in his best Danish. 'Can you buzz me in?'

'*Why would I do that?*' He could hear him pause to drink something. '*How stupid do you think I am? Don't you think I know you're out to get me? You have been for as long as we've known each other, and now you finally see your chance.*' He drank again, big gulps. '*But you know what? Like I already told you, you're too late. There's nothing here for you. Someone else beat you to the punch. I've already confessed everything.*' He sighed, almost blew into the receiver. '*So no, I'm not letting you in. Not under any circumstances. I'm never opening this door again. Not ever. Not for anyone, do you hear me? It's over now. Completely over. So you can just go home. Just fuck off home with you.*'

He hadn't understood most of it. Only that Sleizner was home and apparently refusing to let him in. And something about other people beating him to the punch. But it didn't matter. The important thing was that he was in his flat.

He only needed a few attempts with the lock pick before the pins were pushed up to the shear line and he could turn the cylinder. He folded the doormat over and wedged it under the door before continuing into the lobby.

In a parallel reality, he would have stopped and looked around wide-eyed at the breathtaking lobby, which made him feel like he'd stepped right into a Stanley Kubrick film that had ended up never being made. But in this reality, his mind was busy contemplating the relative positioning of the buttons on the entry phone, and the fact that the position of Sleizner's button would seem to indicate that he lived on the top floor.

When he was halfway to the lift, it suddenly rumbled to life and began to descend. It could be someone who'd just come home after a late shift and sent the lift back down, but to avoid even the risk of running into anyone, he opted instead for the stairs leading up to the first walkway. There, he waited to make sure it wasn't Sleizner on his way out.

As expected, no one came out of the lift, and the door remained closed. He continued along the walkway to the next set of stairs, which took him up to the second floor. From there, he hurried on to the third flight of stairs, which just like the others seemed to start in a random spot. Which meant he had to do quite a bit of running back and forth on the various floors before he'd finally made his way to the topmost walkway and Sleizner's front door, which was equipped with a code lock.

With a movement that was as instinctive as it was unplanned, he tried the handle, and the door opened almost as if of its own volition. He entered with his gun drawn and slowly closed the door behind him. The light was on in the hallway, and from what he could see, most of the other rooms in the flat were lit too. But apart from the faint humming of a vent up by the ceiling, everything was quiet.

A door stood ajar on his right. He opened it with his foot, ready to shoot if there was someone lying in wait behind it. The room was barely bigger than a cupboard and contained, among other things, coats, an ironing board and a vacuum cleaner. He continued into the hallway, the walls of which were lined with diplomas and awards from Sleizner's school days, his time as a handball player, and his career with the Danish police.

The door to what looked like a bedroom was wide open. He stepped inside and looked around, noting that four of the wardrobes along one wall were open and several underwear drawers were pulled out. A few items lay scattered on the floor along with suit trousers and ties, and a half-full bottle of Absolut Vodka was propped up next to the pillow on the unmade bed, below a ceiling mirror and a crystal chandelier.

He put his hand on the sheet and noted that despite the open bedroom window, the bed was still warm. That, coupled with the half-full bottle of vodka, suggested this was where Sleizner had been when he woke him up just over twenty minutes earlier. Then he'd likely staggered out into the hallway to answer the entry phone. He'd probably brought the bottle with him, since it was far from empty. He'd clearly heard him drinking during their conversation.

But what had happened after that? Sleizner had seemed heavily intoxicated, but for whatever reason he'd returned to the bedroom to put the bottle down. Why would he have done that, and why hadn't he just gone back to bed after their conversation, since he wasn't going to let him in? And most importantly, where was he now?

He went over to the en-suite bathroom, popped his head in, and had just decided it was empty when the bedroom door behind him slammed shut. He threw himself down on the floor, ready with both hands on his gun. But when nothing happened, he slowly got back up, went over to the door and gingerly opened it.

A rush of air hit his face, and he realized it must have been the draught from the open window that had made the door close. He hadn't noticed the draught earlier. Or the burnt smell. But once he was back in the hallway, he could clearly pick out the vaguely acrid smell, which grew more pronounced as he moved deeper into the flat.

The smell turned out to be emanating from the kitchen. But why the multigym was placed in front of the cooker, or why the ceiling above it was blackened by smoke, was beyond him. Nor could he figure out the severed straps that lay discarded on the floor alongside what appeared to be burnt remnants of red-and-white-striped cloth.

Something had clearly been on fire in here, but there was no time to ponder what or, more importantly, why. He was after Sleizner. Everything else would have to wait.

The living room was empty too. The stereo, which was equipped with a valve amplifier that must have cost half a year's salary, was on, but silent. He continued through the curved flat. A study here and a guest room there. Yet another hallway and even more doors.

He stopped outside yet another bathroom. The light from the crack under the closed door pooled on the floor outside. There was no obvious way in. Granted, the door was unlocked, but no matter how fast he was, he'd have no chance if Sleizner was poised to attack on the other side. But what choice did he have, he asked himself as he threw open the door and jumped in, gun first.

No Sleizner. Not in the jacuzzi or behind the shower wall. What he did find was chaos. Not the chaos of a messy person, but chaos sprung from what could only be described as utter panic.

There was a first-aid kit in one of the two sinks. The drawers underneath had been pulled out, their contents spread across the mosaic floor. There were scissors, toothbrushes and bloodstained towels. Empty pill jars, all kinds of pills, and shards of glass from the smashed full-length mirror on the wall. The toilet was unflushed, filled with urine and long strips of loo roll, and among the bloody smears on the seat he could make out what appeared to be bits of burnt skin.

While his mind struggled to fit the jumbled impressions into a coherent narrative, he picked up one of the jars from the floor and noted that it contained Oxycodone Actavis, one of the strongest and most addictive painkillers a doctor could prescribe.

A door slammed shut somewhere in the flat. Maybe it was the bedroom door again. From what he could recall, he'd left it open. But a cross breeze required two openings, and so far the only one he'd seen was the window in the bedroom. He found the explanation in a room with a dartboard, a pool table and a small corner bar.

The glass balcony door was only open a crack. But the crack was more than big enough to create a strong draught that swept through the flat, and, what's more, it was big enough for someone to squeeze through.

The balcony overlooked the water and Vesterbro on the other side of it; it was approximately five feet wide and seemed to run the length of the flat. In addition to a table and four chairs, a pile of cushions, a gas grill, a few tomato plants and two folded sun loungers, there were also a couple of empty planters, three sacks of firewood and a plastic storage box.

There was no sign of Sleizner.

He sat down on the damp lid of the storage box and felt exhaustion begin to creep back in. Even though he'd slept, it was a struggle to keep his eyes open. He wasn't just tired like he was about to nod off. Every last joint and muscle was exhausted. Tired of this crap. Of hunting and hunting and never catching the scent of his prey. Of giving a shit.

Maybe that was why he hadn't reacted at first to the pile of cushions that lay exposed to the elements on the wooden deck next to him, why it took so long before he asked himself why they weren't where they were supposed to be, namely in the storage box he was sitting on.

From what he could see, there were two sun loungers and

four regular balcony chairs, which tallied with the number of cushions in the pile. In other words, the explanation wasn't that there was a lack of space. Unless...

He stood up, turned to face the storage box, and leaned down to open it, gun in hand. He threw the lid open as quickly and forcefully as he was able, to give Sleizner as little time as possible to prepare.

A musty smell wafted up at him, but other than that and a necklace glinting at the bottom, the box was empty. He bent down, holding his breath to avoid the smell, and picked up the gold chain.

Kim Sleizner may well be the kind of person who walked around with a gold chain underneath his shirt. The only thing that didn't fit was the Ganesha pendant dangling from it. The Hindu elephant god who represented wisdom, intelligence and learning.

He turned his attention to the pile of cushions and touched the top one, which was more or less as damp as the lid he'd been sitting on. Which meant the cushions had lain unprotected outside the storage box all night and maybe even longer. But what that meant, he was too tired to figure out. If it meant anything.

After closing the lid, he went over to the railing and gazed out across the water glittering far below in the light of countless lamps. An eternity away, yet fully visible, his hotel towered like a giant Lego brick above all the other buildings in the city centre. He could even make out the tiny dot of light that was the floor lamp he'd left on in the window.

The tall buildings, the lights and the smell weren't the only things that set a city like Copenhagen apart from Helsingborg. The soundscape was different too. This was a metropolis, with all that entailed. Like the sharp screeching from the railyard on the other side of the water, the constant sound of traffic, and the sirens, the ever-present sirens.

It wasn't like New York, but not far from it either. It didn't matter what time of day it was. You could almost always hear the distant howling from somewhere, as though there was always a fire or a bank robbery happening somewhere.

He could only guess what it might be this time. That said, the sirens, which had been distant at first, part of the aural backdrop, were quickly growing louder, until they sounded like they were only a few hundred yards away. He leaned out over the railing, and it wasn't long before he could see blue light reflected in the choppy water.

They were close now. So close they were turned off.

The notion that they might be after him had only just begun to take shape when it was interrupted by a completely different insight as the unmarked police car with its flashing blue lights approached along the cobbled pier and stopped in front of the building.

It was then, lit by the car's headlight, that he saw the body on the pavement below, twisted into a position that wasn't really a position but rather a pile of something that had once been human.

He didn't know how to react, so he just stood there staring. As though a bug in his software was causing him to freeze up. As though all the contradictory feelings cancelled each other out and the only thing he could do was to look down at the two police officers who moved towards the body, powerful torches in hand, while a light-blue van pulled up behind them.

It was the voice that roused him in the end and made him turn towards the pool room and the rest of the flat. The voice that loudly and clearly announced it was from the police.

56

MORTEN HEINESEN CLIMBED out of the car, turned on his torch and started to walk across the cobblestones. The same uneven cobblestones he'd sprained his ankle on during a run a few years earlier. Behind him, he could hear Julie Bernstorff close her door and follow him. The sound of her heels against the rounded stones made the pain on the outside of his right foot flare up again. As though it had lain dormant all that time, just waiting for him to come back here and injure himself once more.

The alarm had reached them a few minutes after they'd left the police garage. A neighbour two floors down from Sleizner had been working late and had witnessed someone falling past his window head first.

He'd ordered the Special Intervention Unit into the stairwell and up to the flat to make sure no curious neighbours stuck their noses in before they'd secured the scene. It was his first time here. Unlike several of his colleagues, he'd never been invited to one of the legendary Christmas parties in the luxury penthouse of the spectacular converted silo.

He squatted down and turned his torch on what had once been Sleizner's head. In line with the neighbour's statement, it had hit the ground first, and with such force there was hardly anything left of it. But he recognized the suit and the red-and-green chequered tie. And the Soprano Rolex that ticked on as though nothing untoward had happened.

STEFAN AHNHEM

Was this his fault? Was that why he felt so uncomfortable? Had he painted his boss so far into a corner he'd seen no other way out than to take his own life? He'd done everything in his power to keep his planned arrest to a select few. And still the information had somehow found its way to Sleizner.

He turned around and saw that Hemmer had unloaded his metal equipment cases and was waiting next to Bernstorff. 'You know what to do. I'm going to head up and have a look at his flat,' he said, and he started to walk around the building towards the main entrance, past the ambulance that was waiting to take charge of the body.

A second ambulance was parked further down the street. He'd only requested one, but then, judging by the distant sirens, more resources and staff were on their way. So the news had spread.

He took the lift all the way up, was informed by the head of the Special Intervention Unit that the flat had been secured, and stepped through the door. 'Hey, Magnus.' He stopped and turned around. 'You should probably set up a cordon down there.'

'Okay. But don't you want me to leave two officers up here?'

'No, it's all right. Just keep an eye on the stairs and make sure there's no unauthorized access.'

Once the head of the SIU had waved the two other members of his team over and left him alone in the flat, which was what he'd been waiting for, he set his jaw and began to look around.

The flat was extravagant and ridiculously large for one person. And even considering his ample salary, the décor should have been out of Sleizner's price range. There was no time to go through it all now. That would be up to Hemmer and his assistants tomorrow.

Instead, he continued through the hallway, into the living

426

room and over to a glass door that opened out onto the balcony. He'd decided to start at the end point, the last moment, and then move backwards in time through the flat from there.

After pulling on gloves, he pushed open the door and stepped into the night. The balcony looked pretty much like one would expect a balcony of its size to look. Some outdoor furniture, a pile of cushions, planters of various sizes, the plants in them wilted, and a bin bag full of recyclable bottles in the far corner. In other words, nothing that stood out or piqued his interest.

In an attempt to envision the course of events, he went up to the railing and looked over the edge, down at the site of impact. Which turned out to be a number of feet further to the right, so he adjusted his position until he was right above it.

He estimated the drop to be about 130 feet and was struck by the courage Sleizner must have had to summon to climb over the railing and throw himself out. He'd seen it in photographs from the attack on the World Trade Center. People jumping out of windows to escape the fire, some like Sleizner, head first, towards certain death. He would never have dared to do that. Not even if he wanted to kill himself.

On the street below, a third ambulance had arrived, and three people were approaching Hemmer and Bernstorff, who, dressed in coveralls, were examining and taking pictures of the remains. He couldn't hear what they were saying to each other, but Hemmer's body language showed him going from gently querying to deeply upset in a matter of seconds.

He took out his phone and called Bernstorff, who seemed to be staying out of the discussion.

'Yes, this is Julie,' she said, and he could see her step even further away from the others.

'This is Morten. What's going on?'

'*There are some people from Forensics here, and they're saying they're taking over.*'

'Who?'

'*Oscar Pedersen.*'

'Pedersen? What is he bloody doing here at this hour?'

'*He says he's doing the autopsy.*'

'Sure, he's the head of forensics. But that doesn't mean he can just come in and take over. He will, like everyone else, have to wait until you're done examining the scene. So just stand your ground and take your time.'

'*Okay, but I have to hang up now.*'

The call cut out and he saw her turn back towards the others.

That Pedersen liked to perform an autopsy personally once in a while was all well and good. But that he was on the scene in person to pick up the body, and in the middle of the night too, was, as far as Heinesen knew, unprecedented, and it demonstrated very clearly that the news of Sleizner's death had reached the top brass.

But maybe he shouldn't be surprised about that. After all, Sleizner had been one of the public faces of the Copenhagen Police, and this was obviously an event that would overshadow most other things. The question was whether he and the other members of his team would be allowed to continue their investigation, or if they would be forced to...

His line of thought trailed off as his eyes came to rest on the storage box, or rather, its lid. Something about the sheen of the damp on it didn't seem right, and when he went over and squatted down to study the dew that had deposited thousands and thousands of tiny water droplets all across it, he could clearly see that someone had been sitting on it.

Just then, his phone buzzed in his trouser pocket. He

considered ignoring it but realized that wasn't an option when he saw it was National Police Commissioner Henrik Hammersten calling.

'Yes, this is Morten Heinesen,' he said with the phone pressed to his ear as he examined the storage box and the dry area in the middle of the lid.

'*Hi Morten, I'm not sure if we've met. My name is Henrik Hammersten. I'm sure you know who I am.*'

'Of course.' He bent down to grab the lid with his free hand.

'*I've just been informed about Kim Sleizner's tragic suicide, and from what I understand, your team is on the scene.*'

'That's correct. We're already—'

'*That's great, Morten. Really great,*' Hammersten interrupted as Heinesen prepared to open the lid. '*I'm calling to inform you that from now on, another team is going to take over the case, so I want you and your guys to leave without—*' The call cut out when the phone slipped out of Heinesen's hand and hit the wooden decking.

He had no chance to react before the armed man jumped out of the storage box and struck him so hard with the side of his handgun the world went dark.

57

FABIAN ROUNDED THE pool table and hurried back through the flat. There might be more police officers, or there might not. One problem at a time. Now, it was all about trying to get out as quickly as possible.

He'd struck the detective harder than intended. But going back to make sure he was okay was tantamount to giving up. Whether the man was unconscious or not, he'd be trapped.

There would be nothing he could say to clear himself of the charge that he'd pushed Sleizner over the railing. That he'd exacted revenge in a moment of blind rage. Untrue though it was, it came far too close to the truth. What else could he possibly have been doing in Sleizner's flat in the middle of the night? How had he got in? Why was he even in Copenhagen? He was standing in quicksand, and any attempt to explain himself would be like so much ill-advised flailing.

Too many things pointed to him being guilty. Everything from his motive to his actions over the past few days. He was practically convicted already, and his only hope now was to make sure he wasn't arrested.

'Stop,' the detective behind him called out. 'Stop right now!' In a way, it was a relief to hear that he seemed okay, though that brought with it other problems. 'Get down on the floor! I said, get down, right now!'

Fabian kept moving forward, past sofas, bookshelves and

dining room tables with candelabra, around a corner and down the next hallway in the labyrinthine flat.

The bullet missed him by inches and burrowed into the wall in front of him. Just as he would have if the roles had been reversed, the Danish detective had aimed for his legs. He managed to evade the next bullet by throwing himself to the left, into the hallway that led to the front door. The second bullet hit an electrical outlet, causing an explosion of sparks. Then all the lights in the flat went out.

Back on his feet once more, Fabian hurried on towards the front hallway. It was too dark now for his pursuer to fire any more shots. But it was a brief respite. The moment he opened the door, the light flooding in from the stairwell would make him the easiest of targets. But what choice did he have? The bullet must have hit his left upper arm the moment he launched himself out onto the landing, just before he landed on the floor and kicked the door shut. He didn't feel any pain. But he could see that the bullet had ripped entry and exit holes in the beige fabric of his jacket.

And as soon as he was back on his feet, he began to bleed. At first, it was just a few drops winding their way out through his sleeve, landing on the floor like tiny islets. But before long, the slow trickle turned into a rivulet. So he tore off his jacket, wrapped it around the wounds, and held it taut with his teeth while he tied a double knot to staunch the bleeding. All while hurrying down the stairs to the next floor.

'Hey! You!' a voice said from somewhere below. 'Stand completely still and put your hands above your head!'

Fabian didn't have time to see much more than that it was an SIU officer, wearing a helmet and a bulletproof vest and carrying an automatic rifle, before he dived down behind the railing. The voices below were multiplying quickly, and even though he couldn't hear what they were saying, it was clear they were on their way up to surround him.

Staying low behind the railing, he crawled across the floor towards the lift as the voices grew louder. Once he got to it, he reached up with his uninjured arm and pushed the button, which lit up with a faint blue glow as an electronic signal rang out and the doors slid open.

'Get down on the ground and put your hands behind your head,' shouted the first officer, who was running towards him with his gun raised.

But Fabian was already inside the lift, pushing the button to go down. The doors began to close as bullets ripped deep holes in the lift walls. These men were not trying to incapacitate a possible suspect with a bullet in the leg. They were hunting a terrorist.

Unfortunately, he couldn't detect any signs that the lift was going down. There were no vibrations, no movement. No display counting the floors. He pushed the bottom button again, but nothing happened. Instead, it was the officer outside, shouting to the others that the *subject* was on his way down in the lift, that finally let him breathe a sigh of relief and stand up.

He used the brief respite to pull his blood-soaked jacket tighter around his wounds and adjust the straps of his chest holster to turn it into a makeshift sling. Then he pulled out his gun and prepared to shoot his way out through the lobby the second the doors slid open.

It was him or them.

The terrorist or the heroes.

He jumped through the doors the moment they slid open. But not into the lobby. He stopped and looked around, realizing he was in an underground garage. How had he not thought of that before? Of course a property like this one had an on-site garage.

With his eyes sweeping back and forth and over his shoulder, he moved towards a pedestrian entrance next to the main garage door. Once he was outside, he filled his lungs with damp night air and started to walk slowly up the ramp, towards the distant sounds of shouting and various communication devices.

He'd made it a third of the way up when a car turned onto the ramp and drove towards him with its high beams on. He quickly turned back and heard the car behind him accelerate, and even though he'd lost so much blood, he ran the last few yards, only to discover that the garage door couldn't be opened from the outside.

With trembling hands, he pulled out his lock pick, but dropped it as tyres screeched behind him and a car door opened. As though it were the only thing left for him to do, he continued to tug at the door without turning around. As though he had to keep trying, even though fate had finally caught up with him.

'Maybe you should give that a rest and come with us instead,' a voice said in decent Swedish. A voice he hadn't heard in several years and had missed dearly.

He turned around and saw Dunja standing next to an ambulance. He was about to ask where she'd been the past few years. Why she hadn't answered his messages. How she had known to find him there. But he didn't know where to start, so instead he hurried over without a word and climbed into the ambulance.

'Get on the stretcher and strap yourself in.' She pulled the doors shut behind him and moved up to the passenger seat. 'Turn on the lights and the sirens.'

'Are you sure?' said the Indian man behind the wheel.

'No, but do it anyway.'

The Indian turned on the sirens and the flashing blue lights, turned the ambulance around, and drove back up the ramp. Fabian strapped himself to the stretcher as best he could and lay down in an attempt to relax. Which turned out to come more easily than he'd thought it would. To just lie there with his eyes closed, to let go and let whatever happened happen, filled him with a sense of peace.

After a while, he noticed the vehicle slowing down and eventually coming to a stop. But he was too tired to care. There were voices from the cab and information was exchanged with someone outside the vehicle. He was too tired to stay alert, ready to run.

When the sirens fell silent and they slowed down once more, he realized he must have dozed off.

'You're injured,' Dunja said, and when he opened his eyes, he saw that she was leaning over him, undoing the straps. 'Sit up so I can have a look.'

'When did you get so good at Swedish?'

'Who said I was ever bad at it?' She untied the jacket around his arm and inspected the gunshot wounds.

'How did you know where to find me?'

'How did you know that was your only way out?'

'But that's just it. I had no—'

'See that screen?' she broke in, nodding towards a screen that showed Sleizner's front hallway, kitchen and underground garage by turns. 'After he confessed, we kept an eye on him to make sure he didn't do anything stupid. We never dreamed he would jump.' She shook her head. 'And then you turned up in the middle of everything.'

Fabian looked at the screen, where the feed was now

flickering and then breaking up into static. 'You said something about a confession. What confession?'

'Fabian, you're not the only one with questions,' she said, cutting up his shirt sleeve. 'May I suggest that we hold off on asking them until we're sitting in front of a fireplace with a glass of whisky?'

He was about to object, but before he could speak, she'd squirted iodine into his wounds and a searing pain overwhelmed him.

'Just so you know, sewing was never really my thing,' she said, opening a sterile package containing something that looked like a curved needle and some kind of thread.

'Is that really necessary?'

'It's this or bleeding out.' She held the needle up to the light. 'And what good would you be to me dead?'

'Good? What do you mean—?'

'Look, we just saved you from having to spend the rest of your life in a Danish prison. So now it's your turn to help us. Simple as that.'

'He'd already jumped when I got there.'

'Maybe. But how does that help us when I'm a terrorist suspected of murder and you're a man who was in the wrong place at the wrong time?' She stuck the needle in next to the entry wound and began to stitch him up.

'What did you do to him?' he said in an attempt to distract himself. 'He said someone had beaten me to it, over the entry phone when I called. That I was too late. And there was a smell in his flat, like—'

'Something burning?' Dunja cut in while she reached for a pair of pliers and cut the thread. 'That reminds me of our agreement. You might not remember, but I decided we were going to hold off on the questions until we're in front of a crackling fire with glasses of whisky in our hands.' She angled his arm out to gain better access to the exit wound on the back of it and continued her work. 'You should count yourself lucky no one seems to have figured out who you are. On the police channel, you go by one of two names: *the man* or *the subject*. So hopefully, you'll be able to just go home and pretend nothing happened as soon as we're done here.'

'Speaking of which, we're almost there,' put in the Indian man driving the ambulance.

'Where?' he said, looking from Fareed to Dunja and back again.' Where are we going?'

'To a parking garage on Østerbro,' Dunja said.

'Or more precisely, to a secret basement that doesn't exist,' Fareed added.

'What basement? I don't understand what you need my help with? Sleizner's already dead.'

'True. But his two goons are still alive, and according to Sleizner, they can be found on the basement level of a property that was renovated seven years ago. At which point, not only were the stairs and the lift redone so they no longer reached the basement floor, but the entire basement floor disappeared. At least, from the blueprints that were submitted to the planning board.'

Fabian was about to ask what the point was of doing something like that but decided against it.

'So now you're probably wondering why anyone would spend so much time and money drastically altering the layout of a property by removing any way to access the basement, other than through a parking garage on the other side of the street,' Dunja went on as she snipped the last thread and began to wrap gauze around his arm.

'Dunja, you're not the person I met two years ago.'

'Good. Both of us have changed then. Who knows where this might lead?'

He looked her in the eyes. Saw that just like him, for a few seconds, she toyed with the idea of a very different future.

'Thanks for the help,' he said, realizing how naive he'd been. 'I really mean it. With all my heart. But I'd like you to pull over now.' He climbed down from the stretcher and turned towards the back doors.

'That's the second time you've thanked me. Do you realize that?'

'Dunja, what is it you want me to say?'

'Nothing. The best thing you can do right now is shut the fuck up and listen.' She paused and took a few deep breaths to compose herself. 'The first time I helped you out, I ended up being fired by everyone's favourite person, Sleizner. Since then, I've been forced to live more or less outside the law. But don't feel bad about it. I'd do it again if I had to. You solved that case and arrested the perpetrator. If it hadn't been for the help I gave you, that murderer would still have been on the loose and would likely have picked you and your old classmates off, one by one.'

'And now you want me to help you.'

'We're a man short, and from what I've seen, like me, you have nothing to lose.'

'I came here to hold Sleizner accountable. Now he's dead, and if there's one thing I know, it's that I have no more business here.'

'And what about these two?' Dunja handed over a grainy CCTV image of two men in military get-up. 'They executed Qiang Who, one of us, right in front of our eyes, on Sleizner's direct order. They stabbed a knife into his throat and left it there while he bled out. Can you imagine that? With a fucking knife in his throat. Look at this, if you don't believe me.'

'Dunja, I believe you,' he said when she handed him another grainy printout, this one showing an Asian man kneeling with his hands tied behind his back, fighting for his life with a knife through his throat.

'And you think we should just let them get away with it.'

'No,' he said after a quick glance at the picture. 'That's not why I can't help you.'

'Oh no? Okay. So may I ask—'

'Because you're wrong,' he broke in. 'Theodor is gone.'

'What?' Dunja clapped a hand to her mouth. 'What are you—?'

'He killed himself a week ago.'

'Oh my God.' Dunja came over and put her arms around him. 'I had no idea. Was it Sleizner?'

'It doesn't matter any more,' he said. 'The only thing that matters is that I have a daughter. I have no doubt she's both disappointed and angry with me. But she's alive, and I wouldn't risk losing her for anything in the world. Do you understand?'

Dunja looked him in the eye for a long moment without speaking, then nodded.

'But thank you for everything.'

'You already said that,' she replied, and she opened the back doors.

'It bears repeating.'

'You're welcome, again. For everything.'

He nodded in an attempt to fill the silence while he climbed out of the ambulance and stepped out onto the street. 'Who knows, maybe we'll meet again sometime.'

'Time will tell.' She pulled the door shut, then the ambulance indicated and drove off into the night.

58

THE LIGHTS TURNED from red to green in the usually heavily trafficked intersection. But during the darkest hour of the night, there was no audience. Like the rest of Østerbrogade, the intersection was deserted. No cars or cyclists as far as the eye could see. No lonely pedestrian sauntering across the empty street after a far too wet night.

The desolateness was like a stifling blanket. As though humanity had been annihilated overnight and the traffic lights just kept on changing, oblivious.

The one exception was the ambulance that slowly rolled through the intersection and turned into Gunnar Nu Hansen Square and then hung a right down the ramp of the 24-hour parking garage, whose door slid open silently like the maw of a giant whale large enough to swallow the vehicle.

Once it was inside, the ambulance parked as far from the auto repair shop as possible, and when the headlight had winked out and the engine gone quiet, Dunja and Fareed climbed out, closed the doors and hurried on, hunched over, hiding behind pillars and cars.

They had no concrete plan. The incursion was born of instinct. Of a shared conviction that Sleizner had told the truth when he'd said this was where the two men in camouflage would be. That their base of operations could be found here, in the secret basement lair.

They had no reason to doubt him. Dunja had never seen him as beaten down and deflated as when they finally managed to get the smouldering nappy off him. The pain must have been unspeakable, and it would certainly have been a long time before he considered raping anyone again.

But that had been the worst of it. Sleizner would have lived, and his wounds would have healed. It would have taken some time, but if there was anything he would have had lots of in prison, it was time.

Instead, he'd chosen to take his own life. She'd never know if it was the burns that drove him to it, or the fact that the threat of another go with the nappy had prompted him to confess to everything from the murder of Hesk to ordering Qiang's execution. Maybe it was a combination of the two.

Fareed raised one hand and quickly squatted down behind a car. Dunja did the same, but didn't understand why until she straightened up enough to see through the windows of the car she was hiding behind.

A lorry was parked with its back to the loading dock. She couldn't see any movements, on the dock or around the back of the lorry. And the driver-side window reflected the fluorescent ceiling lights, making it impossible to see if there was anyone inside.

She signalled to Fareed, and they continued to move towards the lorry in short, quick sprints behind the rows of parked cars. Once they reached it, she could establish that the cab was empty, and after trying both doors, that it was also locked.

A club, had been Sleizner's answer to the question of what they got up to in the secret basement. *A very exclusive club.* She had her suspicions as to what kind of club it might be, but it was the only question to which he hadn't given a straight answer. And the lorry didn't exactly help to clear things up, either.

Fareed climbed the steel staircase to the loading dock and had already pulled out his lock pick kit when she joined him. 'What do you think?' he said, studying the different needles in the fluorescent light. 'Do we go in?'

She made no reply. She honestly didn't know what they should do next. How they should act to avoid falling into the same trap as Qiang. She walked up to the lorry, touched the large padlock and put her ear to the metal door. Were they clearing out the basement? But then, why was no one here? Had they just gone home for the night? Or had Sleizner's death made the work grind to a halt?

She could hear no sounds from inside, but the silence wasn't reassuring. Quite the opposite.

'Let's start with the lorry,' she said finally and stepped aside to make room for Fareed, who immediately went to work on the padlock.

Despite liberal application of lubricant and three lock picks working at once, it was a long time before he could turn around and hold up the opened lock. Then he lubricated the hinges of the door while Dunja undid the espagnolette, and they opened the doors together.

Apart from a metal box in one of the far corners, the lorry was empty. Even so, Dunja stepped in and let the hard, rusty inside envelop her with a growing sense of unease. When she reached the box, she kicked it open with her foot. It contained a stack of removal blankets, a roll of black bin bags, some plastic water bottles, a box of tampons, and three rolls of kitchen towel.

She couldn't be sure, but the images the contents of the box conjured were as horrifying as she'd always expected, considering that Sleizner was involved. But maybe her expectations blinded her. Maybe the blankets were to prevent furniture from getting scuffed and maybe the water was for the removal men.

Then again, maybe not.

The question was answered when she noticed the writing on the rusty walls. The tiny, scratched letters that were almost invisible, but that turned out to be all around her. *Makeba*, it said on one side of a heart, and *Tatiana* on the other. And underneath, *Oksana, Elaya, Polina, Zendaya, Ramineh* and so on. The names seemed to cover large parts of the wall. She hurried back onto the loading dock. 'Fareed, we can't wait any longer. We have to go in.'

Fareed walked over to the metal door and got to work with the lock pick. After a few attempts, he was able to turn the lock and push down the handle. But for some reason, the door still wouldn't open.

'Hold on, I'll give you a hand.' Dunja hurried over to Fareed, braced with one foot against the wall and pulled as hard as she could on the door, which still refused to open more than a couple of millimetres.

'It's not budging,' Fareed said. 'It's probably bolted shut from the inside.'

'That means they're in there. Come on,' she said, hurrying down the steps. 'There's another way in.'

59

HEINESEN FINGERED HIS throbbing cheekbone as he followed the trail of blood out of the lift and across the concrete floor, torch in hand. His cheek was very swollen. The cut on it would have to be cleaned out and taped up; he might even need stitches. But like the calls from Hemmer and Bernstorff, it would have to wait. Right now, everything except the trail of blood on the floor in front of him would have to wait.

The trail led him past a number of parked cars, through the pedestrian entrance next to the main garage door to the ramp to the street, where it continued up the left side. But then, it suddenly stopped, or no, hold on...

He squatted down, let the beam of light from his torch sweep back across the dark-red stains on the concrete, and realized the bleeding man must have turned back down the ramp. Closer inspection revealed two different trails right next to each other. One with less time between droplets, one with considerably more.

If it was true the bullet had hit the man in his left upper arm, the trail suggested he'd walked up slowly and then, about a third of the way up, had turned around and run back down. And then the trail ended.

In other words, the person in question hadn't had a car waiting, he'd been picked up by someone else. Someone who had appeared when he was on his way up, and whom he had tried to run from.

Heinesen had left the station with his team and the Special Intervention Unit to arrest Sleizner and bring him in for questioning. But they'd arrived to find Sleizner dead on the street beneath his own balcony. It had so obviously been suicide that neither he nor Bernstorff nor Hemmer had given it a second thought.

Sleizner's association with Jakob Sand had painted him into a corner. There was no way out of it for him, and he'd preferred killing himself to facing the humiliation, to being forced to answer all their questions. It was drastic, but in a way so like Sleizner, to choose dying over losing face.

But he was no longer so sure.

Now, it would seem the man on the balcony had likely been behind Sleizner's fall. But no amount of speculation could tell him who that man was, how he'd got inside, or most importantly, what his motive may have been.

With a hand on his aching cheek, Heinesen continued up the ramp and looked over at the cordoned-off area at the front of the building. It had only been just over thirty minutes since they'd arrived at the scene, but it was already teeming with people, uniformed and plain clothes, all rushing about, looking like they knew what they were supposed to be doing among the countless police cars and ambulances with their flashing lights.

It was a response so massive it must have been ordered by the top brass, which was obviously what Hammersten had called to tell him. And sure, the fact that Sleizner was dead and might even have been murdered was serious. But the size of this response was proof of something else. Something much bigger.

'There he is,' someone called out behind him. 'Torben, he's over here.'

Heinesen turned around and saw Bernstorff and Hemmer running across the jet-black asphalt.

'Morten, what's going on?' Hemmer said, trying to catch his breath. 'Where did all these people come from? It's like someone blew up the royal palace.'

'I know.' He stepped in closer and lowered his voice. 'The answer is that I have no earthly idea. I suspect the orders are coming from the very top, but we'll have to wait and see. How did your examination of the body go? Did you get to finish?'

'Far from it.' Hemmer exchanged a look with Bernstorff.

'We were told to stop what we were doing and leave the area,' Bernstorff said.

'By whom?'

Hemmer looked over his shoulder before answering. 'Suddenly, this other technician showed up with a gaggle of assistants and just took over. We're not even allowed in the flat now.'

'It has to be Mads Jensen.'

'The Director of Public Prosecutions?'

Heinesen nodded. 'He categorically denied my request to bring Sleizner in for questioning. It didn't matter that I promised to keep it internal until we knew more. He said it would inevitably leak and be damaging to the police. And now this.' He gazed out at the flashing vehicles, which had begun to attract reporters and photographers. 'But you know what,' he said, turning back to Hemmer and Bernstorff. 'Let them have at it. There are no answers here anyway. If you go get the cars, I'll call Magnus.'

'Okay, but maybe this time you could tell us where we're going?' Hemmer said. 'Assuming that you trust us, that is.'

'Absolutely,' he said, nodding. But before he could say anything else, he was interrupted by his phone and saw that it was once again Henrik Hammersten. 'This is Morten Heinesen,' he said, trying to sound neutral.

'I assume you know who this is, so I won't waste time on introducing myself again.'

'Okay,' he said, pointing skyward to indicate to the others who was on the other end.

'Like I said the last time we spoke, it has come to my knowledge that you and your team were the first on the scene on Islands Brygge.'

'Yes, that's correct.'

'And I'm given to understand that this was the case because you were conducting your own investigation, aimed at Kim Sleizner. An investigation that, I'm told, was neither authorized by your superiors nor approved by a prosecutor.'

'That is correct, too. For obvious reasons, I couldn't inform Sleizner, who was my superior. Instead, I contacted Mads Jensen to—'

'Who did you contact?'

'Mads Jensen. The Director of Public Prosecutions, but he—'

'I know who Jensen is,' Hammersten broke in with an annoyed sigh. *'And I also happen to know that he expressly ordered you and your team to vacate the scene. And you have so far, I'm told, refused to comply with that order.'*

'I simply didn't see any other—'

'What you see or don't see is irrelevant. You were given a direct order. But instead of following it, you decided to bumble your way into something that could have ended in disaster.'

'Hold on, I don't follow.'

'Yes, I can tell. And since you seem unable to take in and process information, I'll spell it out for you. We've been watching Sleizner for two years. For obvious reasons, this work was delegated to an independent unit, which means that

right now, you're lucky he offed himself before you barged in and ruined everything. So in order to avoid any more misunderstandings, I want to lay out the two options you have going forward. Either you start to toe the line and contact the officer in charge at the scene to see if there is anything you and your team can do to be of service, or you hand in your resignation to me no later than eight o'clock this morning. Is that understood?'

'Absolutely,' he said, and signalled for Hemmer to hold out his diving watch, which told him it was half past four. 'That means I have three and a half hours left, and in order to avoid any more misunderstandings, let me be clear: I intend to continue working until then.'

The answer came in the form of silence, followed by a short click.

60

THE LOCK ON the door to the auto repair shop was far less of a challenge for Fareed than the padlock on the trailer had been, and it wasn't long before he and Dunja were walking past tools, jacks and cars, breathing in the smell of motor oil.

Like two shadows, they hurried through the dark reception area, across the worn linoleum, past the visitors' chairs and around the counter to the bullet-riddled door.

'So this was how Qiang got in.' Fareed looked around the cluttered office.

'Behind that poster.' Dunja pointed to a naked blonde with enormous breasts lying on her back on the bonnet of Jaguar E-Type with her legs spread under the words *No airbags needed*.

Fareed ripped it off the wall and punched in the code 7895, which Sleizner had assured them would still work. There was a faint click behind the filing cabinet, and Dunja just had to give it a light shove to make it slide into the wall, revealing an opening.

They hunched down and entered. Darkness enveloped them as it must have enveloped Qiang. Behind them, they heard the cabinet slide back into place and come to a stop with another click. Dunja had hoped the exit would remain open, to accommodate a hasty retreat. But they'd have to cross that bridge when they came to it.

She took out her phone to use it as a torch, but changed her mind when she realized her battery was down to just a few per cent. Instead, she pushed on through the darkness, with her hands on the rough walls, which closed in more and more. Eventually, they met in a dead end, at which point she stopped and looked around, even though it was impossible to make out anything in the dark.

Qiang had found a door; it had stood ajar and opened into some kind of control room. She'd seen it on the screens and remembered every step he'd taken. But that was over forty-eight hours ago, and much could have happened since then. It seemed unlikely Sleizner and his men would have simply sat back, twiddled their thumbs and hoped things would work out.

She hadn't considered that before. How odd it was that they'd locked the metal door from the inside but left the code for the filing cabinet unchanged. Given as how they were well aware this was the way Qiang had got in, they should have at least changed the code.

Had it just been an oversight in their frantic efforts to cover their tracks, or was it part of a plan? A plan aimed at her and Fareed. Had they in fact intended to lure them in through this entrance? Sleizner had done everything he could to lead them here, there was no denying that.

'Fareed,' she said and turned around, but she trailed off as a warm, pleasant light flooded in through a growing gap in a door diagonally behind her.

'I think this is where we go in,' he said and opened the door completely.

She recognized the room with the grey walls and the blue carpet, and the door to the adjacent control room, where Qiang had been attacked and knocked unconscious before his cameras cut out, was, just like that time, open a crack.

But unlike that time, several slots in the relay racks gaped empty and the loose ends of cut cables dangled limply here and there. That said, the control panel in the middle was still there, complete with screens and flashing units.

But just like the deserted intersection with its traffic lights, the place felt abandoned. As though the diodes would continue to flash forever under a growing blanket of dust.

Fareed went up to one of the screens, on which the percentage next to a blue bar changed from 89 to 90. 'It's copying something,' he said and started to rummage through the equipment until he eventually stuck his arm in between two computers and pulled out a portable hard drive that was plugged in and working at full capacity.

'How big is it?'

'Two terabytes.'

'So how long will it take it to copy the last ten per cent?'

'Hard to say exactly.' Fareed shrugged. 'An hour or two?'

'I assume it's encrypted, but do you think we could have a look at the contents while it's still going?'

'I'll see what I can do.' Fareed took out his laptop and plugged it into one of the hard drive's free ports.

Dunja tried to follow what was happening on Fareed's screen, but when the strings of indecipherable number and letter combinations became too long, she instead decided to have a look around. The problem was that she didn't know what she was looking at. Other than that it was a jumble of technology: cables, screens, and various modules displaying the same kind of meaningless letter combinations as the one holding Fareed's attention.

While she waited for him to finish, she sat down in the chair by the control panel and studied the rows of knobs and faders all the way to the top-right button, which was labelled *power*.

It was the first one she understood, and therefore the first one she dared to push.

The control panel lit up like a Christmas tree, and the static on three of the screens in front of her disappeared as they turned a solid blue. A number of tiny red displays had lit up as well, one next to each channel fader, running the length of the panel. Displays with symbols that formed words she actually understood.

Entrance the first channel said, and after she slid the fader up and pushed a few buttons at random, the middle of the three screens flickered to life, showing the dimly lit room with the purple sofa Fareed and Qiang had entered. *Sacrifice* the next one read, and once she found the right button, the screen switched to showing the room with the stone table ringed by candelabra. The next two were labelled H_1 and H_2, but the images from them were too dark for her to make anything out.

She pushed the button marked *Bar*, and one of the screens showed a softly lit bar lined by about ten bar stools and deep leather armchairs in the background. She continued through *Recreation*, *Spa* and *Hall of Crystals*, which looked like a ballroom with large crystal chandeliers hanging from the ceiling, heavy crimson drapes along the walls and a cluster of round tables in front of a stage at one end.

Then followed a number of channels with women's names, such as *Amelia*, *Charlotte*, *Emma*, *Aria*, *Stella* and *Delilah*. All looked like windowless cells, the décor dark with gold accents, mirrors on the walls, and a double bed in the middle of each room.

One of the buttons she pushed made the symbols on the little displays change to C_1, C_2, C_3 and so on, up to C_{16}.

Part of her knew instantly what the cramped rooms with

the dirty floors, metal toilets and bunkbeds with stained sheets were.

What she saw on the screen was impossible to ignore. They were cells in which at least two people had been locked in what appeared to be inhuman conditions. With only minor differences, they were all identical up to and including C8. Empty cells that, judging by how filthy they were, had been in use for years.

But C9 was different. Not because of how it looked. On the contrary, the cells were so alike she was unsure whether they were in fact different rooms at first, but everything changed when the pillow and tangled sheets in the upper bunk began to move.

'Dunja, check this out,' Fareed said behind her. But she didn't want to take her eyes off the screen. She wanted to see if there was really someone... 'Dunja.'

Eventually, she did tear her eyes away to look at Fareed's laptop, where a video was playing that showed eight men raping a young woman.

'I thought it was encrypted.'

'It was. But clearly not encrypted enough.'

The woman's vacant eyes showed that her mind was elsewhere as she let the men do whatever they wanted until they grew tired of it and left her alone. Except they didn't grow tired, they kept penetrating any orifice they could find. Sometimes just one at a time, while the others enjoyed a cigarette and had their champagne flutes topped up by a tall, scantily dressed woman with her blonde hair pulled back, sometimes all eight at once.

'Isn't that Jenny Nielsen?'

Fareed nodded. 'And that's our very own Director of Public Prosecutions.' Fareed pointed to one of the men, who was about to straddle the young woman's face. 'Whatever his name is.'

'Mads Jensen,' she said, and she realized she recognized most of the men. 'And that's Ryan Frellesen from Danske Bank, unless I'm mistaken.'

It was the cream of Danish society, from Stig Paulsen, head of the TDC Group, to Kai Mosendahl, Director of the Danish Customs and Tax Administration, and Minister for Foreign Affairs Morten Steinbacher.

'This is far from the only video. There seems to be no end to it.' Fareed clicked open a file system filled with MPEG-4 clips with titles like *ChristmasParty2009*, *S&M-Ryan3* and *JensenGoesTooFar*.

'Try that one.' Dunja pointed to a file entitled *Klinge1*.

The video showed the Head of Operations at DSIS on his back in one of the private rooms, straddled by the woman found dead next to him in his car.

She was riding him, and from one of the speakers came the sound of Klinge moaning as she moved. He had his eyes closed and was so into it he didn't notice the woman was suddenly holding a gun in one hand.

He didn't open his eyes until she shoved the barrel of the gun into his mouth. He resisted then, but the bullet had clearly already been fired, making parts of his brain spatter out across the bed and the mirror behind it.

The shot was no louder than a New Year's cracker, but before the woman could even climb off the lifeless body, the door behind her was thrown open and Jakob Sand could be seen bursting through it. She fired another shot, but missed, and when she tried again, the magazine appeared to be empty.

Jakob Sand reached her moments later, pulled the gun out

of her hands, and shoved his pocket square into her mouth. The woman kicked, flailed, and scratched at him. But Sand was stronger and yanked her off the bed, and the moment she hit the floor, he was on top of her with both hands around her neck. When her arms and legs finally fell limply to the floor, he straightened up, smoothed down his hair and tuxedo, and left the room.

It was still unclear why the woman had shot Klinge. Apart from that, the video instantly solved the murder case Hesk had been working on. The fact that Jakob Sand had been behind the murder of the woman would not only cause a media storm but also breathe new life into the old suspicion that he had killed a prostitute.

But even so, Sand was not her first concern, it was that Sleizner was nowhere to be seen in the video. And it was the same with the other files. She didn't see Sleizner's name on any of them.

She had turned to Fareed to ask if he'd had the same realization when a woman's voice rang out through a speaker behind them.

'Get down. I said, get down!'

They turned to the screens above the control panel and saw the blonde woman, now dressed in figure-hugging gym clothes, approaching the bunkbed in C9.

'It's her again.' Dunja pointed to the woman's back. 'Jenny Nielsen.'

'Wait a second.' Fareed looked from the screen above the control panel to his own laptop, where Klinge and the woman were still lying lifeless in the frame. 'Is that in real time?'

'Yes, it's five past five, right?' Dunja pointed to the timestamp in the corner of the screen.

Fareed consulted his watch and nodded while the young

woman in the top bunk tried to get away by crawling into the furthest corner.

But there was nowhere to hide. Jenny Nielsen had soon grabbed the woman's feet and pulled her out of the bed. Then she slammed the woman's head against the concrete floor until she passed out so she could drag her out of the cell more easily.

61

IT WAS ONLY a half moon, but it still provided most of the glitter on the lake that had been dug in the middle of Copenhagen sometime in the sixteenth century as an additional moat to protect the city from the Swedes, among others. Fabian stood by the eastern edge of it, gazing out across the water. Further down the shoreline, a young couple had taken their clothes off to go for a cooling swim, too drunk and maybe too in love to care about how filthy the water was.

He thought about a similar summer he and Sonja had spent together in 1994, in Stockholm. Every day had set a new heat record, and every night they'd stayed up to watch the football World Cup in the US, and after Sweden won the bronze medal, they'd headed out into the night and stripped naked on Skeppsholmen, intoxicated by the heat and each other.

Now, he was neither drunk nor in love, just on his way back to his hotel to check out and go home. Home, to save what could be saved. Sonja had already made her decision, and he couldn't blame her.

They'd both tried. Done their best. More than their best. They'd compromised, forgiven, started over, talked, quarrelled, reconciled. They'd fought the good fight. Together and separately. Towards the inevitable end. Because in his heart of hearts, he'd always known they wouldn't make it, and he was convinced she felt the same.

The question had been when it was okay to give up. When would the children be old enough? When would one of them meet someone else? When would failing feel preferable to living a lie? And maybe, maybe, they'd finally reached that point.

But it was different with Matilda. With her, he couldn't just make a decision, tear up the contract and divide their joint assets. She might never want to see him again. She might never again pick up when he called. But that didn't change the fact that she was his daughter and he would always be her father.

He pulled the gun out of his jacket pocket and was about to hurl it as far into the lake as he could with his uninjured arm when he noticed the picture of Qiang bleeding to death with a knife in his throat on the ground next to his feet. He picked it up and was just about to rip it to pieces when he realized he'd overlooked the most important thing about it.

And instead of throwing the gun away, instead of getting rid of the picture and going back to his hotel, Fabian turned around and started running back towards Østerbrogade. Back towards the parking garage Dunja had told him about. As fast as he possibly could.

It wasn't the knife, the blood, or Qiang's tortured face that finally made him see what all the different clues in Sleizner's flat had told him about what had really happened on that balcony. It was the barely visible gold chain with the little elephant god pendant around Qiang's neck. That was what had finally made everything fall into place. Where Qiang had been stored and, more importantly, why. Questions he hadn't even known to ask until he already knew the answer.

The answer that made him realize he wasn't done yet.

That he had one more thing to do.

One last thing.

62

ONE OF THE rooms had mirror walls and housed two weight benches and a punchbag that hung suspended from the ceiling. And weights. Dumbbells, kettlebells and straining barbells. And she found a kitchenette with a small table on which sat two half-full coffee cups. Both cold. A third room contained nothing but two wardrobes across from each other. Hanging inside them were suits, overalls, underwear, toiletry bags, and on a lone hanger, a fishing vest and a hat lined with lures. The beds in the two small bedrooms were unmade and judging from the heavy-duty clothing scattered across the floor, this was, as Sleizner had told them, where the two men lived.

But there was no one there now. Since leaving Fareed in the control room, Dunja had searched every nook and cranny of the secret facility behind the auto repair shop. The only sign of life she'd seen had been in the cells on the screens. The cells had been filthy and primitive. These rooms were clean, the walls were painted various shades of grey, and carpets covered the floors.

She did her best to ignore the voice in her head that said maybe the cells were located somewhere else entirely, putting all her faith in the door at the other end of the hallway she was rushing through.

It was the last one, and if it turned out to be a dead end, she didn't know what to do. There was no plan B. No plan

A either, for that matter. The only thing she and Fareed had eventually been able to agree on was that he should stay in the control room and wait for the hard drive to finish copying, and if she wasn't back by then, he should get as far away from there as he could and make sure the contents ended up in the right hands.

She was supposed to locate the cells. That was all that mattered right now. Down to the cells and that Jenny Nielsen. What was going to happen when she got there was anyone's guess.

At least the door opened when she pushed the handle, and when a motion sensor made the lights on the other side flicker to life, she immediately recognized the long tunnel under Østerbrogade from Fareed and Qiang's previous visit.

Once she stepped into the tunnel, she noted that the metal door that opened onto the loading dock was, as they had surmised, bolted from the inside. But she wasn't trying to get back out into the parking garage; she wanted to get into the basement that wasn't supposed to exist.

After covering the fifty or so yards to the other end of the tunnel, she punched in the code 7895 and was relieved to find that it worked here too. Like Qiang and Fareed before her, she pushed the heavy curtain aside and continued into the dimly lit room with the dark walls and the round purple sofa in the middle of the floor.

The door to the room with the sacrificial altar and the implements of torture stood ajar. But since she'd already seen that, she opted for the other door, which took her into yet another hallway. This one had doors all along its right side. Doors with brass name tags. *Amelia, Charlotte, Emma.* She didn't need to open them and see, she already knew what she'd find behind them, so she hurried on through a maze of hallways and rooms that brought to mind a casino designed to let gamblers enter but never leave.

A spa facility, a common room, a number of winding corridors and a massage room later, she found the ballroom that had been labelled *Hall of Crystals* on the control panel. It was just as impressive and timeless as the name made it out to be. A soaring ceiling, impressive crystal chandeliers, round tables with small red lamps, and a long bar and groups of armchairs at the far end.

The décor struck her as a mix of decadence and boudoir, but more than anything, it radiated wealth. Obscene, over-the-top wealth. The kind of wealth that could buy anything. But it was behind a heavy curtain at the back of the lit stage that she finally found something that told her she was on the right track.

A lift.

A lift that only went down.

Because down was where she was going.

Down to where it hurt the most.

Once she stepped out of the lift, it was like a different world. Granted, this one seemed as deserted as the one above. But gone was the dim lighting and the dark, gold-patterned walls. Here, the walls were clinically white, and recessed lighting bathed everything in a harsh white light.

She entered a gleamingly clean, whitewashed shower room with five wall-mounted showerheads in a row along one wall and as many toilets lined up across from them. The third wall was lined with sinks, and in the middle of the room were five bidets.

She instantly recognized the room. This was where it had happened. The scene she would never be able to unsee had played out here. But she didn't stop, she continued past a high-pressure shower and a few jerrycans with red warning triangles on the labels.

The room next to the shower room, also completely white, was equipped with a large overhead light attached to the ceiling via a sturdy arm, a gynaecological chair, and a metal table on wheels on which about ten long, thin surgical tools were neatly lined up on a towel.

Then followed a short corridor that led past a large window into a room with a plastic-covered bed surrounded by cameras on tripods to another lift, which, like the first one, only went one way.

Down.

How far down was hard to say, but further than she'd expected. Or maybe the lift was just unusually slow. Or maybe it wasn't travelling straight down but rather diagonally to one side. It was hard to tell in the faintly flickering light. But in the end, after what felt like several minutes, the lift stopped, and when she stepped out, the heavy, stagnant air and the acrid smell confirmed she was in the right place. That this was what she'd been looking for.

The walls, floor and ceiling surrounded her with rough concrete. Condensation that had trickled and dripped, dried, and trickled again. Sedimentation that would give any technician analysing them nightmares.

Sparsely placed, naked bulbs overhead lit a hallway narrow enough for a submarine. Barred doors on both sides opened into cells devoid of life. Of dignity. Of the last measure. More hallways. More cells. In one corner, a pile of trousers, tops, dresses, knickers and socks. Stained and tattered. Black bugs of a type she'd never seen before crawling around.

Even so, she squatted down to look for clues. Anything she could identify. That could give her a name. But distant voices made her straighten back up and continue down the hallway, following the pungent smell around a corner and into another tangle of hallways that in the end it took the sound of gunfire to lead her through.

And there he was, about thirty feet away, the ring finger on his right hand missing, wearing heavy boots, camouflage clothes and a gas mask. In one hand, he was holding a five-litre jerrycan, the contents of which he was pouring into a hole several feet across in the middle of the cracked concrete floor.

Every cell in her body was poised to rush in and attack. To do anything, so long as it made that man suffer like Qiang had. But she couldn't. Not yet. Not until she'd figured out what was going on.

But how was she supposed to do that?

How can a person comprehend the unfathomable?

The room was large, at least six hundred square feet, and like the rest of the sub-basement, it was made of concrete. A rushing, almost bubbling sound was coming from the large opening in the floor, which at least explained the stench, the unbearable, caustic stench that made every breath feel like a step closer to the end.

A few feet above the opening, a thick, round wooden lid hung suspended from a steel wire that ran through a block up by the ceiling to a winch mounted on the wall on her left, above a long row of jerrycans marked with red warning triangles.

The second man, also in camouflage, was standing at the back of the room. He was shining his torch on the young women lined up there without a shred of clothing on, their hands and necks shackled to a long chain secured to the wall behind them.

The terror in their eyes as they watched the man examine

one of them said more than Dunja was able to take in. As did the screams that came out of their taped-up mouths as a muffled, mournful murmur when he undid the chain around the woman's neck and hands with a fluid motion.

'Here's another one.' The man nodded to the scar in the shape of a cross between the woman's breasts and kicked her over to his colleague by the hole.

The woman shook her head and screamed something behind the tape. Something inaudible in an incomprehensible language they all understood. She was begging for her life. To escape judgement. But she didn't stand a chance. Against all the muscle. The bullet to her forehead. The hands shoving her over the edge.

The whole thing was over in seconds, and just as a distant thud came from the opening in the floor, the man standing over by the women shouted: 'Wratlov. Behind you.'

But Dunja had already reached the man by the hole, and with a firm grip on his right forearm, she pushed it up behind his back so hard his shoulder crunched out of joint, and his gun hit the concrete.

The man, whose name was apparently Wratlov, screamed inside his mask and tried, despite his limp arm, to turn around and overpower her, but his gun was already in her hand, the muzzle pressed against his temple.

'Okay, let's calm down,' she said, locking his unbroken left arm behind his back. 'And you, drop your weapon,' she shouted to the other man. 'Your gun! On the floor!'

'Famous last words.' He dropped his gun with a smile. 'Just so you know, you're not getting out of here alive.'

'That may well be.' Dunja fired a shot that made the gun by the man's feet skitter away across the floor. 'But let's take this one step at a time. Start by releasing them.'

The man hesitated, looking back and forth between the women, his partner, and Dunja.

'You do the sums as much as you like. Go ahead, consider all the factors and fill in every blank so you can figure out the most likely outcome. Or I could just tell you that no matter what conclusion you reach, I have absolutely nothing to lose.'

The man weighed his options for a few more moments before turning around and starting to undo the chains. Then something struck the back of her head. Something hard that made her skull crunch, or maybe that was when her head hit the concrete. She wasn't sure. All she knew was that suddenly she was on her back with a blinding pain in her head and eyes so unfocused the man standing above her was little more than a diffuse shadow.

'Hello there. How are you feeling?'

She tried to place the voice, but her thoughts refused to obey, straying every which way.

'You should be happy I only used this little rascal.' The diffuse shadow held out something that looked like a shiny marble ball and leaned down until she could see who was smiling at her.

But she refused to accept it. She shook her head frantically. Realized how much the back of her head hurt. But there was no helping it. It couldn't be true. Her eyes were deceiving her, that was the only reasonable explanation. It couldn't be true. Maybe that was why her head defied the pain and kept shaking. As though to convince her that what she was seeing was a lie. An inverted mirage escaped from her worst nightmare.

'I wish you could see yourself.' Sleizner chuckled and shook his head, mirroring her. 'You almost look as though you were staring at a dead bloke. "Ooh, I see dead people."'

But it wasn't a lie. He was alive. She couldn't understand

how it was possible. But the prick was alive. Unless she herself was dead and just hadn't come to grips with it yet. That this was what it was like the last few seconds before awareness winked out.

'Yes, that's right. It's just little old me.' Sleizner spread his hands. 'So, we meet again, eh? Nice, no? I don't know about you, but I've never been much of a believer. But when I look at myself in the mirror, it's as close to resurrection as it gets. Don't you think?'

She made no reply. Wasn't about to let him drag her into his little game. Instead, she reached for his trouser leg. A tug, that was all that was needed. He was too busy congratulating himself to notice her hand. One little tug, followed by a kick, and he'd lose his balance and topple over the edge.

'No, no, no.' He pulled his foot away. 'That's not how this—'

That was all she heard before the ball in his hand struck her a second time.

63

FABIAN JOGGED ALONG Østerbrogade, scanning the street for anything that might be a public parking garage, while his brain tried to recall the details of what had happened in the flat on Islands Brygge.

The conversation he'd had with Sleizner via the entry phone, during which Sleizner had assumed he was someone else. Someone he'd apparently been expecting. Someone called Morten Heinesen. Probably the detective who had arrived twenty-five minutes later. The lift that had been on its way down but hadn't let anyone out on the ground floor. The open wardrobe, the clothes on the floor, and the bottle of vodka left in the wrong place. The necklace with the Ganesha pendant.

And the smell.

Above all, the smell in that storage box.

Everything suggested it was impossible. That desperation was making him think the pieces were part of a puzzle. A puzzle that didn't exist. That made no sense at all, no matter how you looked at it. But suspicion had found a toehold inside him, and whether or not there was anything to it, he had to find out for sure before he could go home and start the rest of his life.

So far, four cars had passed him. All of them taxis, of which one had pulled over into the cycle lane, assuming he wanted a ride, since he'd looked over his shoulder and watched it drive past him.

This time, it wasn't a taxi that made him stop and turn around; it was the flashing blue lights from a number of emergency vehicles. They were still too far away for him to count them, but he guessed three.

They shouldn't be looking for him. He'd left his phone in the hotel room, turned off, and no one had followed them in the ambulance. That said, someone could have called the police. Someone who'd recognized him, which would mean the Danish police had identified him.

Unfortunately, he was in the middle of a public square and would be in full view when the flashing emergency vehicles passed. So he ducked down behind a shrubbery, only to discover it hid the entrance to the garage he was looking for.

He heard the cars approaching, and when he realized they were turning off their lights and pulling into the square, he saw no other solution than to trot down the concrete ramp and hurry over to the pedestrian door next to the main garage door.

He'd seen the first car before, from Sleizner's balcony, when it pulled up to the dead body on Islands Brygge. So that was the Morten Heinesen Sleizner had been expecting, the detective who had later chased him through the flat. The black van probably contained the trigger-happy Special Intervention Unit.

He was grateful the door to the 24-hour garage was unlocked so he could get in without difficulty. But at most, it bought him a few seconds; he could already hear tyres screeching on the ramp outside.

In an attempt to buy himself some more time, he climbed up on a wall-mounted fire extinguisher and ripped out the cables to the motor that opened the door. Then he sprinted over to the auto repair shop, where he'd spotted a broom he could stick through the handle of the pedestrian door so that didn't open either.

Before long, the sound of upset voices reached him, then someone started to pull on the door. The broom held, and Fabian backed away, well aware the clock was ticking.

Since Dunja had mentioned something about the garage being connected to a secret basement via a tunnel under Østerbrogade, he began his search in that direction.

He soon came across a lorry parked by a loading dock. Not necessarily significant in itself, but when he noticed the lorry's rear doors were wide open, he didn't hesitate to pull out his gun and disengage the safety while he climbed the steel steps to the loading dock.

But there was no one there, not on the dock and not inside the lorry, so he continued towards the metal door while the sound of pounding from the entrance to the garage continued to echo between the concrete walls. As expected, the door was locked, so he went back to the lorry and stepped into it.

Any questions he might have had about what kind of goods the lorry was intended to transport were answered the moment his eyes grew used to the darkness and he noticed the women's names scratched into the rusty walls. But then, Sleizner had already crossed every line and done what everyone had thought impossible. Why not this, too?

What did surprise him was the name in the far-left corner, about three feet from the floor. It was the only male name he could see. And it was a name he recognized from his final year up in Stockholm.

Diego Arcas.

Diego Arcas was now an inmate of Hall Prison, serving a sentence as one of the brains behind an extensive trafficking network they'd busted in 2009. But apparently it was still active, aided and abetted by Sleizner.

He had no idea what the cross scratched above the name might mean, and he had no time to ponder it, because at that moment, the metal door on the loading dock behind him opened. He turned around, but in the backlight, he could only make out the contours of a woman with her hair pulled back, walking towards him.

'Get on the floor! Face down! Spread your arms and legs!' he called out, aiming his gun at the woman, who stopped right outside the lorry. 'Get down on the floor,' he repeated in English, and only then did he register the two projectiles with long, spiral-shaped metal tails that were flying through the air towards him.

One bored its barbs into his left leg and the other bit into his right hip. The electric shock that followed surged through his body and made time stop, and even though he was fully conscious when his legs buckled under him, cramping and seizing, he was unable to do anything but collapse limply to the floor.

64

FAREED'S EYES WERE red from staring at the screen while he waited for the pulsing blue bar to go from 99 to 100 per cent. A wait that had so far cost him twenty-five and a half minutes and eighty-three blinks. It had taken the bar twenty-seven minutes to go from 98 to 99, so he should be close now. On the other hand, the time each percentage point had required had ranged from two to thirty-three minutes, which meant the final step could just as easily take over an hour.

In other words, he had no idea how long it would be until the copying was completed so he could unplug the hard drive and get out of the control room, back to the ambulance. The only thing he knew for sure was that unless it dinged soon, his eyes risked melting out of their sockets.

A loud thud that sounded like a distant explosion made the floor under his feet tremble. But maybe it was just a door slamming shut extra hard. Hopefully, it was Dunja on her way back. Best-case scenario, she'd found the two men and taken her rage out on them, so they could leave this godforsaken shithole together.

He hadn't liked the idea of splitting up in here. Alone, they were less than half as strong as they were together. He didn't need to remember what had happened to Qiang to know it was a bad idea. But Dunja had refused to listen and had sworn she would be back before the copying was done.

But her words had been as meaningless and empty as a candidate's promise on the eve of an election. She'd even kissed his cheek before rushing off. She'd never done that before and it couldn't be interpreted as anything but a final farewell. Which was why he was immensely surprised to hear what he thought might be the sound of distant footsteps in the hallway outside.

He went over to the door and popped his head out. He could definitely hear something. Unfortunately, it sounded like more than one person. How many was hard to say, but at least a couple. And now he could hear voices too. Male voices communicating in monosyllabic staccato, like soldiers giving each other orders.

An electronic ding made him turn back to the screen, where the pulsing bar was finally filled. He frantically ripped out the hard drive, shoved it into his backpack along with his laptop, and hurried back towards the open door with the bag slung over his shoulder. But by the time he reached the threshold, he realized he had to turn back.

The men were too close. He could hear them clearly now. They were no more than fifty feet away. Maybe less.

He looked around the small room for somewhere to hide. He, who normally never panicked, was now barely able to move. Let alone think a single coherent thought.

It was all Dunja's fault. Ever since she came into his life, he'd been too busy to do his yoga or meditate. And now here he was, sweat glands pumping, and as though it were a game of hide-and-seek, he crawled in and hid under the control panel.

But this wasn't hide-and-seek. He didn't know what it was. Other than that he was going to end up with a knife in his throat if they found him, which was why he pressed himself even further back, in behind a desktop computer and a pile of loose cables. Or would they do something else, just to surprise him? Stab him through the eye instead, maybe. Or why not...

It was anything but deliberate, but the moment he heard the men reach the doorway, he stopped thinking and breathing altogether and just sat there like a petrified Houdini who during his grand finale had suddenly come to realize this wasn't what he was supposed to be doing with his life.

He didn't breathe again until he was sure the steps had continued past the door, but moments later the steps stopped, replaced by voices once again exchanging a handful of clipped sentences.

Not long after, a pair of heavy boots entered the control room and stopped in the middle of the small space. He could hear the man breathing and scratching his stubble. He was once again holding his breath, controlling every muscle in his body so he wouldn't accidentally brush against something that might make a noise.

The silence felt like a game of chicken, in which the first person to make a noise lost. He won the game when two loud thuds reached his ears.

That he'd actually lost only dawned on him when he realized the thuds had been the sound of the man's knees hitting the floor. But by then, it was already too late. The man was on his hands and knees, staring him right in the eye.

65

FABIAN ONLY HAD time to register yet another extravagant lamp passing by overhead before everything went dark again. When he managed to force his eyelids up once more, the blonde woman in front of him had dragged him even further into the dimly lit maze of hallways by the rope around his ankles. Then everything went dark again, as though there were a glitch in his brain.

Each time he blacked out, he also lost control of every muscle below his waist. As though he were experiencing an endless epileptic seizure, stuck in a loop of convulsive twitching, triggered by the pulsating current between the two wired metal barbs.

'Listen,' the tall blonde woman in front of him said into her headset. 'I was just getting things ready for transport, okay? And then I saw this bloke poking about inside the lorry.'

But something had changed. Maybe his body was getting used to the electric shocks. Or maybe the taser was running out of battery after being in maintenance mode for several minutes to keep him incapacitated.

'I have no idea,' the woman continued. 'It was just open.'

The shocks were definitely growing weaker; when he came to after yet another attack, he could even move his right arm a little.

'No, no driving licence, no nothing. But I think it's that Swedish detective, Risk.'

If only he'd been able to pull himself up, he could have yanked out the barbs and regained control. But it was out of the question; the muscles of his torso had a life of their own.

'How the fuck am I supposed to know? How is that my responsibility? I'm taking him to the shower room, and you take him from there, okay?'

What he did manage to accomplish, even though everything went dark again, was to grab hold of one of the many draperies and hold on long enough to hear it fall to the floor, rod and all.

'Fuck... I have to go.' The woman in front of him stopped and turned to him with a weary sigh, completely unprepared for the blow.

The curtain rod hit her across the ear. 'What the fuck?' Not particularly hard, but hard enough that she was suddenly more focused on her bleeding ear than on parrying his next blow, for which he used both hands, defying the pain in his injured arm to shove the end of the rod into her face. She groaned faintly before staggering to one side and collapsing in a heap.

66

'No idea. But I trust you'll take care of... Good... Fifteen more minutes, tops. That's all I need.'

It was just a few feet away from her.

'Yes, if you haven't heard from me in fifteen minutes, you can come down. But not before then. Is that clear?'

The voice that had risen from the dead.

'No, she's still out, so you go ahead as planned.'

The voice that should have been silenced forever.

'I don't give a flying fuck about what he did or didn't tell you. I'm in charge here, and I'm telling you I'm going to deal with her. In my own way. Okay?'

She was on the floor, on her side, with her arms tied behind her back and something cold and hard around her neck. The corrosive smell told her she was somewhere near that opening in the floor. Escaping was out of the question. The smallest movement risked drawing his attention.

'That's your problem. Sort it out. I want fifteen minutes alone with her down here.'

She tried to open her eyes but couldn't tell if she'd succeeded. Couldn't see anything. Other than grey, nebulous patches. As though she were looking into her own brain.

'Now you listen here.'

But the pain, it was there. Somewhere. Like a distant storm. But why wasn't it more intense, considering how hard he'd hit

475

her? Had she lost sensation? Was that why? Was she even able to move?

'No, you listen to me. I'm not going anywhere until I'm done here, and I won't be done here until she's awake so she can look me in the eye when I—'

The voice broke off, replaced by footsteps against the concrete floor.

'Well, well.' The voice was closer now. 'If it isn't Sleeping Beauty, waking from her slumber.' Much closer.

Dunja turned her head and felt the cold chain around her neck shift. Felt it running down her back to her hands and feet. Felt his breath.

'Apparently it makes no difference how much I hate you, every time I see you, I can't help but think how good we could have had it,' he went on, and she heard him straighten up and take a step away from her.

She blinked, realized her eyes were open, and blinked again. The grey fields were slowly coming into focus, and after a few more blinks, she could make out more than just a blurred outline. His sweaty forehead, his chapped lips, and his smile. The superior smile of a person who knew he was holding all the cards and was overcome with pleasure at the thought of what was about to happen.

'But we already talked about that, and there's nothing worse than people endlessly repeating themselves. And I'll be all right. Not you so much, though.'

'You killed yourself,' she said as he hung his jacket up on the winch handle on the wall behind her.

'Yes, I suppose I did.' He picked up a gas mask that lay next to a row of jerrycans full of hydrofluoric acid and checked it over before turning to her. 'Don't you get tired of yourself sometimes? You know, that feeling of being stuck in the same old rut, repeating yourself over and over like a senile parrot.' He waited for her reaction, but she said nothing. 'No? Okay, fine. I do on occasion, though, and I definitely would if I were you.'

There was no one else in the room. No young women in chains. No men in camouflage. Just her and Sleizner. And his smile. That smug fucking smile that would have made anyone else's face sore.

'So the whole dying thing is actually an idea I've been toying with for a while. Because it would feel so good to just reset everything and start over.' He removed his cufflinks and rolled up his shirtsleeves. 'You know, shed my skin, become something else entirely. I mean, just a hundred years ago, I would have been dead and buried at my age. No wonder we have mid-life crises. Some try to work through it with therapy. Others get divorced, change their careers, or move out to the country to ferment things or take some ridiculous fucking pottery class or whatever. I apparently had to die to find my new life.' He chuckled and shook his head. 'And thanks to you and Jan Hesk, all the pieces fell into place. A bit sooner than I'd planned, true. But what does that matter in the grand scheme of things? And your little Chink friend, of course. Let's not forget about him.'

She was sorry she'd said anything. That she'd given him a reason to lay it all out for her and revel in his own cunning. But her silence wouldn't have been enough to stop him. Nothing could have kept him from boasting. It was the whole reason he was there. That she was still alive.

'As you already know, some pretty important people are members of our little club,' he continued, opening a bottle of water.

Was he bluffing or did he know she and Fareed had found the videos?

'Dunja, seriously.' Sleizner heaved a sigh and drank. 'Have I really overestimated you this badly?' He came over and squatted down next to her. 'Or have you underestimated me yet again? Of course I know which videos you and your little curry boy saw on that hard drive. No need to look so surprised. Why else do you think I rolled out the red carpet for you and made sure the door codes weren't changed? Here, have some water.' He put the bottle to her lips and poured. 'There's no reason to die thirsty.' Most of it trickled down her cheek, but what little she managed to swallow at least washed down the worst of the dust in the back of her throat.

'Fareed. Did you catch Fareed?'

'Fareed Cherukuri. That's his name, isn't it?' Sleizner stood up, knocked back the last of the water and threw the bottle in an arc over her and into the hole. 'Or maybe I should say it was his name.'

'Answer me. What did you do to him?'

Sleizner chuckled and gave her three slow claps. 'And the Oscar goes to... Come on. Who is this performance for? Yourself? I certainly don't find it very convincing. The truth is, if we're both being honest, that you couldn't care less about your tea-slurping Indian or that elephant bloke. They were just a means to an end for you. Disposable. So just drop the act already.' He glanced at the old Nokia screen. 'Look, we don't have all night, so let's stick to the subject. Which is to say my little demise.'

'Kim, forget I asked. I honestly don't give a toss.'

Sleizner chuckled. 'You're a funny one. Anyway, I needed two things to pull it off. A body and a plausible scenario.' He moved in behind her. 'The body was never much of a problem. Pretty much any old corpse would do.'

She could hear him unzip his trousers and urinate into the hole.

'As it happened, I used your chubby little friend. Granted, he was nowhere near as fit as me, and his skin was yellower than diarrhoea. But Oscar Pedersen will see to those details. He's always been a loyal member of our little club, and he has already identified my body. Speaking of which, didn't you work with him on your very first case?'

She nodded. It didn't surprise her at all to learn that Oscar Pedersen was one of them. The first time she'd met and shaken hands with him, she'd felt dirty for days afterwards.

'He asked me to send his love when he called to tell me I've been cremated and am ready to be put in the ground,' he continued as he squeezed the last few drops out of his bladder and zipped his trousers back up. 'And in case you're wondering, I can assure you it didn't hurt half as much as your attempted incineration.'

'Is he alive?'

'Who?'

'Fareed?'

Sleizner rolled his eyes. 'Here I am, about to tell you how I managed to build such a credible scenario, and you're back to harping on about—'

'Kim, I want you to answer me. Is Fareed alive or not?'

Sleizner shook his head. 'You'll never make me believe you care one wit about his... condition. The only thing that gets your juices flowing is the idea of getting to me. You might as well admit it.'

'You think you know me,' she said. 'But the truth, if that's what we're discussing here, is that you have no idea who I am.'

Sleizner burst out laughing and shook his head. 'Sweet little Dunja.' He knelt down, bent over and kissed her cheek. 'The truth is I know everything there is to know about you. Probably more than you know yourself. And how is that, you ask?'

'No, I don't.' She shook her head. 'I'm not asking anything. So we might as well wrap this up. I don't know what you have planned, but let's just get to it so we can be done.'

'The only thing I need to do to see straight through you,' he went on as though he hadn't heard her, 'is to look at myself in the mirror. Turn my gaze inward, as they say.' He stood up and backed away a few feet. 'You see, you and I, we're not so different as one might at first assume. I'd say we're more similar than we're different. Take sex, for instance. I get horny and like to take what I want, and I'm not ashamed of it. And you.' He pointed at her. 'You're the same way. When the mood strikes, you see it as your right to hit the town on a Tuesday night and choose someone. The only difference is that you're a woman and I'm a man, which means you get to carry on unpunished.'

'Has it ever occurred to you that people might prefer having sex with me to being raped by you?'

'Well, I never got to finish what I started at that Christmas party a few years ago. From what I recall, we were only just getting warmed up when Hesk burst in, playing the hero. If not for him, you would have experienced something very different from your pathetic Tuesday shags. I promise you.'

'I have no doubt.'

Sleizner replied with a smile and turned around to fetch another bottle of water. 'So close to death and still so cocky. It must feel good to be so full of yourself and so convinced you're on the "right side" and one of the "good guys".' He unscrewed the top and drank.

'I don't know if I'd call myself one of the good guys. But at least I'm not a monster like you.'

'Monster?' He pondered that for a moment before nodding. 'Sure, why not? I certainly never thought of myself as good. I'm happy to admit it.' He walked over to her again, squatted down, and carefully poured water into her mouth. 'Being kind has always bored me somehow. "Kind." I mean, what the fuck is that?' He shook his head. 'The word alone is annoying. Thinking about others and getting in the back of the queue. "Who am I to..." Come on. Is that how you would describe yourself? Is that why you're here? To help the weak? All the people out there who can't be arsed to work, who just want to live off welfare and be coddled until they're so fat they can't even get through their front doors? Is that why you're tied up here, thinking about what awaits you once I roll you over that edge? Because you're so bloody kind? Hardly.' He stood back up and drank the last of the water before tossing the bottle.

This time, she counted the seconds.

'Evil, on the other hand,' he went on. 'Now that's interesting. That's where things are happening.'

Five... Six...

'That's where the forward motion is.'

Seven... then she heard it land.

'Natural selection, survival of the fittest. I'm talking Charles fucking Darwin. I'm talking development. Progress. Evolution. You name it. It all rests on a foundation of evil. We have evil to thank for everything. Like this.' Sleizner spread his arms. 'If not for evil, none of this would have existed.'

'That sounds pretty good to me.'

'Dunja, nothing would have existed. No Copenhagen, no buildings, no cars, no phones. Not even a little dildo to stick up your cunt. And that wouldn't have been much fun, now would it? Though it doesn't really matter, because neither one of us would have existed, and no one else either, for that matter, good or evil. No animals. No plants. Nothing. The world, the universe, or whatever you want to call it, wasn't built on goodness. Quite the opposite. And you know that as well as I do. And do you know why?' He sat down next to her. 'Do you know why none of what I'm telling you is news to you?' He leaned down and looked her in the eye. 'Because whatever delusional self-image you're toting around, evil has always been an important part of you. Maybe the most important. I saw it in your eyes the first time you stepped into my office, and I saw it a few hours ago when you set that nappy on fire. How good it felt to watch me suffer, even though you hadn't planned it. How you enjoyed it more than you'd ever enjoyed anything before. How you enjoyed defeating me. Finally exacting your revenge. I don't know if you agree, but I don't think you've ever been as true to yourself as you were in that moment. And even though it hurt, and God knows it still does, it was wonderful to see you accepting your nature for once, instead of fighting it. It was, how to put it, the very picture of harmony.'

She wanted to argue. Protest and spit her arguments in his face. Show him how wrong he was. Prove how radically different they were. But all she could do was nod. Anything else would have been a lie.

She had relished her revenge. Watching him suffer had been invigorating. She'd crossed one line after another without the slightest pang of conscience. She had long since stopped considering what was legal or illegal. As long as she held the moral high ground. As long as she was doing the right thing.

But she'd lost the moral high ground the moment she set him on fire. That was the moment she'd crossed a line there was no coming back from.

She had become like him.

It had never been clearer.

Like the man she hated above everything else.

'It was why we became police officers in the first place. Wasn't it?' He gently stroked her cheek with the back of his hand. 'Not because we're good people who want to make the world a better place. It's like soldiers. Not one of them wants peace on Earth. On the contrary, if that were ever to happen, they'd be so bored it wouldn't take them long to start shooting at each other. You and me, we're the same. Being on the side of right and working for the good in this world might sound like a wonderful idea, and most of our colleagues have said it and repeated it so many times they've started to believe it. But the truth, since that's what we're talking about, is that it was evil that first drew us to policing. Wasn't it?'

She nodded again, and he leaned down.

'Being close to what's forbidden.'

All the way down.

'To the life-and-death struggle.'

Face to face.

'To the taste of blood and the smell of corpses.'

Breath to breath.

'The closer, the better.'

She opened her mouth and met his lips, letting his tongue find its way in. At first, he was tentative, as though he didn't want to be too forward, as though he didn't dare to believe it was different this time. That she wanted nothing more than for his tongue to play with hers, to claim her mouth. To fill her up. Then he finally relaxed and started to go at it. She replied in kind, offering resistance. Offering exactly what he wanted.

She couldn't remember where, but somewhere she'd read the jaw muscle was the strongest in the human body. Not even the thigh muscles, which were far bigger, could exert the same force on an external object. Even so, she was surprised by the sudden taste of blood when her teeth sank into him, into his tongue.

It was the same thing with his panicked scream. She wasn't prepared for it or for his violent attempts to break free. But more than anything, she was unprepared for her own reaction. That she didn't let go, but rather clamped down even harder. That she had no problem breathing through her nose so she could swallow his blood without choking.

He couldn't have been more right, she had time to think before biting down one last time. About how evil made her feel at peace with herself and about how much she enjoyed his suffering.

She spat out the severed piece of tongue. Was struck by how small it looked as it landed in a pool of blood on the concrete floor. Small relative to the screams coming from Sleizner where he sat bent over on his knees with his hands in his bloody mouth, as though he needed to touch what was left with his fingers to comprehend what had happened. The penetrating, wordless screams that were so full of pain it spread to her.

She rolled over and kicked him hard with both feet. The whole thing happened so quickly her mind failed to keep up. But he went quiet, as though someone had pushed the mute button, the moment he disappeared over the edge and fell into the hole.

Once more, she counted the seconds.

Four... Five... Six...

But she didn't hear him hit the bottom.

Seven... Eight... Nine...

Instead, she heard something else. Was that him breathing? Ragged, shallow breaths. On the verge of panting. Like her own.

With her hands and feet still chained behind her back, she scooted towards the opening in the floor. It took a while, but once she could peer over the edge, she spotted him a few feet down, clinging to the rough wall. Below him, there was nothing but endless darkness.

'Please...' He sounded intoxicated, panicked. 'Please, help me...' His words were slurred. 'I'll do anything... Anything, if you just help me... Please, I'm begging you...' Blood bubbled out of the corners of his mouth and trickled down his throat. 'I don't want to die... Not like this... You have to help me. Do you hear me? I need your help...'

All she had to do was lie there and wait. Watch him fight to hold on. Watch his nails go whiter and whiter until he finally lost his grip. It could take two minutes or ten. He was stronger than he looked. Maybe even an hour.

'The key...' he continued. 'In my jacket... there, behind you...'

She turned around, saw his jacket on the winch handle and started to scoot across the floor. She was faster this time. As though her shoulders, abdominal muscles, back, her entire body was getting used to having her hands and feet tied. Once she reached the jacket, she rolled onto her back, pulled it down with her feet, and searched the pockets with her hands still behind her back.

She found the key almost immediately. Within minutes, she'd managed to fit it into the padlock behind her. Once it was unlocked, she made short shrift of the rest of her shackles and moments later, she was back on her feet.

A searing headache reminded her of the blows to the back of her head. She gingerly explored the area with one hand and noted that quite a bit of blood had gushed from the two cuts in her scalp, but that the bleeding had almost stopped.

She probably had a mild concussion. But nothing a couple of stitches and a week of rest wouldn't cure.

She returned to the hole in the floor and looked down at Sleizner, who was still clinging to the wall.

'Please...' he repeated in that intoxicated voice as he stared up at her. 'You're free... it's up to you... but please get me out of here. I'll do anything you want. I've already confessed. Because that's what you wanted, isn't it? To see me convicted.'

She turned around and started to walk towards the exit.

'No, Dunja. Don't go... Come back. Don't go. This isn't you. I know you're not like this,' he called after her. 'You want to do the right thing... You always have, and if you walk away, you'll regret it... I promise... For the rest of your life...'

She stopped next to the winch, grabbed the handle and started to turn it. Each revolution lowered the massive wooden lid that hung from a steel wire another inch towards the opening in the floor.

'No, Dunja... Don't close... Please... I don't want to die. Do you hear me? I don't want to...'

She tried to shut down her thoughts and just keep turning the winch. Lower the lid and let him disappear forever. He was already dead.

But what did that make her?

Who was she?

Really.

Not just now. After all of this.

When this was over.

Who would she have turned into?

67

FAREED SAT ON the floor, his hands tied and his back against the wall, and he'd never been so terrified of doing something wrong. The slightest movement risked provoking the man in camouflage squatting in front of him, going through his backpack.

So far, neither one of them had spoken, and he wasn't going to be the one to break the silence. Speaking without being spoken to was asking for trouble. If he was asked a question, on the other hand, any question, he was going to answer it honestly and without obfuscation. Trying to be clever wasn't an option for a person in his position.

Even if they asked for the password to his laptop, he'd give it to them without hesitation. That would be problematic, and he could only hope they didn't discover that he'd decrypted their hard drive and stolen some of its contents.

If they did, his chances of survival hit zero. And he wasn't ready to die. Not yet. They'd already taken Qiang, and maybe Dunja too; he might be the last man standing. The only silver lining was that he was, in fact, still alive. Maybe they'd realized he was more useful to them that way. Or maybe they just wanted to draw it out to toy with him. So they could deal the final blow when he least suspected it, like they had with Qiang.

The man looked up from his backpack and fixed him

intently. Fareed was too slow to react; he should have lowered his eyes immediately. Staring back meant instigating a power struggle. But if he looked down now, he might as well give the man the finger. So he sat there in a wordless contest that was only interrupted when the man's partner stepped into the control room.

Unlike the first one, he wasn't dressed in heavy boots and coarse camouflage clothing, but in regular trousers and a jacket. Fareed had figured they were both military, but maybe this wasn't the other half of the pair, but rather a third man. Maybe this was their boss, who had come to decide what to do with him.

How, when, and where.

'Do you work for Dunja Hougaard?' The man took another step forward and looked down at Fareed, who nodded.

'What's your name?'

'Fareed. Fareed Cherukuri,' he replied. His whole body was beginning to shake from the strain of sitting so still.

The man squatted down, studied him, and nodded with grim determination. 'My name is Morten Heinesen,' he said, and unlocked his handcuffs. 'I'm from the Copenhagen Police.'

'The police?' Who was this man? How could they have missed him? 'You're from the police?' Fareed didn't know what to think.

'That's right,' Heinesen said with a nod. 'You and I have a lot to talk about, but before we do, I'd like you to tell me where Dunja is.'

'I don't know.' Fareed shook his head. 'I have no idea. I don't even know if she's still alive. I kept telling her not to go. That it was too dangerous and we should stick together. But as usual, she didn't listen. She never does. Even though she knows they killed Qiang, when he—'

'All right, let's calm down and take this one step at a time,' Heinesen broke in.

'Calm down?' Fareed stared at him. 'That's the last thing we should do. We have to help her. Don't you get that?'

'And how are we supposed to help her when we don't know where she is?'

'She's down here somewhere. She has to be.' He looked towards the exit. 'She just left, and I haven't seen her since...'

'Fareed, we've searched every part of this basement, and the only person here is you.'

'Then you haven't looked hard enough. Because they're here somewhere. I know they're...' He trailed off as he spotted one of the three screens above the control panel. 'There he is. See? There's one of them.' He pointed to the screen where the contours of a man could be seen hurrying through the shadows of one of the many dark hallways.

68

DUNJA LET GO of the winch and turned to the opening in the floor. What was right and what was wrong here? How was she supposed to know? What did it matter anyway, when she had no choice? If she wanted to be able to live with herself, her only option was to grab the chain on the floor and wrap it around her arm as she walked up to the edge, from where she could lower the end of it to Sleizner, who was somehow still clinging to the wall.

'Are you ready?' he said in that slurred voice, and she nodded. 'You have to plant your feet and brace... Promise me you will... That you'll brace... Otherwise we'll both fall.'

'Come on already,' she said, placing her right foot behind her left. 'Before I change my mind.'

Sleizner, whose entire body was shaking with effort, finally dared to reach for the chain, first with one hand and then with the other, and she began to haul him up. As though this were why she had been working out so hard.

No part of her trusted him. No part of her said what she was doing was right. She knew him far too well, knew what he was capable of, so she made sure to keep him at arm's length, the chain the only link between them. If he tried anything, she could just let go and let him disappear into the hole.

But he didn't try anything. He just clung to the chain. Once he reached the edge, he was too exhausted to climb the last bit. She tried to pull harder, but to no avail.

'I can't...' he said, on the verge of a breakdown. 'You have to come here... You have to help me... Please...'

She looked into his pleading eyes and nodded, even though it hurt. But she saw no other way. If she didn't do something, he'd lose his grip and fall.

'If you try anything, I swear,' she said, approaching him with tiny steps, still holding the chain taut. 'You'll be going straight down.'

'Please, before I fall...' he cried, with blood streaming out of his mouth. 'I can't hold on much longer...'

With her left foot right next to him, she slowly bent down, put her arm under his and helped him over the edge.

Sleizner collapsed in a shaking pile on the concrete floor. 'Bloody hell... Thank you... Bloody fucking hell...'

'Kim, I want you to lie down and put your hands on your back,' she said, prepping the handcuffs attached to the chain.

'Absolutely,' he said, nodding. 'I just have to...' He pushed up onto all fours. 'My tongue... The piece you bit off...' His body shook and he rocked back and forth like a wounded animal. 'Just have to find it, before we... Before we... Where is it? You know, the tip of my tongue? Maybe they can sew it back on. Don't you think? Huh? That they can sew it back on? They should be able to, right? If we can just find it...'

'I'll take care of it,' she said, and nodded. 'If you just lie down, I'll see to it.' She pulled a tissue out of her pocket and went over to the bloody puddle.

There was no question what the dragging sound was that she heard behind her the moment she bent down to pick up the bloody piece of tongue. Sleizner was on the move. He hadn't got far, but he was probably trying to get back on his feet.

Her reaction was pure instinct. Under no circumstances was she going to let him get away. And yet it turned out all wrong. Both the angle of impact and her centre of gravity, but above all, the trajectory. Because rather than trying to escape, to move away from her, Sleizner shot up from the floor straight towards her, and his right arm passed just an inch or two from her face.

The miss was her chance to counter. But she didn't, because she spotted the curved edge gleaming in his hand. The karambit he'd threatened her with at the detention facility.

Then she noticed the slash across her stomach.

At first, it was a thin line.

Then there was blood everywhere.

But she felt nothing. Not until she saw the almost foot-long gash through not just her hoodie and T-shirt, but her skin, which opened up like a big red mouth all the way into her stomach and intestines.

She hit the floor with her hands over her open abdomen. Blood everywhere. Organs sliding out. Sleizner, who grew increasingly diffuse as he walked towards her.

'Wow... beautiful...' he said. 'Practically a caesarean... It's a shame you weren't pregnant. I could have got two birds with one stone.'

She could hear him laugh like after a bad joke on TV.

'If only you'd listened to me,' he went on, bending towards her. 'If only you'd accepted evil and let it direct your actions.'

She could see him coming closer. At the same time, he grew less sharp, as though he were about to fade into grey.

'But you couldn't. Could you? Even though you knew, you had to reach out.'

She tried to say something, but nothing happened. Not so much as a sound.

'Even though you knew this was how it was going to end,

you still wanted to polish that halo and be able to look yourself in the mirror with a clear conscience.'

She couldn't see him any more, just feel his presence, if that. As though her senses were seeping out of her, one after the other.

'Like when you toss a homeless person a couple of coins and feel so good and righteous about it, you're practically bursting with pride. Pathetic is what it is. Pathetic and as sickeningly saccharine as scarfing down four pounds of sweets.'

Vaguely, she saw the curved edge of the knife, glinting in the light of the fluorescent overheads, right next to her face.

'So the only thing you deserve is to stop existing.'

By the time he lowered his arm and pressed the cold edge of the blade against her exposed throat, she'd given up and passed out.

'To disappear into nothingness. Missed by no one.'

Which was why she didn't register the loud bang or the bullet that burst through Sleizner's forehead like an alien, leaving a crater in its wake. Or that despite the hole in his head, Sleizner burst into one of his patented laughs and remained straddled across her. Or that Fabian, who was entering the room, fired another round at Sleizner, who just kept on laughing.

She was oblivious to all of it.

Even to the third bullet, which from point-blank range shredded everything in its path as it ripped through Sleizner's head. But still didn't manage to shut him up. As though the muscles in his face and throat were stuck in a groove. It took two more bullets to finally silence him.

But by then, Dunja was somewhere else entirely.

69

AFTER FIRING THE five shots, Fabian felt completely empty. A vacuum in which everything had been paused. A walking husk that should long since have lain down and given up. But he was still standing, and even though he'd never done what he was doing before, he worked on autopilot. As though he were pre-programmed.

His impressions of the world around him were disjointed. Occasional bursts of input, filtered down to an absolute minimum. Like the faint hissing sound, like an effervescent tablet in a glass of water. Normally almost inaudible. Here, a turned-up, corrosive hiss emanating from Sleizner, who was dissolving somewhere at the bottom of that darkness. He could almost hear the hydrofluoric acid eating into his body.

Or the toxic fumes, which, even though they were heavier than air, stubbornly wafted up out of the hole and through the many filters of the gas mask. Into him.

Even so, he emptied a third can down the hole.

To silence any nagging doubts.

The faintest possibility.

He'd already ripped off his jacket, after making sure Dunja was still alive. And his shirt and trousers. Packed and tied them as hard as he could around her midriff. To stop the bleeding. To buy time.

He took off the gas mask, winched the lid closed, and

picked Dunja up off the floor. Even though he didn't have the strength, even though the gunshot wound in his arm had opened up again, he carried her out of the room and into the narrow hallway, through the stench, past the cells.

The door to the lift was open, just like he'd left it. Inside, he bent down over her after pushing the top button with his elbow. But he could find no signs of breathing or a pulse. Just limp, lifeless muscles. A long, unbroken beep from some instrument that told him it was too late. That he might as well give up.

He put her down on the floor as the lift slowly climbed upwards. Too slowly. As though it didn't really want to and was doing everything it could to slow down, stop, turn back. To delay. He pressed his lips to hers, felt the warmth, and pushed down the thought that she would soon be cold. The thought that there was no point. He filled her lungs and saw her chest rise. Once, then again. Tried to tell himself it had to work. Pumped her blood around with hard, fast chest compressions. Thirty in a row.

It had to work.

It just had to work.

He saw the blood trickle out from under the clothes around her abdomen. Pooling on the floor of the lift. A growing puddle of loss. Of death. The lift was still barely moving. Barely perceptible tremors along their never-ending ascent. There was nothing he could do except to continue rescue breathing. Compressions. Fighting the clock. The voices in his head screaming over each other that it was too late.

Maybe it was the vibrations from the lift as it finally stopped, or maybe it was her heart starting back up. He didn't know. Could only hope as he moved through the harshly lit, hospital-like corridors on the next floor. Hope beyond hope.

There was no one else there. Just him and Dunja. And

the next lift. This one was faster. The door opened almost immediately, giving him no time to check her pulse again. Instead, he hurried down from the stage, through the large ballroom with its crystal chandeliers, and into the dimly lit tangle of hallways.

He could feel the blood from his gunshot wound. Trickling down his arm, each droplet draining him of a bit more strength as it dripped from his elbow. But it was nothing compared to Dunja. He didn't even need to look down to know she'd lost pints. Feeling her body trying to slip out of his arms was enough.

Just like before, everything suddenly went dark, and when he came to, he was falling, but he managed to right himself and pushed on through the labyrinthine hallways. Stopping wasn't an option. Instead, he blinked a few times to stay conscious. But it didn't help. His vision was growing blurred. Same thing with his hearing, which now only let through the lowest frequencies.

The long tunnel was so narrow he had to move sideways to keep her head from hitting the wall, and on the other side he was greeted by flashing blue lights and armed SIU officers shouting at him to drop her and get down on the ground with his hands behind his head. Threats of shooting him if he didn't. The same people who'd already hunted and shot him.

But he couldn't let her go. Not now. Didn't dare to do anything but push forward to the sound of his own breathing and the ever more distant voices. Towards the steep staircase. On his left, a group of young women with blankets wrapped around them; on his right, two men in camouflage clothing lying face down with their hands cuffed behind their backs next to the woman in gym clothes.

He heard them yelling. Not at him. At each other. He tried to call out for an ambulance but wasn't sure anyone could hear him.

Had to stop halfway down the steps, which disappeared from under his feet as he wobbled and fell headlong into darkness.

Woke up to the sound of voices. Shouting voices. Fluorescent lights passing by overhead. Tried to get up, but straps kept him on the stretcher that was taking him backwards over uneven ground. All he could do was turn his head.

Flashing police cars and uniformed officers blocked his view in one direction. Turning the other way, he saw Dunja, surrounded by paramedics administering IVs and using instruments that made her body arch as the current between the two paddles surged through her.

He felt the vibrations from the ambulance's engine starting as the doors closed. Only then, when he was on his way out of the garage, up the ramp, and out into the light of the breaking dawn, only then did what he'd waited so long for finally happen. What he'd tried to reach, to feel.

Quietly, almost imperceptibly to anyone else.

A single tear so small it had long since dried when the next one followed.

The process had begun. There was no stopping it now. As the ambulance turned on its sirens and raced down Østerbrogade, Fabian cried.

For everything that had been and everything that lay ahead. For all the efforts that had never been enough. For his failures, which had destroyed so many things. He cried at the realization that none of it could be undone. He cried for Matilda, who'd been right all along, and because whatever he did, whatever decisions he made going forward, this was how it was always going to end.

And he cried for Theodor.

His darling Theodor.

Finally, he was able to cry for him.

EPILOGUE

THE HOURS THAT followed were characterized by efficient calm. Suspects were arrested, the basement was thoroughly searched, and the group of young women were examined and looked after. Some of them turned out to be malnourished and others deeply traumatized. All were given whatever care they needed.

Even though the police response continued to grow over the course of the morning, as news of the raid on Østerbrogade spread to all units and agencies, everyone involved knew exactly what to do under the leadership of Morten Heinesen. It was a role he'd never played before, and which he only then realized he was made for.

The National Commissioner's threat to fire him came to nothing. Instead, Heinesen was asked to lead the subsequent investigation along with Bernstorff and Hemmer, and as the material Fareed had seized was processed and analysed, the arrests began in earnest.

Nothing was the same after that. Jakob Sand and Director of Public Prosecutions Mads Jensen were the first to be picked up, followed almost immediately by Head of Forensics Oscar Pedersen. Then Ryan Frellesen, CEO of Danske Bank, Stig Paulsen, CEO of TDC Group, and Kai Mosendahl, Director of the Danish Customs and Tax Administration.

The arrests continued all the way up to government level, with Foreign Minister Morten Steinbacher as one of the more active members of the club. The whole thing turned into a scandal that not only mired the Danish Police Authority in its worst public confidence crisis ever but also swept through large swathes of the Danish elite with such force the event would become known as the Copenhagen Bloodbath.

A scandal that turned out to involve everything from human trafficking, bribery and economic crimes to tax evasion, murder and soliciting to murder. There were international connections as well, to, among other places, Stockholm and the case Malin Rehnberg was working on. But that's a different story altogether.

After a number of sleepless days and nights filled with endless questioning, Fabian and Fareed were cleared of all charges and released. Some question marks remained around Sleizner's death, but since his body was never found, the case was eventually dropped.

Tissue samples from the walls of the hole, from the top all the way down to the bottom, proved that he had definitely been in it. But that was where the trail ended, because the hole turned out to open straight into Copenhagen's sewer system.

No one knows where Fareed went after his release. Nor what happened to the urn containing Qiang's ashes, which vanished while awaiting burial.

One of the many rumours floating about has it that Fareed's in Sri Lanka, where he has taken over a tea plantation after spreading Qiang's ashes in a reserve for orphaned elephants. Another claims he went underground and founded international hacker network *Insidious Elephant*. A third says all the rumours were started by the man himself.

The only person who at the time of writing has not been heard of by the police is Dunja, because after several complex surgeries she's still on a ventilator in the ICU at Rigshospitalet, under the watchful eye of both the hospital staff and Mikael Rønning, who visits at least three times a week.

Every time, he goes through the same two-hour procedure. First, he throws out the flowers on the nightstand and replaces them with fresh ones. Then he sits down on the edge of Dunja's bed, takes her hand and tells her everything, from the latest twists and turns of the investigation and which heads have rolled to who he's dating at the moment, convinced that somehow she will hear every word and soon be back on her feet.

When Fabian returned home to the terraced house on Pålsjögatan 17 in Helsingborg, the bed in the guest room had been made up for him. He slept for almost twenty-four hours before he was ready to get up and have dinner with Sonja and Matilda.

Neither of them asked about the events in Copenhagen. Maybe because it was all over the news anyway. Instead, they talked about the preparations for Theodor's funeral. What they wanted, and what they thought Theodor would have wanted. For the first time in ages, they were able to spend time together without fighting, and over the two weeks that followed, they all worked to make the funeral as beautiful as it could be.

It's still too soon to say if it was the start of something new for them. Maybe it was just a better ending.

In early September, Fabian decided to buy a Maxi 108, a sailboat that could handle the strain of a trip around the world, if he ever felt like going. Sonja gave up after a few short trips, defeated by seasickness. Matilda, on the other hand, turned out to have a knack for sailing, and that autumn she and Fabian spent weekends together on the boat, which they agreed to name *Theo*.

Other than that, not many days went by without Fabian

visiting his son's grave in Pålsjö cemetery. He often caught himself having sat there for hours. There was something there, among the graves and mausoleums, that helped him find peace. An inner harmony he'd never come close to feeling before.

Nothing pulled at him there. Nothing shouted to get his attention, to drag him away. And for the first time, he experienced some kind of connection. It was impossible to say if it was with Theodor or with himself.

But it was something.

Something healing.

ACKNOWLEDGEMENTS

THE GREATER PART of this book was written during the pandemic years of 2020 and 2021. Not that this affected Fabian Risk, since the book is set in 2012. What it did affect was me and my writing process, though I have, so far, managed to avoid contracting COVID and am still waiting for the vaccine.

My stories are usually chaotic. In the fictional world, everything is turned upside down and inside out and my job as a writer consists in large part of attempting to solve problems and impose order. To do so, I need at least an illusion of structure out in the real world.

To me, it has never been clearer than during this past year that life truly is stranger than fiction. If I ever needed convincing, all I had to do was turn from my manuscript to the first newspaper article I could find to have it proven anew, and this has, to cite Erica in the prologue, been kryptonite to my writing.

Being unable to travel and visit my adult children in Stockholm, my mother in Helsingborg (even though she lives right across the sound), or my friends in Spain, where I usually spend my most intensive writing periods, has been very difficult. Being unable to meet you, dear readers, has not made it any easier.

And yet, in the end, a book was written. A book I feel

genuinely proud of, too, and for that I want to thank those closest to me who (don't ask me how) were able to deal with both me and, more importantly, my neuroses in a way that helped me through the process.

I couldn't have done it without you.

Mi, you don't just support and cheer me on. You read, share your thoughts, and discuss the plot with me, and even though we disagree sometimes, it always turns out you were right in the end.

Sander, thank you for always asking how my work is going, and for promising to read all my books once you're old enough.

Noomi, thank you for all the breaks you've provided by bringing me a new drawing or fantastical creature to add to the collection on my windowsill. Every time I look at them, I feel like anything's possible.

Filippa, this year we've mostly talked on the phone, and even though our conversations always fill me with new energy, I can't wait to see you in person again soon.

Kasper, thank you for being there when I need extra support. When I complain about how badly it's going and how the book isn't turning out the way I thought it would – you always remind me that it's like that every time.

I also want to thank the team at Forum, led by my publisher Adam Dahlin. You all do tremendous work. Andreas, editor of all my books, you have been my rock, but this time you've truly outdone yourself.

A big thanks also to Tor, Julia, and Marie at Salomonsson for putting so much effort into disseminating the books about Fabian Risk across the globe and for caring about everything from cover details to what watch Kim Sleizner wears.

And finally, I want to thank you, dear readers, for

demonstrating so clearly over the past year that no matter what happens, there's always a need for a good story.

Stefan Ahnhem
Copenhagen, March 2021

ABOUT THE AUTHOR

STEFAN AHNHEM grew up in Helsingborg, Sweden, and now lives in Denmark. He began his career as a screenwriter, and among his credits is the adaptation of Henning Mankell's *Wallander* series for TV. His first novel, *Victim Without a Face*, won Crimetime's Novel of the Year, and became a top-ten bestseller in Germany, Sweden and Ireland. The series went on to become a top-three bestseller in Germany and Sweden, and a number one bestseller in Norway. Stefan Ahnhem has been named Swedish Crime Writer of the Year, and has been published in thirty countries. The Fabian Risk novels have sold more than 2.3 million copies worldwide.

ABOUT THE TRANSLATOR

AGNES BROOMÉ is a translator of Swedish literature. She holds a PhD in Translation Studies, and has translated a number of works including *The Expedition* by Bea Uusma, which won the August Prize.

21982320578903